GOD
SEX
AND
PSY
CHO
SIS

A Novel

Todd Crawshaw

CrowsnestPublishing.com

WE

ARE ALL

BELIEVERS

(SEARCHING)

FOR MEANING

AND

SEXUAL

(WITH DESIRE)

FOR A REASON

AND

CRAZY

(BY DEGREES)

FOR

LOVE

TABLE OF CONTENT

Dissociative Identity Disorder, also known as Multiple Personality Disorder, is a condition wherein a person's identity is fragmented into two or more distinct personalities. People who suffer from this rare condition are usually victims of severe child abuse. It is one of the most controversial psychiatric disorders with no clear consensus regarding its diagnosis or treatment.

PART I

FAYE:
Playing Dead

GOD, SEX & PSYCHOSIS

"Woe to the innocent

who hears that sound!"

— Homer, The Odyssey
    (Song of the Sirens)

ONE

The sky was a beautiful mess of black ink. It had spilled across a paper-thin world. Light escaped through holes made by angels so God could look down upon His creation.

The father laughed and called his son a little idiot. The earth was round and the universe incomprehensible. There was gravity and galaxies and light-years and didn't they teach this shit at school? His father fondly smacked his son's head, then staggered off towards the house while pointing with his beer bottle at the stars and saying what they were looking at was the past. The light they were seeing took millions of years to reach Earth. For all they knew the universe was dead. The breaking news hadn't reached them yet.

The boy stared with confused wonder into the blackness until he awoke to the sound of birds. The sky was blue, almost white, with a hint of yellow. Crystals of dew were on the top of his sleeping bag. He lay still, listening to the silence, the morning calm, waiting for the world to end. But nothing happened. He was alive.

Unlike his sister, always pretending, playing dead. Her antics had made him laugh. She'd made up ghost stories too, scaring them both before abandoning him for the house to sleep in her warm bed. It was another day. Dead was what happened to their grandmother. Her words a faint memory like last night's stars. She had told them her face had once been as smooth as porcelain, like the head of the doll tucked beside him. He rubbed at the chipped scar on her cheek to comfort them both, but it only made him feel worse. For he had broken his promise to protect her.

The sun was quivering over the trees like a lost balloon drifting upwards to reach the center of the sky, having almost made it, before his mother's first scream of the day. It burst the silence. His father shouting back. They fought like raccoons, clawing and screeching. He pulled the nylon flap over his head and inched deeper into the warmth of his sleeping bag and hugged the doll. Her body was soft like a pillow. Only her head was fragile.

She was Mira, named after the mythical princess of wonder and visions. And when he dreamed Mira would be there, to protect him. Never ordinary, but magical. Her painted lips told him about angels, warned him of dragons, and took him to places unseen by others. Where the animals lived. Not the kind his father killed, but the ones who hid on the other side of the world, invisible to humans.

Their pink eyes appeared first. He saw the shape of their furry bodies. Rabbits huddled in the darkness. Their ears turned upward and alerted. Their whiskered mouths trying to tell him something. Then a door slammed.

The boy's head emerged cautiously, peering out from the hole in the ground. From far away he watched his father moving within the shadows, banging into chairs and rummaging through trash cans. The sun had fallen in the sky. It was behind the arms of an oak tree. The voice of his sister was faint, coming from inside the house.

He closed his eyes and prayed for God to make him invisible. Dappled sunlight fell upon him through the rustling leaves that clung to branches. His cheek touched the cool grass. Its damp green scent flooding his nostrils as he slid beneath the surface to muffle the noise of clanging bottles.

The rabbits were friendly. Their eyes sympathetic. The eyes of his grandmother, his aunt, his teacher, the neighbor who came to the door when the noise from their house erupted into violence. They were urging him to enter another hole that went deeper. There was no time to hesitate. They were gesturing, *Hurry!*

The explosion startled him. He jerked upright, brushing flecks of wet dirt off his face. On the ground nearby lay the remains of a squirrel. Half its head was blown off. Across his sleeping bag were particles of fur and blood.

Footsteps shook the ground. The rifle barrel moved recklessly in the direction of his head. His father flicked the headless animal into the woods with the tip of the gun. His tears only made it worse. His father telling him to stop whining and be a man. Dogs ate dogs, the weak inherited shit, and he'd better learn that fast.

The boy was told to get up and go inside the house. He tried to hide Mira but his father saw the doll, poking it with the gun barrel. As he walked barefoot across the crabgrass, the boy clutched Mira to his chest. His father followed close behind asking him if the doll was his sister's, asking why he played with dolls, asking what the hell he wanted to be – a boy or girl?

The boy looked for help. His twin sister was nowhere in sight, in hiding too or off playing with friends. He could see his mother slumped in an armchair inside the house facing the television.

Demanding answers, the father grasped and tugged the boy's long hair. Male or *fe*-male? Because if he wanted to act like a girl, to be like his sister – it could be arranged.

From one pull of the trigger.

Flung around, forced to face his father, he was pushed against a picnic table. Held by the throat, the boy felt the gun barrel pushing through the open fly of his pajamas. The cold muzzle pressed against his flesh and he screamed.

The boy lost his grip, letting go of Mira, and watched in horror as the doll's face struck the red bricks and shattered to pieces.

Black ink and stars gushed from his head.

Egon thought he heard the voice of God. In a soft rumble that had formed words, telling him not to fear, to relax, to listen, to trust. He was in the shadows of an oak tree beneath its crown of dark brambles. He looked up to locate the source of this phenomenon as the voice began to fade like a sputtering airplane. The branches were arched and formed the dome of a cathedral with stained-glass views of blue sky and sunbeams streaming through its windows.

Blinded for a second, Egon shielded his eyes. In the sparkling blackout, he smelled blackberries mixed with the scent of sage, along with whiffs of dust stirred in the air by his feet. The mountain trail was cooler inside this shady grove, but sweltering beyond its shelter. Even birds weren't talking much, being quieter than normal, hiding from the heat. His forehead was damp with sweat. It was morning, not even noon. He stopped to watch a squirrel scamper up the trunk of a tree and chatter at him before he ventured out into the endless blue sky with the full force of the sun upon him.

Egon never thought his sister would actually do it, run away, but now she had, and he was searching the woods looking for her. Being twins, they were supposed to know each other's thoughts and feel what the other was feeling. Which was stupid. He rarely knew what Faye was thinking or feeling. Contrary to what he'd overheard on the school bus, the older kids saying twins were "telepathic." He had to look up the word in the dictionary. The meaning was clear. They believed twins could transmit thoughts supernaturally. Which meant these other kids thought they were both freaks.

Faye didn't care. But Egon did. He wanted to know what else people thought about him and his sister.

"Faye!"

It was pointless to shout. If Faye wanted to be found she would be found. But that didn't stop him from searching overhead as he passed under branches because Faye liked to climb trees. She'd hide, then jump down to startle him. That was how she played.

With the sun at his back, Egon observed his shadow as it took the lead, attached to his feet and the ground. He flailed his arms and watched the elongated figure mimicking his gestures, mocking their connection. It reminded him of the conjoined twins he'd seen on TV. Because of a birth defect, two girls were forced to share a body. They had separate heads and hearts, but only two arms and two legs. Each girl had her own personality and independent sensations. Somehow they had learned to play the piano, ride a bike, swim, even drive a car. They were considered a medical mystery.

Egon couldn't imagine sharing a body with his sister. It would never work. They were too independent. He told Faye about seeing these two girls inside one body but she wasn't interested. She said she already felt like a freak and didn't need reminding.

On their ninth birthday, his sister gave up playing with dolls and stuffed animals. She wanted to become magical.

That was three years ago. They'd been walking along this same path. "Nine is a magical age," she'd told him. "And a lucky number. The highest single-digit. It's the symbol for dragons who have super-natural powers."

"Chinese mythology," he told her. "I knew that. There are nine muses in Greek mythology too. So what?"

"And nine choirs of angels. It proves my theory."

"You have no theory."

"Do too. Special powers don't come unless you seek them out. How many lives do cats have? Nine."

Egon laughed. "Not the ones Dad shoots."

"We don't know for sure. Maybe they already had nine—"

"And nine circles of Hell."

"You're a killjoy."

"I am not. It's what they told us in church."

Egon looked at his sister and each time it felt strange. Because they looked alike. They came from different eggs and were fraternal twins. Yet they had the same blue eyes, almost silver. Same shape to their face except Faye's lips were fuller. And they had the same black hair, roughly the same length, except on this morning his sister had decided to tie hers into a ponytail. It swished back and forth with each turn and flick of her head.

"You look like a horse."

She made a face. "Then so do you."

"With your ponytail."

"It's fun. You should try it."

"Boy's don't wear—"

"Then stop trying to look like me."

"I'm not."

"Cut your hair then."

"Lots of boys have long hair."

He swatted her hand away from touching him.

"Don't."

"So prickly," she teased. "You're a porcupine."

"Am not."

"Are too. You expect the worst and see the worst."

"That's not true. Look. Over there."

Egon walked off the trail to a cluster of bushes and pointed at a large spiderweb. Its iridescent strands glistened in the sunlight.

Faye was unimpressed. "So?"

"It's a work of art."

"It's a stupid spiderweb, Egon."

"I bet you didn't know that silk threads are stronger than steel if they were the same thickness. Spiders are weird. Did you know they've been on Earth for like more than 350,000 years?"

"And where before that?"

"All I'm saying is they've been here a lot longer than us."

"What are you saying, they're smarter?"

"No, but we can learn from them."

Faye touched her palms together in prayer. "Oh great wise one, come out wherever you are. Teach us your secrets. You're smarter than my brother, I know that. Because he's an idiot."

"You sound like dad."

Faye was laughing. "You're a nerd. Better?"

Egon pretended to ignore her and examined the web. "Spiders eat their webs too. Did you know that?"

"No."

"They recycle the silk to build new ones. It's true. See, I told you spiders were weird."

"That's more than weird. It's gross."

"Not the males. Only females build spiderwebs." Egon smiled and poked his sister.

She hit him back. "It figures. Girls do all the real work. Boys are useless."

Egon pointed into the bush. "There. See?"

"See what?"

"There he—I mean, she is. Hiding."

Faye blew air at the spider. "We see you. Stop spying."

"Did you know Little Miss Muffet was a real girl?"

Faye scrunched her lips. "Who?"

Egon took a gulp of water from his thermos. "You know, from that fairytale. Her dad was a doctor. He crushed up spiders and had her eat them. He thought it was a cure for the common cold."

"Men are morons."

Faye grabbed his water bottle and drank from it.

Egon took out his pocket compass and watched the arrow spin to the north. "Except he was right. Sorta. Spiderwebs really do have healing powers."

Faye widened her eyes to express disbelief.

"I'm serious. Their silk has properties that can stop bleeding. When placed over a wound."

"Liar."

"It helps coagulation. The silk has vitamin K—"

Faye swept the spiderweb up in her hand and wiped it over her brother's face. "There—go heal yourself." She squealed and ran off laughing.

"That's not funny!"

Egon spat, laughing too, brushing off the sticky web and chased after his sister before finally stopping, knowing he'd never catch her. She was too fast.

Egon stood there, recalling the memory. They had been nine. They were now twelve.

He could almost picture her disappearing into the trees off in the distance, after running through the tall green grass, now golden. He wiped sweat from his forehead and decided to go look where she had gone that day. He trampled a new path through the brittle stalks of wheat that cracked and hissed. While trudging along the hillside that dipped down, then rose up, then down again, he heard the clicking of insects but couldn't spot or hear a single bird.

"Forty-eight hours," said his father. "You wait forty-eight hours before you call someone a missing person. Police, they won't do a damned thing or take you seriously." His father had been reclined in his armchair. His, because no one else was allowed to sit there. He was on his second beer and third shot of tequila. "In case you ever vanish, and you don't make it back within that time frame. Or, let's say you do show up after running away. Then hell, I'd be forced to bury you myself. Advance warning." His father had grinned to show he was half joking, bending back his head to swallow tequila before wiping his mouth, followed by a laugh.

Time was running out for Faye. It was close to forty-eight hours since she'd gone missing. Egon could hardly blame her. He'd heard her muffled cries from the night before. Egon knew what his father had done. He now realized he'd been doing it to her for years.

The following morning his sister had refused to come out of her bedroom. She had yelled at him when he entered. "You do nothing. You let him get away with it!"

Egon snapped back, "What am I supposed to do?"

"I hate you."

"I'm not him, Faye,"

"You will be."

"No, I won't."

"You're a boy. Next a man. I hate my life!"

"Faye."

"Go away!"

Egon stood helpless as he watched his sister throw herself onto the bed and cry into her pillow. When she looked up and saw he was still standing there, she screamed at him. "I said—go away! Leave me alone! I never want to see you ever again! Ever!"

Egon had shut the door behind him, never actually believing he wouldn't see his sister again. He blinked, looking up at the sun, into the blinding light before shutting his eyes. He had to wait a moment to collect his senses. When he opened his eyes he felt light-headed and dizzy.

He came upon the grove of trees. The clustered oaks made him think of cattle herded around a source of water. The stream was now a mere trickle. He slid down the riverbank avoiding rocks and ruts to reach the water. He walked downstream and came to the millpond his sister had discovered when they were five years old. It was one of their secret hiding places even though a few other kids knew about the swimming hole too. The stream had been dammed into a pond by someone, and so the water level remained pretty much the same year-round.

But Faye wasn't there. At least, not in plain site. He knew she could be hiding, but he had his doubts. She'd left the house in the middle of the night. Her purple backpack was gone. Drawers had been left open, half shut, with clothing missing. Her favorite frayed blue denim jacket was not in the hall closet. He assumed she'd taken food from the kitchen too. He'd done his best to cover for her by pretending to bring food to her room and telling both his parents she wasn't feeling well. His mother was half drunk by dinnertime. And his father said nothing. Except to lift his gaze from the football game to give him a suspicious look.

Egon gazed at the millpond, searching its shore. It was wider than their backyard and deep in the center for diving. Egon wanted to strip to his shorts and swim. But he resisted, climbing one of the oak trees instead. Several branches extended over the water. One had a rope swing. Egon positioned his body where the crook of higher branches spread out from its trunk. It gave him a mostly clear view of the entire pond, while keeping him camouflaged, unseen unless someone happened to look up.

Assuming Faye hadn't reached the highway and hitched a ride, Egon guessed she'd be somewhere in the woods, and would gravitate to this pond eventually. Because of the heat. And the water. So he sat and waited, cooling off in the shade.

Having dozed, he awakened to a barking dog. Looking down, he saw a golden labrador drinking at the shore. Next came a girl. She stood beside the dog and petted its head. Egon recognized her. She was a year younger and went to the same middle school.

Egon watched the girl pick up a stick and toss it into the water. The dog dove after it. After retrieving the stick, she threw it in again. She did this several times before moving away to sit upon the ground. The lab came out of the pond and dropped the stick in front of her, then shook his body – spraying water on her.

"Gershwin!"

The girl shrieked and laughed. Gershwin? Strange name for a dog thought Egon. The name of a musician. He recalled seeing her carrying a case for an instrument, maybe a flute or clarinet. He had watched her on the playground with her friends and thought she was pretty. But because of their difference in age and sex, they were never really part of the same social group.

Egon held his breath. He realized what the girl was about to do. He remained still, unlike her dog, who squirmed as she commanded to him to "Stay." After a careful examination of her surroundings, she removed her shirt, next her bra, exposing her breasts with their budding nipples. She kicked off her shoes and removed her shorts. Except for white panties, she was naked and waded into the water. Glancing back at her dog, she pointed and commanded, "Stay! You be my watchdog. Bark if you see anyone coming."

The dog seemed confused, cocking its head as she lowered her body into the water and swam away. Gershwin leapt into the pond and dog-paddled after her.

"Gershwin! I told you to stay! Go back!"

She laughed as she scolded her dog. His disobedience amused Egon too. He wanted to take part in this fun, leap into the water and surprise them both. Instead, he continued to watch from above. The girl held her breath and dove, legs kicking upwards, exposing her pink bottom before she disappeared underwater.

More than thirty seconds had passed and she hadn't surfaced. Egon began to worry. Her dog too, swimming in circles, aimlessly looking for her. Then she shot up, gasping for air, laughing.

She swam back to shore, Gershwin splashing behind her. She emerged from the water and found a patch of dry grass to sit on with sunlight shining through the patchwork of trees. Gershwin plopped down beside her. While drying off in the heat, she gazed around, appearing to admire the beauty, the seclusion, then tilted her head back and closed her eyes.

As she absorbed the warmth of the sun, Egon absorbed the sight of her. He thought she looked like a goddess he'd seen in a painting. Her golden hair hung in wet tangles from her head tilted upwards. Both arms were extended behind to prop her body, her chest arched, with water drops glistening on her skin like jewels.

The world felt mystical and magical, and Egon became aroused. He felt the stirrings of love and lust, unable to take his eyes off her. That is until she opened her eyes – blinking and refocusing – seeing him in a tree!

She screamed, covered her breasts and stood. Her dog barking, unsure what was happening. The girl was scrambling to get dressed, ducking into her t-shirt, stepping into her shorts, grabbing her bra, slipping on her shoes, then running away.

She ran up the riverbank and was gone.

It happened fast.

The barks from Gershwin faded into the distance. The silence that followed was disquieting. He wondered if she had seen his face? Had she recognized him? He felt embarrassed, ashamed, perched in a tree like a monster. A gargoyle. An aberration of nature. A boy transformed into an ungodly creature, cursed by the gods.

His metamorphosis was aborted by a voice.

THREE

It was a girl's voice: "Why are you sitting in a tree?"

Egon looked down at his sister standing by the pond. She was wearing a pullover pleated dress he didn't recognize. She'd taken off her purple backpack and dropped it beside her. It took a moment for him to register she had actually returned.

With a smile on her lips, she added, "That girl must really like you. The way she ran off screaming."

Egon hopped to the ground. "Dad's going to be really mad."

"Why? What did you *do* to her?" she teased.

"Nothing. I was talking about you. Running away."

"I didn't. Let's go swimming."

Egon stopped her. "We need to get back home."

Faye brushed his hand away. "You don't own me."

"Faye, I know what Dad did to you."

"I'm Jenna. Not Faye."

Egon stared at her. Her hair had been tied into braids. And on her head, she wore a wreath of wildflowers, stems woven together. Not something Faye would do. She had a spritely squint of a grin. Egon frowned and asked, "What's wrong with you?"

"Nothing's *wrong* with me," she said. "What's wrong with you? Are you in love or something?"

"What do you mean?"

"With that girl. Who is she?"

"It doesn't matter."

"It matters to me."

"I was afraid you'd never come back."

"That's sweet," she said.

"Faye, why—"

17

"Don't call me that. Faye was captured by the Spriggans."

"The who?"

"Don't you ever listen to your mother?"

"What are you talking about?"

"How they steal children and leave changelings in their place. That's what happened. That's who I am."

"Dad's not going to buy that crap."

"Why should I care? Faye ran off. She got captured. And I escaped. End of story."

"You were raped, Faye. Dad *raped* you."

She turned from him to rummage through the backpack. "I'm not *her*. I told you. I have no idea what you're talking about." She dropped the pack. "They stole everything. That's what they do."

"Who?"

"The *Spriggans*. Do you have any food? I'm hungry."

Egon patted his pockets. "A candy bar, I think." He pulled a melted Snicker's bar from his pocket. "You want it?"

"Of course I do. I'm famished. "Faye snatched it from him and tore off the wrapper, sucking and licking the gooey mess, as much as she could get into her mouth. With her face smeared with chocolate, she stopped to look at him. "Why didn't you run away too?"

Egon couldn't understand why his sister was acting so strange, or what kind of game she was playing. All he could think to do was play along. "Faye didn't *tell* me she was running away."

His sister licked chocolate off her fingers. "Yes, she did."

"She told me she *never* wanted to see me again."

"Listen to what she's *really* telling you. I like your sister. So do the Spriggans. That's why they exchanged her for me. What? You don't believe me?"

"I don't know what to believe. *Jenna*."

His sister went over to wash her hands and face in the pond. "Thanks."

Egon followed her. "For what?"

She rose from her crouch to wiggle and dry her wet fingers in the warm air. "Pretending to believe. And coming to look for her." She took hold of her brother's hand and kissed his fingertips.

He pulled his hand away. "What are you doing!?"

"Trying to make you feel better. I lost brothers and sisters too. All the water faeries, except for me, were killed. When they found out I had been a princess they turned me into their slave. They made me do horrible things. It was horrible."

"Faye, come on."

"I'm *not* her." She pouted, then smiled. "But I'll pretend to be her, your sister, if that's what you want."

Egon didn't know what to say or think. Faye was acting weird. Not herself. She liked to play act. But never like this. She seemed out of her mind. "What happened to you last night? I mean, you know, when you were captured? By the … ah, Spriggans?"

"I wasn't."

"But you said—"

"No. I was *already* there. I told you that. They traded me for your sister."

His sister picked up the backpack, swung it over her shoulder. Then she dropped it to the ground and said, "I don't need her bag. It's full of nothing. Are we going, or what?"

Egon pointed to the wreath in her hair. "You made that?"

"They told me to wear it. A crown of flowers for the dethroned princess. To make me look innocent. But I'm not."

"You're not, what?"

"Innocent." She widened her eyes to appear playfully sinister, then grabbed his hand. "Okay. I'll go home with you."

Egon let his sister pull him along. Quickly she let go and sprang like a sure-footed mountain goat to the top of the riverbank. From the shadows below, Egon saw his sister glowing in the blazing sun, her dress sparkling as if set on fire.

"I'm so happy to be free!" she shouted. "Hurry!"

Egon struggled to get his footing, slipping twice before reaching the top. "Slow down, okay?"

"I haven't seen the sun for so long. Come, I'll race you!"

"No. Faye, it's too hot!"

But his sister ran off. She followed the rut of dried grass he'd trampled down earlier. He was only halfway across the field by the time she had reached the main trail. She waved back at him, then disappeared. Egon was soaked in sweat when he reached the path. Faye was standing on one leg, balanced on a log. When she saw him, she hopped off. She seemed unfazed by the heat.

"This is fun," she said. "Which way?"

"You know which way. Down. Aren't you hot?"

"Water faeries are unaffected by heat. I'll race you."

"No! Faye. I mean, come on. Stop doing that. Please?"

She came over to him. "Are you mad at me?"

"No. Slow down. Walk with me."

"Okay. It's so beautiful. I really love it here."

She walked beside him with an airy bounce to her step. As if she might sprint off any second. Egon observed his sister's movements, noticed her fingers, splayed and pointed, so straight her digits were arched backward, tapping the air, as if creating soundless music. He couldn't recall the last time he'd seen Faye this happy. He hesitated to say anything, not sure if he should break whatever spell she was under but felt compelled to ask her.

"What will happen to Faye?"

His sister looked him in the eyes. His eyes were the same blue. They were the same height. She blinked. "I don't know. Spriggans can be nasty."

"How nasty? What did they do to you?"

She looked into the trees. "I don't want to talk about it."

"Did they hurt you?"

"I *said*, I don't want to *talk* about it."

Egon stopped to take a drink of water from his plastic thermos he had clipped to his belt. "You want some?"

Faye examined the bottle with it twist-top and spout, as if it was the first time she'd ever seen such a strange contraption. She put the nipple to her lips and squeezed, sucking. "Umm, water."

"Faye, talk to me. Tell me what happened."

His sister rotated the plastic container around in her hands as if she was turning the question around in her mind. Before aiming the bottle and squeezing hard – squirting him in the face.

She giggled and dropped the bottle, then ran downhill.

"Damn you, Faye. Stop running away!"

Though she'd surprised him, the water had felt refreshing. And, at least, she was acting more like the sister he knew, thought Egon. While trudging down the path, he saw several butterflies, a squirrel, finally glimpsed a bird, but saw no other humans hiking on this hot afternoon. Any second he expected Faye to leap out from behind a tree to surprise him, but she never did.

They were more than a mile up the mountain, far from their home. When he reached the last stretch of the fire trail he noticed torn flowers and stems littering the path. Same colors as the wreath his sister wore. He came around a bend and saw her standing at the bottom of the hill. In her hand was what was left of the garland from her hair. Both arms hung at her sides. And she wasn't moving. It was as if she'd turned into stone. Into a statue. He approached her and lightly touched her shoulder.

She let out a startled gasp. She looked at him, then down at the broken wreath of flowers in her hand. She dropped it.

"Where am I?"

"We're almost home."

Egon was puzzled by her blank expression. Tears were welling in her eyes, trickling down her cheeks. Her lips began to tremble. Egon placed a hand on his sister's shoulder and she fell into his arms and sobbed against his body.

"It's going to be okay," said Egon.

Faye shook her head to say it wasn't.

Egon held his sister until her body was calm. She pushed away and seemed embarrassed and confused. She clutched the sides of her dress. "Why am I wearing this? Where's my backpack?"

"You left it by the pond."

"When?"

Egon took hold of her hand. "Let's go home."

Faye pulled away, "No!"

"Faye, come on."

"What are we doing here?"

Egon was exhausted, getting annoyed again. "Because you ran away. Two nights ago. Stop playing games."

"I'm not."

"We need to get home," said Egon.

Faye refused to budge. "Dad will kill me."

"I've been covering for you. I don't think Dad or Mom know you were gone last night."

"Where was I?"

"Faye. Stop it. It's getting late."

He pulled her along. She didn't resist this time. His sister now felt like a zombie he'd captured, the way she shuffled her feet as if she was incapable of monitoring herself. Their house was at the edge of the woods. It was one of the older homes, built before the tract houses which had turned the area into a sprawling neighborhood.

They came off the trail and passed across an undeveloped patch of land that was flat and surrounded by a grove of trees. The place where kids played softball and soccer. No one was playing today. It was too hot. Vacant, except for them, kicking up dust.

Egon decided they should sneak in through the back door. He pulled Faye with him, squeezing them through a hole in their wood fence. They next crossed the length of dirt and crabgrass his parents jokingly called a backyard. He glanced back at Faye, put a finger to his lips, before opening the screen door. It made a wrenching noise. To Egon, it sounded like a haunted house.

The interior was dark. No lights were turned on. Even with its two stories, their shack of a house was dwarfed by the forest of oaks, pines and eucalyptus. Light rarely found its way through the dense foliage. Egon was hoping they'd made it back before their father arrived home from the service station he worked at. Their mother would be drunk, most likely unconscious in front of the television. He heard nothing, not even static nor the usual chatter from a soap opera or game show.

It was then he noticed the dark shapes of his parents standing in the living room. Followed by his father's gruff voice.

"Where in the *hell* have you been?"

"We were worried sick," said his mother.

"Gone for two days! Two nights! Answer me!"

This was directed at Faye. Egon felt his sister squeeze into him, trying to hide behind his body.

Their mother sighed. "We were about to call the police."

"Not me. She was." The silhouette of their father came closer. The faint light revealed the rage on his face. "You think I'd let you do that? Make me look *foolish*. Again. The cops showing up – for nothing! Get out of my sight! You're grounded. Go!"

Faye pushed away and ran up the stairs.

Egon remained still. "Why are you mad at me?"

"Get out of my sight! Go—I said!"

"I did nothing wrong."

"Are you challenging me, boy?"

"No, I—"

"Shut the *fuck* up. You want to end up like your sister?"

"Ray!" howled his mother.

Egon stepped backward. "I went looking for her."

His father bolted toward him. Egon fled up the stairs but then stopped halfway.

His dad shouted, "Move! Keep running!"

Egon screamed back, "I know why she left! It's because of you! It's what you do to her at night!"

"You shut up! I'll deal with you later. Go!"

Egon ran to the top of the stairs and stopped. He crouched at the wood banister. He listened to his parents arguing.

"What is he talking about, Ray?"

"Nothing."

"Kids don't run away for no reason!"

"What's that supposed to mean? You blaming *me!?*"

"Should I?"

Egon heard a loud slap, followed by his mother's scream.

"You bastard!"

"Bitch!"

The sound of broken glass – something thrown against a wall – made Egon back away and retreat into Faye's bedroom. He saw her on the floor wedged between her bed and dresser. Her knees were up against her chest, a pillow clutched to her face. She was shaking. Her eyes were swollen from crying.

Egon told her, "We'll be safe tonight. He won't come after you. I won't let him hurt you again."

Faye looked up and glared at her brother.

Egon flinched, startled by more glass breaking. "I promise."

"I wish you had never found me."

Someone spoke and Egon looked up. He focused on where he was, on a school bus. He listened to the clamor of voices, the shouts, and laughter within this confined shell. Nobody was talking to him, so he looked back down at the book he'd discovered in the library. A medical book about mental illness. He was searching for answers. Something was wrong with his sister. She had become increasingly moody. Her playful spirit was gone. She'd refuse to get out of bed, and complain of headaches and cramps. Her voice would go weird. She'd pretend to be Jenna, this water faerie. Or someone else. And she'd forget things. Then lie about it.

One morning Egon caught her looking in the bathroom mirror while brushing her teeth. She spit into the sink, then turned, seeing him at the door. It was as if she hadn't recognized him.

A finger poked his head. It came from the seat behind him.

"Hey, Geeko, whatcha doing?"

Egon closed the book. "Nothing."

"Looking at porn?"

"Ha-ha. Are you ready for the test?"

"As long as you are."

The boy grinned down at Egon who'd craned his neck upwards. His name was Jay. Not exactly a best friend but close to one. They were preassigned lab partners and Egon let him cheat off his paper. This won him some popularity points and the nickname, "Geeko," which he didn't mind. Jay was actually Jayden, one of those unisex names, so he went by Jay. He played football, had a slew of friends, and sometimes the two of them hung out after school.

Jay came around and sat next to Egon. He lowered his voice to ask, "Hey, man. What happened to your twin? Like, it's been awhile since I saw her."

"She dropped out. Wants to be home-schooled."

"No shit," said Jay.

"She talked my mom into letting her."

Jay nodded. "Maybe I'll come over. Pay her a visit?"

Egon shrugged. "Yeah, whatever."

Jay grinned. "Cool. Tell Faye I'm coming."

"No problem."

"We could all go for a swim. At that pond in the woods. I mean, if you're up for it."

"Sure, I'll let her know."

"Cool. Hey, we're here. Later. See you in chem class."

Jay stood as the bus pulled into the schoolyard and came to a stop. Jay was the first to exit as the compressed doors hissed and slapped open. He ran from the bus to join with his friends already congested in the courtyard.

Egon opted to circumvent this gathering of the tribes with their many cliques since the first bell was about to sound. He went to his locker. From his backpack, he took out books and exchanged them for others. About to slam shut the metal door, he was slammed – blindsided by a body block. His locker closed with a bang during the commotion.

"Hey. Watch where you're going, *freshman.*"

Egon recognized the three boys, each a junior. Sid Meyers, Brad Fuller, Stan Romano. They stopped to surround him. They waited to see how he'd react to their challenge. They were friends of his cousin Roger, also two years older, and who attended the same high school. Egon glanced down the hall.

"Roger ain't here. You're on your own, punk."

Egon held his temper and acted unfazed. "Hey, Sid."

Sid grinned. "Enjoying high school?"

"Yeah, you guys make it so much better." Egon smiled.

Sid laughed. He fake-punched Egon, then hit the metal locker with his fist, before departing with his two friends. The one named Brad turned and shouted, "Better watch your back!"

"Thanks, Brad. Sage advice."

"Weirdo!"

Egon muttered back, "*Asshole.*"

He knew them all. Since forever. Except Romano, who was a transplant from the east coast. But they were all older, and they'd always be. And they'd never let him forget it, this age-old pecking order. Sid had been a bedwetter as a kid, during sleepovers, and got teased a lot. He'd grown into a bully, now pissing on everyone else. Why his cousin, a nice guy, at least, to him, was friends with these jerk-offs Egon couldn't understand. Maybe because Roger played football with them. Some kind of bond between jocks.

The encounter left Egon on edge, distracted and bursting with pent-up anger. He tried refocusing on the upcoming chemistry test. On the transformation of energy. How it could never be destroyed or created, only transferred and converted to other forms. Egon had become fascinated by the properties of matter. Its changeability.

Lost in thought, he moved within the flow of students, weaving to avoid the oncoming bodies. His shoulder brushed against others as he walked down the hall to his first-period History class.

Seeing a wall-mounted water fountain, he stopped for a drink. The cold liquid got him thinking. About the three states of matter – solid, liquid, gas. Ice changed into water then into steam. A process that was reversible. And the chemical composition was unchanged. Only the physical state of each was different.

Egon thought of Faye. The bell rang and he froze. He realized something similar was happening to his sister. Like chemistry. Like she was this substance that transformed into other things.

He recalled what their teacher had said. It was a law of science. Energy could change form but never be destroyed. That was Faye.

Able to alter herself while her core, her elemental self, had remained the same. Had Faye discovered what she'd been searching for while lost in the woods? The secret to becoming magical?

The second bell rang and it snapped Egon out of his reverie. He found himself in an empty hallway.

He was late for class. It would be another detention slip.

But luckily, as he snuck into the classroom, their teacher faced the blackboard writing names of historical figures. He slunk into his seat. Instead of a pink slip, he received a fist bump from the boy who sat across the aisle. Mr. Quinn wanted to discuss the Revolutionary War today, but Egon's mind drifted onto subjects that mattered more to him. Like his wayward sister. Domestic issues. Current events. To things happening *now*. These Founding Fathers had their day. They *were* history. Literally. Like remnants reflected in a rearview mirror seen from inside a fast moving car.

History taught him what? About the human tendency to herd. Assembling into communities and countries to survive as a species. And how repelling forces – religious, racial, sexual and ideological differences – split the magnetic pull, creating friction and wars. Still, people kept herding, to seek shelter, also to dominate and exploit. Man's inhumanity to man was legendary, well documented.

It baffled Egon, this divergent disconnect of the human spirit. Along with the atrocities were the acts of kindness and self-sacrifice, humans willing to die for another. Religion and philosophy were the subjects devoted to solving these mysteries. A multitude of proposed hypotheticals had been the result, but nothing definitive.

Science was basically about understanding energy. The control of flowing electrons and photons to illuminate the darkness or heat a house. Or to construct weapons of mass destruction. There were now integrated circuits that opened the gates to an even greater flow of knowledge and awareness. Yet, it was clear to Egon, humans still didn't have a clue as to why they existed.

Biology was all about organisms, and how they functioned, with cells working like factories to build up symbiotic relationships. And since everyone was made from the same organic stuff, daisy-chains of spiraling atoms, each life form was reliant on the other.

Mathematics was the study of how symbols and formulas could calculate space and time. For shooting rockets and orbiting satellites. Coded languages that had evolved to spawn electronic devices now capable of performing tasks and cognitive thinking of a superhuman. Totally mind-boggling, thought Egon, this human race he had been born into.

He glanced across the aisle and saw his friend drawing planes dropping bombs on people across the pages of his history book.

And art class? It was all about aesthetics. Was love beauty? Was fear ugly? What about a tarantula? A butterfly. Malicious viruses. Marriage. School shootings. Sex. Death.

Was everything, Egon wondered, somehow related?

A siren wailed. It stopped class. Mr. Quinn instructed them all to remain calm. "Walk—not stampede!" No one looked concerned. Some kid was always setting off a fire alarm, as a prank, or to avoid taking a test. It reduced them to cattle, Egon felt, as they were herded through doors, down hallways, then out into the paved and green pastures of the playground.

While he waited outside with the entire school assembled there, Egon spotted Sid. He was among his delinquent friends and grinned, flashed Egon a thumbs-up sign, then extended his middle finger.

Egon looked away, fairly certain this was not what God had had in mind. Life on Earth was no Paradise.

The world was broken.

His sister was too.

The explosion sounded like the wrath of God.

The detonation was fierce.

It sounded to Egon like a thousand firecrackers set off at once. It resulted in everyone being dismissed from school, told to go home. The police arrived at his house later that evening.

His father gripped the open door, "Can I help you?"

"There was an incident at the high school today."

His father stared down the short officer, ignoring the tall one. "My son told me. It's on the news. What's this about?"

"Sir, we have reason to believe your son was involved."

"Bullshit," said his father.

Egon shook his head. "No way."

His father stared back at the two officers.

"Sir, we've discovered evidence to the contrary."

"What evidence?" said his father.

"In his school locker."

"My locker?" said Egon.

"Shut up," his father told him. "Be specific."

"Blasting caps."

"What?"

His father slapped the back of his son's head to shut him up, then demanded to know, "Why were those in your locker?"

"They weren't," said Egon. "It's a mistake."

"Is your locker number 375?"

Egon acknowledged with a head bob.

"Three blasting caps were found inside," said the tall officer.

His partner added, "We searched every student locker. Aside from a few knives and drug paraphernalia, your locker was the only one with these illegal items, linking you to the crime."

"I didn't *do* anything," said Egon. "Those aren't mine."

"Then whose are they?"

"I don't know."

"Then who, besides you, could have placed them there?"

Egon went silent. He recalled his locker being slammed shut by Sid, Brad or Stan. He shook his head. "I don't know."

"We'd like to have a look inside," said the short officer.

"Not unless you have a search warrant," said his father.

The tall officer reached into his coat pocket. "We do."

Egon began to panic. He had nothing and everything to hide. He didn't understand what was happening. He heard his sister shout from upstairs. "What's going on? Who's at the front door?"

Nothing incriminating was found after the search of his room, his sister's, his parent's, and every other room in their house. All that remained was the airstream trailer which his father kept bolted shut with padlocks. A place his father would disappear into at night and on weekends, and then lock the trailer door from inside. Neither he nor his sister was allowed to enter or know what he did. Egon and Faye would sometimes sneak up close and put their heads to the metal siding to listen to the sounds emanating from within. Whirring and grinding. Pinging and sparking.

"We need to search in there," said the short officer.

"The hell you do," said his father. "Off limits. Private."

"Not anymore." The short officer placed a hand on his gun as the taller one pulled out his black baton and tapped the metal door. "Either you open this door or we will. One way or the other we're having a look inside."

His father paused to glare at his son.

Egon knew at that precise moment all hell would be let loose. Upon him. Later. Because he was the one responsible for causing this invasion into his father's personal space, his man cave. Violating the shrine of secrecy no one was allowed to witness.

Egon felt Faye nudge his side. She too was eager to know what their father kept hidden.

Their father snapped at them, "Get in the house!"

"Sir, we need your son to stay right where he is. And we need you to open that door right now."

The short officer had drawn his handgun. The excitement was palpable. Neighbors had emerged from inside their houses to watch. His father was fuming, rattling at the keys he kept on a chain to open the first lock, before twisting the combination to undo the second. Admitting defeat, he flung the door open.

"I hope you're happy," he snarled. "Cause I'm not."

His father went inside first with the officers in tow. Egon and Faye peaked inside.

The tall officer had to duck. "What is it you do in here?"

His father spat back, "The hell's it look like? It's my workshop. My lab. I'm an inventor."

The short officer queried, "What sort of inventions?"

"None of your damned business."

The tall officer remarked, "I'll be god-damned. Quite a setup you have." He seemed in admiration of the collection of equipment, tools, the order, precision, touching various items. "What's this?"

"A micro lathe," said his father. "Don't be expecting a guided tour. And I'd appreciate it if you didn't touch anything."

The short officer pointed. "Is that a riflescope?"

"The makings of one. I'm a ballistics specialist. Ex-Marine."

"Combat?"

"Vietnam. You?"

"Iraq."

This got them talking shop, fighting extremists, war missions.

"I have paperwork to document all of this. Registered patents. The works. You won't find anything incriminating."

And they didn't, even apologizing for the intrusion when they exited the trailer. "Sir, we appreciate your cooperation."

"And your service overseas," added the tall one.

Egon's father said nothing to that. He clamped back both locks and turned to his neighbors. "Show's over! You can all go home."

He turned on the officers. "Are we done here?"

"For now," said the short one.

The other said, "We may want to question your son again."

"Make sure you have something substantial next time you do. My son would never do anything stupid like that. Those blasting caps could have been planted there by anyone."

"Forensics is checking for prints."

"Swell," said his father. "Good luck with that. What was it got destroyed?"

The tall officer turned at the squad car. "Excuse me?"

"On the news, it said nobody got hurt. What got blown up?"

"A boy's lavatory," said the short one, before ducking inside to take the diver's seat.

His father snorted a laugh. "All *this* for *that*. Toilets? Shit."

Except his father wasn't laughing now. He was chewing his lip, waiting to be alone with his son, waiting for the officers to exit the interrogation room. The moment they left he turned on Egon. "You swear on your life you never *touched* that girl?"

The question was confusing, vaguely phrased, and Egon stalled, saying, "Only to help her. I had to touch her, Dad."

"You *know* what I meant. Did you? Rape her?"

"No! I swear."

"Okay. Then *who* the hell did?"

Egon stalled again. "I don't know. It happened like I said, just like I told the police and everyone. I didn't see anything. I wasn't *there*. The girl said that too? Right? What is she saying?"

"They're not telling us."

"Why not?"

"Because they think *you* did it!"

"I didn't." Egon began to sob.

"Stop crying. Man up. They'll be doing DNA testing on you."

"I don't care. It'll prove I'm innocent."

"Maybe. Why were you wandering in the woods?"

Egon wiped at his tears. "I wasn't wandering."

"Then what were you doing?"

"I always go there. You know that."

"The police, as well as me, are having a hard time believing you happened to stumble upon this girl lying naked in the dirt."

"It's the *truth*. You can ask her. *Ask* her."

Egon directed his last remark at the mirror. He knew how this worked, that he was being watched and listened to behind the big glass panel on the wall. He wasn't stupid.

He swiped at another tear. "I'd never do anything like that." He looked directly at his father. "*Rape* someone."

His father averted his eyes, put hands to his knees and stood.

"Especially not her." Egon regretted having said it.

His father looked at him. "What's that supposed to mean?"

"Nothing."

"You meant something. Not this girl, why?"

"Anyone, I meant."

"You said 'her.' This girl. Who is she?"

"Her name's Clara."

"How do you know her?"

"She's just a girl. Someone from school."

"You said especially *not* her? Why?"

"Because." Tears were on the verge of pouring again.

"Damn it, Egon. Tell me! Why?"

"Because I love her!"

SIX

In the moonlight, he saw Faye lying on her bed.

Egon had climbed through her bedroom window. He used it to sneak in and out at night. The branch of an oak tree allowed him to leave their house without his parents knowing about his departures and reentries. This escape hatch was the best thing that had come from their relocation. After a bomb blast at the high school, then a girl getting raped in the woods. Even after declaring his innocence and cleared for lack of evidence in both cases, rumors of his guilt had persisted. So his father relocated the family to a new town. How his father could afford this new home on a hill was a mystery to Egon. It was a mansion compared to their previous dump of a house.

Normally he would have hurried past his sleeping sister to make it back to his own room in case one of his parents happened to wake. But there was something about her stillness that troubled him. Also, the sound he thought he heard. He wasn't sure it was coming from his sister until he approached the bed. There was also a musty smell. The scent of alcohol. He looked down and saw her eyes rolled back, revealing only an eerie sliver of white between her shuttering eyelids. The rest of her body was rigid.

Was she dreaming?

If she was, it was nightmarish. She looked possessed. Blankets and sheets were tucked around the mound of her body and her neck. Arms buried tight at her sides. Like a mummy. Except for her legs. Noticeably parted. He noticed the sheets of the bed had been pulled out at the ends. Only her head was exposed.

He wasn't sure if he should wake her. He touched her shoulder. It was bare when he pulled down the blanket. Hesitating, he lifted the sheet and saw her naked torso exposed in the starlight, reflected off a quarter moon all alone in the dark sky. He didn't need to look any further to know his sister had been raped by their father.

Again.

Gazing at his twin felt otherworldly. It was like looking down at himself. Tears were welling in his eyes. His fists were clenched. He felt paralyzed. With rage. With sadness. Fear.

"Faye. Wake up. *Faye.*"

She remained as she was, in some deep fitful sleep, or trance. Egon didn't know what to do. He wanted to shake her but resisted. He half expected – hoped, prayed – his sister would open her eyes and grin, to let him know he'd been punked. That was how she used to play. Done in fun. He thought back to when they were younger. How she would make him laugh.

When they were six years old, Faye had a collection of pennies. One day she insisted they walk to the park near a shopping mall. He watched as she placed the coins on the ground. Then they sat on a bench to see who would pick them up.

Egon: "No one is going to stop and pick up a penny."

Faye: "Wait and see."

Egon: "They're practically worthless."

Faye: "Not to the people who believe in magic."

Egon: "Nobody cares about pennies."

Faye: "I'm not leaving them for *nobody.*"

Egon: "This is dumb."

Faye: "It is not. See that woman. She found my penny and now she feels lucky. See? What's wrong with that? *Huh?*"

Egon saw the woman examine the penny and smile, then laugh, looked around, then walk away. Egon frowned. He looked at Faye who took his hand, turned it over and placed pennies in his palm. White paper had been scissored into a circle and glued to each coin. Using colored pencils, his sister had printed notes: *"Make a Wish," "Lucky Coin," "Be Happy," "I'm Magical."*

In hindsight, Egon realized her intent was sweet and thoughtful. Her curiosity was playful. She was imaginative and he admired her sense of adventure. She'd pretend to communicate with animals and got people to stop and watch her talking to dogs, birds or a squirrel. Faye wanted to convince others she had special powers. Either that or have them wonder if she was crazy.

Egon would sometimes take part in these pretend games, but he was never as good as his sister, so he'd usually be nearby watching and laughing.

He once asked her why she did it, acting foolish, and wanting to fool people. They had been on the floor playing a game of Fish. She looked up from her hand of cards with a straight face. "It's for you. To make you crack up. You're my only real audience."

Faye had the ability to make him feel special. Also the opposite, teasing him about his fear of snakes and his worries about her make-believe games. He feared they would lead them into serious trouble. She'd laugh. "Light'n up, bro. Don't go *dark* on me, Ego."

That was her nickname for him because as babies she couldn't pronounced his name. It had become a joke. His parents began to call him that too. *Ego.* He hated it when they did, or even kids, but didn't mind it when his sister did. Because she said it with affection. Because early on they'd been close. They'd share secrets. And Faye, for awhile, had him believing that maybe she *could* communicate with animals. He'd watch as animals appeared to listen, tilt their heads, then react as if they *did* know what she was talking about and was asking them to do.

Egon knew it was crazy to think his sister was somehow special. But Faye *was* different. She was fearless with her love. Full of life and daring.

He envied her. Until she began to fall apart.

Egon: "What's the matter?"

Faye: "Leave me alone. Don't touch me!"

Egon: "Jeez, light'n up, sis. Don't go *dark* on me."

Faye: "*Fuck* you."

He couldn't recall what age they were. Maybe eight. Or nine. It was the first time his sister had used that word. *Fuck*. Certainly a favorite word voiced around the house, used freely by their father. So it didn't shock him that much. Other kids used the word. But it sounded foreign coming from his sister. Until she began to use the word a lot.

It changed her sense of play too. Inside diners, she'd hide notes for customers to find, that read: "Your fly is open." She'd giggle and watch as the man she'd targeted stare at his crotch before looking up, looking embarrassed. Finding this little girl staring back. Faye would stand and say loudly, "Stop playing with yourself and looking at me. Pervert."

Another time she'd left a note that said, "I admire you. You're so brave to go out in public dressed as a slut." And as they got older, having reached their teens, Faye would double-down on her pranks. At restaurants, she'd try to spark an awkward romance. She would leave two notes, one for a customer, the other for the waiter. Her hands had become as swift as a magician's, distracting the eyes of the unsuspecting. She'd pretend to accidentally bump into a table. She'd apologize and put notes under drinks. Or she's scribble messages on cocktail napkins and slip them into check holders that the waiter or waitress would collect and find.

"Do you believe in love at first sight? Meet me outside."

Faye made bets with her friends that this waiter and customer would be compelled by curiosity, and a desire for love, to be drawn outside. Most of the time she lost the bet. The customer might wait, lingering outside, before giving up. Or the waiter might step outside, to find no one there. But every so often, both parties would appear. Hands might touch. Faye and her friends would scream from inside their parked car after waiting, watching, and passing around a joint.

With a laugh, Faye would say, "Look! I win. God, I feel like Cupid! I'm buying myself a bow and arrow. Someone should go tell them the world is one big lie. Who wants to go? I dare you."

These were the impish and devilish games that Faye had begun to play, which kept getting darker.

By the time they turned thirteen his sister became obsessed with music. She discovered the heavy metal bands. Anthrax. Megadeth. Slipknot. Bands with hellish names and lyrics to strike fear into the hearts of their parents. At least, that's what Egon imagined. Because he sensed Faye derived no real joy from these albums. She played them as if they were weapons used to annihilate her enemies.

But Jimi was different. She loved Hendrix. Egon could tell she was enthralled by him. By his lyrics, the melodies, blasting The Jimi Hendrix Experience loud inside the confines of her bedroom. *Purple Haze. Foxey Lady. Little Wing. Castles Made of Sand. Voodoo Child.* She'd play these songs over and over again until their father could stand it no more and shouted: "Turn that shit off!"

Egon had come out of his own room to listen because Faye had turned up the volume. As he entered her room, Faye grinned at him. She'd sing – screaming – to the lyrics – "*Now if 6 turned out to be 9! I don't mind! I don't mind!*"

Her bursts of laughter had been infectious.

They were now sixteen. And his sister had been broken.

It was his father's doing. Egon's arms were stiff against his sides, clenching and unclenching his fists. He'd promised Faye that he'd never let it happen again. He had promised to protect her. But he had failed. He now knew what he had to do.

But he was scared. He didn't know how to do it.

Kill their father.

PART 2

EGON:

Trial Separation

What is madness

but nobility of soul

at odds

with circumstance?"

— Theodore Roethke
from the poem In a Dark Time

As I watch her, he watches me. We form a strange triangle. My sister's crazy. Fears for her life. So she hires a private detective. I can't see him but I know he's there, parked across the street, inside a blue-grey Jaguar. It's one of the older models. An XKE, not in great shape. The blue paint has oxidized. All its windows have been tinted dark. Its bulging curves, like muscles, have a few dents. It makes me think of a stalking animal, past its prime. He's been following me for days. And unaware, like most of us, he is less predator than prey.

As for me, I'm seated at Enrico's, a sidewalk cafe on Broadway. It's my favorite haunt. A ghost of a place. It's been renovated in an effort to recapture the golden years of San Francisco. Sporadically visible is the sun, seen through wisps of fog and cumulus clouds high above me in the blue sky. It's a warm morning. A rarity. And I've come disguised, hidden behind mirrored sunglasses. My long hair is tucked beneath a Giant's baseball cap. I hold a Sunday newspaper spread wide as I peer over its top. I try to see the wisdom and beauty of it all. But it's a parade of weirdos mostly. Tech addicts poking their smart phones as if they were remote controls controlling them. Zombies talking out loud into headgear. Bums working the curbs. Tourists wielding cameras. Barkers at doorways touting illicit thrills. Strippers sashaying their magnificent tits.

It's incredible how we've evolved as a species, become fruitful and multiplied. To advertise our promiscuity, marquees and life-size posters of naked men and women span the entire block.

So why am I here? Because of Faye, my twin sister, inside the bar, reposed like a bitch in heat between pawing males, all laughing with drinks in their hands. Bloody Marys. It's late morning and she's already sloshed. Unbelievable. Granted, it's her birthday. Mine too.

But knowing she's out whoring around in public, imagine how that makes me I feel.

"Have you decided?"

The question startles me. "Ah, Nick, you're back." I know this waiter. Having identified the source of the inquiry, I relax, smile.

"Something to eat?"

"Maybe later. It's my birthday."

"Congratulations. You're alive. Special plans?"

"Some friends are throwing a surprise party for me later."

"Not much of a surprise then."

"I'll be surprised."

"How was Union Square this morning?"

"I gave myself the day off."

"No performance? You'll be missed."

"Thanks." I set down the paper. "I'll have a double expresso. To celebrate my sister's *passing*."

"Come again?" Nick grins as if waiting for the punchline.

"Born on the same day. She's my twin."

"She died?"

"No. We're temporarily estranged, is all."

"I didn't know you had a sister."

"That cabaret restaurant along the Embarcadero?"

"Teatro ZinZanni. What about it?"

"She does this act with a boa constrictor."

"That's your sister?"

"Yeah, Faye."

"I've seen the posters. I thought ..."

"What?"

"Nothing."

"She rents a dressing room nearby. She had a lunch show today, I thought. I came to surprise her and wish her a happy birthday. My attempt to make things right between us."

"Good luck."

"Yeah, like that's going to happen. She's inside getting drunk. I need to use the head. You heard the news, right? That serial killer struck again."

"No shit."

"Late last night."

"Where?"

"Ghirardelli. Near the wharf."

Nick shakes his head. "Sick world."

We get distracted by the sight of a beautiful woman walking by. She's one of the dancers going to work. I call out, "You brighten my day. You're like the sunshine." My complement gets her to smile, then flip me off, with a kiss to her finger. I'm heartened by her blush. As she walks away I joke with Nick, "How do you stay focused? I'd lose my mind working at this roadside attraction."

Nick laughs, and I prepare to get up. Having spoken my piece, I, Egon (a name I hate but am stuck with like a permanent tattoo), refold the sections of worthless news, twist them in a roll and wedge them beneath my arm, then start to rise. But the sun at that precise moment decides to burn a hole through the grey matter of clouds and beam to earth into my eyes. My hand is slow to shield, a reflex after the fact, and I'm blinded – forced back into my chair. I descend once again into the shadows of the cafe awning, the visor of my cap, and the darkness of my glasses.

"Why do you hate your name?"

For a second I forget who I am, or where I am. To disguise my disorientation, I feign blithe indifference. I scan the room to regain my bearings. I recognize the office space. And this lovely woman. Her beauty overwhelms me. My expression turns playful.

"Do *you* like my name?"

"I do," she says. "I'm interested to know why you do not."

"I thought it was obvious."

"Not to me. Explain."

My smiling inquisitor is coy. This was all Faye's idea, my being here. I was told this is relationship counseling. I tell her, "I actually think it was my parent's idea of a joke. I happen to know we were a mistake."

"A mistake?"

"Me and my sister."

"I don't follow."

"Our arrival into this world wasn't welcomed with any fanfare. My mother went on a drinking binge. And my father. So overjoyed by our birth, he abandoned us in celebration. Dropping us off with whoever would open the door. That's what I was told."

"By whom?"

"My aunt."

"And she raised you?"

"Sort of. After my grandmother and parents died. I guess having twins was more than my mother had bargained for. My father used to dump us off at our grandmother's house. Which was often."

"What memories come to mind?"

My tongue probes the scar, hardly noticeable now, on the inside of my lower lip which I push out to show her.

"Being dropped by my mother. I still have the scar."

I point and, obligingly, she leans closer to glimpse this vestige from my infancy. As she imagines the psychological scars, I imagine her body beneath her professional attire – dressed in the business suit of a man except for the silk blouse and skirt – and how she is in bed. Her breasts are well-developed, pronounced, unlike Faye's. Her eyes have a tint of green. She makes me think of a tiger. It's the way she observes me. She also chews the end of her pencils.

"And you remember this incident?"

"Not everything. But the fall. Tasting blood and crying. The commotion. Screams. My father hitting my mother."

"How old were you?"

"A year, or two, maybe."

"You have a remarkable memory."

"Not really."

"What else do you recall?"

"Not much." I hear the shrieks of my sister, then her sobbing moans, followed by silence. Until it's deafening. Life-altering pain that never leaves me.

"Did your father hit your mother often?"

"Until the day he died."

"And you witnessed this?"

"He beat me too."

"Did your aunt and grandmother know?"

"Probably."

"You never told them?"

"No."

"Why not?"

"Elementary. I tell them, they tell him, he slaps me harder next time. What would you do?"

She doesn't like answering my questions, choosing to treat them rhetorically, giving them a dignified nod before asking her own.

"You said your grandmother died?"

"She did."

"Your aunt, is she still alive?"

"In a nursing home. If you'd call that living."

I raise my eyebrows to express my ambivalence at how we strive to hold onto things that elude us, like life itself, instead of letting go. My expression is also to encourage her own views. But she taps the eraser against her teeth before scribbling something in her notebook. It's a defensive move. Needing time to think of her next question, she resorts to this. She's done it before. And I find it fascinating. A cute habit. She's so serious like a schoolgirl striving for high marks. And it reminds me of the first time I saw her in the woods. Curiously observing, listening to the sounds of nature, collecting flowers, she was like a lost angel. I knew right then I'd fall in love with her.

"Can we get back to your name?"

"If we must."

"The reason why you hate it?"

"I hate it because I hate myself. Isn't that the answer you're looking for?"

I say this as a joke, but she's not in the mood for humor.

"Only if it's true."

"Are you fond of *your* name? Doctor *M*. Skyles?"

I've coaxed a smile out of her. A minor victory.

"Yes," she tells me.

"What does the 'M' stand for?"

"Miranda. I prefer Mira."

"Ah, pronounced like a *mirror*. That's amazing."

"Why?"

"That was my ... my grandmother's name."

"Really?"

"I love that name. It's pretty."

"Thank you. But can we discuss the reasons why you don't like your name?"

"Sure. It's the reason we're here. For you to psychoanalyze me. Since my life has gone to hell. Thanks to Faye. But, keep in mind, I am not the psychotic one."

"You believe Faye to be psychotic?"

"I'll let you be the judge."

"Go on."

"She wasn't always like this. When we were kids she'd do crazy things. But Faye was never mean. She had a sweet disposition that was fun and quirky. Then things changed."

"Changed how?"

I shake my head and smile at the ludicrous notion of being able to pinpoint an exact moment, a definitive answer, as to when it all went wrong. Mira returns my smile, perfectly willing to wait until she gets what she wants out of me.

Since these sessions began, I've avoided mentioning our past. We share a history. But I wonder if she knows how much I'm aware of who she is, or was. Could this be part of the process? To see which one of us blinks first and looks away?

"You know, Mira, I did take a psychology course in college. You were there. At the same time."

"I remember you."

"Okay. I wasn't sure. You knew my sister, right?"

"Yes, Faye and I met. Toward the end."

"You two were friends?"

"Briefly."

"Wait. Did we ever meet?"

"Once."

The fact I can't recall rattles me. "When?"

Mira's smile has a dismissive ease that transports us back to the present. "It's not important. That was a horrible time for me. A lot was going on in my life, as you probably know."

I nod, respectful not to dig up the past, letting the murders on campus stay buried. I smile, in an attempt to lighten the mood, and say, "I believe those psych courses I took were an attempt to try and make sense of my sister. To see if I could figure her out."

"Did they a help?"

"Not much. But it did make me appreciate this psychoanalytic process. What you do. I majored in the liberal arts and philosophy. Which you probably already know. Faye told you?"

"She did not."

"I wrote my philosophy thesis on Artaud and Nietzsche, entitled Masks of the Soul. It was published in a scientific journal."

"That's impressive."

"I thought so too at the time. Meaningless now. My projects were theatrical in nature. Still are."

"You're a street artist, you said?"

"One definition."

"You perform here in San Francisco?"

"Wherever I am. It began in college. I got interested in theater. Faye followed me there. She pretended to major in fine arts."

"Pretended?"

Her time at college was a joke."

"Why do you say that?"

"She had no interest in graduating. She'd sometimes audit a course I was taking. She'd do it to confuse people, getting them to think she was me. Doing pranks like that."

"Like what?"

"Pretending to be me. Come dressed as a guy. Which she could pull off. Then I'd show up. People thought they were seeing double. Faye thought this was hysterical."

"And you?"

"The joke got old. College, for Faye, amounted to taking drugs and doing improvisational acts. She's an exhibitionist. One time she painted a wall-size canvas with multicolored oil impressions of her buttocks. She called it 'Kisses To Succeed.' It caused a minor furor when she entered it in a student competition."

"Why is that funny?"

"Faculty names were stenciled over each impression of her *ass*. 'Professor Skinner, Comparative Literature, 6 Credits,' Professor Little, Biology 101, 5 credits, and so on. Faye somehow managed to pass all her courses without really trying. Go figure."

"Are you implying she had relations with her professors?"

"Who knows. She has a hyperactive libido, I know that much. Except she's more of a devious tease. Men tend to scare her."

"How would you describe your own sexuality."

Screw this. My teeth clench in a grim smile as I debate whether to get up and leave. The whole reason I'm here is a complete farce. This is *not* relationship counseling. No, it's because Faye got arrested for assaulting a man, and was issued a court order requiring her to attend anger management therapy. My sister doesn't think I know what she's up to. And she'd be right. I don't. Which is why I come. To figure out what the hell it is she's planning. She's always got some scheme going. Who knows, maybe the two of them meet afterward for cocktails and laugh about me.

"The fact that I'm a woman asking you personal questions, does that bother you?"

"No. Why would it?"

"It bothers some people."

"Men, you mean."

"Both genders. It depends on the individual."

"On what?"

"On your willingness to trust me. I'm only here to help. Our conversations are strictly confidential."

She's right. I don't trust her. Besides, I can't imagine how any of this is going to help reconcile our so-called trial separation. Mira, no doubt, is wondering what I'm thinking. It would be my luck to get a shrink who's psychic.

"Faye won't find out about any of this?"

"Not unless you want me to tell her. Or, if you decide to tell her yourself. Confidentiality is essential for this process to work."

"I'd rather Faye didn't know what we talked about."

"Then she won't."

She does have a nice smile. I'm guessing braces as a child, and rich parents. Perfect grades in school. A fat teenager. Exercises now and diets avidly. She once wore glasses. Blinks from contact lenses. She was an ugly duckling who turned into someone beautiful. Made over, like her mind. Which is unbelievably *unrelenting*.

"You're an artist, you said."

"I did."

"How would you describe your art?"

"As indescribable." My words and smile has charmed her again. She warms a bit as if willing to play now. "I'm an illusionist. Also a sculptor. A ventriloquist. An actor. A lot of things."

"A performing artist."

"Essentially."

"And Faye is too?"

"A performer, yes. But an artist? Hum. Currently, she's in this circus-like dinner show. Doing her thing with snakes."

"Snakes?"

"It's like a dog act, except with snakes." Mira's expression tells me additional information is needed. "We used to perform together. For instance, we created this piece called The Garden. Based on the myth of God's first leading man, Adam. And the wannabe Eve, who gets cast as a bit player, in a supporting role, told to be submissive. Are you following me so far?"

Mira nods.

"Then along comes the proverbial 'third wheel,' in the form of a Serpent, or snake, who offers temptation. Faye worked with the boa constrictor. It was a play that explored this sexual madness."

"Sexual madness?"

"Sexual differences. Man. Woman. The discrepancies. Sex is, I mean, probably the most important subject of all. Without sex, we wouldn't exist. Right?"

"Go on," says Mira, never satisfied with mere clues.

I rub a hand through my hair. "What I'm saying, if our bodies didn't come equipped with these erogenous zones, these areas of ecstatic pleasure, we might not have the desire, nor the attraction, to engage in these intimate acts. Acts of carnal knowledge. It's a built-in survival mechanism for our sustainability. To hump like bunnies. Procreate. Which requires there to be sexual differences."

"I see. You implied Faye is not an artist, only a performer? Can you define what the difference is?"

"Faye and I have divergent views as to whether or not a higher power exists and if anyone, or anything, might be running this show. On Earth. I do."

"You believe there's a God."

"Same way I feel an artist should be willing to sacrifice himself, or herself, to become a conduit."

"A conduit?"

"To originate and flow. To attain creativity."

"And Faye, you feel, is not a conduit?"

I smile to convey sadness. "I sound like an asshole. Faye is – was, amazing. As a kid she was fearless. I love my sister."

"And now?"

I shake my head. "She has fears."

"Are you jealous of your sister's success?"

"No. Why would I be?" I surmise Mira detects I'm lying.

"Tell me more about Faye, when she was a child?"

"What do you want to know?"

"As brother and sister, were you close?"

"Well, we came from the same womb. Lived in the same house. Had the same parents. In close proximity. I'd say, yes."

"I meant emotionally. Was there much sibling rivalry?"

"Sure. We fought. But we were close."

"Being fraternal twins, was that difficult?"

"You mean because we look alike? Yeah, when people assumed we were identical? It made things weird."

"Weird, how?"

"Identical means the same. Physiologically?"

"Yes. But aside from that. How else?"

I expel a laugh. "Seriously, I don't know where to begin."

"Try closing your eyes."

"Why?"

"Like we've done before. You can trust me."

I comply but don't particularly like her methods of induction, playing her fishing-for-memories. It reminds me too much of Faye, and her make-believe world, when everything began to unravel.

"Take a deep breath. Let your muscles relax. Feel your mind traveling deep into the past. Tell me whatever comes to mind."

"Okay. I'm remembering something."

"Good."

"It might help explain our differences."

"I'd like to hear."

Of course, she would. It's what she lives for, to probe into the lost souls of others. "We'd take these walks into the woods."

"How old are you in this memory?"

"Five, maybe."

"Your parents let you wander off alone?"

"They didn't care, as long as we made it home for dinner."

"Go on."

"We lived at the end of a housing development, next to a vacant lot. Beyond were hills and forests and a few creeks. It was Spring. I can picture the creek being high. Hypnotic, the way water drowns other sounds and pulls you in. You know what I mean?"

"Yes."

"We're following the stream, exploring rocks, catching frogs, and we come to this millpond. It's unreal. Like something out of a storybook. The water is so clear. We can see the bottom. It's deep. And the shore is lined with stones, lush greenery, and wildflowers. These huge oak trees arching above, shading and enclosing us with privacy. You'll think I'm making this up. But it was real. At least, I think it wasn't a dream."

"It's what you remember that's important. Go on."

"It's a beautiful day, and warm. Like we've discovered paradise. And we decide to go swimming."

I hear a voice. A girl is sitting in a tree, scribbling, taking notes, watching. I am momentarily lost in transit between past and present, becoming self-conscious.

"We didn't have swimsuits. We started to dare each other. Faye stripped first. It was ... weird."

"Weird, how?"

I hear a faint voice again. I search the sky. "Weird because ... We're alone. Surrounded by nature. This beauty. And something is not right. Faye. Standing there naked."

I open my eyes.

Mira asks, "What?"

"It's stupid."

"Nothing you tell me is stupid. Go on."

"It struck me, at that moment, how we *weren't* the same."

"Sexually, you mean?"

"Right." Like now. I look at Mira. She's so matter-of-fact. Her legs crossed in front of me. She has a vagina, not a penis. There is no embarrassment. Same as Faye. She dives right in.

I shake my head. "It was more than that."

"In what way?"

I glance at the clock on the wall. "It doesn't matter."

"Close your eyes again."

"Why?"

"Please?"

"Fine." The world goes blank except for the thought of Mira undressing, as Faye had.

I peek. She is not.

My eyes close and return to darkness visible.

"Don't force anything. Let your mind go where it wants. Relax, feel your body float as I count backward from one hundred. Ninety-nine ... ninety-eight ... ninety—"

A pink shape. Her body moving through dark water. I follow, naked, gaining on her. We touch. Laugh. Push away. She splashes my eyes. Then she disappears. Underwater. Her pink shape undulating towards the shore. I churn along the surface, a clumsy swimmer, in pursuit. She squeals when I reach her. She splashes me again and I swallow water, choking. When I recover she's laughing and wiggling something at me. I scream.

"Egon, what is it?"

I'm not sure where I am when I open my eyes. Left with a vision from my past, the present floods back at me in a rush.

"Faye had found a snake."

"And?"

"She was taunting me."

"How?"

"Laughing. I told her to get rid of it."

"The snake?"

"Yes, but she wouldn't. Because she realized it was something she could use against me."

"Use against you, how?"

I picture the black snake again. "It could've been poisonous. A Water Moccasin. But I doubt Faye knew or thought to care."

"You said she uses this against you. How?"

I sigh. This is her profession. How can she not get this? "When I said we were different, *that's* what I meant. Yes, sexually. But it's the way Faye looks for your weakness. That's how she plays."

"I'm not sure I follow."

"Faye discovered I'm afraid of snakes. So what does my sister do? She decides she wants to have them as pets!"

"Would you like another?"

I flinch. The therapist is gone.

I blink at the sparkle of empty glasses on the table, at the people engaged in noisy conversations all around me.

Nick is gone too, replaced by another waiter. "Sir?"

"Another what?"

"Drink."

I turn and look inside the cafe. Faye has left the bar.

"Again. Would you like—"

"I heard you the first time." I notice the sun has shifted towards the west. "I don't want a drink. What time is it?"

"Almost three."

"How is that possible?" I glance at my wrist before realizing I don't wear a watch anymore.

"Time flies. It happens. Something to eat?"

"No. I'm leaving."

"Then I'll be right back with your check."

"For what?"

The waiter stiffens, composing himself with a surly smile. I feel as if I am about to be swallowed whole by a whirlpool of stars.

I refocus on the waiter.

"Is there going to be a problem, Sir?"

I'm 27, about the same age as this man. *Sir?* His tone irks me. On the table is a glass with remnants of ice. I detect a hint of orange in this glacial melt. A *Screw Driver* would be my guess.

I shake my head and give the waiter a good-natured smile. I fear these sessions with Faye's therapist are doing more harm than good. "Sorry. It's been one of those days."

"Forget it. Nick told me it's your birthday. I can relate."

I doubt that he can.

Clifford surrendered to the pull of gravity and closed his eyes. He was exhausted, reclined in his car seat. Three consecutive nights of surveillance had taken its toll. The windows were rolled up and the Jaguar's interior continued to heat like a warm bath. His mind evaporated and rose into a steam cloud while the weight of his body sank into the lulling waves of tuck-and-roll upholstery.

He heard church music and indistinct voices drifting by.

In this netherworld of semiconsciousness, Clifford mulled over the details of what he knew so far. In this state of calm he was able to see his life as a forest, an overview, versus an obstruction of trees. Able to see how the dots, seemingly unrelated, connected. There had been a series of recent murders, all males, occurring in San Francisco. Three so far, all within six months. Evidence had been leaked into the news. The investigators believed it was the work of a serial killer. Each neck expertly snapped. Similar bruises from blows to the jaw. Yet no indication of a prolonged fight or struggle. No skin or blood specimens found under the fingernails. Hair and fiber samples led to no matches in the DNA database. No leads, except for a key element bonding the murders to one perpetrator. All the victims had an "X" carved into the skin, cut after each death. Minimizing the release of blood. Never in the same location. Behind an ear, in between fingers, inside the scalp. Evidence that had almost been overlooked. The first two victims had been exhumed to verify this theory on the killer's trademark signature.

Clifford felt the prickle of hairs rising on his skin. He shifted in his car seat. He was envisioning the women's face as he opened his office door. She had come without an appointment, desperate to hire him. Another domestic abuse? A philandering spouse? These were the usual cases. But no. To document her brother's behavior. They were estranged. Over "irreconcilable differences," she had told him. Before adding that she "suspected" – correct that, "feared" (because she was certain) – her brother was the serial killer.

A siren wailed past, rupturing what felt like the larva shape of his unformed being into premature birth. The bright daylight outside his car was almost blinding. Clifford squinted and caught a glimpse of the screaming ambulance zig-zagging through the Sunday traffic. He felt like a stunned insect on its back, having a multiplex of tinted eyes. Outside everyone was moving fast to be somewhere. Except for him, transitioning into human form as he stretched and yawned, not wanting to be thrust back into this absurd human race.

Until he remembered why he was parked on Broadway.

Clifford shifted up his seat. He cranked down the window and searched the cafe through his binoculars. Through its high-powered lenses he scanned the diverse mix of faces along the sidewalk. But his suspect, a street performer named Egon Norwood, was gone.

The man was an enigma. Clifford was envious of his face. It was beguiling and framed within a wild length of androgynous dark hair. His body had the lithe muscularity of a ballet dancer. And, despite the charm and amicable demeanor which he projected onto others, Norwood was essentially a loner. Also unpredictable. The man had a knack for disappearing unexpectedly.

In frustration, Clifford tossed his binoculars aside. He rubbed his eyes. The warmth of the car interior no longer felt pleasurable. Now it was stultifyingly hot and oppressive. He had begun to sweat. He loosened the noose of his tie and unbuttoned his collar. His gut hung over his belted pants. Rolls of fat had accumulated after sitting for hours inside his car doing nothing but watching and eating junk food. Trickles of sweat oozed from his crevices of flab, and it made him feel as if he was about to melt into something formless.

He punched the horn, then regretted it. The rash act resulted in unwanted attention. Passersby peered into his car. He turned the key. The starter whined, grinding out a complaint, prior to quitting in a defeatist *whirrr*. It was a worn-out sound that could have emanated from his own internal battery.

Clifford grasped and shook the steering wheel. At the apex, his fingers locked together, fighting off rage. It would be futile to plead with an Atheistic Nonentity. So he clenched his hands in prayer and raised his head toward the possibility of there being an Omnipotent Creator who might *deign* to toss him a bone.

His eyes opened. They wandered across the convertible top. He noticed a hole in the fabric. From vandals? Deterioration from age? He threw back his head with a groan. He would now get soaking wet each time it rained!

He sucked in air and tried the starter again. *Click. Click.*

"Thanks. Again. For *nothing*."

From inside his car, Clifford popped the hood and winced at the sound of prying metal. Damage from being sideswiped months back by an uninsured motorist. He pushed open the door and squeezed out. Hoisting up his pants by the belt hooks, then tucking in his shirt which never wanted to stay in place, he glanced up at no particular spot in the sky.

"Are you enjoying this?"

A religious man, Clifford felt the burden of Original Sin. After Adam, who got mankind banished from the Garden (a big thanks to Eve), Clifford believed *this* was life on Earth. A smorgasbord of Hell. A world now overrun with weeds.

Clifford trusted few people. One was a childhood friend who had worked his way up from a low-level position to be an ADA for San Francisco District Attorney's office. In confidence, he'd called Clifford to ask a favor. To investigate a man, *this* man, Norwood, who had become a person of interest in the serial killer investigation. This friend, who worked as a prosecutor, also suspected there was a rogue operative within the crime unit investigating these murders. So, he'd asked Clifford to spy on the police too, and any associates involved in this serial murder case.

Another trusted friend, a local cop who was privy to 911 calls, kept Clifford alerted to homicides occurring in the city. But even if he identified himself as a private investigator, or disguised himself as a reporter, he was smart enough to know that anyone frequenting crime scenes after a murder ran the risk of casting a net of suspicion upon themselves.

Clifford felt like an idiot.

He now suspected the police had begun to suspect him.

Glaring at his smart phone, Clifford was tempted to toss it into the gutter. And accomplish what? Everyone was under surveillance. Satellites were circling the Earth and able to pinpoint his every move and whereabouts. Government agencies were tapping phones lines and tracing electronic transmissions, emails, Internet activity, then sifting through the data.

God might be ignoring him, but other humans were not.

He lifted the hood and peered into the complex system of metal, hoses, and wires as if he knew something about engines. It took him a full minute to locate the battery. He jiggled a few wires, which got his fingers dirty, rubbed the side of his pants, then shut the hood.

"Hey, Bro! Jag-man, how's tricks?"

The man was large, dressed in black leather. And happy about something by the looks of it, the way he sauntered up and came to a stop in front of Clifford.

"You is one *bad* sight."

Clifford glanced behind himself. He became quietly terrified to realize this imposing man was addressing him. The man was flanked by a bevy of creatures. There was a woman in leopard-skin tights, gold pointy boots, and a lion's mane of teased hair who smacked her red lips as she chewed gum. At her sides stood two male studs who wore tank tops, their muscles flexing like restless horses. Behind this foursome was a taller man sporting a mottled orange dinner jacket with no shirt, bare-chested, yet wearing a casually knotted tie.

The only commonality, Clifford assessed, was their sunglasses. Their eyes were all opaqued behind black, blue or mirrored glass.

"Lighten-up, Jag-man. Mechanical problems. Stay cool. Allow me to perform my magic."

Nudging Clifford aside, the big man's stubby fingers probed for the hood release.

"The lever," said Clifford. "It's inside. Under the dashboard. But, hold on. Do I know you?"

"Jag-man, you is one funny dude. Is he flying, or what? Take a look at 'em eyes. That face. Flying, for sure. You out of orbit again. What you on?"

"Listen," said Clifford, hoisting up his pants and taking a step backward. "I have no idea what you're talking about." He touched his coat, then realized he'd left his gun in the glove box.

At a loss, Clifford smiled back, deciding to play it cool. He let this man in leather squeeze inside his Jaguar, jiggle the gear shift and turn the key.

Click. Click-click.

The man extracted himself from the car. "Not even a purr. Dead as dead can be. You'll be needing a jump."

"Pardon me?"

"*Juice.* The spark of life!"

"Jumper cables," said Clifford.

The man snorted a laugh. "Jag-man, you be spinning so fast you be entering slow-mo. Coming down, or *up*, on something. Go inside with my friends. My treat. Titillate him back to his senses."

Clifford was given a friendly shove and gave no resistance. He felt as inconsequential as a leaf caught in the current of a jungle river. As he was moved down the sidewalk he realized he was being steered toward a red door surrounded by blinking lights. The marque above read Garden of Eden.

Of course – a strip joint! These were hustlers, pimps, strippers and whores surrounding him, and acting friendly to get his money. He felt for his wallet.

"Jag-man, why you so paranoid?" The big man leaned in close and whispered, "You working on another case? Same one?"

Clifford knew he had a keen, if not psychic, intuition. And for a detective, these paranormal flashes provided invaluable insights. But how did this stranger know he was a private investigator? Then it hit him – jolting him like a lightning bolt of acuity.

An intentional deception. This man was in law enforcement too. A friend of a friend. Associated with the man who had hired him. An undercover cop who was portraying himself to be something he was not: a street pimp. Facial recognition began to take form.

This business of subterfuge got very confusing at times, thought Clifford, answering back in a hushed tone, "I am." He paused at the curtained doorway, whispering back to this undercover cop, "How'd you know I was working this case?"

"Your disguise." The man winked, then reverted to the role of a street hustler. "Enjoy the show, Jag-man. What you need right now is a *jump*. If my girls can't get you up, nothing can!"

THREE

Faye was out to have some fun. The world felt delightfully out-of-sync as she brushed through velvet curtains to escape the club's nocturnal darkness and welcome sunlight. The warm air caressed her skin and she fancied herself departing an air-conditioned plane to vacation on a tropical island. The three men she'd befriended at the bar were at her heels and willing to follow her anywhere.

She licked the red fullness of her lips and smiled to herself. How the slightest touch of her fingers could arouse a man fascinated her. A casual pat to the wrist or knee while engaged in idle conversation would draw them in. Yet when they reached for her, she laughed and brushed their hands away, rebuffing their advances in this game of foreplay, a want to touch her in places she refused to let them go. The thought of these three men pulling her to the ground like a pack of wild dogs alarmed and aroused her.

She felt a rush of hot blood coursing through her body, pulsing through theirs as well. For she could see the swelling in their pants. A vulnerability exclusive to men. She was amused at their plight to subdue an erection. This restraint was proof of their domestication. They would not molest her in public. Nevertheless, she enjoyed the danger of testing fate.

Today, being her birthday, she wanted to start the party off early by making new friends. Her old ones she would hook up with later. These new fake friends were like trial software she'd downloaded off the Internet, and now free to use on a dare. A dare she had made to herself that morning. To celebrate her independence. To have fun. And to prove she'd overcome her fear of men. The challenge was to play with them in a normal fashion. And no longer be a victim, or feel victimized, ever again.

Mira, her court-assigned therapist, made it very clear she could never regain her lost innocence, but she *could* rebuild her self-image. So she was on a quest to recapture her youthful exuberance and love of life. Yet she found it hard to discard the annoying inner voice that kept telling her she was a pathetic little whore.

She came alone and took a seat at the bar, ordering a Bloody Mary. She wore a low-cut blue silk dress held up by thin straps at the shoulders. It was short in length to expose her bare legs and thighs. Her high-heel shoes had leather laces that rose to encircle her calves. A heart-shaped locket dangled from her neck. Murmurs had already begun to circulate as she swiveled coyly upon the barstool to assess her fellow customers. She was making small talk with the bartender who was a friend and had gifted her a free drink after telling him it was her birthday. He'd struck a match and held the flame toward her as a joke. "No cake. But you do get one wish. So what'll be?"

Faye swirled her cocktail with the celery stick, considering her options, then blew out the light. With a straight face, she said:

"To fuck."

Her remark caused a stunned silence. She turned her eyes on the three men who were seated nearby at the bar and smiled.

"You see? It worked. I'm *fucking* with you right now."

This got them all laughing. And it got the party off to a start. Innocuous fun. Strangers meeting by chance. After introductions and the preliminary what-is-it-you-do-for-a-living exchanges, Faye had suggested the four of them explore more clubs then take a cruise on the bay. Someone mentioned Alcatraz, a landmark she had yet to visit, so that was the plan.

Faye was now intoxicated, having indulged in shots of Tequila. Feeling the afterglow of the Roaring 20s, a garish nightclub that had weakened her resolve with its nighttime ambiance, she yearned for more excitement and free drinks, and strippers swinging from poles. As they were walking down the sidewalk, Faye was stopped by the sight of her detective – hired to investigate her brother – and saw him entering the Garden of Eden. How her hired help was spending his time and her money made her angry, then amused.

"Men," she huffed.

"What's that, Angel?"

Faye glanced up at her blond boy-toy who clearly had it wrong. He was the angel, innocent to her moods. His boyish face and fluffy hair attracted her in a perverse way. Fallen wings after sex were not uncommon in the insect world nor in hers.

"I simply said '*men*,' nothing more, nothing less."

She recalled his name to be Devin. She took hold of his tie and he laughed as she playfully pulled him along as her pet on a leash.

She walked into the Condor. The red velvet curtain parted down the middle as they all entered a cordoned-off alcove. Further access was restricted by a doorman guarding the rope. Seen in the darkness was a petite large-breasted woman under blinking lights on a low stage minutely gyrating to pulsating music. As the song faded the dancer pushed away from the pole and pivoted in her high-heels to exit with a look that revealed her boredom.

The fat man at the rope was giving them his sales pitch. He had somehow managed to squeeze his body into a knock-off Armani suit a size too small, that perhaps once fit, a toothpick moving from his hand to his mouth while he talked.

Faye interrupted him. "Is she the best you have? I could dance better than her in a coma."

The doorman pulled out his toothpick and stared at her chest, then gave a contradictory grunt.

One of the men in her party found this amusing and shared a laugh with the doorman. "You got *that* right."

His name was Dick but wanted everyone to call him Richard. Faye realized this man in her group was a potential liability.

The doorman added, "Honey, you wanna dance for me, you get

yourself some of them silicone implants."

"Listen, *Honey*, I could have you begging for mine."

The doorman scoffed. "Honey-bun, a snowball's chance in hell would be a safer bet."

Dick let out a laugh, siding with the doorman. She was getting dangerously close to kicking one of them in the balls.

"Angel, I'm with you. Let's leave."

"Not yet," said Faye, yet soothed by Devin's devotion.

"I say we vacate." This from Roger, her muscleman, employed as a bouncer at the Warfield theater. "Let's try another club."

Faye might have, had it not been for this heretic in their midst, acting like he was in charge, now telling the doorman, "Hey, buddy, I'm not averse to phony tits. But I'd fire that bitch. That cunt has attitude problems. She acts like she's above it all."

"Maybe she is," Faye countered.

"Is what?" said Dick.

"Above it all," said Faye.

Dick laughed. "What—*now* you're defending that twat?"

"I am," said Faye. "Against men who use ugly names to degrade women. That's how women deal with rape. They become survivors, not victims, and rise *above* it all. Above men, like you."

The heretic huffed, "Yeah, well, some women *ask* for it."

"How would you know?"

"Sweetheart, this isn't my first rodeo."

"Are you saying you've raped your share of women?"

"Let's say I have. What of it?"

His cocky grin enraged Faye. A few minutes ago *Richard* would have grovelled at her feet to have sex. She wanted to scratch his face. Permanently scar it.

His laugh was a taunt. "That scare you?"

"Not at all." Faye smiled sweetly. "Haven't you heard? It's not the male spider. It's the female who *devours* her mate."

The doorman intervened. "Look, all of you, either pay the price and come in—or go."

Faye patted his fat cheek. "We'd *love* to—"

The doorman swatted her hand away.

"Once you hire some talent."

"Get the fuck out. And don't forget what I said about getting those breast implants."

"I'd save it for your teeny-tiny little *penis*."

Faye winced at the bright sunlight and pulled down sunglasses off her head to screen out the glare.

"Angel, forget that creep. You're perfect the way you are."

Faye was heartened by Devin's loyalty.

"Absolutely," said Roger.

"Oh, yeah, abso*lutely*," echoed Dick in a mocking tone.

Faye's fun mood was radically shifting into a furious migraine. She wanted to rid herself of this foul-mouthed misogynist.

"I mean it, Angel. You're a beauty. You are."

Her blond admirer provided the balm she needed to snap out of her funk and regain her confidence.

Faye stopped at a store window and felt like a kid again. She was reminded of cotton candy and saltwater taffy on display along a boardwalk at the beach. She took hold of her angel's hand and the others followed them both inside.

An entire wall from floor to ceiling displayed magazine covers of naked men and women in numerous poses of sexual engagement. Faye ran her fingers over the glossy images with murmured interest. She stopped to open a few magazines on the rack. She felt the heat of her male companions as they looked over her shoulder. Their hot breath lifted the hairs on the back of her neck.

Faye brazenly selected a magazine entitled ORGY, opening its centerspread, which showed five men of different ethnicities fondling a girl who looked sixteen, yet her recumbent pose showed she was more than just culturally open-minded.

"Now *that* looks like fun, "quipped Faye.

The three men stumbled over their words in competition for a witty riposte but managed only to muster incoherent assents. Faye teased them with a laugh and set the glossy rag onto its holder, then turned toward a wall of inflatable dolls, crotchless lingerie, and bondage devices.

"You have quite an assortment of playthings."

"Yes, Ma'am. We do."

The clerk was a shrunken old man, wearing a Greek fisherman's cap shadowing his forehead. He was chewing on a stubby cigar that had burned out. Faye was amused by his uninhibited candor and enthusiasm for these products. She imagined him standing behind a carnival booth tempting all comers to step up and win a Kewpie doll.

"How much does she cost?"

"Lolita doll? She runs forty-five ninety-nine. Plus nine ninety-nine for her optional vibrating pussy."

"She has a vibrating pussy?"

"Yes, Ma'am. She does."

"That's very impressive," said Faye.

"I don't make 'em, only sell 'em."

"I don't suppose batteries are included?"

"No, Ma'am."

"Those look challenging," said Faye, pointing to an array of oblong devices pinned to the wall as if they were balloons she could toss darts at and pop. "What's that one called?"

"Super Dong. Twenty-one ninety-nine."

"And that one?"

"That would be The Tormentor. Excuse me. The Intruder. They begin to look alike after awhile."

"Yes, I can imagine. How much?"

"Seventeen ninety-nine. Batteries sold separately."

"I'm not sure," said Faye. "Which one do you like?"

Her angel was visibly uncomfortable, sweat glistening on his forehead, yet eager to please. "They all look fine to me."

"Shows how much you know. I like the looks of that shiny one. Next to that prickly thing."

"Goldfinger. That's a popular item. A real bargain for twelve ninety-nine. A very good choice."

"Oh, yeah," the heretic said with a laugh. "The imitation ebony handle gives it a real classy touch. And with its polished head, you could easily get it to slide right up your ass too."

"Or yours," Faye retorted.

Dick shook his head. "Not my style. But I sure wouldn't want to deprive *you*. Hell, I think you should get it. All cunts deserve to get it up the ass now and then."

"Is that so?" Faye's eyes burned into his as she hatched a plan. "I have a better idea. Why don't *you* buy it for me."

"What's my incentive?"

"As my birthday present." Faye turned to address them all. "I propose you each buy me a gift so we can go back to my place for a party. Birthday suits required."

"I'm game." Dick smugly pointed to fur-lined straps with velcro fasteners under the glass counter. "Those, Dollface, are for you."

Roger, her muscleman, had trouble deciding so Faye pointed to a horsetail whip. Along with a bridle with a mouth bit, head straps, and reins.

"The *fuck?*" said the heretic.

"Can't a girl enjoy a little bondage?"

"So long as I hold the whip," said Dick.

"Oh, definitely, you can, and *will*," she teased.

Devin purchased the Goldfinger dildo.

"Oh," she told him, "I want body paint too."

"What the hell for?" The heretic, voicing objections again.

"It's *my* party," said Faye. "I want bright happy colors to shoot from spray cans."

Faye pointed to several colors and Devin purchased them all.

"Now," she said, "who wants to win my heart by flagging down a cab?"

On the ride across town, Faye gave fellatio to Goldfinger. Then, on a dare, she pretended to pleasure herself with her new toy, faking an orgasm. She won a bet by getting the cab driver's face to turn red and break into a sweat while peering into his rearview mirror. As a tip, Faye tossed Goldfinger over the seat into the cab driver's lap.

Their party of four piled out of the taxi in bursts of laughter. While Roger settled the cab fare, Faye dashed ahead up the stairs to a Victorian house. She located the key above the transom, opened the door and slammed it shut, then turned the deadbolt.

She listened to their frantic knocking and pounding, followed by pleading and whining for her to let them in. She agreed to under one condition. They needed to stay seated in the living room and remain quiet while she stripped naked and danced for them.

"I might stand on my head for that," Dick laughed and gave the door a solid bang.

"I bet you would," she teased.

"Angel, we'll do anything you say. Just let us in."

"I believe *you*, Devin," said Faye. "But can I trust the other two to obey my wishes? Will you all remain quiet while I dance?"

"Yeah, no worries."

Faye recognized the husky voice of Roger, her muscleman. But more importantly, she believed him.

"Let–us–the–*fuck*–in already!"

The voice of Dick again and his fist against the door.

"I'm serious!" said Faye. "If you don't remain seated and silent throughout my entire performance until the music ends, there will be consequences to pay. A penalty. Agreed?"

"What penalty?" voiced Devin.

"Yes, god-damn-it! We agree to the terms of your *fucking* game. Now open up!"

"You heard Dick agree," said Faye.

"It's Richard!"

Faye unbolted the door and retreated up the stairs. Halfway up, she turned to watch. The heretic pushed past the others to enter first. She waited at the landing as they climbed the stairs. Richard leered at her. "What's my incentive for staying quiet while you do your little dance? You giving out party favors?"

"You get to have your way with me afterward." Faye directed them to the living room. "Now, everyone take a seat. I'll be serving. Who wants wine? Hard liquor? Cannabis? Cocaine? Ecstacy?"

After playing host and serving them a variety of intoxicants, and partaking herself, Faye announced it was time to be silent. Devin and Roger settled into their seats. Richard remained standing, swilling his whiskey. He set the glass down and clapped his hands.

"Time to dance. Do it! Strip!"

Faye was busy sorting through a wall of stacked record albums. They surrounded an elaborate sound system with a fancy turntable. Richard slapped her bottom. "I said, *move* your ass."

Startled, Faye jumped, caught off guard as he grabbed her arms, turning her around and shoving her into the wall.

"What are you doing?" she said. "No touching!"

"The hell there isn't."

"Let go!"

She was overpowered by Richard who grinned.

"Stop being an asshole," grunted Roger. "Sit down and shut the fuck up."

"Yeah, come on," added Devin.

The heretic let go of Faye and laughed. "Hey, I'm just *fucking* with you. Giving you your birthday wish."

Richard grabbed his whiskey and plopped down onto the sofa. "Yeah, all right, let's see that dance."

Shaken, Faye smoothed her dress. To calm her nerves, she took a sip of wine. The fire in her eyes was reignited and she raised her index finger to her lips. "Patience, Richard. It *is* a virtue." She then went back to sorting through the records.

"Jeezuz," griped Richard, shifting his body on the leather sofa. "Pick a fucking song already—and *dance*."

"No more talking," said Faye, selecting an album. She slid the record from its sleeve, then found the right track to place the needle. "An oldie but goodie. Romeo Void. This is my favorite. It's called, *Just Too Easy*. It has a rapid two-one beat that—"

Dick muttered, "Christ, get on with it."

Faye turned and yanked the needle off the record. It made an amplified shriek.

"I'm serious!" Faye pointed. "Interrupt me again, *Richard*, and I will make you pay. For your sins."

The heretic rose to his feet. "Lighten up, Sweetheart."

This propelled the bouncer out from his chair to grab and shove Richard back onto the sofa. "Stay put! And zip it! Or I'll toss your sorry ass onto the street."

"You and who else?" The heretic smirked, looking up, playing it cool. "Whoa, Incredible Hulk, cool your green engines, my man. I was getting up to pour myself another drink."

"Later. Play by the rules," said Roger.

"Whose rules? Hers? We outnumber this—"

Roger faked-punched Richard with his right hand, followed by a light slap with his left. He held up a finger as a warning. Richard scoffed but did nothing.

Faye smiled. She was pleased to see Dick was realizing his place in this pecking order. "I will let that go as a warning. But, you each gave me your solemn oath. And I intend to collect on my bet if you fail me and lose."

She waited for her bouncer to settle back into his seat.

"Ready? Set. Go."

Faye placed the needle back down on the record. For the first few revolutions, the song now had an audible *scratch-scratch–pop*. She closed her eyes to feel the rhythm and mentally absorb the lyrics, which were strident, confident, sexy. Her hips swayed to the beat as her head flung backward, shaking her long hair in defiance as she stretched her arms above her head and mouthed the words of the female singer, *"It was just too easy, to break your heart ..."*

Faye crossed her arms over her breasts to reach her shoulders, pealing off the straps to her slip-on dress. While she shimmied to the beat her fingers moved down her thighs to lift the hem, exposing a peek of black-lace panties.

In a sultry, sensuous strut, she moved across the oriental carpet and took hold of a grand piano with both hands. Twerking her hips, she leaned over the black-lacquered instrument and lay her cheek on its surface.

"Maybe she's gonna *fuck* the piano."

Devin shooshed Richard.

Continuing to sway, Faye reached up to pull down the top of her dress, as if pealing off snakeskin, and exposed her breasts.

The heretic stifled a laugh. "Shit, those are some seriously itty-bitty *titties.*"

Faye covered her chest, pulled up her dress, and returned to the turntable. She kicked it fiercely – sending the needle skipping across the record in spasmodic bursts of noise. Holding her dress with one hand, she pointed with her other at the heretic and shouted, "That does it! You lose! I warned you!"

The heretic raised his hands. "You got me. I surrender. Don't get your panties in a twist, Dollface."

"Don't '*Dollface*' me!" screamed Faye. "You two are witnesses.

You heard him make a promise to be quiet – even after I gave him several warnings! Now he has to pay."

Richard scoffed and rose to his feet. "Give it a rest. You'll have a fucking orgasm."

"No, *Dollface*," said Faye, "You're the one who'll be having the fucking orgasm."

The heretic downed his glass of whiskey, set it back on a table, then proceeded to unzip his pants with a lurid grin. "All right, then. Show me those little titties. Drop to your knees, and get over here. Let's do this thing—*now*."

Faye reattached the shoulders straps of her dress and stared at his erect penis, poking from her guest's unzipped pants. He wagged it at her like a dog eager for play, wagging his little tail to taunt her. She informed him, "The penalty for breaking your promise to me is for you to become my slave."

"Your what? Fuck you. No fucking way." He glanced at the others. "Hey, there's no fucking way we're—"

"Not *them*," clarified Faye. "Only you."

"Like hell." Richard stuffed his swollen genitalia back into his pants and nervously zipped himself up. "The fun's over."

"Wrong," she countered. "It's just begun."

The heretic turned to leave. "I'm outa here, *bitch*."

"Stop him!" Faye pointed to Roger, who responded promptly by blocking his path to the door.

"Out of my way, asshole!"

"Don't let him leave," said Faye.

Richard, not sure of his next move, acted unconcerned. He kept watch of Devin who approached him from behind. "Hey! Back off. You may be tall, but you're a pussy! You too, Incredible Hulk. You act tough, but you're no threat to me. Only *dumb* – to be taking orders from this – this *cunt*. I'm warning you. This won't end well for any of you!"

"I like my odds," said Faye. "And don't call me a *cunt*."

The heretic kicked over a table, "I don't know what you are! You're fucking *nuts* – I know that much!"

"This name calling," said Faye. "Devin – a *pussy?* And Roger – *dumb?* It must stop. You need to be taught some manners."

"Fuck you. Back off, Hulk! I warning you, I'm connected."

Faye was curiously amused. "Connected? To what?

"The mafia—bitch! Heard of it? Now back off! Before you all regret it."

The heretic saw his threat wasn't working.

Faye told the bouncer, "This is what I want. We move Dick into the dining room to receive his punishment."

Richard was backing up and cornered. "Why're you listening to this shit? What's in it for you? Nothing. You can't—"

The heretic made a dash for the stairs. Roger tackled him to the floor, wrestling until he had Richard's arm twisted behind his back and restrained.

"Ouch—*shit!* Let go of me you fucking ape!"

"Very impressive," said Faye to Roger, then addressed Richard. "To answer your question, *Dickie.* The two of them get me as a prize for keeping their promise. Unlike you."

"We did promise," said the angel.

"Fuck you! Ouch! You too, shit-head"

Roger forced Richard to his feet. "If you want, I could dislocate his arm."

"That won't be necessary," said Faye. "I abhor violence."

Roger pushed Richard toward the room Faye had pointed to. "You should've stayed in the bar. You've been a real pain in the ass to be around, you know that?"

"He *has*, hasn't he," said Faye.

She led them through an arched doorway to examine a massive oak table. It had sturdy legs carved into claws for feet. She swept off the centerpiece arrangement of dried flowers and candleholder. They crashed to the floor. She pushed the table and was pleased by its resistance.

"Here will be perfect." She patted the tabletop and turned to her angel, "Your task, my pet, is to secure those bondage straps to each table leg." She turned to Richard, restrained by Roger. "Thank you for your present. I can't wait to try these out."

"I don't find this amusing," said Richard.

Faye placed fingers to her lips. "Oh, Dickie, but I do."

"God-damn-it, last warning! Let me go or I'll—"

"What?" Faye feigned distress. "You don't look to be in a very good bargaining position."

Richard struggled unsuccessfully to free himself. "You're going to regret this you cunt!"

The bouncer jerked the heretic's arm up a notch to shut him up, then asked Faye, "What now?"

"First, I want to seal off his foul mouth." Faye opened her bag of goodies. She took out the horse bridle with it reins, dangling the apparatus before Richard. "Open your mouth and take the bit."

He spit in her face.

"Aren't *you* the filthy beast." Faye wiped her cheek. "Keep your mouth open this time."

Dick clenched his teeth.

Faye gave the headgear to Devin. "You'll know when to insert the bridle." She reached down and took hold of Richard's gonads. "Last chance. Open wide."

When he didn't, Faye squeezed.

The heretic howled. Faye held on as if riding a bucking bull as Roger pulled the arm up from behind.

Devin forced the ball bit into Richard's mouth, quickly synched the bridle straps around his head, then jumped away as if retreating from a rabid animal.

Faye let go of Richard's genitals. She looked him in the eyes and petted his muzzled face. "I will have you broken in no time."

The heretic looked dazed and began to wobble. Faye turned to examine the table and realized something was missing.

"Angel, come help me."

They returned from the living room carrying an ottoman. They slid it onto the center of the table.

Roger was struggling to keep Richard standing. "Hey, what the hell's going on with him?"

"I confess," said Faye. "I spiked his drink, a touch. Now, where I want him is face down on the ottoman, arms and legs secured by those velcro fasteners to the four corners of the table. Do whatever it takes to get him there. Are you ready? Set. Go."

Handicapped as he was by barbiturates, Richard managed to free an arm while being hoisted onto the tabletop and elbowed Devin in the face. Roger responded by knocking the wind out of Richard – shoving him into the table, then into submission. Richard was docile after that and was moved into position, his legs and arms bound.

"Bravo!" Faye clapped ecstatically. "You were both marvelous. Now, who wants to join me in having some fun?"

Faye climbed onto the table to unbutton her captive's shirt. He groaned, writhing in resistance, so she tore it off, ripping it to shreds until his torso was bare. She next unbuckled his belt and unbuttoned his pants. To force them down, she ripped apart the crotch and pulled what remained to his ankles. She then tore off his boxers, leaving only the elastic band.

Thrilled with her conquest, Faye gave his bare bottom a spank and hopped off the table. She retrieved her bag of birthday gifts and removed a can of paint. The little ball clanged inside as she declared, "Your mission, if you choose to accept it, is to remake this ugly beast into the beautiful creature he was meant to be."

"And what's that?" asked Roger.

She sprayed his scrotum blue. "My Little Pony."

This got them all laughing, except for Richard. Faye stopped to shake another can. "Darn, I wish I'd thought to get glitter. Oh, well, we'll make do."

Delighted by her artistic start, she shook more paint cans and moved to the other end of the table, where she sprayed his black hair with streaks of silver and gold. Devin and Roger merely watched, a bit stunned by Faye's aggressive play. She tossed them each a can of paint, encouraging them to join her. They regarded each other with skeptical looks, before laughing and applying swirls of graffiti to Richard's torso.

"Angel?" said Devin, "Are you sure about this?"

Faye paused to take a gulp of wine. "I've never been surer of anything in my life."

She went back to working on the purple and yellow bullseye she was spraying on Richard's posterior. When completed they all broke into infectious laughter. Richard voiced inarticulate threats through his gagged mouth. Faye slapped his rear end.

"*Stop* that," she scolded.

Faye went around the table. She grabbed the reins and jiggled his head. "My little pony, are you going to behave now?"

Faye jerked up his reins as Richard snarled at her. "You refuse? Angel, hand me the whip."

The heretic's eyes widened.

She took hold of the requested item and examined the plastic handle. It had a slight curve, thick as a banana with a bulbous end. She teased her captive's face with the long fibers.

"Oh, my," she exclaimed. "This is not a whip!"

Roger had flopped himself down into a dining-room chair and was holding a goblet of wine. "What do you mean?"

Faye giggled. "Thank you, I love it! It's the *perfect* party favor. Who wants to play Pin the Tail on the Donkey?"

The invitation, and its implication, took a moment for everyone to register. Richard's head strained upwards, eyes showing alarm, comprehending what was to come. He thrashed violently to break loose from his bonds, realizing he was to be the donkey.

Faye swished the horsetail across his face and told him, "Oh, *Dickie*, don't be such a party poop."

Faye rounded the table. "What was that comment you made? Something about women deserving to get it up the ass now and then. Whatever did you mean by that remark?"

Richard's words were garbled.

"Silly me," Faye said, scooping the glass of wine from Roger's hand. She took a gulp. "Donkeys can't *talk*."

Devin walked back from the kitchen holding a bag of corn chips and a container of onion dip.

"I'll go first," said Faye. "Since I'm the birthday girl."

"You want a blindfold?" said Roger.

Faye laughed and handed him his wine. "And miss seeing this? No, but I will be needing *that*." She took the onion dip from Devin and dipped the horsetail handle into its container. She aimed, then pushed its primed plastic end into the center of the bullseye.

The muffled howls rose in pitch, escalating.

"*Relax*," said Faye, shoving the tail in deeper. "Enjoy it. Isn't that what you tell all the women you rape?"

She left the tail hanging from him. She poured herself a glass of wine and declared, "I win." She admired her art, then meandered back to Dick's gagged head slumped over the ottoman. She jangled the reins to gain his attention. She lifted his head and he lunged at her – stopped by his restraints.

His thrust startled Faye enough to spill her wine. She set her glass down on the table.

"You *nasty* little pony," she scolded. "Shame on you. I thought I'd broken you. This will surely do the trick."

Roger had begun to pace, conflicted and troubled by what he'd become a part of. "Enough. It's time we end this."

Faye brushed past him. "I agree."

"No more. Let him go."

Ignoring the bouncer, Faye walked over to the counter dividing kitchen and dining room. She removed a large carving knife from its wooden block.

Devin expressed alarm. "Angel, what are you doing?"

"This stud needs to be put out to pasture. Neutered. He can't be *molesting* the mares."

Richard was thrashing at his restraints.

Roger waved his arms and shouted. "Hold on! There's no way I'm letting you—"

"Do what?" She avoided him by scooting to the opposite side of the table. "It's a routine surgery. To *fix* these nasty ponies of their ill-bred ways."

Faye flipped up the horsetail with the blade. She smiled with a wink at Roger and Devin, both confused, ready to intervene.

"Hold still, Dick," she said. "You'll only make it worse. Angel, I'll need a bucket of ice. Also rubber bands for a tourniquet."

Faye placed a finger to her lips to show she was only joking. She walked around the table and lifted Richard's head. She pursed her lips and touched his tears. "My poor little pony. You've been crying. Are you going to keep your promises now?"

She danced over to the counter, sliding the knife into its holder. "Almost done." She removed a new iPhone from her purse, poked its buttons, and began filming every angle, finishing with a close-up of his face. "Big smile. And ... Cut!"

She pinched his nose. "You were terrific. Oh, FYI. Don't dream of revenge. Because if anything happens. Let's say I die ..."

Faye took a gulp of wine and collected her purse. "This movie, starring you, my little pony, you *jackass*. It will go viral. All over the

Internet. Enjoy the rest of your day. Are we ready?"

This was directed at Devin and Roger. They were not moving, still stunned by what had transpired.

Faye batted her eyes. "What?" She looked at her creation bound to the table as if noticing for the first time the beauty of her work. "Did *we* do that? He's so pretty. Richard, you should see yourself. You're a real piece of art."

No one was laughing.

Faye giggled. "Come on, it's funny."

Roger turned and walked from the room saying nothing. Devin trailed after him, glancing back with a sheepish look.

"Angel … I don't know. Sorry."

Faye followed after them, realizing she'd taken it too far again and misbehaved. "Fine, we'll untie him. He had it coming."

Roger stopped to ask, "Is it really your birthday?"

"Yes. Why would I lie?"

Roger grabbed his coat. Devin was leaving too.

"Guys." Faye laughed. "Come on. I guess this means no cruise on the bay to see Alcatraz?"

Clouds are amassing above the bay. In formations of radiant white, edged with iridescence, swollen at the base with dark purpose. Moving mountains of water vapor. They were once believed to be the dwelling place of gods, titans, and giants.

I point, showing Semele. "Where the gods used to roam."

She gives me a WTF look.

The two of us are walking along the Marina Green. "And now God is everywhere," I add. "Inside all of us. According to Jesus. Of course, he hadn't factored you, being such a hard sell."

"Shut up," she tells me with a smile.

We keep walking.

"Beautiful," I say to defuse the topic of religion. Semele, a non-believer, thinks I am delusional. But she's wrong. I am ambivalent. Semantics aside, even atheists who believe in nothing – no God – is something. A belief. "Most of our ancestors were delusional."

She bumps into me. "Yours. Definitely."

"I like the Hindus. They believe the world is illusionary. They might be onto something. Who really knows?"

Semele stops. "Can you feel this?"

"What?" I stop too.

She slaps my face. "That. It's reality."

I laugh and touch my tingling skin. "Heartfelt."

"For being twenty minutes late today."

"I overslept."

"You take too many naps."

"I do night shifts. Morning shows. I need to."

A strong wind off the ocean buffets us, filling both our workout jackets like sails. We lean into the wind to fight this palpable force then almost fall on our faces when the gust subsides just as quickly, to show us how vulnerable we are against the whims of nature.

"If there's no God, what's the purpose of our existence?"

Semele glances at me. "Nothing."

"Come on, all these impressive creatures with tentacles, claws, spouts, fins, legs, snouts and mouths. Eyes to see beyond ourselves. Minds to distinguish what is what. There has to be more to us than mechanisms to survive."

"Why?"

"Exactly."

"No, Egon. *Why* does it matter?"

"Vision? Our ability to see? There must be a reason."

Semele stops, sighs, takes a breath. "For us to enjoy ourselves? Can't you simply enjoy the beauty around us?"

Seagulls are squawking from above, battling the wind.

I copy Semele's example and gaze around, admiring these birds in flight and the afternoon wind upon the bay. "The Zen masters say our vision of the world is only a map. Not reality."

Semele inhales and starts walking again. "A map to what?"

"You got me."

"Do I? Really?" Semele gives me that funny look I know well, her mind toying with the notion of where I'd go if she *did* have me, how I'd fit into her life, whether I'd clash with her furniture.

"Yes, you do," I say. "That said, all things are mutable."

"Especially you."

I point to the leaves tumbling over the lawn. "Their attachment to a tree has come and gone, run its course. The essence of free will, or lack thereof, as envisioned by Spinoza. Every existence is finite. Simultaneously infinite. Mutable. You see?"

Semele stops to kiss me on the lips. "I don't know this Spinoza. I'm only trying to understand you. I'll see you later?"

"I'll be there."

"No more naps. Happy birthday."

I watch Semele run off, stepping up her pace, the last length of her exercise is a sprint to her front door. I stop to admire her body, her energy, her spirit. I turn around to face the Golden Gate Bridge and watch a squadron of pelicans hovering in the sky and dropping with meteoric speed into the bay to swallow up fish.

A flying object startles me – a dog who leaps, snatching in its teeth a whizzing frisbee about to hit me in the face. The slobbering black Lab drops the plastic disc and bounds over to nudge his foamy snout against my leg. He wants to be rewarded for his act of bravery and skill. I rub his floppy ears.

He lowers his head to sniff the ground, warning me. Saving me from stepping onto a land mine, of the organic non-explosive kind. Planted by one of his friends. A whistle from far off gets the dog to react and retrieve the frisbee then run away.

And I am left alone again with my thoughts.

I stop at a pink gravel path to balance on one leg while I lift my other and survey my sole. In this awkward position, I feel the ground shake and set my foot on the ground. A woman is running at me. Her smile seems a bit too fanatical, muscles tensed from exertion. She is wearing an athletic bikini, and proud of her toned physique, tan and glistening with sweat. In the brief time, before she passes me, she examines my face and body. We both turn our heads. She slows, jogging backward, offering me a chance, it would seem, to make an offer, to say something. She pouts comically, turns, and runs on.

Women find me attractive for some reason. After college, while working for a theater constructing sets, a cohort convinced me to try my luck at modeling. The pay was potentially more lucrative. A few snapshots later and a new career was launched. I had representation. I auditioned for ad agencies, was directed by directors, was shot by photographers, and prepped by makeup artists who groomed me for the bright lights. My nose would get powdered, my skin creamed, and my hair combed or fluffed or spiked, depending on the product I was hired to sell. I too had become a commodity. Encouraged by my advisors and handlers, I starved myself and devoted hours in the gym to define my biceps, pecs, and abs. I became eye candy.

Women loved me. So too did the men.

You can only be a golden leaf and float downstream for so long before you start to sink from saturation, caught up in one seductive eddy after another, becoming lost in the cross currents. Destined to drown. And I would have, had it not been for Faye. She saved me. She told me to quit. To follow my dreams. Be an artist.

I love my sister for that. But that was then.

A car screeches to a halt as I step off the curb. A horn blasts, but I ignore it.

"Are you trying to get killed?"

I'm not technically inside the crosswalk, but close enough, and I have the right-of-way. But this motorist has forgotten. People need to be reminded of the rules or we'd have anarchy.

"Hey, I'm talking to you! Maybe I won't stop next time! I'll turn you into road kill!"

To tell this man to fuck off, to be more courteous, drive slower, would have what effect? The opposite. It would only flare his rage. I wonder if he feels invulnerable in his vehicle, holding the wheel and leaning on his horn? Somehow we are made to feel safe traveling around in our semi-protective bubbles, yet never knowing who we might find ourselves suddenly face to face with, staring at their eyes, into their soul, and feel the consequence of our actions. Does anyone listen in a shouting match? I don't.

I stop to check for mail. When the box reveals nothing, I am reminded it is Sunday.

The days go by fast, shot full of holes.

It takes me awhile to find the right key. We have keys to let us in and keys to let us out. We've become wardens to our own prisons.

Birds and squirrels must peer down from branches and power lines to wonder what the hell we do inside these boxes, moving from one box into the next.

The third key fits into the deadbolt and turns without a click. It wasn't even locked. I'm forgetful. If I didn't stare into a mirror from time to time, I'd probably forget who I was. I think of Mira as I do. Apropos, for she has become a reflection of me, like this hall mirror. She is seductive, bewitching, someone who believes she is capable of exorcising my demons.

As I stare at myself, I imagine her reflected back. "Mira, you know that I'm in love with you, right?"

"'*Mirror, mirror* on the wall.'"

Hunter's voice startles me. I find him grinning, sitting midway up my flight of stairs.

"*Jesus*, Hunter! You scared the shit out of me."

"Happy birthday, pal. 'Who *is* the fairest one of all?'"

"How'd you get in?"

My friend cocks his head. "Your door was unlocked."

I turn the deadbolt. "Right."

"I'm not alone." Hunter nods to the side.

A rustle of white moves in the darkness of this alcove.

"Hi, Ego."

Jenna rises off a cushioned bench. One hand lingers behind her to brush the stucco wall with her fingertips, as if she requires this contact, needing constant grounding. Hunter's girlfriend has moods that alternate like a holograph.

She touches my shoulder. We receive a light spark. She giggles, kisses my cheek, and plops her body on the stairs below Hunter.

"Pretty as ever," I tell her.

"Charmed," she says.

It's a game we play. I will never have her as a lover. She is all Hunter's and he knows it.

"Why do you love the mirror?" Jenna asks.

"It's Egon's shrink," says Hunter. "Her name's Mira."

"Therapist," I clarify. "And she's Faye's, not mine."

Hunter huffs a laugh. Perched on the stairs, he reminds me of a gargoyle, legs splayed, elbows on knees, chin resting on his fists.

"Is she pretty?" Jenna leans into Hunter and he wraps his arms around her.

"What difference does it make?"

"So—she *is*," Jenna intuits and fluffs the gauzy ruffles of white fabric above her knees. She has come dressed as a ballet dancer. She reminds me of an angel sitting on a cloud.

"She's only interested in my mind," I tell her.

"She might want your *body* too."

"Not everyone's demonic like you, Hunter."

"I'm flattered," he says.

"Are we playing Faust?"

"No, Jenna," I step toward them. Hunter has on a biker's jacket and black jeans, leather boots. "What are you going as?"

"Myself." Hunter grins through his bristles.

"Do you mind moving?"

Jenna rises in her satin slippers. When my sister was little she'd play make-believe and pretend to be other people. One was a water faerie named Jenna. Who drove me crazy.

So does *this* Jenna.

Hunter rises too, with effort, hoisting his weight, mostly muscle, and towers above both me and Jenna. As we climb, he tells me, "I'd be careful what you say to that shrink. She can't unshackle you from your misery, my friend. That's on you."

"Thanks."

He glances down at me, "Careless words will be greeted by the scourge of her whip."

Jenna giggles.

"Your pessimism is always refreshing," I tell Hunter.

Jenna, in between us, says." I don't agree with Hunter. Take the bedlamites. They had the unique freedom of being able to curse the king and get away with it."

"The *hell* are you talking about?" Hunter reaches the landing and scoops up a handful of mints from a bowl. He pops them, one by one, into his mouth.

I too am puzzled by Jenna's logic or lack thereof. Her method of reasoning has a tendency to create more confusion and headaches in those who attempt to understand her, and for friends to toss things at her – like matchbooks and ice cubes. I tend to be more forgiving since Jenna often inspires me.

Jenna and I reach the landing and stop.

"Ah," I deduce. "Like a court jester? Since the truth they deliver is packaged in foolish humor."

"Exacto," says Jenna, pleased with me. "They pose no threat. Never taken seriously. Lunatics possess the only true freedom."

Hunter laughs and tosses a mint at her.

"Oh!" She ignores both Hunter and the green mint stuck like an ornament in her blond curls. "It's like how I can't stand Hunter for being so boorish. Because it encourages me to fight back. Which is good, because you have to, or you might as well give up and die. Like the fish, how they evolved. We'd never have crawled onto land if we hadn't been forced to do it, to survive. And if we hadn't, where would we be today? Nowhere. Dead fish."

"What a *mind*," taunts Hunter. "What little there is."

Except Jenna's twisted logic makes me realize what it is Mira is encouraging me to do – to fight back.

All of a sudden, we hear a strange moaning noise.

"What was that?" says Jenna.

We walk into the living room to investigate. I see the ashtrays, empty wine bottles and glasses, the residue of drug paraphernalia.

The audio system is on – its red light pulsing. The turntable is askew. I lift the needle, remove the record, and examine the scratch marks. I switch off the power. But the moaning persists.

Hunter points to the dining room. Burglars? I look to see if my art collection is in place. Sculptures on tables, paintings and antique masks hanging on the walls, untouched. Nothing is missing that I can detect.

The noise is oddly human, a foreboding groan that spooks me. I stare at the masks on the wall. The carved-out eyes seem haunted. Masks that were once worn by shamans to lure primordial spirits. An enchantress. The antelope. A goblin. The duel faces of tragedy and comedy. All moaning in unison.

Jenna touches my shoulder. The masks return to what they are, blank faces, motionless and spiritless. The moaning is coming from another room. Jenna tugs my jacket, gets me to move. Hunter enters the dining room and I hear him laugh.

Curiosity overtakes my fear. Jenna lifts a hand to her mouth. There is a creature stretched upon my dining room table, on its belly, arms and legs stretched, bound to all four corners. It resembles an enormous erotic sculpture. Except alive, thrashing at its restraints.

Puzzling. How the hell did it get here?

Hunter and Jenna are already circling this strange beast whose mouth is biting a rubber bit and snarling, its head girdled in straps, its coiffured hair sprayed gold and silver, and its body elevated upon my leather ottoman. Its naked skin is colorfully defiled in graffiti. Jenna and Hunter stop to admire its black tail.

Jenna bursts into more giggles and it breaks the spell. I see the chimera for what is – a naked man bound and gagged.

Faye's doing. Her kind of animal.

"What the hell happened?" I ask. "How did—"

The man growls like a chained tiger. Instinct warns me that I'll be sorry if I release him. But what choice do I have? He can't stay here. Where will I eat?

"All right, all *right*, calm down," I tell the man. Hunter and Jenna take seats to watch. "Hey, would you mind helping me out?"

"Yes," laughs Hunter, "I mind. He's all yours."

"Faye's handiwork?" asks Jenna.

"What do you think?" I unbind a leg, ripping apart the velcro around one ankle. He kicks free. I realize my error in thinking he had a tail. Something is stuck up his baboon-striped ass.

"Hey!" I tell him. "Hold still. You're angry. I *get* that. But this wasn't my doing, all right?"

He bucks and kicks as I unfasten his other leg.

"Stop it! I'm the one untying you!"

Reluctantly I come around to unbind his wrists. He swings his fist at me once I undo his arm and I step away. He savagely tears off the velcro that grips his other wrist, frees himself, starts to get up, but topples off the table, apparently unaware – or having forgotten – his pants were around his ankles.

"Are you okay?" I move to help but decide it's better I stay clear. "I can't hear what you're saying."

Hunter gives me a comical thumbs-up gesture, entertained by the drama unfolding. The man claws and unfastens the bridle off his head. Next, with the bit and ball removed, he is free to speak, yet he says nothing, bewildered in his rage. Perhaps animal sounds had best expressed his emotions.

He yanks out his tail and is about to throw it at me.

"What the hell!" I raise my hands to prepare to avoid being hit. "You should be mad a *Faye*—not me!"

His mouth contorts. His eyes go weird, regressing again into an animal's bewilderment.

"*Shit!*"

His first word.

"God-damned-you-son-of-a-fucking-bitch-slut-whore!"

His second word, a compound expletive. His hand slams upon the table. As if further exclamation was needed. He turns toward me with his fists raised, ready to lung at me.

My calm response to his aggression seems to throw him off. It feels like I've been miscast in a cheap movie, not of my own making. My pacifism doesn't equate. He stares at me like I'm an actor who's adlibbing, not following the script. My unwillingness to engage into combat stops the action as if a director has yelled, "Cut!"

Conflicted, my antagonist desires to attack me but also wants to maintain some dignity. He has forgotten to pull up his pants. He looks at his body defiled like subway walls. His pants are bunched around his ankles. The remnants of his boxer shorts circle his waist. His penis is blue. He flings the tail to the floor and pulls up what is left of his ripped pants, buckling his belt to hold them up.

Self-consciously, he glances around. Jenna is sipping a glass of wine. She has the hint of a smile as she glides by the island counter, using her free hand to make contact.

In an attempt at civility, I ask the man, "Who are you?" Which is ridiculous, given the circumstances.

He lunges at me. I deflect each swing of his fist with an outward motion of my wrists and arms, then back away. I remain calm, more curious than afraid. Hunter is there to back me up if things get out of hand, so I don't panic.

I raise both hands, palms out, to defend myself in what is called the praying mantis stance. "Hey. I don't want any trouble."

"Too late!"

He sends another windmill swing at my face – which I knock away with a decisive twist of my arm. I retreat, palms raised.

Frustrated and confused by his inability to harm me, he turns to search for something. His shirt. Also, there is Hunter, impossible to ignore. At six foot three, menacing even when seated, he is on the edge of his chair, hands on his knees, prepared to launch up if the need arises. I actually feel sorry for this man. His silk shirt is torn to shreds. He whips his body around to kick me in the head. But since I anticipate his move his foot connects with the wall.

"Hey, man. I realize you're pissed off." I gesture toward Hunter. "But you're outnumbered. *Think.*"

The man looks around, then back at me.

"This isn't my doing," I remind him.

He cocks his head.

"Faye. *She's* the one who did this to you. Right?"

He squints. "Who the *fuck* are you?"

"I'm Egon."

"What?"

"Faye is my twin sister."

"The fuck she is!"

"I know, we look alike. Listen, my sister has problems. She was drinking, right? Something set her off. She needs help."

He wants to attack me, I can see that, but his will to strike stalls. He's confused by my palms moving like the heads of two pythons. In frustration he screams, "Fuck you! Fuck this!"

Shaking with rage, he is on the verge of a nervous breakdown, which doesn't portent well. Hunter launches up from his seat. The man backs away.

"Where's the phone!?"

I'm confused. "You want to use my phone?"

"No, fuckhead! The video! Where is it?"

I signal with my hand. "Hold off, Hunter. I want to know what the hell he's talking about."

The man looks spooked, body wildly painted, a walking canvas. Hunter cracks his knuckles. Jenna moves closer, sipping her wine as if she's at a dinner party and amused by this uninvited guest.

The man moves further away, avoiding us all, shaking his head with a sick laugh. "You're fucking *crazy*. That's it."

Transference. It's a psychological phenomenon I've seen before. It happens when a person unconsciously redirects his own feelings onto another. He's been victimized by Faye. She leaves men in need of restoring something that can't be restored.

Walking backward, he turns and descends, talking to himself in the stairwell, no doubt debating how to navigate through the world with torn clothes and a body defiled with graffiti.

He yells, "Just wait! You've no idea what I'm capable of! You tell your fucking *sister* she's *dead!* Count on it! Bitch!"

The door slams. Hunter and Jenna are no longer amused. They shake their heads.

Hunter points to the mess. "Your sister, she's fucked up."

Jenna sips her wine. "But Ego loves her."

I squint at Jenna. "Not so much anymore. And it's not like she doesn't have her own place, you know."

Jenna gives me a sad pout.

Hunter kicks the horsetail. "These clowns she fucks with? How many more before—"

"Someone kills her?"

"Or *you,*" he adds.

Jenna turns away. "It's so sad."

It is. Faye has made my life a living nightmare.

Hunter grips my shoulder. "That guy's a land mine. He's going to detonate. You need to contain the situation. ASAP."

Jenna says, "Could be he's all bark."

Hunter shakes his head and clenches his teeth. He gestures with a finger, slicing his throat. "I'll take care of it."

It was an hour past midnight. A full moon shining down like a spotlight on a stage. Clifford was hiding in the shrubbery on a small peninsula. He was peering across the lagoon through his binoculars, observing Egon Norwood, who was walking through the colonated open rotunda of the Palace of Fine Arts. It was an exotic structure. Anachronistic. Architecture inspired by the ancient ruins of Greece and Rome. It loomed above the lagoon within a park surrounded by residential dwellings. Built for the 1915 Panama-Pacific Exhibition, it had survived to become a historical San Francisco oddity.

The grounds were lush. Two long colonnades extended from the rotunda like wings. At the base of the corinthian capitals were walls supporting large urns and steps ascending to nowhere. Sculptures of sorrowful woman wept into vessels atop the colonnades. Above the arched rotunda, and beneath its domed top were friezes depicting Contemplation, Wonderment, and Meditation.

It was not the first time Clifford had followed Norwood here. He frequented the park almost daily. His attraction to this rotunda caused Clifford to research the Internet for clues about this structure. One discovery was the name the artist gave for the entablatures: "The Struggle for the Beautiful." Clifford wondered if it held any significance.

Magnified in his binoculars was his suspect, whose face was painted white. It reminded Clifford of the latest murder victim. The image of the dead man's face still troubled him. Clifford had been notified of the 911 call and arrived shortly after the police. Tourists from Miami had discovered the body sitting upright on cement stairs with his back against a wall. The newlyweds, on their honeymoon, had taken a midnight stroll from their hotel near Ghiradelli Square along the beach.

The wife had wanted to avoid the stairs and this ghoulish man. But her husband, a veteran of the Iraq war, had escaped roadside bombs and refused to be intimidated on his home turf, so he gripped his wife's hand and pulled her up the stairs.

The man remained motionless, his eyes wide open, and his neck freakishly twisted. "We thought he was trying to scare us," said the woman, her teeth chattering. "His face looked like a hideous mask. I mean, *look*," she told the police, her body turned into her husband who was consoling her.

Clifford was acting as the dutiful reporter, scribbling notes, but stopped to take another long look at the victim. His eyes were as empty as black holes in space. Anti-matter collapsing. A nothingness that had emotionally agitated Clifford's internal organs. He became nauseous and walked away to vomit in the sand.

A chilling premonition had seized him. Clifford had seen what the victim now saw. People – the police, paramedics, eye witnesses, bystanders – all wearing masks. Body costumes. Cloaked in flesh. Behaving as if they were not disposable, not phantoms walking this Earth alone, and not perishable at any second.

Clifford blinked. He refocussed his binoculars on Norwood, as he had the previous night, at the exact same time the serial killer had struck. As before, Norwood arrived with three magnificent women. Each dressed in a flowing white gown. Each moving like ghosts in the moonlight. Each magnified in his lenses as he shifted from one face to the next.

His suspect's white face stood out from the rest of his body, dressed in black, his shoes and gloves too. Which made Norwood appear disembodied in the moonlight. In contrast to the women, cloaked in white, who were as ethereal as goddesses.

It was a performance, or rehearsal, based on Greek mythology, Clifford determined. From what he had witnessed the night before, he'd investigated and realized they were depicting The Three Fates. They predated the gods and were once believed to control the life thread of every mortal from birth to death. And they held a power not to be trifled with.

Clifford shivered. Faye Norwood had forewarned him of her brother's strange behavior. The man's white face, magnified in his binoculars, seemed like a specimen under a microscope. Opaque. Nondescript. Undeterminable. But as alluring as a freakish creature seen inside a circus sideshow tent.

Clifford had an eerie sensation his own life was being spun by a thread, measured in length, cut with shears. By these three women. The Spinner, the Measurer, and Death. He pictured sparkling debris. The aftermath of a collision. Had his intuition gone off the rails? Clifford let go of his binoculars. It hung from his neck like a noose. His heart was pounding. His thoughts racing. It was a premonition. Butterflies fluttered inside his stomach. He sensed he was about to be thrust upon a stage. Onto a scaffolding. About to die.

To calm his nerves, Clifford reminded himself this man couldn't be the serial killer. Norwood was right here during the last murder. He had observed him for more than two hours. His pager, alerting him to the 911 call, had buzzed him during that time. The kill had taken place two miles away. And by late morning, the forensic team confirmed what everyone had suspected. An "X" was found, carved into the victim's skin. The killer's trademark.

The deceased was identified as a pedophile, a convicted felon, recently released from prison. Clifford even recalled this man, a pre-school teacher who had molested children and photographed their naked bodies.

Clifford unzipped his bag and removed his camera. He attached its zoom lens, then assembled the tripod behind the camouflage of shrubbery. After adjusting his lens setting, then its shutter speed, he pushed a button to take a time-lapse exposure.

Similar to the previous night, the three women moved around while Norwood, this mime, remained seated above them on a wall. Controlled by a timer, the camera did its work automatically. Which allowed Clifford to peer into his binoculars.

He was startled to see Norwood, perfectly still, staring back.

Could this man see in the darkness?

Shaking off the notion, Clifford moved his binoculars onto the Three Fates. While he watched them interact, he reviewed the events of the day. Norwood had left his house mid-morning. He rode a bus over the hill to Broadway street. At a sidewalk cafe, he was joined by one of the Fates, the one who held the golden shears. They exchanged a kiss, talked awhile, then parted. Shortly afterward, fatigue had set in which caused Clifford to doze. He awoke several minutes later and Norwood was gone.

When he located Norwood again, several hours later, the man was walking along the Marina Green with another Fate, the one who held the Thread of Life. Both wore exercise gear and were walking and talking. She departed, and Egon returned to his home.

Nothing out of the ordinary, until Clifford witnessed a man exit the building a half hour later. He was shirtless, holding up pants torn at the seams. His body was spray-painted in wild colors. Shocked by this sight, Clifford nearly missed getting photos.

Norwood left the building roughly an hour later. Clifford trailed him to a restaurant where he joined others. In this group was the women Clifford had seen at the sidewalk cafe. She was dressed as she was now, in a white robe, the Fate known as Death, carrying golden shears. She stood at the window. He watched as she sipped her cocktail, snipping her scissors and laughing. He noted others dressed in strange outfits. Someone in a motorcycle jacket with chains, a gypsy in a turban, a man wearing a blue renaissance jacket with a white embroidered shirt, and a ballerina.

A costume party, Clifford suspected. While the festivities went on, Clifford drove off to buy a milkshake, fries, and a cheeseburger. He returned to sit in his Jaguar munching on junk food while using the telephoto lens on his camera to watch. Norwood had meanwhile changed into the costume of a mime.

Hours passed.

It was late. He was bored and ready to leave. That was, until the Fate masquerading as Death moved into frame, against the window. She was naked beneath her gown – the realization made apparent by the interior lights.

He choked on a french fry. He grabbed his camera and adjusted its telephoto lens, extending in length as he zoomed in on her hips and breasts, capturing rapid-fire exposures.

When she finally moved out of view, Clifford let his camera fall. Breathing hard, he felt aroused.

When the restaurant closed, Norwood left with her, this Fate, snipping the shears at her side. They staggered, pawing each other, kissing as they moved down the sidewalk. They disappeared inside his house. The front door closed behind them. Clifford felt thwarted. Ostracized. Angered. Especially now, after becoming involved in this man's life and witnessing his companion's beauty. A women who'd never remove her canopy to expose her body like a delicious dessert – disrobing in a half shell like Venus – for *him!*

A lust-filled jealous rage caused Clifford to unbuckle his pants. He dug below the soft folds of stomach fat to locate his penis and rubbed himself, stimulating images of this woman developing fast in the darkroom of his mind.

A car alarm erupted the silence.

It whooped and honked.

Clifford scrambled and stuffed himself back together. Smelling fumes of guilt, he ignited his Jaguar and drove off.

He was startled back into real time, into the present, by a white swan honking. It was moving in the dark waters of the lagoon. Its question-mark neck was rotated toward him.

"*Shoosh,*" he hissed.

The swan made a u-turn and came back to honk some more. "Be *quiet*. Go away. Please."

To his surprise, and relief, his polite request did the trick, for the swan moved on, leaving him alone. Or so he thought. From behind he heard a soft shuffling noise.

Clifford turned and saw three youths – one black, two white – standing above him. Their metal knives reflected the moonlight.

SIX

It was all arranged. Egon had agreed to meet Faye for lunch at Cafe de Paris L'Entrecote. Not one to wear a watch, she stopped a passerby to ask him the time. It was as she suspected. Her brother was late. It was several minutes past noon.

Seated beneath a pink umbrella, Faye drummed her fingernails on the plastic tabletop. A cheap and repetitive sound that began to augment her annoyance. She was the only one seated outside. She glanced around for sights of interest. At the center of the patio was an enormous palm tree that rose between the several pink umbrellas to form its own umbrella of green fronds.

Amusingly phallic, she thought. There was even a brass placard nailed to its thick trunk to commemorate some prominent citizen or politician for its erection. Next to the palm tree was a lamp post that had its own metal umbrella. She realized it was a propane gas heater, not a light. She shivered as the waiter arrived. He was holding rolled napkins full of silverware.

"I'm expecting someone," she said.

He set down two menus. "A cocktail to start you off?"

"I'll wait. Could you get someone to turn that heater on?"

Her server stopped what he was doing to consider the tarnished metal pole with its mushroom cap standing idle, before responding in a blasé manner, "I'll ask management. It *is* chilly, isn't it?"

"Yes."

Faye watched as he arranged the table settings by turning each utensil next to each plate just so.

"*Very* chilly," she added.

"Who would have thought it to be overcast this late?"

"Not the weathermen," said Faye. "They promised sunshine."

Having unfurled both napkins and arranging the contents, the waiter gave Faye his full attention. "These weather people, what do they know? If they get their forecasts wrong, they still get paid, and for doing what? Predicting this? I mean, *really*."

"Results are important," said Faye. "The heater?"

"You should come inside where it's warm."

"I like it out here. It's quaint."

"Let me see what I can do. Nice makeup. I like what you've done with your eyes and lips."

"Thank you."

"I'll be right back. Meanwhile, don't let any extremities freeze that are important."

She smiled at his humor and shivered, rubbing her bare knees, then her shoulders. The sky was still swirling with thick grey fog, unwilling to dissipate and be gone.

"Damn you, Egon," she muttered.

Faye discreetly glanced at the rooftop across the street. She was searching the theater's ornate facade for signs of her detective, who was supposed to be positioned there. She glimpsed what she thought to be his head and looked away. He had awakened her at six in the morning to inform her that he had been mugged.

"So?" she told him. "Why tell me?"

He hastily explained that he was without camera equipment. That last night teenage thugs had stolen everything.

"Then you had better go buy new equipment or rent some fast. Today's shoot is important. And don't expect *me* to pay the bill for your incompetence. You're a detective. You should be able to defend yourself." She hung up on him.

Faye had a smile on her lips. She felt she'd made the right choice in hiring Clifford Hill, Private Investigator. She'd been intimidated upon first meeting him. He had a physical resemblance to her father. But when she realized Clifford had neither the backbone nor bile, she imagined her father reincarnated, coming back to Earth as a patsy, gutted and boned like a fish, for her to play with and even the score. It amused her to see how far she could use him.

A black railing separated her from the sidewalk. She could easily reach and touch each person passing had she wanted to. Removing a hand mirror from her purse, she checked her makeup. Over the rim of the mirror, the moving faces held a minimal interest. A few people paused to glance at her. She liked being recognized. She wondered if they had seen her perform at Teatro ZinZanni. Or read the article in the entertainment section of the Chronicle. Or seen her face on one of the many posters displayed around the city.

Adjusting to this attention, Faye met their eyes with a smile but nearly shrieked at the aberration that stood before her.

"Egon—you ass! You startled me."

It was the same sullen face she had come to associate with her brother. Opaque white. Except for his lips painted black, along with his eyes, one with a tear-drop. The face of a mime.

Faye added, "Only a fool walks around looking like one."

"Don't start."

"Is this to embarrass me?"

"Why are you sitting out here?"

"Because I like it."

"You're shivering."

"No, I'm not."

"Let's go inside."

"I want to eat here."

"Faye, for Christ's sake."

"Stop complaining. Sit down."

Egon took the seat opposite her. "It feels like winter."

"The fog's going to break any minute."

Egon shook his head as Faye shook her purse to locate cigarettes within the clutter of items. She tapped out one from a pack, saw him staring and said, "What?"

"You said you were going to quit."

"Yes, and when you said you'd meet me for lunch I expected you to come as a normal human being, not a freak."

"You know I work on Mondays."

"Play, don't you mean?"

Egon zipped up his coat, then reached for the fork to stroke the prongs with his thumb. "I perform."

"Like at the zoo? As a janitor."

"I'm at the Academy of Sciences now. Their night shift. It's nice and quiet. I like it."

"The *Academy*. My, my. A step up."

Egon grimaced. "Faye, don't mock. It's ugly. I don't like seeing that side of myself."

"With that face?"

"Come watch us tonight."

Faye tapped her cigarette. "Why would I do that?"

"It's our debut. We're doing The Three Fates."

"You're *doing* them? All three, at once? Impressive."

Egon hadn't intended to laugh. "Come on. We've missed you. You'll like it. Greek mythology. Comedy and tragedy. Yes?"

Faye dug through her purse for her butane lighter. "There is no greater power than the Sisters of Fate, you told me. Three old hags. Which one do you play?"

Egon gestured with open arms. "Can we have a truce?"

Faye flicked sparks from her lighter. "You tell me."

Egon rubbed his hands. "Let's go inside. It's freezing."

Faye fought off a shiver. "I said no."

"You know that I'm mad at you, right?"

Fare returned his stare. "Not as *pissed* as I am with you."

Egon clenched his fork, set it down. "Now what?"

"You *know* what."

"No, Faye, I can't *imagine.* What?"

"The inheritance? It's what you didn't do."

Egon pushed away his fork. "You can't blame me for that."

"I do. Your attitude is typically *male.* If you'd been born a girl you'd know how I feel."

"Our dad was a bastard. You know that. It was a total shock he left us anything."

"Us? The estate went to you."

"Technically."

"Not technically. And not an equal split."

"It's in a trust fund. The attorneys—"

"Fuck them. I get *fucked.* Again, by him. Posthumously."

The waiter returned, setting down two glasses of water. "My boss is debating about the weather. I'll be sure to inform you *if* and when he makes a decision. Which may be never. In the interim can I get you something from the bar?"

"Yes." Faye tapped her fingernail on the wine menu. "A bottle of chardonnay. That one."

"I don't want any," said Egon.

"Sure you do. It will warm us up."

"Two glasses? Or one?"

Faye bristled at the waiter's smarmy expression. "*Two.* Do you have a problem with that?"

"Absolutely not. Wine for two. I'll be back to tell you about our specialties."

As the waiter left, she ignited her cigarette and squinted at Egon. With a snap, she snuffed the flame. "Look at you, plastered white in your mask of silence. Truth is, you have nothing intelligent to say."

"You wanted to meet, Faye. Why?"

"We'll get to that." She sucked in smoke.

Egon drank his water carefully to avoid smearing his black lips. "You've missed meetings. Do you ever plan on returning?"

"The group was going nowhere."

Egon rotated the water glass. "We're thinking of auditioning for that TV show. You know, the one where you can win a grand prize of a million dollars and headline a show in Las Vegas."

"You sound desperate. You must be jealous."

Egon picked up his menu. "Seriously? Faye, you're in an off—*off*—Broadway dinner show. Nobody is jealous. And you're not a star. Trust me on that."

"I let others determine what I am."

Egon set down the menu. "Again, why am I here? Why are we doing this? What is it you want?"

Faye opened her menu. "Maybe I've missed you."

"Yeah, like I *missed* you. When I came home and found a naked man tied to my dining room table!"

Faye bit her lip to stifle her laugh.

"Your boyfriend wasn't amused. Nor was I. You broke things and left my house a mess."

"I thought you liked janitorial work."

"This has to stop, Faye. What the hell happened?"

"He was a misogynist prick. He ruined my birthday party."

"Meaning, you got drunk and wasted. Again."

"Fuck you. So what?"

"You're out of control. Hunter and Jenna agree."

Faye sipped her water with a grimace. "How am I supposed to take you seriously, Egon, when you show up looking like Casper the Ghost? That man was a worm. And he got what he deserved."

"That *worm* told me to give you a message."

"I'm really not interested."

"He threatened to kill you. *And* me."

"Calm down." Faye took out her cell phone, tapped the screen and held it up for Egon to see.

Egon leaned forward. "You're incredible. You made a video?

Now I know what he was screaming about."

"I emasculated him. He's no longer a threat."

"Wrong."

"I know what I'm doing."

"Oh, sure you do. Like getting yourself arrested."

Faye blew out smoke. "He was another misogynist prick."

"I don't fucking care. This has to stop."

"Why?"

"I'm worried about you."

"That's sweet."

"Because it affects me too. And I don't particularly enjoy having to attend your required therapy sessions."

She raised an eyebrow.

"What's that supposed to mean?"

"Hypocrite. Admit it. You're in love."

"Don't change the subject."

"Have you?"

"Have I what?"

"Told her yet?"

"Who?"

"You're childhood sweetheart. *Clara*." Faye blew smoke rings at him from across the table.

Egon fanned his face. "You can't smoke out here."

She sucked on her cigarette, then dropped it in her water glass. "Everything I do is for a reason. I got myself arrested on purpose. Being my brother doesn't give you the right to tell me what I *can* or can't do. We get to *fuck* whoever we like."

Egon pushed back his chair. "Fuck you. Have a wonderful day. Oh, and a belated happy birthday. I'm leaving."

"Wait! You can't. We haven't eaten."

Egon stood. "I lost my appetite."

"Sit down! We need to talk about money."

Egon dropped back into his seat. "What a surprise."

"How do you expect me to pay for my apartment?"

"You're a star. Gainfully employed. Congratulations."

"I have expensive tastes." Faye lit another cigarette. She tilted her head back as she inhaled. "What about you? Spending money on those *god*-awful masks. Your taste in art, Egon, is atrocious."

"Nothing like your extravagant taste in *breaking* my things. You destroyed my turntable."

"It was a relic."

"It was a *classic* VPI and worth—"

"Shit." Faye gave a laugh. "I rearranged it. Besides, you still owe me. I'm entitled to half the inheritance."

The waiter returned to set down two stemmed glasses. They all waited in silence as he unscrewed the cork, set it down, then poured wine in both glasses. "Are you ready to order?"

Fay took hold of her wine glass, annoyed by the waiter's bad timing. "What happened to your specialties? You've yet to tell us. And there's no heat. Still. Did you forget that too?"

Egon said, "Give us a couple minutes."

"Delighted," said the waiter. "And there's no smoking."

Faye waved him away. "Thank you. Forgot. Don't you worry, I'm putting it right out."

As the waiter left, she ground her cigarette into the tabletop and brushed it to the ground. "Do you realize how embarrassing it was to have a high-school bitch of a clerk turn up her nose at me and say my credit card was no good. She cut up my card! In *front* of me with a perky sneer. I wanted to slap her."

"You did," said Egon.

Faye raised her glass in an empty toast to nothing and shrugged, then tasted her wine. "This is good."

"You're lucky she didn't press charges."

"You embarrassed me in public."

Egon tapped the base of his wine glass. "Faye, you need help. Your entire life is a brakeless joy ride."

"That's not true."

"I had to cancel the card. You'd have bankrupted us."

"Don't get melodramatic. All that fuck money father left *you* – and not me. I'm the one who deserves it."

"There's less than you think."

"Then tell me how much so I'll know when to stop."

His sister smiled and he laughed. "Faye, you don't know how to stop. It's the way you are with men."

"How am I with men? How would you know?"

"You turn men into animals. Case in point." He pointed to her cell phone lying between them on the table.

"You think I'm a whore, don't you?"

"I've never said that."

"Well, I'm not. Those men were all pigs and jackasses. I simply exposed them for what they were." She slid her phone toward him. "Take another look. It's funny. I should post it online."

"I saw the live version. I wasn't laughing."

"I wasn't laughing either when father *raped* me."

"Faye. Don't start."

"You swore to me. You'd promised. And did *nothing*."

Egon looked away, then back, "I'm sorry."

"You should be." Faye picked up her menu. "I forgive you. We were kids. Except now you think I'm a *whore*."

"Stop it."

"You stop it. I don't squander my sex like you do. I treat it like a jewel to be treasured and adored."

Egon rolled his eyes. "Like your snakes."

"My snakes are important to me."

Egon opened his menu. "Part of your act. Got it."

"Snakes are beautiful. You should try to appreciate them, and all of God's creations."

Egon set down his menu. "Ah, like peeping toms?"

Faye looked up. "Is that an appetizer?"

"Someone's been stalking me."

"Mimes have groupies?"

Egon asked her pointedly, "Did you hire a detective?"

"I can barely afford my rent."

"Damn it, Faye. What's this about?"

"Why don't we decide want we want to eat first— "

Egon slammed his fist on the table. "Faye! I know you!"

She recoiled. "You think you do."

"Come on, Faye. Tell me what's going on. You can't expect me to believe you got yourself arrested on purpose."

"Like I told you, it was *intentional*."

"Jesus. You need help."

Faye ignored the passing looks from pedestrians and returned to view her menu. "Now I'm getting help. Those anger-management classes I've signed up for are doing me a world of good."

"It was a court order. Issued by a judge."

"If you don't like the results, shoot the messenger, not me."

Egon laughed, shook his head. His sister knew which buttons to push. "You told me it was relationship counseling."

"It is."

"Why can't you be truthful for once in your life?"

Faye's sanguine smile had transformed to a strained expression. Her hand trembled as she raised her glass of wine. "Maybe it hasn't occurred to you, *Egon,* that I'm only putting on a brave front. Deep down, I'm frightened."

Egon squinted.

"I am. It's true. I'm terrified."

"About?"

Faye removed a piece of paper from her purse. It looked like something a child might have made. Individual letters scissored and pasted down to spell out a message:

YOU WILL DIE BITCH!

As Egon reached for it, Faye tucked it back into her purse. "Did you send this to me?"

"You can't be serious."

"Then I'm right. It *was* him."

"Who?"

"You know who. Father."

"He's *dead*, Faye."

"We never saw the body."

"Mom killed him. You saw the photos."

"Doctored."

"Faye, get real."

"*You* get real! They made it look like he was murdered."

"I saw the body."

"He had Mom killed too." Faye rubbed her arms.

"She killed herself."

"That's what they *want* us to believe."

"Who's they?"

"The military. He's still active, doing special operations."

"Dad was discharged with PTSD."

"Faked. His job at that service station was a cover. He was a ballistics expert. Also a spy."

"No way."

"His death was a hoax."

"You're forgetting the inheritance."

"Which proves my point."

"This is ridiculous. Why—"

"Listen to me! He was worth millions from those gadgets he invented. And we – meaning *you* – received a fraction of that money. His disappearance was part of a conspiracy. He's *not* dead. He got placed in protective custody or something."

"Faye."

"And now he wants me dead too. I know it."

"You're being paranoid."

"Fuck you! He's a pedophile. A sick bastard who said he'd kill me if I ever told anyone. And I *did*."

"He's not alive, Faye.

Faye pulled from her purse several papers clenched in her fist. "Then what's this? Look at the last one I got. Look!"

Egon sighed and leaned forward. The individual cut-out letters read: "U R DEAD – X"

"See how it's signed? Like the serial killer, Egon."

"Really, Faye? You never suspected this might happen? It wasn't Dad who sent you those."

"So it *was* you. You admit it."

"Faye, how many men have you humiliated like the one I found on my dining-room table? Enough for at least *one* of them to want you dead."

"Does that include you?"

Egon grimaced, his anger mixed with pity for his sister, at what she'd become. He shook his head to indicate "no," but then added, "That's not to say it hasn't crossed my mind."

Faye grabbed her cell phone, stood, and held it at him. "Would you mind repeating that, Egon? I'm not sure you said it loud enough for me to get a clear recording of your confession! I can't wait for a judge and jury to hear this!"

Egon pushed back his chair and knocked the phone out of her hand. It flew over the black railing and landed in the street. The wheels from passing cars crushed it.

Faye flung her wine glass, then her silverware at him. "Bastard! You helped him kill mom too! Didn't you?"

Egon slapped his sister. Struck so hard, she stumbled backward and tumbled onto the bricks. He pulled money from his wallet and tossed it at her. He left a fifty-dollar bill on the table.

"About seven hundred. It's for you. For today's session."

Faye fought to get to her feet and screamed. "See, I knew you'd end up just like Dad!"

Bystanders had stopped to watch. Egon's scowl transformed into a grin as he explained, "She's an actress. I'm helping my sister rehearse a scene in which she plays a raving bitch. How was it? Convincing?"

He zipped his lips and smiled, indicating it was done in jest. He then attempted to leave but was blocked by an invisible barrier. His hands felt the glass, examined the walls, searching for a way out. He worked his way through the maze, finally escaping the cafe patio and stepping onto the sidewalk.

Egon tipped his beret, gave a theatrical bow, and departed to the sound of applause.

Faye gathered up the money and stuffed it into her purse, then pushed through the adoring crowd who clapped for her too.

"Fuck off," she told them.

Attempting to be anonymous, Clifford came to Union Square dressed as a tourist. Around his neck hung a camera. He wore dark glasses, khaki shorts, and a tropical shirt with colorful parrots.

The balmy afternoon was unusual for San Francisco, an Indian Summer occurring in late autumn. For a Monday, this urban park had a fair number of drifters, shoppers, and sightseers. It took up the entire block. The park was surrounded by streets that rose and fell, part of the city's charm, along with the sound of clanging cable cars, tour buses and a congestion of traffic.

Clifford ascended the wide stairs at the southwest corner which led to an expansive area paved with marble tiles. The west and east ends had small cafes. Easels were clustered in one section where painters were showcasing their artwork. The park's centerpiece was a towering corinthian column with a bronze woman standing on one leg and balanced on a ball. She held a wreath, a trident in her other hand. Clifford lowered his gaze and was surprised to see someone skating – as if on ice – across the center of the promenade.

It was Norwood, dressed as a mime, moving gracefully on roller skates. People stopped to watch as he circled with his arms raised, a leg lifted, gracefully turning, portraying a competition ice skater – doing spins, butterfly jumps, almost falling, recovering, finishing with an axel leap and a rotating spin.

Clifford moved aside to sit on a metal bench and watch.

The audience clapped. As Egon took a bow, the Three Fates emerged from different corners of the park dressed in white gowns. One held an oversized spool of thread, another a large ruler, and the third a gigantic pair of scissors. Their beautiful faces were masked to depict them as old and ugly.

Clifford's body released a shudder.

The shudder coincided with the physical presence of a man who sat next to him on the bench. The man's legs crossed at the ankles as his torso fell back against the rails – jolting the bench.

"Death."

"Excuse me," said Clifford.

"Ah, he speaks." The man pointed at the robed women holding the scissors. "Her."

The man had a bald head, his face shaved, except for a patch of black hair pointing south like an arrow beneath his lower lip. His sharp chin jutted forward, indicating that Clifford look elsewhere – at the three women circulating about the park. Clifford looked.

"Yes, I believe she represents death."

"That's right. Which means someone is gonna die."

The man's remark made Clifford uneasy.

The man held up a card. "She handed me this."

Clifford read the headline.

I AM DEATH

In smaller text it said: *One of The Three Fates.*

The flyer was an announcement for an evening performance in Union Square at nine o'clock. "It's for a play," Clifford said.

"You never play with death."

Clifford felt beads of sweat on his forehead. "It's a Greek myth. These three deities were believed to choose man's fate."

"Are you part of it?"

"Excuse me?"

"The performance?"

"No," Clifford laughed. "An observer, same as you."

A tattoo of flames rose from the collar of the man's long-sleeved shirt. On his wrists were blue-forked tongues poking out from heads of green snakes.

Clifford averted his eyes from the tattoos and saw people staring at the two of them. It occurred to him that maybe this man was one of the performers, planted as a ruse.

"Do you believe in signs?"

Clifford regarded the man. "How do you mean?"

He flicked the card. "She knows who I am."

"She's giving those to everyone."

"No. She's summoned me. Let's see who she targets next."

Clifford felt compelled to look.

Many refused to accept the handouts from these women. A card was finally taken from the Fate who held the golden scissors. When the recipient read the flyer he tore it up and tossed the pieces.

"There! That one."

"Who?" asked Clifford.

"Fucker's a goner. He never shoulda done that. No good."

Clifford felt the bench move. The man stood. He picked a coin off the ground. He held it up, turned it over and spat a laugh. He tossed it in Clifford's lap. "Now who in the *fuck* would do that?"

"Do what?" Clifford looked at the coin. The copper had a piece of paper glued to one side with a hand-printed word:

WINNER

"Fucking pathetic." The man snatched the coin out of Clifford's hand. "A goddamned worthless penny." He was about to fling it into the crowd but stuffed it into his pocket instead.

Clifford wished the man would leave.

The man looked down. "You don't remember me, do you?"

Not words Clifford wanted to hear. "Should I?"

"As soon as I got out, I came here. Ask me why?"

"Why?"

"To find you." He held the flyer up to Clifford's face.

Where, and in what circle of hell, had he met this man? thought Clifford. He tried to shake off his fear, but it was unshakable. Maybe this was a game. To instill fear in others.

As hard as he tried, Clifford could not summon a recollection of when or where he had met this man. Yet a clue had been dangled: "*When I got out.*"

Out of where? An insane asylum?

Clifford rubbed his knees. He noticed people staring as if they were expecting more to happen.

Finally, it struck him. The man's voice had triggered a memory. He recalled the laughter of boys and the sensation of water cascading around his face. The time he had nearly drowned when his head was held underwater, in a toilet bowl, in a school lavatory.

Clifford blinked. The memory drained all at once. Death was in front of him with her monstrous face looking down. Spectators were watching. Clifford presented a frozen smile. Her blue eyes, inside the mask, stared into his. She placed her scissors on the bench, separated her gown, and straddled him. She held the backrest and rotated her hips, performing a lap dance.

The crowd of onlookers applauded and laughed.

Clifford broke into a sweat, knowing what was under her gown. Nothing except her naked body. Despite his efforts to control his emotions, she stimulated his passion.

Upon dismount, she exposed a tent she'd pitched upon his khaki pants. His erection was like a standing ovation.

She touched his nose, handed him her card, then strutted away. Among the crowd of bystanders watching was a white face. The teardrop eye winked before the mime held up invisible binoculars to magnify Clifford's embarrassment.

EIGHT

Mira is intrigued by my question. I ask her again.

"Do you like what *you* do for a living?"

"Yes, for the most part. I do."

"Why?"

"Psychotherapy is challenging."

"In what way?"

"You, for example. You're challenging."

She gives me a direct look, followed by a smile. I realize I've met my match. Although she is slight in stature with a demeanor that is nonthreatening, she has the hint of an elfin grin. A sweetness which belies a mind with incredible power and depth. I know now, after peeking through a crack in her fortress, there are hidden forces that are discreetly kept hidden. It's something I recognize in myself. She too is full of danger.

This could be fun.

"You said 'for the most part.' What part don't you like about your profession?"

"You. Asking me these questions."

I reciprocate with my own smile. "Did you choose psychology as a career because there's a history of mental illness in your family? And you, being the responsible one in a line of crazy siblings, decided to fight for the afflicted?"

Her lips twist playfully. "I'm an only child. You got that wrong. I became fascinated by the stars when I was young."

"Let me guess. You were a child prodigy. And you come from a long line of psychics. No, strike that. Witches?"

"My mother *was* a bit of a witch. But, no."

"I've got you talking about your mother. This is good."

She responds with a laugh. "You're charming when you want to be. I was drawn to astronomy not astrology. At college, I realized the mind was as infinite as the universe and just as fascinating. Which led me to psychology becoming my focus of interest."

I detect she has falsified her biography somewhat, yet I let it go. "So, there you are. In a nutshell."

Mira smiles then compartmentalizes the frivolity and resumes the mask of her profession. "Let's get back to you."

"Why not Faye? It's the reason I'm here, right?"

"Precisely." Mira is back in form, her pencil repositioned, ready to take me down with a scribble of words. "How would you describe your relationship with your sister?"

"She drives me crazy. She's my sister. That's not to say I don't love her. I don't know who she is half the time."

Incredibly patient, Mira is observing me intently, listening to my every word like Athena, the breast-plated goddess of wisdom.

I go on without prompting. "She was born two minutes earlier and likes to remind me she is the older twin, thus the wiser one. She keeps prodding me to be more adventurous."

"Would you say she's a motivating force for your art?"

"Faye? No. Some ineffable ghost-like signal, both essential and inevitable, that's what motivates and guides me."

"Explain."

"That's the best I can do."

I wait while she jots down notes. She looks up and taps the pink eraser of her mechanical pencil against her teeth. "As an artist, with your performances, what do you hope to achieve?"

"Wake people up. To entertain, educate and inspire."

"Wake them up, how?"

As I explain myself, the tip of Mira's pencil comes to rest upon the cleft of her beautiful chin. "We're born into a state of wonder. We dive into snowbanks and piles of leaves. We skip and we twirl on impulse. We're delighted, as children, by simply being alive."

She nods.

"Then everything changes."

"How do you mean?"

"Pain. Restrictions. Demands. Regimentation. Expectations. Disappointments. Disillusionment."

"Which is part of being alive, and maturing, yes?"

"Of course." She is the tenacious daughter of Zeus again, who sprung fully grown and armored from her father's head. Athena, the virgin goddess of reason. I want to bring out her fun side, the elfin goddess. "Okay, as a hypothetical, would you act on an impulse to shed your clothes and dance naked?"

I receive a glare of holy light from the polished helmet she wears for protection. "Why would I?"

I admire her curiosity. "For the fun of it?"

"I don't see the point."

"There is no point. Our sense of play calcifies as we grow older. It's sad. It doesn't take a genius to look around and see people going through the motions. Like the walking dead unable to feel how they once felt."

Mira relaxes a bit. Jots down more notes. When she looks up, she says very calmly and directly, "As intelligent as you are. And you are, there is no mistaking that. Highly-functioning in many areas. While in others areas you are not functioning as well. And that you, like Faye, are in need of help. Can you acknowledge that?"

I was wrong. Her attacks are quick and decisive. Her remark has blindsided me into silence.

I rebut, "We *all* are in need of help, Mira."

"True. But can you accept that you are too?"

I hold a smile. "Maybe. Maybe not."

Her elfin coyness returns with a grin. "Which is it?"

"A definite *maybe*. Put that down."

"I will," she says. "It's progress. We're getting somewhere."

"How is this supposed to help Faye?"

"That depends entirely on you."

"I thought you were the guiding star. No?"

"I'm only Faye's therapist. I'm here to help you both discover the root cause of your issues and dissociation."

"Are you married?"

"Why do you ask?"

Those defensive questions of hers I find endearing.

"I'm merely curious." If she has nothing to hide she will tell me. By avoiding the question will convince me she's not being forthright in her effort to help.

She returns a reserved smile "I can't think of a reason why you shouldn't know. I've had proposals. But I've never married."

I shake my head.

"Why is that amusing?"

"If you've never been in a long term relationship like marriage, or had siblings, it makes me wonder how good you could possibly be at this relationship counseling."

Mira stiffens, mentally securing her helmet. When she returns a smile it is slightly askew.

"I was joking. Sorry. Faye sometimes acts like we're married. It comes from being twins."

"I see," she says, resetting herself. "Would you like to talk about Faye?"

"Not really." The thought of her angers me. I picture the naked man I'd found tied to my dining room table. "How about death?"

"What about it?"

"Do you believe in an afterlife?"

Mira gives it some thought. "I'm not sure. Do you?"

"We're like snakes shedding our skins. Or butterflies yet to be, lost in the fog of our cocoons."

"In a state of transition?"

"Metamorphosis, sure. Maybe God is going through one too. Transforming from a Him to Her, or something else. Who knows?"

"And you believe there's a God?"

"Until proven otherwise, why not? We have mobility. But we're still inside a womb. And all the screaming pain we hear inside our head, it's like birth pangs."

"What kind of screaming?"

"The kind Zeus felt right before his son split his head open with a mallet and out popped Athena in all her brilliance."

I smile, but Mira doesn't.

"Do you hear voices inside your head?"

"I was speaking metaphorically. But, yeah, I'd say there's more to us than we can imagine. We're a compilation of symbolic entities. I like what Jung said: 'Archetypes are the constellations in the blind sky of the mind.' You've heard of him?"

Mira smiles. "I have."

"You have a beautiful smile, by the way."

"Thank you."

"So, back to these nebulous stars, our dreams, which we find wandering up and down the subconscious stairwells of our DNA, these twisted strands of chemicals. Like batons passed along by our predecessors. Holding the essence of who we are. Jung called it our collective unconscious. We're a composite of many things."

"I would agree," she says to contribute.

"Many voices. And not all of them are screaming."

Mira is busy taking notes, so I wait for her.

"Or something like that," I add.

Mira looks up from her notebook. She has that beguiling look about her again. "What you said was poetic."

I feel she is toying with my internal circuitry. "Thanks," I say before shutting my eyes. I press fingers against these orbs, pressing into the pain. Why is she flattering me? It feels like a chess move. She's letting me win, letting me think I am when I'm actually losing. I can hear Hunter sneering. He thinks I'm capitulating, love-struck, therefore, willing to be led to the slaughter.

A wild impulse washes over me – a need to blast some useless carbon from my mind. When I open my eyes I see I have upset Mira. Her lips are parted. Her eraser is severed.

"Who am I talking to?" she asks.

I close and massage my eyes. "What do you mean? It wasn't me. It was probably something Jung said." I glance at the wall and see I have about five minutes left. When I turn back she hasn't moved. She's waiting for me to say something. So I say, "Did you know there's this belief in primitive societies that several souls can coexist in one person?"

Mira nods, leaving the door open for me to enter.

"I have a collection of masks. Primitive societies interest me."

"The collective unconscious," she says to reconfirm.

"Right." I take a moment to rub my temples to ease the residue of pain. "People think they know who they are. But we don't have a clue. We have no idea what lurks in the labyrinth of the soul."

"You said 'lurks,' which would imply you feel there's something ominous at the root. True?"

"I used that word arbitrarily."

"I don't believe you did."

She's unrelenting. "Fine. What do *you* think I meant?"

"I think you know. You believe there is something there you are afraid to face. Something that might devour you."

"You mean like a Minotaur?"

"Yes. Something you must defeat in order to get better."

"Because you think I'm sick in the head? Like Faye."

She fidgets with her pencil, then says, "You've mentioned to me that you experience blackouts."

"Not that often."

"But your life would improve without them?"

I'm looking for a way out, a diversion. I rake hands through my hair. "That Minotaur? I know the myth. He was deadly. Theseus had a ball of golden thread to unwind as he went through the maze. And after he killed the monster, that thread guided him to safety, out of darkness into light. Are you going to provide this thread?"

Her eyes are sympathetic. I glimpse something is troubling her. She has her own demons to deal with. We *are* alike. Her eyes look away to her notes, not wanting me to see what's inside of her.

When she looks up again, she tells me, "I don't think Faye wants to disappear. Or to lose you. You need each other."

Her comment is meant to distract me from probing into her own problems. "Ah, we're back to Faye. Okay. You're right. She likes the competition."

"No," she says. "That's not what I meant. You *need* each other. To feel whole again."

"Right. Well, good luck with that."

"Call it a woman's intuition."

I laugh. "My mother used to tell me that."

"Why is that funny?"

"Because she used it as an excuse to get drunk. Saying it helped her communicate with the spirits. She was a lush."

"Did you love your mother?"

"Sure. She never hit me. So there was that. She could be fun, but she didn't provide us with much protection either."

"Do you feel she loved you?"

"In her way."

"In what way was that?"

"I indulged in her fantasies. She had dreams of being a dancer, a heroine on the silver screen, a gypsy, a nun. It changed day to day. I think she wished I'd been born a girl too, like my sister."

"Why do you say that?"

I hesitate. She's eager to hear my confession. How much do I want to confess? What will she think of me afterward? Then again, what difference does it make?

"I don't want Faye to know about this."

"You can trust me."

Right. I can trust her not to tell Faye, but she can't wait to run and tell her colleagues.

She says reassuringly, "It must be very personal."

"Sort of. When my sister was away at a friend's house and my father was at work, my mother used to dress me up as a girl. She'd get drunk and ... she'd put on records. Have me dance. Wearing ... this ... a ballet dress."

"A tutu?"

I feel blood flood my face. "I don't even know why I'm telling you this."

"It helps to talk about it."

"Maybe for you."

"What else did your mother have you do?"

"Things like that. She used to parade me in front of neighbors dressed as a girl. It was unforgivable. I hated her for it."

"Did your father know?"

"One day my mother took me on a picnic in the woods. Then, on the way home, she ran into a tree with her car. And ..."

"And?"

I can feel a migraine coming straight at me like a freight train, its whistle piercing my skull. I press fingers into my eyes.

Faye opened the door. She was sipping a martini.

"Oh, good. It's you. Come in."

Clifford glanced at the semi-transparent fabric and realized she was wearing lingerie. "Have I come too late?"

"Heavens no, you're right on time. What can I get you?"

Clifford was stunned that she made no effort to cover herself. She walked away and he stepped inside her apartment. He observed her backside moving against the sheer négligée as she walked toward the bar. The underwear she wore exposed her posterior.

"Would you like a martini?"

"Uh, no. Thank you. Nothing."

Photos from a binder slipped from under his arm and fell to the carpet. He dropped to his hands and knees to gather them up.

"You *deserve* one," Faye told him. "I insist. How can you stand to do the work you do without having a cocktail?"

Clifford looked up from the floor. "Scotch. If you insist."

"I do."

"With ice. I'm part Scotch myself. Scottish, I meant. On my father's side."

"How interesting." Faye set a glass on the bar and poured from a triangular-shaped bottle of Pinch. Her detective was still crawling across her floor when she looked up. "*Oopsy-daisy.*" I overpoured. I hope you're thirsty."

"I'm not much of a drinker."

"I feel sad for men who don't drink. Please get up off the floor and close the door. I'm feeling a draft."

Faye dipped a finger into his drink and tasted it as she strolled into the living room. "I've always been attracted to men who drink scotch. Why do you think that is?"

Clifford wasn't sure if he wanted to know. He shut the door, then hoisted up his pants, tucking in his shirt. His client was waiting for him. "Did I catch you at a bad time?"

"Don't be silly. I was expecting you. Here."

The glass was filled to the brim. "Thank you."

"I hope you don't mind me saying, but your office gives me the creeps. That's why we're meeting here."

Clifford glanced around, taking in the spacious room and view of the bay from the apartment tower. "How far up are we?"

Faye sipped her martini. "High enough to *kill* myself if ever I decide to jump."

Clifford choked – spilling scotch on route to his throat. He looked down at the carpet.

She made light of his mishap with a laugh. "Don't bother. I rent. I meant nothing personal about your office. Please, be seated."

Clifford sat on her sofa. His body sank into its accommodating cushions. "That's all right, I understand."

Faye sat in the love seat opposite him. She crossed her legs. To avoid staring at her thinly-veiled nakedness, Clifford studied the room's decor. His eyes went from the white marble tabletop (where he set his drink) to the white carpet (now spotted with scotch), next to the furniture upholstered in pastels (one holding him), then to the walls with impressionistic paintings (a colorful collection).

His hand shook as he raised his glass to his mouth to slurp more scotch. "You have a lovely place."

"It comes furnished. Oh, but I want to show you this."

Faye abruptly uncrossed her legs to stand as Clifford upturned his glass. He caught a glimpse of more flesh. Scotch dribbled from the corners of his mouth.

She returned holding a wooden sculpture and set it on the table between them. "It was the only piece Egon bought that I liked. Isn't he marvelous?"

The polished ebony was sculpted into the shape of an upright man whose arms were outstretched in an expression of celebration, exhibiting a proportionately-large erect phallus.

Clifford set down his cocktail and muttered polite appreciation, then averted his eyes. He began to sweat.

"So," said Faye. "What have you detected?"

"I beg your pardon?"

She raised the back of her hand to her forehead to dramatically portray a woman in distress. "Shock me. I'll try not to faint. What incriminating items do you have to show me?"

Her evening gown separated, exposing her brassiere and a hint of more skin. Clifford coughed, looking down, rummaging through his folder of photographic evidence. "I wish I had more. Sorry."

"I abhor sorrowful men. What about the other day? That scene at 'L Entrecote. You captured *that* incident, I should hope."

"It's right here."

Faye flipped through the stack of photos. "Why is everything so far away? I can't recognize Egon *or* myself. How is a jury supposed to tell who is who?"

"I told you, my camera equipment was stolen. And, accidently, I purchased the wrong telephoto lens—"

"What are you prepared to do about this?"

He took back the photos. "I could have them blown up."

"Destroyed?"

"I meant enlarged.

"Well," said Faye and downed her martini. "You had better do something. These won't do."

She took back one of the photos. She squinted at what looked to be herself sprawled upon the bricks, her chair overturned, Egon tossing money at her. The image was grainy and blurry. She grabbed another picture to scrutinize.

"You witnessed his rage," said Faye.

"Yes, he—."

"*Snapped*. And threatened me."

"What did he say?"

"I had it recorded. But he knocked my phone into the street, and it got crushed by a car."

"I missed seeing that."

"He even *admitted* he wants me dead."

"That's crucial evidence."

"I know."

"The data might be recoverable. Where's your phone?"

Distracted by a thought, she lowered the photograph and stared at Clifford. "What?"

"The data from your phone might be recoverable."

"I tossed it in the trash."

"Oh, well." Clifford sipped his scotch.

"I fear he plans to murder me too."

Clifford set down his drink. "Why do you think your brother is the serial killer?"

Faye looked at him with annoyance. "I don't think. I'm certain. Tell me what else you have?"

"I found these in his garbage can."

Clifford was having difficulty peeling off whatever it was stuck to the manila folder.

Faye laughed. "Oh, my god, I thought it was you! That smell. Do you make it a habit of digging through trash?"

"No." Clifford took offense. "But valuable evidence is often ascertained."

"*Ugh*. What is that?"

He offered but she refused to take it.

"Magazines. Stained with a bit of food residue."

"Get to the point. What do they have to do with me? Nothing,

I should hope. Let me freshen your drink."

Clifford was too slow to stop her. "I'm fine."

"Well, I'm not. I need another."

"I believe your brother removed the type from these magazines to compose those death threats."

"I'm impressed," Faye said from behind the bar.

"I'll bet the missing letters from these pages will match the type glued to those notes you received. Does your brother has a drinking problem? I found several empty liquor bottles."

"Life is a problem for Egon."

"What do you mean?"

"On the surface, he's polite, contrite, and charming. Underneath he's a monster."

"His hostile outbreaks could be alcohol related."

Faye handed Clifford his drink. She swilled down a third of her martini. "Next you'll be accusing me?"

"No. That's not what ..." Clifford let his words trail off.

Faye removed the speared olive from her glass and bit it in half. "My brother has blackouts. They terrify him. And, they damn well should. But that's not his *real* problem."

"It's not?"

"No. He's a *murderer*. Haven't you been listening?"

Clifford gulped his scotch. "Yes. But—"

"He's also seeing a psychiatrist."

"I didn't know that."

"Why not? I'm paying you to follow him."

"I need to keep my distance. It's hard, sometimes, to tell which door he enters. You should have told me this before."

"I'm telling you now."

"I'll see what I can find out."

Faye stood and paced. "So, that's it? Nothing else?"

"You may not like what I have to say."

"Why not?"

"I had evidence to prove his innocence."

"That's not possible."

"The last murder took place the same night I'd followed your brother to the Palace of Fine Arts. At midnight, during a full moon. He was dressed as a mime, with three women dancing—"

"Get to the point," said Faye.

"The murder, the time of death, corresponded to the hour in which I had photographed him," said Clifford.

"Oh, my god!"

"You see?"

"No," said Faye. "He *used* you."

"What—how?"

"Was my brother moving?"

"Yes."

"While you were photographing him?"

"No. He was seated on a wall."

"For how long?"

"Awhile. I'd set the aperture for a time-lapse exposure."

Faye sipped her drink. "He made a replica of himself."

"What do you mean? Like a manikin?"

"Yes, he's an illusionist. A sculptor too. I need a cigarette. Do you want one?"

"I don't smoke."

"He realized you were following him. He must have. Knowing it would make you the perfect alibi. You—as his witness."

"While he committed the murder?"

An unlit cigarette bobbed from Faye's lips as she said, "Are you grasping the concept? It gave him enough time to do it."

"Theoretically, I suppose."

"No. He did it." Faye removed her cigarette. "What about today? Union Square? And tonight?"

"I don't know what to say." Clifford brought the glass of scotch to his mouth, his hand shaking as he sipped.

"Say it. He tricked you."

"There was a man who distracted me. I did take photographs of the evening performance. It was quite remarkable."

Faye walked away in disgust.

As Clifford watched her leave, he snuck another gulp of scotch. "Your brother and the others are very talented."

Her voice resounded in the hall. "Yes, he tricked you!"

Clifford stared at the walls. The paintings revealed light colors, idyllic worlds, remote from his own. In his client's absence, he had a wild impulse to flee, to escape while he had the chance. But he hadn't been paid. She owned him money which he desperately needed.

When she returned with a boa constrictor around her neck and a cigarette smoking from her lips, Clifford realized his decision to stay had been the wrong one.

"Egon's crazy, but he isn't stupid." Along with the snake, Faye had a folder. From it, she tossed papers into his lap. "Here, these are for you. Check out your theory."

Clifford leafed through the many notes. A series of glued-down letters, each one spelling out a threat: "YOU WILL DIE BITCH" – "I WARNED YOU" – "YOU TELL & YOU DIE" – "MY KNIFE WILL FUCK YOU" – "U R DEAD – X."

"Not your typical love letters," said Faye.

"Can I borrow these?"

"Make sure you don't lose them."

"I won't."

Faye tossed a stack of photos onto his lap. "I want you to look at these too. Tell me what you think."

Clifford could feel his face turning red. Print after print showed different men in compromising sexual positions with Faye dressed as a dominatrix. Each man appeared startled – caught in the act.

"Well?" said Faye.

"Well, what?"

"Are you capable of producing the same results?"

"I beg your pardon."

"Can you take photos like these?"

"What on earth for?"

Faye turned away. "Can you understand how embarrassing it is for me to have to show you these?"

On the contrary, Clifford detected no sign of embarrassment – from her. As he flipped through the photos, Clifford stopped at one in particular. He recognized the face. It was the undercover cop who had approached him on Broadway Street disguised as a pimp. "Wait, I know this man."

"So do I," said Faye, snatching back the photos and fanning her face with them. "He works for the district attorney's office."

Clifford asked, "How do these photos relate to—"

"The reason I hired you?" Faye sat in front of Clifford. Her boa constrictor was draped around her shoulder like a scarf. Except it was writhing. My brother is *controlling*. He's changed since we were kids. He now wants to have total control over me."

Clifford scooted backward on his seat to keep a distance from the boa whose head kept moving. "Do you mean to say that ... he *forced* you to do ... these ... sexual things?"

"Do you seriously think I'd prostitute myself willingly? Yes, he has forced me to do *many* things, which I don't care to discuss. It's way too complicated and upsetting."

"I understand," said Clifford, even though he didn't.

Faye stroked the head of her snake. "I fear for my life. He could strike at *any* moment."

Clifford hoped she was referring to her brother and leaned away. The snake's tongue probed the air.

Faye laughed. "She's curious. Eve, meet Clifford."

"Hello there." Clifford raised his hand to pet the snake.

"I wouldn't do that."

Clifford recoiled his arm. The snake recoiled too. "Is it—she, your snake, dangerous?"

"Only when provoked. She's shy. You startled her. Come here, Baby." Faye snubbed out her cigarette. "She hates it when I smoke. Is that better, Baby?

Faye pulled its head toward her and gave it a kiss. "Would you like to hold her?"

"No. Thank you." Clifford reached for his drink, careful not to provoke a strike. The scotch tasted sharp and strong. Antidotal. He greedily slurped down more alcohol as Faye stroked the glistening scales of her boa constrictor.

I also want you to investigate his psychiatrist," said Faye. "Her name is Miranda Skyles."

"Why?"

"Why, because I don't trust her. We knew each other in college. Briefly. She's devious. I want you to discover where she goes and what she does during her days and nights"

"I can't follow them both."

Faye raised an eyebrow. "Unless ... "

"Unless?"

"They're having an affair."

"Is that what you suspect?"

"I *suspect* you will find out and *tell* me."

Clifford nodded, so distracted by the snake around his client's neck he'd failed to notice, until now, her legs were no longer crossed, and more skin was exposed.

About to take another swallow of scotch, Clifford decided he'd had enough. The alcohol was making his body feel leaden, sinking him deeper into the sofa. In the midst of his descent, he saw her legs separate further.

Clifford sensed, as sure as there was a Hell, God was watching, peeping omnisciently – and, judgementally.

"I should be going," he said.

"What's the rush? Stay for another drink."

He gave it a moment's thought, vacillating, gravity fighting his rocket's attempt at lift-off. "I've had enough. Thanks."

"The night is still young. I can't get you anything else?"

Clifford was halfway up, lost power, and sank back down into the sofa. "There is one thing. I hate this part of doing business. The money. The small advance you gave me was used up awhile ago. I sent you an invoice, which is past due. I'd appreciate getting paid. First of the month payroll and all."

"Payroll? Who else are you paying? Who else knows about our arrangement?"

"No one. My landlord, that's it."

"Your landlord?"

"Being the first of the month. I really ..."

Her snake wavered in the air. He imagined a high-voltage eel as her fingers touched his knee and received a jolt of electricity.

She told him, "I can pay you next week. Unless we can find a way, perhaps, to barter?"

TEN

How did we evolve into such strange creatures? We rely on so many bizarre courting rituals. There is a bar at Fisherman's Wharf with the interior of a rainforest, with tropical ferns, rattan furniture, water falling into pools, and replicas of wild animals lurking about. Am I supposed to be Tarzan looking for Jane? The Financial District has another watering hole with the ambiance of a mad house. Plastic cows graze upside down across the ceiling. Gigantic martini glasses swimming with goldfish illuminate the darkness. Waitresses dressed as nurses in vintage hospital whites attend the afflicted in this over-crowded waiting room. If you seek healing from physicians on call to mix up the medicine, this is the place.

I feel more at home at the Comstock Saloon, where I am now, seated at the bar. The antique furniture, chintz, crystal throughout, makes me feel historic too, a throwback to the Barbary Coast days. A fantasy made more authentic by the presence of the bartender who is dressed in a low-cut green evening dress with her breasts lifted. Strikingly anachronistic is her honey-blonde pixie haircut, streaked with a black accent. It complements her black-meshed elbow-high gloves and tiny pillbox hat pinned on top of her hair.

She is also young and pretty and has my undivided attention. At three in the afternoon, this saloon is almost empty. Our group of artistic misfits has yet to arrive.

"The usual?" the bartender asks me.

I nod. She smiles back. Since I don't have a "usual" and don't know who she is, I play along, curious to discover what concoction she will serve me. I watch her mix and pour and shake the tools of her trade. She places before me a green blended liquid in a martini glass, a curlicue lemon rind balanced on its rim. I take a taste. It's sweet, with a sharp bite, and very potent.

"Mum, that's ... different. I like it. It's called?"

"A Green Fairy."

"You? Or the drink?"

She laughs.

"Have we met?"

She shakes her head. "Absinthe. The drink, not me. I'm Farrah. I started this week."

"Egon."

I raise my hand and she extends hers across the bar. I take hold of her exposed fingers, admiring her painted nails, shiny as emeralds, and kiss the top of her black-laced hand.

She giggles, affected by my antics.

"You remind me of someone." Once I've spoken, I realize who. Mira, the therapist. I can't stop thinking about her. She has worked her way into my mind like a drug to mess with my neurons.

"Who?" Farrah asks.

"A goddess," I tell her.

Her eyes challenge. "Which one?"

"Eunomia. A minor goddess, *but* one of the glorious daughters of Themis. She represented good counsel and the spirit of springtime green. She was beautiful, like you. Are you Greek, by chance?"

She's amused by me. "I guess you know your stuff."

"Some stuff. Mostly useless for daily consumption."

"What is it you do? For a living?"

"Guess."

"Okay. A scholar? You teach at a college?"

"Do I look like a professor?"

She looks me over. "You could be a model. But you look more like a troublemaker."

I laugh. "You're getting warmer."

"Are you a musician?"

"Close enough. I'm a performing artist."

"Are you famous?"

"I work as a janitor at the Academy of Sciences."

"Oh." Her initial flutter of enthusiasm fades.

"By choice. Three nights a week."

Her interest tentatively returns. "By choice?"

"I enjoy science."

"So do I." She is a moth hovering at my flame again.

"I volunteer as a resident artist at the Exploratorium too. And I perform, off and on, during the days and nights."

"As?"

"Come and see. Next Sunday morning."

"I might. A time? Place?"

"Nine am. Union Square."

"What do I look for?"

"Theatrics. I'm an illusionist."

She tilts her head, questioning.

I sip my drink. "Now you see me. Now you don't. An ancient art form modernized to alter how we perceive the world."

"Like a drug?" she says with a coyness.

I tip my glass to her. "Exactly. Mind altering."

She fiddles with a stack of cocktail napkins before glancing up and down the bar to make sure she's not ignoring other customers. Her eyes return to me. "Do you come to the Comstock often?"

"Weekly."

"Alone?"

"No. I'm here with you."

If Farrah had wings they would be pulsating faster. She remains standing, perfectly composed for me to examine her.

"I'm seeing friends. We meet every Wednesday."

"Is this one of them?" Farrah asks.

I turn and see Garrett enter. He's a sculptor. Crazy imaginative.

He welds metal junk into miraculous forms. Whimsical creatures. Monstrous works of art. He's the more monetarily successful one in our group. Despite his taste for expensive clothing, his distressed leather jackets appear old and disheveled, from another era, like his black stovepipe pants and tan leather boots. His pointed Van Dyke beard widens to display a devilish grin upon seeing me.

"Egon. Always the first to arrive."

"And last to leave." I turn to the bartender. "I have a reputation for closing places."

"Who's this?" Garrett takes a seat beside me.

"Garrett, meet Farrah. Aka *Eunomia*."

"Ah, the green goddess." His laugh has a congested sound as if his lungs were caked with soot. "I see the resemblance. You're a vision."

"Thanks," said Farrah. "What can I get you?"

Garrett eyes my drink with distaste. "Being that it is *not* Saint Patrick's Day, I will stick to my whiskey. Jack. Neat."

As Farrah searches for the bottle, Garrett scratches his beard.

"Been following the news?"

"It depresses me. The international conflicts. Political gridlock. Government shutdowns. The reds and blues refusing to play nice. Representatives and their rigid ideologies who won't compromise. They get reelected by the people, for the people, then do *nothing*, for the people. So, in a word, *yes*, I have. Unfortunately."

"Reality TV," said Garrett. "Same damn thing. Whole world's gone dysfunctional."

"Cheer up," I say, toasting Garrett when his drink arrives. "At least we're beyond the days of Caesar crossing the Rubicon, cutting off the hands of his enemies, raping women, and watching babies starve in fields of blood. How a nice despot like Caesar got himself assassinated and then gets glorified in the history books as a hero is another mystery I can't fathom."

"Beware of politics and ambition," says Garrett. "It breeds tiny monsters in the head."

"Thank God we're civilized. No more of *that.*"

Garrett laughs and coughs. "What do you say, Farrah?"

She looks at us both. "Me? Well ... 'I am awaiting perpetually and forever a renaissance of wonder.'"

"Ah!" says Garrett. "Ferlinghetti. I love her already."

I slide my drink toward Farrah. "That's what we're all about, our group of misfits."

She takes up my offer and raises the glass to her lips for a drink of the green absinthe. She squints. "What group?"

Garrett mock salutes. "The Rebel Artists of Perception."

Farrah frowns, tips her head. "Another misfit?"

Garrett and I turn our heads to see Denise coming through the door in her gypsy regalia, moving toward us in her diaphanous dress of layered colors. Her head is covered in a matching silk turban.

"You forgot your cystal ball," quips Garrett.

They kiss and Denise says, "It doesn't take balls to know you're a total miscreant, Garrett, my darling."

As Denise and I exchange kisses, I notice more friends arriving. "We should get a table." Grabbing my drink, I say to Farrah. "Will you be here for awhile?"

"I'll be around," she tells me with a sultry tease. "Go play nice. No more government shutdowns."

I want her. I hesitate to leave but smile and go.

Our group, The Rebel Artists of Perception, move to a booth. We consist of Garrett, Denise, Semele, Megan, Jasper, Hunter, Jenna, myself, others, and an occasional drop-in guest. Faye has resigned. No one takes her seriously, expecting she will reappear at one of the next meetings. But she hasn't attended for over six months.

A waiter approaches. Garrett is our current president and calls the meeting to order by ordering four bottles of wine for the table.

The next act of business on the agenda is discussing any old business. This is followed by silence. Semele demurely folds her paint-stained hands, looking inward, likely envisioning one of her surrealistic oil paintings as a distraction. Jasper (whose real name is plain, I forget, something like Jeff) winks at me. He has on a velour jacket, indigo blue. He believes he is the next great undiscovered poet and reminds us every chance he gets when he's not preoccupied with a story he's writing for the San Francisco Chronicle. Megan, a psychic, makes predictions I've never seen come true. A great actress, though. And a wonderful lover, who is mad at me for not calling her the next day. That was a year ago. Denise, costume designer, and our wardrobe specialist, performs too. Also Jenna, our ethereal princess, who is dressed in trademark white tights and tutu.

Hunter stands and hangs his biker jacket on a hook, then breaks the silence by asking, "Anyone want to mention the elephant in the room? *Faye.* She's been causing trouble."

Everyone looks at me. As if I had the solution to this problem. I respond by saying, "My sister does what she wants. She no longer listens to me."

Megan contributes by saying, "From a woman who plays with snakes. What do you expect?"

Jenna toys with the sweeteners. "Faye thinks she's a star."

"From one review and few posters?" says Denise.

"I couldn't care less," says Jasper. "As long as her antics don't affect the rest of us."

"They do," says Garrett.

"She'll be back," says Megan with an encouraging smile at me, despite her distrust of Faye. "You know we're all here for you, Egon, whenever you need us."

"Appreciated," I say.

Garrett taps his knuckles on the table. "Let's move on."

Semele won't let it rest. "I'm sorry. How is this going to work?

Faye got arrested for assaulting a man. Egon."

"The charges were dropped. She's now getting help."

"What's this about?" Garett laughs. "Enlighten us, brother."

I sip my absinthe. "Money. Our inheritance."

"Ah," says Jasper. "The root of all."

"Everything was left in my name, as the executor of the estate. It's locked up in a trust fund. It's complicated."

"I'd be mad too," Semile says. "If I was your sister."

"Believe me," I add, "Her anger began way before that."

Jasper makes a toast, "To sibling rivalry. It's a bitch."

I laugh but rebut, "Jasper, you're an only child. How in the hell would you know?"

Garrett pings his glass with a knife. "Time to move on."

"Why are you seeing a therapist?" Megan interjects.

I look at her. "Faye's plea bargain required it. We're getting to the root of our family issues. I'm the only surviving blood relative, so I agreed to help."

Jasper becomes diplomatic. "Egon, there's no judgment here. We're an acknowledged group of misfits. But the fact that *both* of you knew this psychotherapist in college. I mean ..."

"Faye knew her."

"That's a rather odd duck of a coincidence. You'd agree?"

"Faye contacted her. It wasn't my idea. Look, while in college, there was an incident on campus. A rape and murder. The girl was a sorority sister of Mira's."

"Mirrors?" said Megan.

"Miranda Skyles. She testified in court as a witness."

"Jesus," says Jasper. "That's a rather curtailed account. Details, man. That's not a story one forgets."

"Jasper, it was a bad time, a media frenzy. *Past* tense."

"All I'm saying. As a journalist, I know when something doesn't add up. It would seem—"

"Can we drop this?"

Our wine arrives and the waiter begins uncorking the bottles. Silence resumes as we watch, and he pours. When the waiter leaves we all raise our glasses.

Megan toasts, "To therapy, may it help pull Faye and Egon back together, to their senses, again."

Laughter follows with more toasts.

Jenna has acquired a dish of sugar cubes. After tasting her glass of Merlot, she continues to stack the sugar into a pyramid. Her actions distract Hunter who is brooding in a dark current of thought as if staring into the black waters of the river Styx, a place no one dares to cross.

Hunter surfaces from the depths to mention the unmentionable. "How about those murders? That serial killer. Cutting an "X" in his victim's skin. Weird, huh? Anyone care to speculate?"

No one does. Garrett looks at me. The others either stare into their upturned glasses or find some object to distract them. As Jenna has, stacking sugar cubes.

I feel a need to defend my sister in her absence. "The answer is categorically – no. Faye sometimes associates with unsavory people. But she's not capable of murder. I know that for a fact."

"Do you?" says Jasper.

"Yes." No one sides with me, only a few noncommittal mutters and head nods. "So, I guess that bring us to new business."

"Agreed," says Garrett with a scratch to his facial hair. "End of discussion. None of us are killers."

"Speak for yourself," jokes Hunter. Shrapnel resides in his head from a roadside bomb while he was deployed overseas. We all know he's killed. Because he reminds us each time he gets drunk.

I attempt to redirect the meeting by announcing, "Garrett and I have been working on a new piece. Based on Donatello's sculpture of David and the beheaded Goliath. It's pretty wild."

"It is," says Garrett. "We're excited by the project."

Semele expresses her enthusiasm with a nod.

"Does Goliath win?" Jasper smiles.

"Nobody wins," I say. "That's the joke."

"I could use a good laugh," laughs Jasper.

"We first need to talk about the Hydra project," says Garrett, always the more practical one. "The logistics of the mechanics, for that puppetry to work, is daunting. First time I've attempted a nine-headed serpent. But it's damn well going to work."

Garrett gives us all a confident nod as I ask Jasper, "Poetry man. How's the script coming along?"

"Inspired," he says. "First reading, next week."

Semele unfurls a scroll of paper to pass around the table. We all admire the renderings she's made of this sea monster, along with her sketches of Hercules. Comments and suggestions are made. Denise shows us swatches of fabric for the costumes.

"The concept, again?" Jenna looks up after poking her finger into the sugar-cubes.

While watching her tiny pyramid collapse, I explain, "Multiple realities. As in, 'Reality has always had too many heads.' It's a line from a Dylan song, *Cold Irons Bound*."

"Like our Hydra," chimes in Garrett.

"It's a myth that underscores our evolution," I add. "Toward a multi-faceted reality."

"Bullshit," says Hunter. "Though I admire the theme."

"As do I," says Megan.

"Good," says Garrett, who gives me a nod. "Because, I received a mysterious phone call from a person working in television."

"Pray tell," says Jasper. "I'm in suspense."

"Somebody posted a video of us performing in the park. It was an anonymous online submission, auditioning us to be on that show coming to San Francisco."

"What show?" says Denise.

"You know the one." Garrett snaps his fingers. "It's called ... American's got something."

Hunter grunts a laugh. "Gall?"

"Talent?" says Megan.

Garrett points his finger at her. "That's it."

"You can't be *serious*," Jasper sniffs.

Jenna holds up a sugar cube to the light, the way a child might inspect a blade of grass, turning it in her fingers to get our attention. "Did you know a collapsing neutron star has a mass so dense that a cube of sugar would weigh fifty-thousand billion tons? I feel like that sometimes." She plops the sugar into her mouth and smiles sweetly. "I say, why not?"

This begins a heated debate. We argue about the pros and cons of television, over exposure, selling out, the commercialism of art, mass media, viral marketing, the ideal venue, maintaining a vision, good intentions that get polluted. Ontology. Why we exist. A myriad of topics. We continue debating and arguing late into the night, which requires dinner and several more bottles of wine.

I am not aware of the hour as our meeting devolves.

Farrah is still working the bar as I approach and take a seat.

"You're drunk," she tells me.

"I confess, Eunomia. That *was* my goal."

"You've succeeded."

"I like you."

"Beyond inebriation, do you have any other goals?"

"You intrigue me. An after-dinner whiskey. Por favor?"

"I should cut you off."

"That's harsh. Perform a miracle. That's it."

"That's what?"

"My ultimate goal."

Farrah frowns at this. "But you said you're an *illusionist*."

"I did say that. I am. Your point?"

"Magic tricks?"

"Miracles *are* magic tricks. Rearranging the molecules. That's the real illusion. Making the illusion *real*. To become real."

"You *are* drunk."

"Love. That's the real illusion." I wave my hand in the air. It lands softly over hers upon the bar. "This falling. A miracle of love. A magical transcendence. Two becoming one. You don't agree?"

"I believe in love."

"Being magic?"

"No," she says. "Love is no trick."

"Tsk-tsk, a double *negative*. That cancels out your '*no*.'"

I win a beautiful smile from her.

"You're saying," she says, "I actually mean '*yes?*'"

"You see? A small miracle. Come home with me."

"I should call you a cab, is what I should do."

"Will you be coming with me?"

"As you can see, I'm still working."

"I can wait."

Faye awoke with a hangover. She moaned at the sliver of sun finding its way through the shades to her eyes. To avoid it she rolled over toward the center of the bed and bumped into a naked body. She had no recollection of bringing anyone home. She opened her eyes a fraction to see who it was and saw breasts.

Faye propped herself on an elbow. This woman in her bed was snoring softly, head tilted on a pillow toward her. The girl was pretty, even in her unconscious state. Her lips were pink and glossy, full and parted. Faye brushed a finger through the blond bangs to see her closed lids, tinted a smokey green. Faye let the hair fall back and the woman moaned and shifted to her side.

Coupled with her memory loss, this naked woman was a source of fascination. Despite her repeated efforts to recall the events of last night, Faye came up blank. Across the crumpled bedsheets, she saw a green dress draped over the arm of a chair. Other items had been tossed upon a table. Black lace from what appeared to be gloves. It sparked something, but the memory extinguished fast and she was left with nothing.

Curious about this female, Faye lowered the bedsheet to expose more of her body. She was impressed by her translucent white skin. Her belly button was pierced with a tiny ring. Her nest of pubic hairs were dark, not matching her blond locks.

She wondered what she had done to this woman.

Faye was reminded of another conquest. She had discovered a pile of discarded clothing – blue jeans, denim jacket, checkered shirt, and snakeskin boots – then a cowboy in her guest room. Beside him was his belt, with its big brass buckle depicting a bucking bronco. A prized possession he'd won. He was from out of town to compete is some machismo event at the Cow Palace. He'd been mouthing off to her at the bar about San Francisco being the "city of fags."

He offered to buy her a drink and told her, "A beautiful girl like you should experience a real man riding you, at least once."

That was his come-on line.

He went on to add, "I'm the title holder of the NFR."

She'd feigned interest. "What's that?"

"The Super Bowl of Rodeos."

Later that night, while sporting his cowboy hat and wearing her dominatrix lingerie, Faye had walloped his ass with his trophy belt. While clutching a shank of his hair, she was determined to break this wild buck into submission, and had.

The recollection of this impassioned play began to arouse her. He'd passed out with his wrists tied to the rails of her headboard. After photographing him in this compromising position, adding it to her collection, she was amused the next morning. She came into the bedroom fully dressed to sit on the corner of the bed and observe this naked cowboy harnessed to her bedposts. His little red rooster was already awake, fully risen and ready for action, while he slept and snored incoherently.

As she had with him, Faye selected a stray pubic hair between her fingertips – and plucked. Her overnight guest sprang up into a startled wakefulness.

"Time to rise and shine," Faye sang out.

The woman's groggy eyes looked down at her uncovered body, then over to Faye's. Her guest's confused expression became sunny, with a warmth that moved toward Faye, a want to touch her body. Faye avoided the woman's hand by sliding off the bed.

"I suppose you'll be wanting coffee?"

The question had an air of coldness. Her guest shivered and pulled the blanket up. She suspiciously rubbed her pubic hairs where her skin stung. Her demeanor returned to a light-hearted disposition.

"Yes, please. Black."

Shuffling naked across the hardwood floor Faye snatched a robe hanging from a hook. She tied the sash on her way downstairs, then brushed fingers through her hair to blindly comb it straight as she walked through the living room. In the kitchen, she swallowed three aspirin while drinking from a glass of orange juice. Grinding coffee beans next, she peered into the dense fog through her window. Over the roar of coffee being pulverized she thought she heard a voice.

Faye shouted, "Did you say something?"

"I did not."

The close proximity surprised Faye. Her guest had followed her downstairs. The woman whispered into her ear, "You act as if you don't remember me."

"Don't think me rude. I've forgotten your name."

"How can that be? When it was *you* who named me."

"I did?"

"*Eunomia.*"

The name sparked a memory. This woman lifted the silk robe. From behind she slid her probing fingers over the landscape of flesh, across the stomach, then traveled down between the legs.

"Ah, *there* you are," says Farrah.

I, Egon, become aware. I realize I've been sleepwalking again. With no idea how I got to where I am. I return her smile. I feel lost. As if I'm inside a book of fiction. No longer the subject of another, but in first-person.

"What time is it?" I ask.

"Almost noon," she tells me.

With one hand she takes off my robe. With her other hand, still attached to my erection, she turns me around and I see she is naked. Farrah pulls me slowly into the living room. She finally lets go of me to lie down on her back upon my couch.

"You were really drunk last night," she tells me as if I needed to be told. She follows this statement with a squint.

"Was I disappointing?"

"Hardly." She beckons me to climb on top of her.

"Did we take a cab?"

Farrah nods. "You *do* remember."

"Did we stop somewhere along the way?"

She spreads her legs for me to position myself between them. As I do, images return, breaking like waves washing up the sand before receding. What's left is a sparkling vision of a cab driver, who stops. And I get out, staggering toward a row of parked cars, one of which I struggle to open.

"Did I ... break into a car?"

She shakes her head and takes hold of my penis. "The car was unlocked." About to guide me inside her, she pauses to ask, "Why did you want the car registration?"

A jolt of ecstatic warmth overwhelms me as I submerge like an electrical cord into bath water, into the body of Eunomia. She makes me want to forget why I exist, yet I need to know.

"Was it a blue Jaguar?"

She sighs "yes" before closing her eyes.

TWELVE

The building shook as another semi-trailer truck rumbled off the freeway overpass. Clifford rolled across the linoleum in his desk chair to reach the remote control on a table. Clenched between his teeth was a chicken leg. He increased the volume but missed hearing the closing remarks of the President of the United States delivering his State of the Union address. The President gave an optimistic smile to reassure the nation the state of the union was good. Enthusiastic applause followed. Clifford remained skeptical.

His nerves were rattled by another horn blast outside his office. About to switch off the television, he changed his mind and made the volume louder, in an attempt to drown out his landlord singing from the room below, bellowing with minimal talent to Sinatra: "... Got the world on a string ... sitting on a rainbow ..."

"*Buzzzz!*"

"What a world! What a life! I'm in love—"

"*Buz-buz-buz! Buzzzzzzzzzzzz!*"

Clifford finally heard the buzzer over all the noise. He sprang to his feet. He looked for his shoes, unable to find them, snapped shut the plastic container of his take-out food and pitched it into a nearby wastepaper basket, wiped his mouth with the back of his hand, then combed fingers through his hair.

"Just a minute!"

"*Buz-buz-buz!*"

Using the handrail, he descended the linoleum stairs which were slippery in his stockings. He opened his office door. On the other side of the iron security gate stood Norwood, the man Clifford had been hired to investigate.

"I believe this is yours," said Egon, sliding the car registration between the bars. He waited for Clifford to take it.

Mystery solved as to why his car door was left ajar. Not the result of vandals breaking into it, Clifford realized, but by this man. He took back the registration form.

"Are you going to invite me in?" asked Egon.

Clifford wasn't sure. He felt exposed without his gun, camera, or disguise to hide behind. Having been found out, Clifford saw no point in playing dumb. So he unlocked (what felt to be) the metal bars to his cage, which allowed this potential menace to enter.

Both remained quiet as they traveled in tandem up the stairs. Watching Norwood from behind, Clifford cringed from the sound of Sinatra being slaughtered by his landlord.

At the top of the stairs, Egon paused to look around at the stark interior. "This is your office?"

"I live here too." Clifford watched Egon examine the bare walls and sparse furnishings. "Have a seat. Take the comfortable one."

Egon looked at the rickety-looking desk chair, the Elizabethan armchair with a cushion, then the worn leather sofa, before deciding on the armchair. Clifford reclaimed his desk chair. He swiveled it around to face his guest who was quick to ask.

"Why have you been following me?"

"Who says I have?"

Egon leaned forward. "Let me make this simple. Faye hired you. I don't know why. But you've been trailing me for weeks."

"A month, and ... eighteen days. To be precise."

"Whatever. You admit it."

"Well, yes, I guess I have." Clifford smiled nervously, scooting his chair a fraction away. "What do you want?"

"Answers. Start talking."

Clifford didn't know what to say. This was by far the strangest case he had ever been involved in. He was first hired to investigate this man, Egon Norwood, seated before him, by a colleague who worked at the district attorney's office. And who had informed him Norwood was a person of interest in the serial murder investigation. Secondly, a woman who called herself Faye, looking suspiciously like Norwood, showed up at his office wanting to hire his services too – to investigate her twin brother, this *same* man. Thirdly, this man, Egon Norwood, who he'd been hired to observe, Clifford realized, had been observing him.

"Well?" said Egon. "What did my sister tell you?"

Clifford wondered if he was being put on. Both of them, client and suspect, were very convincing. Each of them sounded and acted completely different. He half-expected a camera crew to burst out from behind the walls to inform him he'd been *Punk'd*.

Egon leaned forward. "Why did Faye *hire* you?"

Clifford leaned back. "I can't divulge—"

Egon sprung to his feet – surprising Clifford who nearly toppled backward in his spring-loaded chair.

"God-damn-it! Tell me!"

Clifford raised his hands. "Calm down. Don't hit me. I'm required to say that. It'd be unethical if I didn't."

"I don't care about your *ethics*." Egon remained standing.

"Well, *I* do. Or should." The springs in Clifford's chair began to squeak. "I'm sure we can reach a mutual understanding."

"Fine," said Egon. "I'll hire you too."

"What? You can't."

Egon counted out hundred dollar bills and dropped several on the floor in front of Clifford. "She's not paying you much, I'll bet. Five thousand. Will that do for a retainer?"

Clifford sensed he was being played, caught in the middle of a twisted game, but he was over his head in debt. Underwater, in fact. He desperately needed the money lying at his feet. Tempted to scoop it up, he struggled with his base instincts and remained seated.

"Not enough?" said Egon. "Here. Seven thousand?"

Clifford was mentally returning to two nights ago when he had been asked to come to the apartment of his client, Faye Norwood, who'd been wearing a leather-and-lace corset under a sheer negligee. She lived in a highrise near the Embarcadero. After two glasses of scotch, Clifford had felt strange, leaden, and unbalanced. He awoke handcuffed to her bed, and naked, along with a throbbing headache. And no memory of how he got from point A (the cocktails) to point B (overexposed). She'd been standing in a bathrobe filming a video of him on her iPhone when he awoke.

"For my scrapbook," she'd said, before telling him her debt was paid in full for services rendered.

Clifford blinked, still trying to comprehend his circumstances. He assumed he'd been drugged. And victimized, to put it bluntly. He realized he was blushing and his forehead percolating with sweat.

Reseated, Egon said, "What's the matter?"

"Nothing. I was thinking."

"You should know she's a pathological liar."

"Who?"

"My *sister*. You should be aware of that."

"I wasn't. What else should I know? About her?"

"She's an actress. We're twins, as I'm sure you've guessed. We look alike. It can get confusing."

"Yes." Clifford nodded, confused. "I am, a bit. Has she always been, as you said, someone who lies?"

Egon leaned forward, his shoulder-length hair falling into his face which he brushed away. "Tell me why Faye hired you."

"She believes you want to harm her."

"Harm her, how?"

"Kill her."

Egon laughed.

Clifford flinched as Egon abruptly stood.

"My sister's delusional. One more thing to know."

Clifford wheeled backward to his desk. Unlocking a drawer, he pulled out the death threats that Faye (or this man? – he was sure of nothing) had given him. "Do these look familiar?"

Egon came forward. "Let me see."

Clifford locked them back in the drawer. "It's evidence. I can't."

Egon smiled and sat on the sofa.

"What's so funny?"

"Do you think a desk lock would stop me if I really wanted to see those?"

"Then, you've seen them already."

"Don't insult my intelligence," said Egon. "Faye mailed them to herself, most likely."

"Why would she do that?"

"You're the detective. Figure it out."

Clifford watched with unease as Egon stood again. He walked across the pile of money to prowl around his living room.

Clifford stayed still. Every time he moved his chair squeaked. It made him feel weak. "I already knew your sister was an actress."

"Exhibitionist."

"She performs at a nightclub. A dinner—"

"She's a stripper."

"Oh."

"More of a tease than a stripper. So, I guess that's acting. And she's also an extortionist."

"A contortionist?"

"She blackmails. I want you to investigate and find proof."

Clifford's chair wouldn't stop squeaking. "She hired me to take photos of you. The other morning. While you were having lunch at a cafe on Union street."

Egon's frown transformed into a grin. "Ah, that's the reason she wanted to meet me outside."

"I was too far away to see much."

"That's not my problem."

"Those umbrellas, they were blocking—"

"Listen, my sister *is* in danger. She *will* be killed, by someone, if she keeps this up."

"The blackmailing?"

"Precisely. I'm worried about her."

"I thought ... I was beginning to think, you know, this was all ... some kind of an act?"

Egon looked at Clifford. "Everything we do, every day, is an act. Being a voyeur. Isn't that *your* act?"

"No. It's ... my profession."

"Being a peeping tom?" Egon noticed a bullseye on the wall. He went over to pluck darts out from the target. "That entire scene at the cafe. Faye had it staged for you to witness." Egon walked away from the wall. He turned and threw darts into the target.

"Staged? For what purpose?"

Egon pointed a dart at Clifford, then launched it into the wall. "For you. You've been cast into her little *puppet* show."

"I'm not a puppet."

"That's how my sister plays. You're being used, my friend."

"I'm not your friend."

"Whatever. She's fucking with you."

"What about you?"

"What about me?"

"The other night, at the Palace of Fine Arts."

"Ah, so you *were* watching me?"

"What? No." Clifford wiped his forehead with the back of his hand. He remained seated behind his desk. It felt safer there with Norwood armed with darts. Clifford opened the bottom drawer and surreptitiously removed his gun.

"What else has Faye paid you to do?"

Clifford didn't like the insinuation or the way the question was phrased, implying he'd compromised his moral values and possibly broken the law. "I don't know what the hell is going on between you and your sister, but—"

"We're estranged."

"She thinks you're the serial killer."

Clifford tensed as Egon turned. "She said that?"

"Yes."

Egon flung another dart. "Well, I'm not."

If not, Clifford wondered, *what* was he. "Your sister told me she found a dead cat nailed to her front door."

Egon clutched the last dart and walked toward Clifford. "She told me too. And, *no*, it wasn't me. Don't you want my money?"

"That depends on what you're expecting me to do."

"Follow her. Take pictures. Find out who she's blackmailing and why. I need to stop this before someone *does* kill her. I'm trying to save my sister's life. Okay? Is that too much to ask?"

"No. If that's all you're asking me to do." Clifford wheeled out from behind his desk holding the gun.

Egon scoffed. "Do you plan to shoot me?"

"Only if I need to, in defense." Clifford pointed at the dart.

"This?" Egon turned and flung it into a poster.

"Hey!" Angered, Clifford rose from his chair. He then dropped to his knees and began scooping up the money with one hand while holding the gun in his other. "I can't say I trust you. Or your sister. But I'm willing to investigate her if that's all you want."

"That's big of you."

"And discover if what you're telling me *is* the truth."

"It is."

"I mean, you're only hiring me to verify the truth. Right?"

"Right," Egon echoed back.

THIRTEEN

Mira asked, "Have you ever considered that suicide might be the solution to your problems?"

The word "suicide" ruined Faye's moment of reverie. She was hiding behind the role of a woman in distress and scrutinizing her confidant's use of makeup, critical of Mira's lack of imagination, and about to suggest another shade of eye shadow.

Faye told her, "Never. I'm having way too much fun. But it's a relevant question to ask my brother, who I'm sure you've determined by now to be emotionally unstable."

Mira tilted her head. She tapped the eraser of her pencil against her chin. "Faye?"

"Who else would I be?"

"Then you're not—"

"A basket case? No, I'm not. I simply told you I was depressed. Can't a person be sad anymore without their therapist jumping the gun and labeling them suicidal?"

Faye could barely contain her amusement and was trying hard not to destroy this delightful charade. She searched with restraint for her cigarettes, shaking her purse to locate them. Her unsuspecting amanuensis kept jotting down notes to document her behavior in the hopes of psychoanalyzing her true motives.

Mira finished writing. "Can you tell me where Egon is?"

"I have no idea. I don't monitor his activities. Understand that life, for me, is exciting. I don't intend on checking out early. Not if I can help it. Do you have a light?"

Mira reached forward for the crystal lighter kept on the table between them. Her psychotherapist was all business, all woman, the emancipation incarnate of feminine power, composed as she held up the object before her patient and snapped forth a flame.

"Thank you," said Faye. "You would make a good man."

The remark didn't ruffle her analyst, who smiled back, woman to woman, taking the opportunity to advance in her role as the high priestess with her concerned green eyes, all ears.

"When you said 'If I can help it' what did you mean?"

"I told you about the dead cat nailed to my door. It gave me a fright. The message was clear. A death threat."

"Did you notify the police?"

"You can't be serious." Faye leaned forward to flick off an ash. "And tell them what? I'm sure they have more important things to do than hear about dead cats."

"Was the animal yours?"

"No. My snakes would devour it. Egon wants me dead. *That* was the message."

"You're sure it was Egon?"

"I'm sure of nothing. Except that he's jealous. And possessive. He wants to control me. Or have me be nothing. As in *dead*."

"You believe Egon is capable of murder?"

"We all are." Faye held her gaze on Mira. She inhaled smoke then slowly blew it to the side. "You know we are."

Their eyes locked for an uncomfortable few seconds until Mira looked down at her notes. "You said Egon struck you."

"He did."

"The same way your father hit you?"

"What are you getting at?"

"You told me he had a violent temper."

"Yes. He's a monster."

"Your father?"

"I thought you wanted to talk about Egon?"

"I do. Isn't your father dead?"

"No. That's what they want us to believe. He's in one of those government programs where they conceal your identity. They faked his death."

"Why?"

"How should I know?"

"And this worries you?"

"How perceptive."

"Tell me about your father."

"It's a good thing I came prepared with cigarettes. Smoking is a prerequisite when talking about my parents."

"They make you nervous?"

"Neurotic is what they made me. Strike that. I wouldn't want you to get the wrong impression." Faye pursed her lips in a smile.

"You were about to tell me about your father."

"What every psychiatrist yearns to know. Nothing much to tell. The usual horror stories. I learned at an early age not to trust adults. I never knew for certain what was acceptable behavior or what I'd get punished for. The rules changed in accordance with our parent's moods. They were alcoholics. Am I boring you to tears?"

"Not at all. Please, go on."

"When I stayed overnight at a friend's house, it was a revelation to discover you could get up from the dining room table without being slapped in the face. Or realizing that parents expected you to be in bed by a certain hour. Little things like that. And I played along, pretending I was familiar with these parental rules."

Faye paused, inhaling smoke, exhaling. "Egon and I, we'd team up to survive. Imagine this. Our father chased us out of the house with a carving knife. We innocently came across his stash of booze while rummaging through a drawer."

"What happened?"

"He tried to kill us. But he couldn't make it up our back hill and collapsed dead drunk. I was tempted to go back and stab him in the heart. The way you kill vampires. But neither of us could do it."

"Did you feel sorry for him?"

"You're missing the point. I hated his guts. We were afraid he was faking it, to draw us back, so he could grab and kill us. Egon relied on me to be the brave one. He used to tell me I was fearless. But, really, I was terrified. I need another cigarette."

Mira held up an ashtray. Faye deposited a long ash and crushed the remains. "Why did Egon think you were fearless?"

"I was better at pretending. And I fought back. Or tried. Before I'd get overpowered." Faye tapped out a new cigarette. "At this rate, I may go through my entire pack."

"Would you rather we change the subject?"

"Very astute, Mira."

"Your attitude towards men?"

"What about it?"

"Would you say your father, given the way he was, influenced your attitude."

"Toward men? What are you implying? Be blunt."

"I was wondering why ..." Mira flipped through her notebook. "You told me, I quote, 'I enjoy humiliating men.'"

"I know what I said."

"All men?"

Faye tilted back her head to exhale a plume of smoke. "Not all. The ones deserving. Because I find the experience to be ... delicious. Getting *just* desserts. I know you love it too."

Mira said nothing, questioning her with a look.

"Oh, *Mira*, please. Now who's lying to whom? I saw what you did in college. Can we speak frankly?"

"Of course."

"Good." Faye leaned forward to tap her cigarette in the ashtray. "Because I believe, deep down, you'll agree with me when I say this: men are inferior to women. Primitive by comparison. Yet through brute strength, they demand the opposite, insisting they are superior.

It's a sexual farce. I mean, men are born with this extra, protruding appendage, and because of this, they get this notion in their heads they were born *special*. It's ridiculous. Hypocritical."

"Why is that?"

"Because this appendage exemplifies their innate vulnerability. Okay, take Achilles, bravest of warriors, the model of masculinity? You don't seriously believe that story was about him protecting his precious little *heel*, do you? Oh, and that Freudian lie about 'penis envy,' I never fell for that one either. Did you?"

Faye touched Mira's knee. "Oh, my God! You did, I can see it on your face."

Mira shook her head. "No, I was—"

"It's *nothing* to be embarrassed about," said Faye. "We simply have to face the fact that women have been subjugated far too long. Which is why I, for one, have been making an effort to put men in their proper place. Beneath women. So, you see, your theory about my behavior towards men having a direct correlation to my father's hostility towards me is baseless. He was a minor influence at best. But he *was* the first male to make me realize how primitive men are. How perverted our evolutionary—"

"Excuse me for interrupting, but can we—"

"Am I going too fast for you?"

Faye wanted to laugh. She didn't know how much longer she could maintain this masquerade, yet was enjoying the wild ride in her therapist's office.

Mira straightened her skirt. "I was hoping we could bring the conversation back to Egon."

"What is it you'd like to know about him?"

"This repressed anger you harbor toward men—"

"But I *don't* repress it," said Faye. "I try not to."

Mira returned a strained smile, tapped her pencil, then wiggled it between her fingers. "Do you know why you're here?"

"What a question. Does anyone?"

"In my office, for these weekly sessions?"

"A court order. It was part of a plea bargain."

"For anger management."

"I heard the ruling."

"Why are you so angry at Egon?"

Faye inspected her fingernails. "Because he *thinks* like a man. Thinks he's entitled. Yet he's primitive. He even collects primitive art. That's a telltale sign. But, I suppose, he can't be to blame for all of mankind's sins, now can he?"

"But accountable for some?"

"I like how you think."

"What kind of primitive artwork does Egon collect?"

"Masks, mostly. It's a fetish. I'd say he's trying to discover his roots and true identity – his primitive, *inferior* self. Yet when I point this out, the obvious, he gets furious."

Faye tried to peek and see Mira's notes but the pad was angled away from her.

"Aside from assaulting a man with a pool cue, have there been other incidents where you've been violent toward men?"

"Must I answer?"

"That's entirely your decision."

"And if I don't you'll assume the worst."

"Faye, I'm concerned this behavior will go too far one day."

"As in murder?"

Mira gave a neutral nod.

Faye volleyed back. "I thought so. You're in league with the police. Were you assigned to discover if *I'm* the serial killer, Mira? To see if I'm the one who's been murdering all those men?"

"That's not why we're here."

"No?" Faye pulled out her pack of cigarettes, then decided not to take one. "Someone is trying to kill *me*, Mira. Can we focus on that issue?"

"Yes, of course."

Faye smoothed back her hair. "Here's what I *will* tell you about those killings. Those men deserved to die. Horrible men, felons and known rapists. Which is what I told the police. Now, thanks to my big mouth, they think I'm involved."

"You became a person of interest. That's all."

"Because I assaulted a man. Big deal."

"And, it's the reason you were assigned to see me."

Faye removed a hand mirror from her purse and gave a smile intended for Mira. "And now you have me *exactly* where you have always wanted me."

"Excuse me?"

Faye inspected her lips. "We were friends, for a while. Back in college, if you recall."

"I do." Mira saw the time and closed her notebook. "Frankly, I was surprised when you approached me and suggested we be friends."

"Why? Because you ruined my cousin's life?"

"He was a rapist."

"You lied in court."

"I didn't lie—"

"About *that*," said Faye. "I wanted to be your friend because I felt we were kindred spirits."

"Kindred, how?"

Faye snapped the cosmetic mirror shut and returned it to her purse, then lifted the strap over her shoulder. "I admired you. I was curious to know your motives. I followed you to that cemetery. FYI. I was there. I saw what happened."

"Excuse me?"

"I have Mira, excused you. Don't be shocked." Faye glanced over her shoulder at the wall. "Oh, look, the time, how it flies." She stood. "I must go. I wouldn't want to deprive your next patient of their precious minutes."

Faye turned on her toes, pausing at the door.

"Oh, by the way, I was raped by my father. Repeatedly. You'll, no doubt, be wanting to discuss that during our next session. Unless, that is, I'm killed in the meantime. Have a wonderful day, Mira."

This was crazy, Clifford realized. Only moments ago he was looking up at Jupiter and Saturn. Both planets suspended, hanging in the air above him, illuminated within the vast blackened ceiling of the Academy of Sciences building in Golden Gate Park. Now he was staring down at a dead body in a downtown parking garage.

It was the end of the night, but still dark, a morning sky with no visible stars in the overhead fog. At this hour, the Financial District was normally quiet, relatively so, since this was a city. No sirens but red and yellow beacons from squad cars were revolving to light the street corridor below the towering office buildings. The police and forensic team were congregated around the victim. Contorted, on his back, he lay behind the opened doors against an elevator. The man was positioned as found, a short distance inside the sloped concrete entrance to this parking structure.

It was a cavernous space. Clifford was standing on the sidewalk looking in, observing the crime unit picking possible evidence off of the ground and placing it into plastic bags. Among these authorized workers wearing plastic gloves and talking into their recorders as car radios spurted static, Clifford identified the non-uniformed team of specialists. He recognized each of them from the other crime scenes. Except for one, who was new. Four men and one woman. The men wore dark suits with loosely-knotted ties. The woman was bundled in an off-white overcoat.

He recognized her platinum blonde hair, styled short, exposing an elegant neck. Her upturned collar and rain hat partially hid her face. She wasn't the person in charge but the others were considering her words with keen interest. Suddenly a tunneled gust of wind blew apart the wings of her coiffured hair. She brushed away strands from her face. As she did, her eyes looked toward the street and noticed Clifford.

Her reaction was disconcerting. Dressed as a reporter, he held a notepad and had a camera hanging from his neck. Hidden beneath a hat and behind dark-rimmed glasses, he'd assumed he would blend in and be unnoticeable. To show he was there to do his job, he raised the camera to his face.

Through the telephoto lens, Clifford focused on the dead body. The victim wore a sweatshirt bunched at the elbows. The forearms were tattooed with snakes. Their heads and forked-tongues stopped at the wrists. Above the shirt collar rose flames from another tattoo. He next noticed the triangular-shaped patch of hair on the lower lip. The victim's bald head was severely twisted backward.

A broken neck. The serial killer's MO.

Clifford shivered, recalling the psychic vibrations he'd received from this man, now the latest victim, who had sat beside him in the park. Clifford had heard cries, as if from the dead. Then later, during the evening performance of The Three Fates, Clifford saw this man watching the crowd, and intuited he was scouting for a next victim. A jolt of queasiness and intense fear had seized his gut and convinced Clifford this tattooed man *was* the serial killer.

But now he was dead.

Therefore, he couldn't be the killer. It didn't make sense.

Clifford removed the camera from his face. He saw the woman looking at him. She whispered something to the detective next to her. He was the recent addition to the investigative team, and someone Clifford recognized. The street hustler outfitted in black leather, who had approached him on Broadway street when his car battery died. Who he'd seen recently, in a photograph, wearing next to nothing, on hands and knees, with Faye Norwood holding a whip.

At this early hour, Clifford began to distrust his faculties but the man gave him a sly nod, a brusque smile, then turned away.

No longer feeling anonymous, Clifford decided to move on, not wanting to call more attention to himself. He stepped backward to slip around the corner to his parked car. Now powered with a new battery, his Jaguar roared to life and he merged into the commute traffic.

Questions were mounting as fast as the congestion of cars. Why was Norwood's therapist at the crime scene? In what capacity was she working with the police? How much did she know about this serial killer? What was her relationship with this other cop working undercover on the same case? Was he the mole? Clifford needed to confront this Dr. Skyles.

He made a mental checklist of the things he could *not* disclose. For one: she could not know he'd been hired to investigate the crime unit investigating this case. Nor would it be wise to inform her about the latest victim, someone he had known from high school.

Clifford felt out of his depth. He needed advice from someone experienced in this kind of pathological behavior. But how was he to go about approaching this woman, a psychiatrist, without drawing more suspicion upon himself?

A grey sedan appeared to be following him. Staying several cars behind, it turned at every corner he did and was now cresting up California street.

His palms began to sweat, sticking to the leather steering wheel. He had planned to return to his office and examine the digital photos before sending them off to the person responsible for dragging him into this quagmire. He was hoping his friend had new information to explain the multiple sinkholes forming around him.

The car on his tail made itself known. It emerged from the fog with a *whoop* from its siren and flashing lights. An unmarked patrol car, Clifford realized, panicking. He anticipated the worst. He was to be pulled over, questioned, perhaps arrested on suspicion. He slowed to a stop alongside the curb.

The squad car shot past him.

The traffic kept moving.

Clifford remained immobile.

His mind had gone elsewhere. He was receiving a premonition. A shocking new one. Years clicking backward until he channeled a place and time. He envisioned himself as Egon, at the age of sixteen, caged in the backseat of a squad car.

The past and present were uniting into a strong signal. Clifford saw Egon as he was led into a police station. Escorted to a room and asked questions. Had he witnessed the murder? What time had he returned home? Why did he wait so long to call the police?

Clifford could grasp only bits and pieces and surmised the rest. He could sense himself becoming Egon, returning home to discover his mother unconscious on the floor. Her robe splattered in blood. His father stabbed to death in a lounge chair.

Clifford overheard Egon telling investigators pertinent details – the time of day, the hunting knife, the extent of blood, the alcohol consumption, along with other incriminating clues. Except for one. His father's eyes. Egon had wanted to close them.

"That was smart of you, son," said one of the detectives who praised his behavior, encouraging his cooperation. "You never want to tamper with evidence in a crime scene."

Not that reason, Clifford sensed. Egon didn't touch his father's eyelids because he couldn't understand why they had reopened. He had wanted to shut his father's eyes because, even in death, they were looking at him with disapproval and fury.

Clifford jumped, hearing more voices, sensing visions.

He felt himself shrink, unable to stop the years going in reverse. He found himself playing with toys on the floor, reverted to a child. As a juvenile, with his father dead, his grandmother gone too, and his mother accused of murder, the State had taken custody of Egon and placed him in Child Protective Services.

"I'm afraid he may require psychiatric care."

"Egon will be fine." The voice of his aunt.

"He's unresponsive," the nurse informed her. "He calls himself other names."

"He's in shock. He's always been an imaginative boy."

Clifford sensed the presence of others hovering in the air above him, like gods looking down, judging him. He too was there, looking down on Egon whose hand controlled a Tyrannosaurus rex. It was attacking Spiderman, who was able to evade the prehistoric monster by shooting sticky threads onto buildings, before swinging back to surprise the dinosaur. Both of the plastic figures were fighting from his right and left hands.

"Egon?"

Getting no response, the caretaker asked, "How well do you know the boy?"

"His father was my brother. We didn't see eye to eye. But I did come to visit off and on. *Egon*. It's your Aunt Sally."

Clifford glanced up, hearing something. Suddenly both toys, as if losing power, were laid to rest, toppling over. Egon crossed his legs. He hugged his shoulders and leaned forward, rocking back and forth as he mumbled, chanting.

"*God help me ... God help me ... God help me ...*"

"Egon," said his aunt. "God will help you. But you have to help yourself too. Can you do that? You're coming home to live with me. Would you like that?"

Murmuring to himself, Clifford was abruptly transported from his paranormal trance back to the present.

Someone was tapping at his glass bubble. It got him to look up. It took him a moment to adjust to the when and where. He cranked down his side window. "Yes?"

The women in a police uniform handed him a ticket. "You're not permitted to park here."

"But, officer, I was only—"
"Or *stop*. Anytime. Keep moving. Have a nice day."

FIFTEEN

I awake to the sound of buzzing inside my left ear. There is also a background chatter of birds. I open my eyes. My father is in a lawn chair facing me. His eyes are closed, body slumped, with one arm in his lap, the other hanging at his side. At his feet is a liquor bottle. Not quite empty. A puddle of amber liquid remains, sparkling in the morning sun.

The noise in my ear is from a bee, who decides to fly off. I look down and see more bees swarming around me. I'm upright, standing naked, except for my boxer shorts. How is this possible? I turn my head and realize I am tied to our wooden fence. Both arms extended, each wrist secured by black plastic ties with their sawtooth fasteners, the kind my father keeps in his workshop. My ankles are bound to a fence post with more plastic ties.

My mouth won't open, sealed shut with duct tape. What I fear most is what will happen when my father wakes. The bees tickle and make me itch. They crawl across my skin to sample the juice from plums. Squashed and severed. Several are scattered at my feet. I can still hear my sister's screams. She fights hard for me, but she is a girl. Where has she gone?

The memory of last night returns. I am with my sister playing in our backyard, wearing homemade costumes, attempting to kill a monster. A multi-headed serpent. As we cut off one head, two more grow back. The screen door slams. Our father staggers toward us. He's in good humor, drinking from a bottle. He pretends with us, roaring, chasing us. His breath is fire and brimstone, the fumes of hell. And soon he *becomes* the beast, breaking our swords to pieces. We have no defense against his fury as he knocks us to the ground. And it happens, again, his transformation. Branches sprout from his head under the oak trees as the sun begins to sink.

"Ah." My father grunts in a laugh. "You've been reborn."

He is conscious, struggling to sit up straight. I start to tremble. He picks up his bottle, shakes it, and drinks what is left in a few hard swallows. The bottle drops with a hollow clang to the dirt. He rubs his eyes, looks around, confused, staring up at me. His blank look is one I know. He has forgotten what he's done. The momentary shift toward contrition is replaced by a stern smile. And he stands. From his back pocket, he finds a bundled pamphlet. It rekindles something in his mind to justify his actions and redirect his guilt.

He laughs, flipping through the pages before thrashing them in the air. He walks over, threatening to smack me in the face with it. Which he does. A brisk slap, as if meant to punish me for looking at pornography.

My cheek stings. Water fills my eyes. His cold fingers fumble for the edge of the duct tape – ripping it off my skin.

"Where'd you get this trash?"

"Grandma."

"When? She's been—"

"Years ago. At church. They gave it to everyone."

"She filled your head with delusions, did she?"

My father smiles, turns around to cough, then spit. He whirls around with renewed vigor and hurls the pamphlet into the woods. "Let's talk about that. Religion." My father collapses back into the lawn chair and picks up the empty liquor bottle, tapping the glass. "Beliefs in a higher power. A supreme being. I was dumb enough, once, to believe that crap. I enlisted. Joined special forces. Christ. To fight the good fight. Right? Bullshit."

I say nothing. Then, "Are you going to untie me?"

"Maybe. Hear me out."

It's Monday. Not a cold morning, but my body is quivering. More birds are chirping.

He tells me, "I nearly froze to death in Vietnam one night. Yeah. In a tropical jungle. Our unit got ambushed. The sole survivor. Left for dead. I'd lost a lot of blood. Wasn't sure I'd see another day. But I refused to die. Do you know why?"

I shake my head. He smiles, seeing a way out now, a crack in the rubble to dig toward the light of an excuse he will use.

"That's why I tied you up. So you'd know."

"Know what?"

I love my father, but he scares me. I try, but I don't understand him. I fear he is trying to understand himself too.

He chuckles, idly tapping the glass. "Life. It's a precious thing. You're damn lucky to be alive. Embrace it. You cold?"

"No," I lie.

"What were you doing last night? Pretending to be a knight in shining armor? A warrior fighting dragons or something?"

Insects continue to buzz around me. I want to tell him the truth, but I don't.

He leans forward. "Trying to save her? Your twin?"

I say nothing.

"She's dead, Egon."

"I saw her!"

"Son, you don't think *I've* seen things? Weird things? I have. More than anyone should ever have to see."

My father wants to explain it away, make it all right by telling me another war story, the wrongs he has done, which he can't undo. So I listen. What choice do I have?

"Atrocities, Egon. Suicide bombers. Burning flesh. Decapitated little girls. Armless soldiers in shock holding bloody stumps. Images that sicken you. Things you can't erase from your mind."

Nor can he erase what he does to me. Yet I nod.

"*Those* were real, Egon. Not imaginary. Like, like—"

"Dad, you don't understand."

"She's not real!"

"You don't know that."

My father stands. "Right, like Jesus? Preaching about heaven. The great Hereafter. Performing miracles. Walking on water. Sure. About as miraculous as your magic tricks." He points at the house. My mind stutters back to broken images of my magic kit destroyed by my father. During another blackout. "Son, there *are* no miracles. You fight for what you get in life. To stay alive! You fight!"

"Yes, Sir."

My father kicks the fence. "I'm trying to help. To toughen you. To stand up to those bullies. You'll thank me later." He takes hold of my chin and stares intently at me. "Son, *this* is reality.

I fight tears. "How's this going to help? Why'd you do it?"

"Why?" My father chuckles. He removes the military knife that he keeps with him as a memento of his glory days. "Jesus asked the same damned thing. To *his* father."

My father is feeling better about himself, having found a means to justify his actions. "I wanted you to experience what I felt. To *feel* helpless, then *feel* reborn. To know what's real and what's not. And I guarantee you'll never see the world the same again. What I did to you, Son, consider it your Sunday-school lesson."

"It's Monday."

The blade snaps apart the plastic, releasing my arms and legs. To my surprise, he pulls me into a bear hug, slaps me on my back, and tells me, "Go shower. You'll be late for school."

My legs are weak from standing all night but I do my best to run toward the house.

My name is called. It's a woman's voice. Not my mother's.

I look around. I'm somewhere else.

This has to stop.

An angel is staring at me. I realize it's my therapist.

"What happened?"

"Do you remember where you were?"

The memory backwashes through me. "Unfortunately."

"I'm sorry. I had to take you there." Mira's eyes are sad. Her smile is too. She confuses me with a sense of hope.

"Yeah, well, my father was right."

"About?"

"I never saw the world the same after that."

"Hypnosis can be difficult. But it's part of the healing."

"Are you saying this gets worse?"

"There's deeper pain, Egon, locked inside of you."

"Great."

"We do this in increments. The good news is we're getting to the root of your dissociation."

"Dissociation?"

"We're making progress."

"It doesn't feel like we are," I say this with a smile.

"Trust me, we are."

I have trust issues, but Mira must know this by now.

I notice the bandage on her index finger, the one she writes with. It covers her knuckle. Blood has bled through the cotton. She is busy jotting notes into her book, as she is prone to do during our sessions. But her energy is not the same. She is tense, and yet trying to appear relaxed. I notice red marks, faint but visible, on her neck.

"You've cut yourself."

"Oh, this." Her laugh is odd. "I'm clumsy in the kitchen."

"Are you advising me to decline your invitations for dinner?"

Mira shakes her head and smiles.

"It was a joke," I say.

"I realize that."

I ask, "Do you ever feel like you're out of control? Not on the surface. On the surface, you appear normal, as if you're functioning smoothly, professionally. But inside you're falling apart."

"Is that how you feel?"

"I was asking you."

"We're here to talk about you," she reminds me.

"Are you sure about that?"

She gives me a quizzical frown.

"This concerns us both," I say.

She shifts into another gear, masking her emotions, becoming the consummate therapist. "In what way?"

"Mira. What's wrong?"

My question startles her. "How do you mean?"

"You always answer me with questions."

She breaks form, smiles back. "Force of habit. Let's start again. What would you like to talk about today?"

"You. Coming to see me perform. Finally. Tell me."

"Tell you what?"

I smile at her question phrased as an answer. The tables have turned and she's unsure what to make of this switch.

"You were wonderful. I told you already."

"It made me happy you came to see me perform."

Mira is searching for the right gear to move us forward. She is not ordinarily like this. After my performance, I came over to thank her for coming. She seemed dazed, standing like a beautiful gazelle in the middle of an urban forest. I felt compelled to kiss her and did, briefly on the lips. Which surprised her. It has changed everything. She wants to think it has not. But it has.

"Shall we get back to the business at hand?"

"Sure," I tell her. "Fire away."

"Tell me what's been on your mind this week."

"Same as always."

"Which is?"

"Questioning why we exist. Against improbable odds, two cells unite and make us what we are. A fluke."

"How does that make you feel?"

I laugh softly. "Like maybe we're not supposed to be here."

"Shouldn't we feel lucky to exist?"

"I need a good reason."

Mira reacts sympathetically to my nihilism.

"Egon, I want to help you. You know that, don't you?"

"I know."

"So let me."

"Let me help you too." I follow with a disarming, playful grin. "You do love me, don't you?"

"Egon."

She *does* love me, I realize. "Mira, you're good at what you do. I'm good at what I do. We can help each other."

Thrown a bit, she deflects. "Is that why you perform?"

"I have no choice."

"How do you mean?"

"It keeps me alive."

"And, yet, you die of stage."

"Ironic, isn't it? It gives me a reason to live.

"Explain."

"You wouldn't understand."

"I might."

"I know I'm a narcissist. All performers are. The history books are filled with them. These names we've come to know. Desiring to be thought special, notable. The most famous one of all being Jesus. I mean, Christ. He says he's *God* in the flesh. He gets mocked, spit upon, crucified. Is it any wonder? The world was a mess. He comes preaching salvation. Challenging the status quo. Rome. Religion. Promising to make amends, remake the world. His message was flat out rejected. Not by all. But he got deemed a threat. And killed."

"Go on."

"He was offering change. The people wanted blood. Revenge.

187

That's all they knew. It was a viper pit of a world where a few held power, profited from corruption, the rest merely survived, suffering. Jesus was offering a miracle that people either couldn't comprehend or didn't want. People wanted instant gratification. And, basically, not much has changed."

Mira makes a notation. "How does performing, as you'd said, keep you alive?"

"By changing one's perception of reality. For the better."

She leads with a smile. "Do you feel it's working?"

"I'm alive. Were you changed?"

"Somewhat. Yes."

"Good. I keep hoping for a miracle."

"What kind of miracle?"

"You'll be the first to know if and when it happens."

"Why me?"

"That, you will have to figure out on your own."

My air of mystery both intrigues and frustrates her. Mira wants all my pieces disclosed. All my cards turned over. So she can study and reassemble them.

"Can we talk about Faye?"

I shrug. "Sure."

"Has there been any communication with her lately?"

"We've communicated. Sporadically."

"That's good," said Mira.

"Not necessarily. I don't trust her. And she, obviously, doesn't trust me. Not anymore."

"Why do you say that?"

"She hired a private detective."

Mira makes a note. "How do you know this?"

"I confronted him. And he confessed."

"To what?"

"Being hired by Faye. She thinks someone is plotting to kill her.

And that someone, she thinks, is me. Or, our father."

Mira looks up from her notes. "But your father is dead?"

"Not according to Faye."

"I see."

God knows what she writes down or thinks of me. She looks up again, reloaded with more questions. "Is there any truth to what she's saying?"

"That someone wants her dead? It wouldn't surprise me. Faye can be nasty."

"Do *you* want your sister harmed?"

"No. For her crazy behavior to stop. Yes. She's out of control. She does insane things that spiral back to me."

"For example?"

"You won't believe this. A few weeks ago I come home to find a naked man bound and gagged to my dining room table. Left there by Faye and her friends who were partying. She humiliates men. And it puts her in danger. Me too."

As Mira makes more notes, I add, "For the record, it's not me who's sending her death threats. Has she mentioned them?"

"I'm not at liberty to say."

"Okay, that means she has. Nor did I *crucify* a cat on her door. That *is* something my dad would do. Not me."

"But he's deceased."

"Thankfully."

"How did your parents die?"

"I figured you knew. It's public record. My father was stabbed to death by my mother."

"Your mother killed your father?"

"That's what I said."

"And your mother, what—"

"She cut her wrists three months later. After being sentenced to an asylum for the criminally insane. She bled to death."

"How old were you?"

"Somewhere in my mid-teens."

"You don't recall your exact age?"

"I was sixteen. I try not to think about it."

Mira writes more words into her book. "Did you witness your mother kill your father?"

"I wish. I would have helped. No. She'd already killed him by the time I got home."

"Home from where?"

"School. He'd beaten her senseless before he passed out. So there wasn't a struggle. She used his hunting knife."

"You say this with a lack of emotion."

"Yeah, well." I shrug.

"You hated him?"

"I grew to hate him more than I loved him. I'll leave it at that." My heart is pumping fast, like pistons from a revving engine, going nowhere. "No. Let's not. My father molested my sister."

"For how long—"

"Years. I wasn't sure until she ran away. Then I knew."

"You've told me."

"When?"

"During hypnosis."

"Okay. Whole episodes of my past have been cauterized."

"That's common."

"How do you mean?"

"Well, because, you see," she explains with mild enthusiasm, "through hypnosis we're identifying these wounds. Incidents you've tried to erase or cauterize. We need to break apart that scar tissue. For your mind to heal properly. Does that make sense?"

"The fact that it's painful? Yes."

"If left untreated, unresolved, these psychological wounds will fester, continue to get worse, and create more havoc."

"How is this going to help me, and Faye?"

Her smile makes me wonder what canary she has eaten. "We're getting to that. Shall we continue?"

"No more hypnosis. I can only take so much. You know, this sorting through my dirty laundry. It gets embarrassing."

"It's only to help."

She's so earnest and lovely, I want to get up and kiss her on the lips. Yet I remain seated. I mimic her catlike smile. "My concern is, Mira, that you will fall out of love with me."

"Egon. We need to keep our relationship professional."

"Are you saying this can't work otherwise?"

"I don't want to lose my license." She conveys regret.

Hope springs eternal. I can almost see a rainbow in our future. More dots connect and pieces fall into place. But as they do, Faye troubles my mind. I realize I need to warn Mira.

"This is about Faye, isn't it? She *has* something on you."

Mira's demeanor changes. "Excuse me?"

"She does, doesn't she? That's what I thought."

"Egon, what are you're saying?"

"She's planning to use you."

"Use me, how?"

"I'm not sure. But I felt I should warn you."

"About?" Mira is mildly alarmed.

"She might be setting you up. For a fall. So be careful."

"Egon, I don't understand."

"I told you. This is how she plays."

SIXTEEN

Faye bit into the olive of her martini. She winced from its sharp taste while musing about her problems. Her legs were crossed and angled provocatively away from the bar. She vaguely admired the posh ambience and ignored the lecherous eyes of men looking at her over their drinks as if they were dogs begging for a treat.

She was angered that something so basic could go so horribly wrong. Until now her extortion schemes had worked like a dream. The fear of public humiliation had been foolproof. All the masculine bluster and threats were part and parcel of the business she was in. But these men always caved and sent their checks. Never before had she received death threats. Now a cat – nailed to her door!

She had assumed no one would dare risk destroying their career or marriage by challenging her. Was this person only trying to rattle her? She debated whether her life was really in danger.

In hindsight, she clearly saw the flaw of her business model. She hadn't factored in the enormity of her success. And how difficult it would be to monitor all her clients. There were so many. She had no idea how to contain and terminate this anonymous renegade. If she released all the scandalous photos indiscriminately, she would not only penalize her generous donors, it would kill her entire enterprise. And people would suffer. Because the work she did, she rationalized, was altruistic. She was keeping sexual predators off the streets.

She took another gulp of gin and continued to sulk.

A shadowy presence was upon her. By boldly situating his body next to hers, he left her little choice but to look into his eyes.

He wore a tailored suit and reeked of arrogance. He told her, "You look lovely, and lonely. Let me buy you a drink."

"Can't you see I'm busy thinking?" said Faye. "And capable of buying my own drinks, thank you."

Undaunted, his eyes narrowed to the challenge. "Allow me the honor. It's been written in the stars that *two* is better than one."

"I'm on my *second*," bristled Faye. "Go away. And, please, take that charming tail between your legs with you."

The man's suave demeanor collapsed. He snarled back. "Screw you. Crazy bitch. Go to hell."

"Haven't you heard? We've already arrived."

Despite his bluster, the man retreated. Faye pivoted to stare into the elegant bar mirror, at herself, the unofficial winner.

"You're getting a reputation."

Jimmy, the bartender, was her friend and her partner in crime. Always there to give her a drink, along with advice, and to listen.

"It's better to have a reputation, Jimmy, than none at all."

"Hey, it's your funeral."

Faye smiled at his morbidness, delivered like a dry martini.

"Does that mean you won't attend?"

Jimmy wiped a glass with his bar towel. "No. Only that I might be the only one who will."

"You underestimate my powers."

"Suit yourself. Nice dress. You wear black well."

Faye searched for the perfect comeback but got distracted by herself looking back in the mirror. "Hum, so tell me, Jimmy. What is it you've heard?"

"About?"

"Me. You said I'm getting a *reputation*."

"I don't listen to all the idle chatter that much."

Faye laughed. "The hell you don't. You *love* it. Tell me."

"You sure? You know what they say about curiosity."

"What does *she* know?"

"Curiosity, they say, killed the cat."

Faye blanched from the remark.

"Jezzuz, you look ashen. What's wrong?"

Faye downed her drink and slid the empty glass toward him. "Nothing. Another one. Please."

"Slow down. This'll be your third."

Faye grimaced. "Stop counting. Are you now a mathematician? What next?"

Jimmy scooped ice into his steel container, poured gin, splashed in a bit of vermouth, shook the mixture. "Celebrating?"

"Does it look like I am?"

Jimmy placed a cocktail napkin and an empty glass on the bar, speared two olives to insert into it, then poured. "No. You look like hell. As a matter of fact."

"Gee, thanks. I love you too."

"You look worried. What is it? You can tell me."

"Now you're my shrink?"

Jimmy pushed away. "Excuse *me* for being human."

He left to serve other customers. When he returned to locate a bottle, he added, "Last thing I'd want is to be your *damned* shrink. I'm fine tending bar."

"Don't tell me you've given up photography."

He turned abruptly. "That's between you and me."

"I should hope so." Faye bit into an olive. "If you really want to know what's bothering me, I've received threatening notes."

Jimmy's attention returned. "What kind?"

"Death threats."

"Fuck. You didn't *think* to tell me?"

"Isn't that what I'm doing?"

Jimmy left to deliver a drink. On his return, he grabbed a towel, slapped it over his shoulder and glowered at Faye.

"Stop flagellating yourself. It's probably nothing."

"It's *not* nothing," said Jimmy. "What else are you holding back from me? You have that look."

"What look?" Faye sipped her martini. "Oh, all right. I found a dead cat nailed to my front door. Dead."

The bartender's mouth opened but said nothing.

"Close your mouth. You look like a cod."

"Christ, Faye. This isn't good."

"You think?"

Jimmy pulled down his bar towel, began to twist it, suddenly wary of his customers. "Has everyone paid on time? No one's been late? Because that, right there, could be a sign—"

"No one is *late*. No signs of anyone being *pregnant*. Do you think I'm stupid?"

"I don't know, Faye. I'm beginning to wonder."

"You get so testy, Jimmy."

"This concerns *me* too. What now?"

"I'm working on that. I hired a detective."

"You what?"

"Calm down, I know what I'm doing."

"I'm not so sure. You didn't notify the police, did you?"

"Are you joking?"

A man was rapping his knuckles on the bar. It interrupted their conversation. As Jimmy left to take his order, Faye sipped her drink and studied this customer with a beard. He wore a motorcycle jacket with an insignia on the back she couldn't quite make out. The man was large. He wore leather chaps and had keys bunched at his side like a cock-eyed metal scrotum.

She raised her voice, "Jimmy, hurry up and serve Fancy Chaps. I've got something interesting to tell you."

Both men turned their heads. The bartender extended his hand, stopping the bearded customer from approaching Faye. Words were exchanged. The biker's hostility settled into a sardonic grin that was directed at Faye. He raised his glass in a fuck-you toast.

When Jimmy returned, she asked, "What did you tell him, that

I was an easy *lay?* It's no wonder I'm getting a reputation."

"Keep your voice down. I did you a big favor."

"Does he expect me to suck his cock?"

"Quiet. That guy's rough. He's an old aquaintence."

"What's he doing here? He clashes with the decor."

"You can thank me later for saving your life."

"My hero."

"I realize you're upset, Faye. But try not to insult the customers. I'm beginning to think you have a death wish."

Faye poked the nail of her middle finger into her remaining olive and raised it. She held it up to the customer at the other end of the bar and smiled, then sucked the olive off her finger.

The biker squinted back at her.

"Is he blind too?" She turned to Jimmy. "Do you want to hear something funny, also interesting?"

"Sure."

"Did you know that within a pack of hyenas, the female is the dominant gender? It's the same for several animal groups."

"Keep your voice down. Why's that funny?"

Faye pinged the rim of her glass with a fingernail. "Because, it's virtually impossible to distinguish between the male and the female. Because their sexual *organs* are almost identical. You see, the female has a hanging clitoris which can achieve an erection much like its male counterpart. And, they both have scrotums."

Jimmy scoffed. "Where did you hear this?"

"From Egon. He used to work at the zoo. He knows all sorts of weird animal stuff. *Don't* believe me. It's true. I was impressed to know that *males*, at least in the *hyena* society, are considered useless and treated as secondary citizens. I'm serious! The females give the orders, lead the hunts, and make all the rules. The entire pack must defer to the dominant *female*. They salute her by licking her face, then her genitals. The way nature was intended to be. Maybe *Fancy*

Chaps would like to come over here and suck my clit."

The biker slammed his drink down on the counter and rose in a burst of anger.

"Now hold off!" said Jimmy. "No fighting in here. She doesn't know what she's saying."

"The hell I don't!"

Jimmy's hand struck the bar. "Both of you! Stop it. Jesse!"

The man halted. Faye barely flinched, her legs still crossed on the bar stool. "It's *Jesse*, is it? As in Jesse Jane? Were you coming over to salute me with a lick?"

Jimmy had signaled a co-worker and both men were now on the other side of the bar to intervene. "Personal problems, man. It's not worth fighting over. Trust me, Jesse. Let it go."

The man clenched his whiskey glass as if to crush it, then flung it behind the bar. It smashed into liquor bottles. He stormed out nearly breaking glass as he slammed the door shut.

"Dickhead," said Faye.

Jimmy swung around. "What in the *fuck* is wrong with you? Are you happy now? Look at the mess you caused!"

"Me? I didn't throw my glass in a tantrum."

Faye watched as Jimmy apologized to his patrons and returned to his station behind the bar, pissing and moaning as he assessed the damage. Jimmy grabbed for towels and a broom.

"No major damage that I can see."

"Shut up."

Faye's empty glass chimed, rung by the tapping of her fingernail. "When you're finished, I'll have one more for the road."

"Go home, Faye. You've had enough."

"Jimmy, you're sounding like a *mathematician* again."

"You're drunk. Go home."

"Drunk is an ugly word, Jimmy. I am only in-*tox*-icated. There is a *big-big* difference."

Jimmy dumped broken glass into a trash bin. "Yeah, like your god-damned *hyenas.*"

Faye laughed. "That's funny, Jimmy. To have a sense of humor shows we're sane. I enjoy testing the boundaries. To teeter right on the edge of infinity."

"You're there," said Jimmy. "Let me call you a cab."

"That's rude. In no *way* do I resemble one." Faye was startled by a hiccup and giggled. "Oops. A little foreplay."

She peered over the counter at her partner-in-crime cleaning the floor to whisper, "Tomorrow evening, don't forget. Another photo shoot. Investment *banker.* Who's been naughty. And, he's loaded."

Jimmy stood and hissed at her. "*Seriously?* We need to shut this down until we get a handle on what's happening. You have *no* idea who's sending you those threats?"

"I have plenty. Each one has a motive, I suppose."

"This whole venture was a bad idea."

"Au *contraire.* We're doing good. Besides, you have expenses. This place would close in a month without my help."

Jimmy rose from the floor with a new scoopful of broken glass to show her. "And *this* is helping me?"

Faye opened her purse and pulled out a penny. She slid it across the bar. "For you. My donation. It's a gift."

He dumped the glass, then picked up the penny, turned it over and laughed. Written on a piece of paper stuck to the other side, it read: SMILE.

"For the damages. Keep the change."

"You're unreal."

"*Don't.*" She stopped him from tossing it in the trash.

"It's a fucking *penny*, Faye."

"A special penny. You have to promise to keep it."

"Why?"

"It'll bring you good luck. I swear."

Jimmy placed it in his pocket and told her sarcastically, "I can't thank you enough."

"You're welcome."

Reflected in the bar mirror, Faye saw bits and pieces of people moving along the sidewalk. Suddenly one of the unfocused shapes came to the glass. Her hiccups stopped. It was a face she recognized. The last time she'd seen this man he was tied to a table.

She nearly fell over the bar stool as she grabbed her purse and staggered toward the rest room. His eyes had a murderous look, too much to take, especially while inebriated.

The restroom smelled of misplaced urine, powdered soap, and bitter air. A cold wind was blowing in from a half-shut window. The swirling wallpaper made her nauseous. Footsteps were heard on the other side of the door. Faye fumbled inside her purse for the can of mace she carried for defense.

A fist slammed against the door and she dropped the canister. It rolled behind the toilet.

"Open the door you cunt! I know you're in there! I'll count to three before I break it down. One—two—"

The door exploded—splintering down the center.

Faye let out a scream. It caused her head to rise off the bartop. She blinked at the bartender who was banging his dustpan, shaking more glass into a bin.

Faye attempted to smile but couldn't seem to remember how it was done. Jimmy looked at her and shook his head.

"Do yourself a favor and go home."

Now what? A moment ago in such bliss. Angels caressing me in a dream. Ruptured from their world by a merciless buzzer. This damned well better be important.

On the other side of my front door is a young woman in her early twenties, thereabouts.

"Can I help you?"

"You're Egon Norwood. We met."

"Okay."

"Can I come in?"

I feel as if I haven't quite awakened. She has remarkable skin. Like semi-sweet chocolate. Her creamy eye shadow and cherry lips smile at me with a delectable familiarity.

"I forgot your name. Sorry."

"Andrea. Aren't you going to invite me in?"

I open the door wider. She reminds me of one of my carvings. But alive. More beautiful. She returns my curious stare as if I'm the one who should be asking permission to enter.

"What is it you want?" I ask.

Her alluring composure scatters and reshapes quickly like leaves on a tree ruffled by a light breeze. She gives me a playful smile. "You advertised. So here I am, ready to go to work."

She brushes past me. My instinct is to grab her. But I let her go, puzzled by the piece of information she seems to possess that I lack. I follow after her up the stairs, eye level to her bottom that sways to the rhythm of drums beating in my head.

I catch up to her on the landing and find her inspecting my mess. An eclectic array of books, artwork, coffee mugs left unattended, a coat I have been meaning to hang up, a hat tossed on a table.

"I wasn't expecting you."

"I can see that." She has a wonderful laugh, like an Alice who has stumbled into a rabbit hole.

With an impish agility, she maneuvers through my living room, then turns suddenly in her yellow dress which spins outward with a show of legs, as if she's modeling for a magazine. I have to admit it, she is an enticing sight. The morning glow enshrines her body.

"You're quite lovely," I say.

"I know." Her interest shifts to a large photograph on the wall. I decide to accept her arrival regardless of reason.

She distorts her face and laughs. "What am I looking at?"

"The head of a honeybee. It was photographed with a scanning electron microscope."

She tilts her head and studies me as if I'm the one with spiky body hair, compound eyes, and fuzzy antennae. She turns back to regard the other two enlarged heads in this triptych.

"I give up," she says.

"The one in the middle is an ant. That one's a wasp."

"Portraits of your family?"

We exchange smiles. She has a sense of humor, which is good. A warmth about her too. Sounding like a tour guide, I say, "Insects are probably the most successful inhabitants on our planet. Unlike us, they're incredibly resilient. Almost indestructible as a species."

"Are you their spokesman?"

"They don't need me. They'll be the ones surviving a nuclear holocaust, not us."

She considers this, mutely, as if viewing me in a new light, then travels on. With the resiliency of an insect, she has already brushed the negativity aside and turns to give me a cheerful smile, continuing to move about. She stops at the large terrarium and pouts.

"Why is it empty?"

"I built it for Faye."

She frowns, waiting for more information.

"My sister. For her boa constrictor. When she visited. Not that she comes anymore."

"Did she die?"

"We're estranged. She's calling it a trial separation."

I catch her surveying the floor in case I'm not being truthful and the snake is lying in wait, waiting to strangle her.

"You never got another one?"

"Snake? No, I can't stand them. That's Faye's fetish."

She appears relieved. She plops her body with a playful bounce onto my sofa. I remain standing as her arm extends to point at the chaotic assortment of masks and heads all over the walls.

"You have unusual tastes," she says.

"So I've been told."

Andrea's finger moves like a needle on a compass, magnetically drawn to a colorfully foolish mask. The pink papier-mache head of a man mounted on the wall like a wild animal. "A recent hunt?"

"Man's killing himself. Why not make it a sport?"

Amused, she widens her eyes. She brushes my sarcasm aside with a carefree resilience and rises off the sofa to approach a new head, this one hanging from the ceiling by a string. A miniature face, black and shriveled. "What *is* this?"

"It's real."

Her hand retracts but she doesn't scream. She gives me a shitty look, admonishing me for not warning her.

I shrug. "I didn't do it. In case you were wondering."

"Hum. Should I be afraid of you?"

"Headhunters from darkest Africa. One of your ancestors?"

Her composure impresses me. She gives me a waggish smile and darts her eyes at me as she walks away. "I don't shrink heads. I boil them in oil."

I laugh. I follow her as she walks into the den. Surrounding us are clocks ticking, out of time, to different beats, hands pointing to four o'clock, two-thirty-five, half past six. A few have stopped. One strikes and gongs twice. She notices this discrepancy.

"How do you know what time it is?"

"I don't. It's timeless art."

Andrea crosses her arms and surveys the wall over the fireplace. She avoids stating the obvious, that I like to collect things. Masks, specifically.

"Where did you get these?"

"From all over. Do you like them?"

"I'm not sure. I think so."

"The one in front of you is from the Congo. An initiation mask. It was used in ceremonies to solidify the bonds between the living and the dead. The antelope mask was worn during hunting dances and to honor totem ancestors."

She is again magnetically drawn to the centerpiece, to a mask predominately white with black incised lines curving outward from heavy-lidded eyes, with a slit for a mouth. I too am pulled in, awed by its presence.

I tell her, "That one belonged to a secret society. A tribe called Haluba. The mask was used for transmitting messages to and from the spiritual world."

She studies me. Her hand rises to trace lines on my face.

My hand comes up to touch hers, which stays, like a butterfly, pulsing, before fluttering away.

She lingers nearby. "Is this something you believe in?"

"I like to keep an open mind. You?"

She doesn't answer. She is curious about me. I too am curious about her. Who is she? As she wanders back into my living room, I say, "The modern world mocks primitive cultures. It prides itself on the suppression of natural instincts. I find that ludicrous. Given the way we behave."

Her eyes take in the masks again. "All are from Africa?"

"No. From around the world. The one over there, which looks like a monkey, it came from here. Indian tribe. The carnival mask, that grinning one, is from Mexico. Some from Japan, Greece. But the majority come from Africa. Congo, Nigeria, Cameroon."

"Are they valuable?"

"To me they are. For what they represent."

Her eyes question me again.

"They symbolize our hopes and fears. By wearing these masks, a shaman would capture the vital forces of departed spirits and gods. His act of self-sacrifice enhanced his powers and healed the tribe."

"Is that your secret?"

Andrea has nestled herself onto my sofa. She has kicked off her shoes and has tucked her legs under her dress. She reminds me of a cat, more sphinx-like, full of riddles.

"How do you mean?"

"With your magic. Have they enhanced your powers?"

It's a clue to how I know her. She picks up a small sculpture in the shape of a ball off my table. A man carved from wood, hugging himself in prayer, or sorrow.

"Wow," she says and sets him back down.

Her hand moves toward the sight of gold among the cluster of wood carvings. In her palm the antique cross seems brighter, the tiny filigree more pronounced, more beautiful. She handles it reverently, gently, before returning it to its upright position on its stand. Her eyes look up at me.

"Are you religious?"

"It's the human condition. To believe in something. So, yes."

"It's pretty."

"It was my grandmother's."

"She died?"

"Yeah. She was a beautiful soul."

"You must miss her?"

The porcelain face of a doll's head shatters against red bricks and I flinch.

"Are you okay?"

Her remark takes a moment to reach me. "What? No, I'm fine. Would you like a drink or something?"

"It's morning. But sure. What do you have?"

"A pretty good cabernet sauvignon. Also coffee, or tea."

"I'll take the breakfast of champions. The wine."

From the kitchen, I hear the hardwood floor creak. I realize she has risen and is walking again.

"Do you mind if I look around?"

"No, help yourself."

Her unexpected appearance and incessant curiosity trigger my suspicions, but I let it go. While unscrewing the cork, it slides inside the bottle. Wine splashes on my white shirt. The spatters remind me of blood stains. Using a steak knife, I poke through the neck to hold down the cork. I pour, filling two crystal goblets. I taste the wine to make sure it hasn't gone bad. It's good, but the girl is gone when I return to the living room.

Holding the goblets I peer about. I begin to think the worst of her. I scan the room to see if anything is missing. My artistic clutter is still in place. I walk into the hallway and take a sip of the wine.

"Hello?"

"Up here!"

I ascend the stairs. At the top of the landing, I see her yellow dress on the floor. I walk into my bedroom. The bathroom door is open. A matching yellow bra and panties lay on my bed. Her purse is set on my dresser.

I hear the sound of running water. Holding the glasses of wine, I find Andrea standing naked in my bathtub. Hot water is circling her ankles, steam rising to fill the air around her. She beckons me with a crooked finger.

I hand her the goblet of wine. She brings it to her lips and lets the liquid overflow from the corners of her mouth as she drinks. She smiles, wipes her lips, then rubs the spilled wine over her nipples.

Rather unexpected. But I enjoy the show and sip my wine.

Her eyes react to something she doesn't like. "Why do you have a knife?"

"Oh, I used it to push down the cork. I forgot I was holding it." I toss the knife onto the counter.

She seems relieved and swallows more wine.

"I didn't mean to scare you."

"You didn't."

She's lying. Maybe not. Living dangerously might be her thing, also getting naked, exposing herself to strangers. My eyes admire her body.

"This must happen to you a lot," she says.

"Actually, no. You'd be surprised."

"Aren't you going to get undressed? Let me wash you."

I set my wine glass by the sink. I first remove my wine-stained shirt, then unzip my pants, step from my boots, socks, then jeans. Andrea cradles her goblet in both hands as she sips wine. Her eyes peer over the rim and focus on my erection as I remove my boxers. She hands me her glass. I set it next to mine. I step into the bathtub. Before I have a chance to kiss her, she goes to her knees. She grabs the soap and begins to wash me, starting with my feet, soaping them, rising to my ankles, then both legs.

She looks up at me. "How do you do it?"

"Do what?"

"Disappear."

"When?"

"On stage. Dying. And don't tell me it's just magic."

"Okay," I tell her with a smile. "I won't."

She has worked her way up to my genitals and is giving the area a thorough scrubbing. "It has something to do with those masks. Their power. Am I right? You can tell me."

"I might. If you tell me why you're doing this."

"I posted the video."

"Video?"

"For your online audition."

"That was you?"

"Me. I filmed you guys performing in the park and submitted it. I knew you'd get a callback."

"They tracked Garrett down. But ..."

"Why? I want to be a Rebel Artist too."

"I'd say you are."

"Really? You're getting soft. Are you mad at me?"

"On the contrary." Her enthusiasm to please me gets my libido to rise again and momentarily quell my suspicions about this woman and her motives. She scoops bath water, cupped in her palms, and washes the soap off my skin with devotion.

"Thank you. I think."

She looks up with a smile. "Stop thinking. I want you to win." She blows warm air on me. "If you make it to the finals, you said the last act will be spectacular. Can you give me a hint? I won't tell."

I look down at her expectant gaze, looking up. "You're actually inspiring me with ideas."

"Am I?"

"You're very good."

"I'm worth every penny. Five hundred dollars worth."

She laughs. "I'm kidding. I'm not a whore. I came to learn what you do. Will you let me be your apprentice?"

"What other tricks do you know?"

"Close your eyes. I'll show you."

"You're not going to make me vanish, are you?"

"Umm, I could ... if I wanted."

Andrea takes me on a warm vigorous back-and-forth tunnel-of-love ride through dark waters with her mouth. I close my eyes and gradually disappear.

EIGHTEEN

Clifford sensed the time was right to meet this psychotherapist. So he scheduled an appointment. Now facing her, he was seated in one of her cushy chairs. After fidgeting with his coat, he folded his hands in his lap.

"What did you say your name was?"

"Clifford Hill."

"And you're a detective?"

"That's correct."

Clifford, ill at ease, stared into the soft suede backing of Dr. M. Skyles's notebook as she wrote something in it.

"What are you doing?"

Mira looked up at him. "Don't let it bother you. I take notes at all meetings. And you're here because?"

"One of your patients. You're treating a man, Egon Norword. Also his twin sister, Faye? Is that true?"

"How do you know this?"

"I'm an investigator. As I told you, a private detective."

"Are you currently investigating them?"

"I'm not at liberty to say. Has he mentioned me?"

"I am not at liberty to say either, under ordinary circumstances. But yes, Egon has mentioned you. I'm helping him. Both of them, with personal problems."

"Both of them?"

"Are you familiar with the term dissociative identity disorder? Also known by the name, multiple personality disorder?"

"I'm not sure. I believe I've heard of it," said Clifford.

"It's a psychological condition."

Clifford patted his jacket, pulled out his pocket-sized notepad and pen to write down this information.

Mira asked, "How did you come to know Egon and Faye?"

"It's complicated. I'm not sure where to begin."

"Wherever you'd like."

Clifford reached up to touch his tie but felt nothing there, then realized he'd taken it off in his car. "The sister, Faye, hired me first. To investigate her brother."

"For what purpose?"

"To take photos, observe his behavior. I was intrigued by how similar they looked. Almost identical. I became suspicious."

"I can imagine," said Mira.

"Except their mannerisms are completely different."

"What made you suspicious?"

"Well," said Clifford, "I've only met them separately. They live at different residences. The brother has a house near the Marina. The sister lives in a highrise apartment downtown. It hadn't occurred to me, until recently, they could be the same person."

Mira nodded.

Clifford folded his hands, not sure what to do with them. "I got the distinct feeling I was being *pranked*. Possibly scammed. You see, the brother discovered I'd been following him and came to my office. To hire me too. To investigate his sister. Now I'm not sure what or *who* to believe anymore. This entire case has me baffled."

"And that's why you came to see me?"

"Well, yes. It is."

"And have you been following me too?"

"I'm sorry. What?"

"The other morning. I saw you at the crime scene."

"Ah, I thought so. You noticed."

"Why were you pretending to be a reporter?"

Clifford reached to straighten his nonexistent tie. He dropped his hand. "I do that sometimes."

"Wear fake glasses and funny hats?"

Clifford squirmed. "Tools of the trade. Camouflage." He then became emboldened with his own question. "Why were *you* at the crime scene?"

"I'm a criminal psychologist. I was asked to come." Mira then volleyed back. "How did you know about the murder?"

Clifford refused to disclose his source. "It was an anonymous tip. I know people in law enforcement." Now it was his turn to ask. "How long have you been part of the crime unit investigating these serial killings?"

Mira made a note. "When you called my receptionist you said you had important information concerning Egon. Is that true?"

"Yes, I do. But you didn't answer my question."

Mira closed her notebook. "I became involved after evidence was found on the third murder victim. And it appeared to establish a link, connecting these killings to one perpetrator."

"You're referring to the 'X' he cuts into the skin."

"Correct. *That* is why I was brought in. For my expertise."

"Thank you," said Clifford.

"You're welcome. Now, this information you have about Egon, might it be pertinent to these murders?"

"Possibly."

Mira tapped her pencil. "Are you going to tell me?"

"You realize, I am *not* one of your patients."

"I respect that. It was not my intent to make you feel that way. But are we not after the same results?"

Clifford lifted his chin. "Which are?"

"Finding the truth, for one."

"Of course. The truth."

Mira added, "And to help our client. Or, rather, *clients*."

Clifford straightened his posture, having sensed a clue was being fed to him. "Was that an admission they *are* one and the same?"

"Client-patient confidentiality. I'm not permitted to say. You'll have to respect my code of professional ethics."

Somewhat ruffled, Clifford regathered his thoughts. "I too pride myself on doing the right thing. Being ethical."

"Yet you allowed both Faye *and* Egon to hire you. Isn't that a conflict of interest? Unethical?

Clifford blushed. "Ordinarily, but not for the higher purpose of verifying the truth."

"And have you?"

"Have I what?"

"Verified the truth?"

"Clifford gave his knees a rub. "On the surface, it would appear to be a conflict of interest, collecting fees from both parties."

"I would agree," said Mira.

"Unless, they *are* the same person." Clifford removed a folder from his briefcase. "I discovered the sister, aka Faye, is involved in some kind of blackmailing scheme. Extorting money. And, from not-so-innocent victims. Here, let me show you what I mean."

"You have evidence?"

"Does that surprise you?"

Mira waved her hand. "No. Please, show me."

"I've brought photos that, if made public, or shown to a spouse, would cause embarrassment. Liable to be scandalous, if you catch my drift."

"I'm beginning to." Mira tapped her pencil upon her chin, bit the eraser, then stood. "Would you mind excusing me for a moment? I would like to consult with a colleague. In fact, I'd like the two of you to meet. If you wouldn't mind?"

Clifford stood too, to be polite. "Not at all. That's why I came. To get to the bottom of this."

Mira took her notebook with her. "I'll be right back. I want my colleague to hear this too."

They exchanged civil smiles. The door closed behind her.

Clifford muttered, "*Now* we're getting somewhere." He wished she had left her notebook. But, for the first time, his eyes were free to roam about her office. He saw the many stacked rows of books, neatly arranged (alphabetized, no doubt), along with her certificates, and photographs of prominent political figures standing beside her, which, all together, made a strong impression. Informing the viewer she was smart and knew powerful people.

Stretching his legs, Clifford wandered about, surveying her desk by touching ashtrays, paperweights, folders. He noticed there were no sharp objects anywhere. No letter openers. He opened drawers. Mostly paraphernalia. Paper clips and pencils. The file drawer was locked. Clifford took out a small knife, which he carried specifically for the purpose of picking locks.

He easily picked this one. Inside he discovered the file on Egon, and also Faye. He rifled through a stack of notes, thumbing until he found comments which stood out: "*Egon exhibits classic symptoms of D.I.D. Personality shifts are extreme ... Faye is his twin sister.*" Clifford flipped through to other remarks: "*Egon exhibits artistic control ... is charming but calculating ... he is a spiritually troubled soul.*" Also, "*hypnosis has revealed extensive childhood abuse.*"

Clifford flipped to notations on the sister. "*Faye's rage traced to molestation by the father. Has transference issues ... abuse of men ... sexual engagement is unknown.*"

Clifford next found medical journals referencing case studies on deviant sexual behavior. He opened another book and saw photos of crossdressers and transgenders. He became distracted by a penny, seemingly out of place, and examined it. White paper had been cut and glued to one side. Small hand-written words read:

SAVE ME

"What are you doing!" said Mira, entering the room.

They looked at each other, both surprised, she more than him.

A large bearded man stood behind Mira but seemed unperturbed by the situation.

Clifford smiled. "Professional habit. To snoop."

"How did you get into my desk drawer? It was locked."

"It seems you forgot to lock it."

Mira didn't believe him. Her face was flustered, waving an arm in an effort to control him and her emotions, to move him. "Please, would you *please* return to your seat. This is Doctor Ramsey."

"Clifford Hill, private detective." He extended his hand and shook what felt to be the large paw of a bear, who was bespectacled, with a round face and natty beard, trimmed to show where his jaw line should be. He displayed a pleasant, non-threatening smile.

"Curious penny," said Clifford.

"Put that back," said Mira.

"No worries." He dropped it inside the drawer.

"Shall we all be seated?" suggested Mira's colleague, directing Clifford back to his cushy chair. The man wheeled up a matching seat between them to form a semi-circle. "Dr. Skyles, *Mira*, has told me you have some important information. I'd be honored if you'd share it with us."

"It concerns Egon Norwood," said Clifford. "And Faye."

"His alternate," added Mira.

"Alternate?" said Clifford.

"His twin," clarified Mira.

Doctor Ramsey nodded and the rolls of fat bunched beneath his furry multiple chins.

"You see, Doctor—"

"Call me Lester."

Clifford began again, "I fear someone is going to die."

Lester frowned. "Why do you suspect that?"

Clifford directed his eyes at Mira, "Her patient is also *my* client, and she's been receiving death threats." He removed three letters from a folder, along with the remnants of a soiled magazine. He held the items up. "Have a look."

Mira and Lester reluctantly took hold of the items.

"The individual letters were cut from this magazine. I found it in the trash, outside Egon's home. Which suggests either he did this himself or someone is trying to make it look as if he did it."

"In order to frame him?" asked Mira.

"Possibly," said Clifford.

"Is that it?" asked Mira.

"A cat was killed and nailed to his sister's apartment door."

Mira and Lester looked at one another.

"We both know about the cat incident," said Mira.

"You don't consider that a serious threat?"

Clifford watched the two doctors consult surreptitiously with their eyes. Did their psychological training include convert blinks to communicate signals? He began to resent them both.

"I have theories," added Clifford.

Lester stroked his beard. "We would appreciate it if you would share those theories with us."

Share? What was *he* getting from *them* in return? Clifford took back the letters and magazine and said, "It's quite possible that one of Faye's – *Egon's*, whatever – victims, who were being blackmailed, decided to take action. Revenge. It's logical."

"Indeed," said Lester.

"You said there were photos," said Mira, glancing at the binder in his lap. "Do you have them with you?"

Clifford handed each of them a photo. "She has many more like these locked away. I was shocked to recognize the Chief Assistant District Attorney. I believe that's him. In fact, I'm certain it is."

Mira and Lester were silently expressing shock.

Clifford closed his briefcase. "Keep those. Prominent citizens and government officials, who have engaged in these kinky fetishes, are being blackmailed to avoid exposure to public ridicule."

Mira made a notation and looked up to ask, "What else can you tell us about these photos?"

"Nothing." Clifford rose. "Since neither of you are willing to share information with me. This is clearly a one-way street."

NINETEEN

Faye was reclined against satin pillows. She wore a lace and leather corset, a tiara in her braided hair, a jeweled necklace, and a gold armlet. She held a cat o' nine tails. She yanked on the chain clipped to a studded dog collar attached to a man licking her toes.

Her attentive servant wore a French maid's dress, frilly apron, lace cap, and nothing else. On hands and knees, he looked up at her, waiting for instructions. A blonde wig curtained his face.

Faye told him, "I'm not dissatisfied with your work. You have earned the privilege to advance." From a silver bowl polished by her client, she plucked a grape off its vine and popped it into her mouth, then drank from a matching silver goblet. "Eunuch, come get your reward. Make haste!"

Faye jerked on the leash. Her housekeeper obediently groveled between her legs. "Good boy." She removed his wig to pat his bald head as he lapped wine from a bowl placed on the bed. "Drink all of it. Don't disappoint me or I will be forced to *whip* you again."

The man looked up, "Thank you, Your Highness—"

"Silence! How *dare* you speak to me." Faye flagellated his bare bottom with the cat-o-nine-tails. He yelped, lowered his head to the bowl and slurped faster.

How boring it would be, Faye mused, without her carnal romps. She was amazed by these men who subjugated themselves to her sadomasochistic punishments. Case in point, this man before her. He held financial power over others, granting loans to some and foreclosing on others. A man born to a life of privilege, sole heir to a banking magnate, who was in need of repentance. His wife had divorced him, having caught him philandering one too many times. The final straw, that broke him, was having sex with their nineteen-year-old au pair, daughter of his ex-wife's childhood friend.

Faye's business partner, Jimmy, the bartender, managed to find these losers. How he got them to confess their misery while plying them with alcohol was, in Faye's mind, a rare gift. As a consolation for these late-night confessionals, Jimmy would give each wayward soul a card. An exclusive invitation to receive Faye's special services. A ticket granting them absolution and atonement for their sins by confessing and receiving due punishment for the errors of their ways. "*Ultimate Liberation & Sexual Salvation – Guaranteed.*" That was her titillating tagline and promise. And she was more than willing to give these sexual predators their wish.

Faye idly swatted her client's bottom as she mused.

Her father had been rejected countless times by bankers. After each rejection, he would return home drunk. As a car mechanic and ex-marine left with post-traumatic wounds, his greasy hands left black marks on everything he touched. What money he earned he spent on liquor and drugs. What time he had left for his family he spent locked inside a refurbished Airstream trailer with his tools and dreams of inventing a military gadget that would make him rich. After each letter of denial for a patent or a loan, he'd drink himself into oblivion and curse the financial institutions of the world.

Their home suffered his wrath. Broken chairs. Their mother slapped and battered. While listening to her screams, Faye hid under her blankets. Some nights he'd stumble down the hall and barge into her room. He'd tear off her pajamas, then force himself upon her. Most times he was too drunk to do much, so he hit her.

Faye shuddered as she recalled being held upside down by the ankles. Her father had dangled her over the railing of their staircase. He swore he would drop her if she ever told a soul about what went on between them. So terrified, Faye peed and urine trickling down to her face. So disgusted, her father almost let go. Instead, he pulled her over the railing and dropped her onto the hardwood floor, then told her to clean up her mess.

Eyes overflowing with tears, Faye looked up and noticed her client. His face had a look of concern. She snapped the bed with her whip, wiped her eyes, and flagellated his bare bottom.

"How dare you look up at me. Head down!"

Angry at her tears, Faye closed her eyes. As a child, she would escape into the hills to run through the tall grass, then disappear behind the green and golden wavering walls. Finding comfort there, she would cry and watch the wind as it blew overhead.

She detected light, opened her eyes, then shielded them from the sun shining over the edge of her grassy sanctuary. She had forgotten where she was and sat up. Her subservient guest thought the lights were part of the game they were playing and kept licking wine from the bowl between her legs.

Faye shouted, "Stop it. Get up!"

The man looked up in dismay, bewildered by the lights flashing from outside the motel window. Cocking back her leg, Faye placed a foot on his chest and catapulted him to the floor. Draping herself with the bedsheet, she lunged toward the window. Footsteps could be heard descending the metal fire escape.

From the floor, her client asked, "What was that?"

"Keep quiet! I'm trying to listen."

Faye glowered at his fat, quaking body. He was now standing in the skimpy maid's uniform, foolishly attempting to hide his genitals. Quickly sobering to the situation, he collapsed to the floor with a look of shame and guilt.

"Dear, God," he blubbered. "Were those flashes from a camera? Did someone just ... Oh, my God! I'll ... be—"

"Stop whining, you big baby," Faye scolded. "What about me? Why is it *always* about you?"

"I'm the owner of a bank, for God's sake!"

"Well *hurray* for you."

"Do you have any idea who that was?"

"I'm as surprised as you."

"Then ... oh, *Jesus*. This can't be happening. If anyone should, I mean ... Damn! Where are my clothes! Where the hell did you put my pants?"

Faye almost laughed. He looked cartoonish, like Porky Pig as he hopped around in drag. She hugged the sheets to her body. It gave her a sense of control until she noticed the red stains. From wine spilled during the commotion. She dropped the sheet to the floor. Her guest had found his pants and now had one foot caught inside. Hopping past the mirror, he saw himself – pimped up with lipstick and mascara – and crashed into the dresser.

"Watch it! Don't go breaking the furniture."

"I'm sorry. I don't know what to do."

"Get a hold of yourself," she said. "You sound pathetic."

"You don't understand, the possible ramifications of ... what this could do to me ... if ... you know?"

"No, I don't," said Faye. "Why don't you tell me."

"If photos got out. Made public. My career, my reputation ... Oh, my God. This could ... it could ..."

He couldn't get himself to say it. The harsh light of reality was burning his eyes. He sat in a chair and began to sob. Faye tried to imagine him smugly seated behind his desk, within his environment of wealth, making the less fortunate beg.

These executives, Faye thought, were paper thin and disposable. Such mushy targets. "Stop sniveling. You're giving me a headache. Please get up and act like a man."

This bit of advice stung him deeply. He hung his head and saw the dress half-off, his pants half-on. The dog collar and leash hung from his neck. He looked up at Faye.

Faye sensed he was about to crawl across the floor to her feet to be consoled like a baby. She would have none of it.

"Can't you see that I'm as upset as *you* are? Get up. It's time for you to leave."

Obeying her command, he stood. "Do you have *any* idea who that might have been outside the window?"

Faye detached the tiara and tossed it on the bed. "No."

TWENTY

I become aware of the morning congestion as I awake. Cars are honking and I am outside, standing at a street corner in the financial district. I can't recall how I got here, which is less disturbing than the realization I am wearing a dress. It is cold, barely light at this hour. And all I have on is a skimpy blue strapless party dress. I'm holding a small purse and teetering in high heels.

Another honk – which I sense is blasted at me – and I nearly fall. Men in suits, clutching briefcases, newspapers, and their styrofoam cups of coffee, take a moment to stare at me. Adjusting as best as I can to the situation, as if beamed down to Earth from outer space, I wave to flag down a cab. It zooms past me. I pretend to be unfazed. An offshore breeze lifts my dress, which I hold down with one hand as my other rises to signal another taxi.

This one stops. I escape into its back seat. With mild relief, I shiver from the icy vinyl against my skin. I glance down at my bare, shaven legs held together at the knees. My driver is looking at me in his rearview mirror.

"Happy Halloween, Darling. Where to?"

I'm losing my mind. The driver resembles Dracula and gives me a fanged grin, before stepping on his accelerator and bolting us into the rush-hour traffic.

"The Marina District," I tell him.

"You're starting off early," he says, suggestively. "The parties don't normally get going 'till after dark. So I applaud you. I mean, your costume had me wondering. You *are* a guy, right?"

I notice the driver's collar and realize he is wearing a black cape. "Right," I echo. I gaze out the window. I glimpse other irregularities on the sidewalk: a bearded pirate, a devil with horns in red spandex.

"I love this holiday," says the driver with a passing leer at me in his tilted mirror. "I guess you do too."

I ignore him and search through the beaded purse. Among the lipstick, eyeliner, and other sundries I find my cell phone.

"Turn back. I changed my mind. Sutter and Montgomery."

"Whatever floats your boat, sweetheart."

As the cab makes a U-turn, I dial Mira's office number. "Good morning. Can I speak with Doctor Skyles? How long? It's urgent I see her. I'm coming now. No problem. I'll wait."

Because it is Halloween, I feel less a freak. But walking through the lobby, I receive many stares. I play along. Today is one big party and people expect these anomalies, like me, to breach the routine of their day-to-day workflow existence. But underneath the bluster and carefree stage presence, I display for my small audience who rides with me up the elevator to the ninth floor, I am harboring (like a ship broken loose from its mooring) panic at my loss of control.

I enter the reception area of Mira's office and wait, and appear as normal as I can. I cross my legs and scavenge through the stacks of tabloid magazines. I take in the latest celebrity scandal, this year's most beautiful people, the Biggest Loser, and all the other useless news that people can't seem to live without.

My name is called and I enter Mira's office. I am impressed by her composure, her lack of shock, as she ushers me to my usual chair. It feels like an entire minute has passed before she remarks on my appearance.

"I like your costume," she says neutrally.

"That's the problem."

"What is?"

"I wasn't aware it was Halloween. Or that I would be dressed as a woman. When I awoke. Or came to, as it were."

"Shall we talk about Faye?"

"This is her doing."

"Egon, you realize Faye is part of you."

"She's my twin."

"Your sister died."

"Why is this happening to me?"

"When we began these sessions you told me you'd been very close with your sister."

"When we were children."

"And that you'd become estranged."

"She abandoned me."

"We've talked about dissociative identity disorder."

"You mean my blackouts."

"Which you've had for a long time. Haven't you?"

I acquiesce with a curt nod.

She continues by saying, "Over time, and with repeated stress, this syndrome has caused severe splintering. Your ability to function semi-normally and to disguise your disability has worked for you, up to a point. But that's no longer the case."

While she assaults me with a diagnosis I don't want to hear, my eyes scan her office space. Her precision and order are diametrically opposed to my expressionistic clutter. It makes me want to see what her home is like. Much the same, I would guess. As I digest her final assessment of me, I remind her. "My art requires a rather *high* degree of functionality. And our group *is* in the semi-finals of that TV show. So, touché." I grin and coax a smile out of her.

"And that's wonderful," she praises me. "But it's also increased your stress level. For these illusions to work, they need to be precise. Flawless. Correct?"

She has me cornered. "What's your point?"

"You've managed to develop a means of maintaining your sense of self throughout each performance."

"Again, your point?"

"This mechanism of self-control, we can work on that."

"You've lost me."

"My point is …" Mira takes another tact, coming about like a sailboat, its sheets filling with wind, taking us into smoother waters. "Your performances are breathtaking. I honestly cannot figure out how you manage to do them."

"Thanks." I smile. "That *is* the point."

"The dynamics behind how those heads get cut off, then appear to reappear and grow, growing more. Until …"

"I die?"

"It's mind-boggling."

"Garrett gets credit for making that work. Quite ingenious."

"Who's Garrett?"

"A friend and cohort. He's part of our group."

Mira has that scrunched puzzled look. "He's real?"

I laugh. "Yes, Mira, not all my friends are make-believe. He's a sculptor. Engineer. An artist. And the women in that Hercules and Hydra piece are not only actors but costume designers and painters. It's a collaborative art form, what we do. It's not all about me."

"I realize that," says Mira. "Which is wonderful."

"Why? Because I have friends?"

"That's not what I meant."

"It was." I counter with a smile. "But it's okay."

It appears I've won a small victory. Mira resorts to her notes then looks up. "Can we talk about Clifford Hill?"

"What about him?"

"He made an appointment and came to my office."

"Okay."

"Then you know about him?"

"Of course. He's a detective. We've met."

I watch as she calculates, determining the best course of action for her next question. "Then you know he's been watching you?"

"For some time now. Faye hired him."

"He told me you hired him too."

"I did, to investigate Faye."

Mira is in a quandary. "You realize how strange that sounds? Considering your relationship with Faye."

"Ah, because she's the ghost of my dead sister, you mean?"

Mira's smile fades. "Egon, I need to ask you something."

"So, ask." I wait for her bombshell to drop.

"How many more of you are there?"

The detonation is swift, imploding through my guts like a sonic wind, blowing my defenses away, one by one. Devastation complete. Mentally, I am left with nothing more than a wan smile.

"Egon?" she asks, making sure I haven't disappeared.

"I'm here."

"Talk to me."

"You win."

"Win? Why do you say that?"

"You broke me. I'm in pieces. Congratulations."

"Egon, I'm trying to help you, not *win*."

I struggle to make light of it all. "I don't blame you, Mira. I'm a Humpty Dumpty who can't put himself back together again."

"You're not a nursery rhyme. At least, not *that* one."

I admire her tactic. Going for humor, trying to cheer me up.

"This is real," she adds. "*You* are real."

"No longer wooden? I'm now a real boy?"

"Egon, as painful as this process is, this is what it takes to heal. We *are* making progress. We are. Trust me."

I look at her as if *she's* the crazy one. Maybe she is. She seems to know what I'm thinking. She has her own pain. I know this now. She's got problems. I can sense it. I want to help her. So I rise above the surface as if gulping for air and reach out.

Mira takes hold of my hand. "We'll get through this. We will. Please let me help you."

I remain as stoic as a statue. Acid rain drips from my eyes and erodes my marble cheeks. I can take the pain. I want to show her I am strong, that I'm able to help her too. Because I love her.

"The integration of your personalities has started," she tells me. "We're working to make you whole again."

I'm in a strange fog. My mind is hampered by merging voices in my head, everyone wanting to talk at once. "What happens to us all? Who lives, who dies?"

"No one has to die," she says to reassure me. "The goal is to get your personalities to communicate harmoniously."

I laugh. "That'll never happen."

"I don't mean perfectly. Inside every person—"

"Normal people, you mean."

"Everyone. Conflict exists within us all."

"Have you met Hunter?"

"Yes. Briefly. Twice."

"Hunter doesn't scare easily. But *you* scare the hell out of him. Just so you know, he called for a vote to have you killed."

Mira, shocked, fails to write a single word.

"I won't let it happen. You can relax."

She braves a smile, an uneasy one. Her eyes lower to examine my clothing, to make me conscious again I am wearing a dress.

"Can I talk to Faye?"

"You're welcome to try. I'm sure she's listening."

I hesitate to comply. I don't like letting myself go. But Mira has a way about her, with those beautiful eyes, looking into my soul.

Faye avoided Mira eyes, choosing instead to search through her purse for cigarettes. She knocked one from the pack, pulled it to her lips, but couldn't find any matches.

"Light?"

Mira held the crystal lighter up. Faye leaned into it to ignite the tip of her cigarette with the flame. She sat back to inhale, studying Mira as she did, then exhaled, blowing out little rings.

"It's like you're trying to herd cats. It can't be done."

"Hello, Faye."

"Mira."

"It won't work. We're too independent."

Faye watched Mira position the lighter, placing it on the table in the exact spot as before. It seemed that each piece of Mira's puzzling profession had to be arranged within its assigned place. Faye tilted her head to stare at the globular light fixture directly overhead. Its frosted glass and swirls of white were like a mysterious planet, which Faye blew smoke at.

She returned her gaze on Mira. "And here we are again. It's like old times when we'd meet for coffee or drinks back in college."

"I wouldn't say it's the same," said Mira.

"Those were fun times."

"Not for me."

"I keep forgetting. Let's not go there then."

"Can we talk about the photos?"

"Photos?"

"Showing you having sex with men."

"You're mistaken."

"What would you call it?" Mira held up a photo.

231

"Clifford, that little *rat*."

"Is that the Chief Assistant District Attorney?"

"Not his most flattering angle."

"What is this, if not sex?"

"Therapeutic retribution. I don't allow any touching."

"No intercourse?"

"It's not permitted. I can't believe Clifford betrayed me."

"I believe you intended to have him show me this."

"Why would I? That photo is private, as you can see."

"Taken for what purpose?"

"Personal reasons."

"To use as blackmail?"

"Mira, now *that* is a dirty word."

"Faye, this is bad. You can't—"

"My methods are unorthodox. But I do good work."

"It's illegal to extort money, you realize."

"Who says I am?"

"Hill, the detective you hired. He believes you are."

"What I do is my business, and *not* illegal. And besides, our conversations are private, inadmissible in a court of law. Patient-physician confidentiality. Or did I get that wrong?"

Mira said nothing.

Faye leaned forward to grind out her cigarette in the matching crystal ashtray next to the lighter. She made sure to shift it to a new location on the table. Mira repositioned it back to its place.

"You're very anal, Mira."

"Faye."

"Yes, Mira."

"You portray yourself as being Egon's twin sister, but you know that I know better. You are one and the same person."

Faye raised her eyebrows. "What?"

"Don't pretend to be shocked."

"I don't shock easily. You should know that about me. What I require, Mira, is that you make *me* the dominant personality."

"Faye, that's not how this works."

"The host, or whatever you called it. Whenever this *implosion* occurs and all the planets align."

"Integration. Fusion is another term we use."

"And how is that coming along?"

"You need to stop extorting money, or whatever you call it."

"Must I?"

"Faye, even if it's not illegal. It's dangerous."

"Funny you should mention danger." Faye arranged the hem of her dress. "I like your shoes, by the way. Because my partner and I, only yesterday, were considering shutting down our little operation. At least for the time being."

"Because of the threats you've received?"

"And then there is *that*." She laughed and crossed her legs.

"They're real? You didn't send those letters to yourself?"

"I'm not a fool. I'm anything but."

"You must suspect someone."

"I suspect everyone. Being that I'm a *paranoid* schizophrenic." Faye stood. "I need to move around." She strolled along the wall, studying the photo gallery showing Mira posing with public figures. "You've done well for yourself since college."

"Thank you. I've worked hard to get where I am."

"I always knew that about you, Mira. Your determination. It's very fierce. That's why I befriended you." Faye turned to face Mira, still seated, swiveled towards her. "A few weeks ago, there was this man, a misogynist of the worst stripe, a skunk, who I'd humiliated. I had the jackass gagged, stripped naked, and spray-painted while tied to a table. I even gave him a tail. Don't be shocked."

Mira shook her head. "Your alternate already told me."

"Alternate?"

"Your twin."

"Egon, yes, he found the prick. This man had even *boasted* to me about raping women. He had it coming."

"And Egon wasn't aware you had done this?"

"His mind is lost in a cloud half the time. No. He had no idea. He was furious. I'm pretty sure *he's* the one who wants me dead."

"Egon?"

"No. That *jackass*. Things like that happen. That's why I hired a detective. Why are you staring at me like I'm an idiot?"

"I wasn't," said Mira. "Please, go on."

Making her way to the end of the wall, she said, "This jackass, he warns me, tells me he's connected with the *mafia*. I didn't believe him. At the time. Now it's got me worried."

"Did you attempt to extort money from him?"

"Dickie? No. I recorded a video. So he would *not* retaliate. Now I'm seriously thinking I should let the damn thing go viral."

"I would strongly advise that you do not."

Faye wandered back to her chair, sat and crossed her legs. "And why, pray tell?"

"Faye, if this man *is* the same person sending you these threats, he may only be doing it to rattle you."

"Well, he's succeeded."

"And if you release the video on the Internet, he will for sure want you dead. Possibly act upon it."

"You do make a good point. That's why I sought you out in the first place. To get counseled."

"Faye, you were arrested for beating a man unconscious with a billiard stick. You were assigned to me by a court order."

"You're forgetting. You came when I called. Why do you think my *single* phone call was placed to you?"

"I had wondered."

"Because," Faye winked, "I had you trained."

"By that you're implying, what?"

"It started in college. When we became friends. Then."

Mira closed her notebook. "How long have you been extorting money? Were you doing this during college?"

"I'd begun experimenting. Yes, about the same time your little crime spree began."

Mira said nothing, tapping her pencil. "Meaning?"

"Don't be coy. We go too far back. I know you lied under oath in court. And, as I'd said, I *saw* what you did in that graveyard."

Faye and Mira studied each other.

Faye broke off the stare by opening her purse to remove a hand mirror and stare at her face. "Look, you had me crying. My mascara has run." She worked at her eyes with a tissue, then relined her eyes as Mira watched in silence. "I've had Clifford follow you too. He's captured several intriguing photos."

Mira shifted in her seat. "Of what?"

Faye snapped her purse shut. "Now *that* is for me to know, and for you to ponder. In order for you, Mira, to do my bidding."

"What exactly is it you want from me?"

Faye stood. "At our next session, let's talk about those murders you've been investigating. You see, Mira, I do know things."

Faye saw a bowl of candy in a dish on a pedestal by the door. She stopped to sort through the items, selecting a tootsie-roll pop. She removed the wrapper and placed the red candy between her lips, twisting and licking the cherry-coating.

Mira stood, unsure what to do. "Faye, we still have time left. We should talk about this now."

Faye tilted her tootsie-roll pop at Mira as if it was a tiny wand. "It was sweet of you to see me on such short notice. I'd forgotten it was Halloween. I do love to trick. And *treat*."

At the door, Faye turned, then swiveled back.

"Oh, and Mira. If I do not become the dominant personality,

then no one will. Have I made myself clear?"

Faye reinserted her tootsie pop and walked out.

Clifford took cover inside the insect room. He had to scurry into this small enclosure to prevent being seen by Norwood. The Academy of Sciences had been closed for several hours. It was late in the evening and Clifford had remained after hours, hiding in a utility room until it was safe to emerge. He lifted a janitor's outfit from the employee's room to blend in with the other workers and went to spy on Norwood. When his suspect made an abrupt about-turn, Clifford backed into the entomology room.

Clifford was now hiding against a glass case, listening as Egon passed down the hallway. He turned his head and was startled to be inches from a multitude of scorpions, tarantulas, beetles, row after row of bugs, skewered by pins. Each bug had piercing mouthparts and either encased in metallic armor or cloaked in spiky hairs.

Clifford closed his eyes, held his breath, and broke into a sweat. His nerves were already on edge, troubled by the new information which emerged from the latest victim of the serial killer. Clifford had called his source at the DA's office after emailing digital photos he'd taken at the crime scene. He became privy to three discoveries: 1) the deceased, though a felon, hadn't been a rapist nor pedophile, as had the other victims; 2) in the dead man's pocket was a penny – with a note glued to it saying "WINNER" – a rare coin, determined to be worth five thousand dollars, and; 3) a newspaper clipping was found in his wallet that described another murder, with the same MO as the serial killer's, occurring seven years earlier within a college campus in Oregon. This now changed the body count from six to seven.

Clifford felt another mental storm overtaking him. As a child, he had witnessed inexplicable things, such as psychic phenomenons and paranormal activity. Having been a sensitive boy, he would, in great detail, describe these visions to his parents. Because they lacked his vision, they chose to distance themselves and hire professionals who could give him the needed jolts of reality they felt ill-equipped to give. They placed him in the hands of medical professionals and no-nonsense nannies. Clifford learned to distrust all clinical tests, doctor's assessments, and social rules of order. Instead, Bible lessons taught by Sunday-school teachers had had the strongest influence on him. Yet, ultimately, he defaulted to relying on his own instincts.

Clifford knew he wasn't supposed to exist. During a confusing account of the birds and bees, his father had confessed this truth. While listening to the disturbing talk on how conception happened, his father had resolved to never have children again, but not refrain from sex, so he'd decided to have his reproductive tubes cut and tied. This proactive decision caused a heated debate between his parents who, after screaming and fighting, had makeup sex which resulted, nine months later, with his mother giving birth to him.

Clifford hardly knew his three brothers. All of them were more than a decade older. And by the time he'd reached adolescence they were long gone from home. This deepened his sense of alienation. A type of isolation he was feeling now, hiding in a room full of bugs. A containment heightened by stress.

It was stress that triggered his paranormal visions. And though valuable insights came from these visions, it was a gift that was often terrifying. He had no control over the transmutations and the places he'd be delivered into, places not of his own making.

He saw Egon as a teenager, at a new high school. Their family had moved to another city to escape the rumor-mills of toxic gossip caused by a second incident. A girl had been raped. Clifford's head began to hurt from the voice of the father shouting, enraged about this unmentionable calamity.

While channeling Egon, Clifford felt himself being relocated and transported beside an Airstream trailer. Norwood stood picking its lock. Egon was attempting to solve the mystery behind how his father had managed to move the family from a run-down house into a semi-mansion with a pool.

The old trailer had magically transformed into a shiny new one. Egon stood in the dark beside this vehicle. To him, it looked like an enormous silver caterpillar. Signs were posted on it. DANGER. DO NOT ENTER. NO TRESPASSING. Egon learned about trespassing at Sunday school, and how he was not to be led into temptation. But Egon was determined to know what his father kept inside.

The Internet had helped, teaching Egon how to unfasten locks with a tension wrench and a tool called a snake rake. He broke into the Airstream to discover a variety of switches and levers and gears. He picked up a military rifle that had a mounted scope. An LCD monitor directed a laser beam by the touch of a button.

"Put that down!"

Caught spying, Egon froze.

"Get out!"

"What is this?"

"Now!"

"Why can't I know what you do?"

"Out! These are *my* things. Trade secrets." The father grabbed Egon's shirt, brusquely escorted him down the steps, and tossed him onto the lawn. "Do you know what a patent is?"

"Yes, Sir."

"Okay, smart ass. Tell me."

"It's when the government allows you sole ownership to sell and license a product you've made."

"That's right, intellectual property. And that is why *nobody* is allowed to snoop around in there. You got that?"

"Yes, Sir. But I'm your son."

"Who has long hair and plays with dolls."

"That's Faye. Not me."

His father slapped his face. "Don't *ever* mention your sister's name again. Do you hear me?"

"Yes, Sir."

"It upsets your mother."

"Yes, Sir."

"She told me you signed up for football. Is it true? Or a lie?"

"Hunter liked the idea."

His father squinted. "Who the hell is Hunter?"

"Nobody."

"Jesus Christ, Son."

Egon was pulled to his feet by his father.

"I swear, I don't know what to do with you. I thought boxing and martial arts would knock some sense into you. Why the hell did you disobey my orders?"

"I wanted to see what you did."

"I hope it was worth it."

Egon was pushed toward the back of the house. "You're to keep your mouth shut. Your friends *cannot* know what I do."

"I don't have any friends."

"You're pathetic."

"It's because I'm new here. Why did we move?"

"You know damned well why."

"I mean, how can we afford this place?"

His shoulder was grabbed, body spun around to face his father. "Because of a special switch. Designed for Special Ops."

"The military?"

"The Department of Defense bought one of my patents. And they paid a lot."

"Wow. That's great."

"Not for you, Son. Not tonight."

His father unlocked a small door at the foot of their house.

"What are you doing?"

"Get inside."

"Why?"

"For disobeying my orders. I'll see you in the morning."

Shoved, kicked in the rear, Egon squeezed into the crawl space beneath the house. The foundation area was less than two-feet high. He was unable to stand, and when he lifted his head he felt cobwebs. The door slammed and sealed him in darkness.

Terrified, he screamed, "Let me out!" He banged on the door and heard the padlock snap shut.

"*Listen to me.*" His father warned. "You scream again and I'll find a far worse punishment. Count on it. Now take your medicine like a man."

He heard his father walk away. The dank air was full with dust. He began to cry. Then he felt the first of many insects crawl onto his skin, up his legs, on his arms, into his hair.

Come morning, a flood of light came into the crawl-space as the door opened. It was Faye that emerged. She held a black and yellow garter snake. Her father recoiled.

"What the *fuck*. Get rid of that thing. Now!"

"I'm keeping him." She held the squirming snake between her fist and raised it at her father who backed away.

"I am warning you, boy, you had—"

"I'm *not* a boy. I'm Faye! Your daughter. And don't ever touch me again. Or I'll kill you!"

Her father advanced, but quickly retreated to avoid the snake. "Now you listen to me! I will *not* have you—"

"Go *fuck* yourself."

Faye walked around to the back porch. She held the snake in one hand as she opened then slammed the door behind her.

The sharp sound of a closing door startled Clifford. He glanced around and saw he was in a roomful of bugs. Dead ones. Troubling still. The paranormal visions backwashed through his mind like a toilet flush, the watery visions sucked down a cycling hole, suddenly gone. With his senses gurgling, refilling, he relocated where he was, establishing present time.

Needing to escape this claustrophobic room, he peered around the corner, saw no one there, took out a handkerchief, wiped sweat from his forehead, and stepped into the hallway.

He went downstairs and ventured through a submerged world, a replica of Amazon's flooded forest, then through a glass-tunneled enclosure where anacondas and piranhas swam. Beside a tidepool of starfish and sponges was a giant octopus floating in a tank of water. The translucent shapes of jellyfish propelled themselves up and over him as he heard the discordant roar from some machine in a nearby quadrant.

Clifford peered around the corner and saw Egon vacuuming in a tropical environment. There was a waterfall, also a swamp where alligators lounged on boulders. The surrounding cave-like walls had enclosures where reptiles were showcased. Clifford pulled his head back and hid against the fake rockwork and wondered what to do. Should he confront the man?

Clifford touched the gun he'd placed in one of the large pockets of his overalls. He became distracted by the displays.

Window after window showed cobras, rattlesnakes, pit vipers, green mambas. Each armed – or rather fanged – with a lethal poison, injections with neurotoxins to numb and rot flesh. Lovely creatures. Some were coiled, ready to strike. Clifford flinched. He was struck by a new vision. He was inside a prison. He felt hatred toward these killers, whose names were exhibited with their mug shots, including a list of their crimes.

One of the plaques had a mug shot he recognized. The face and body of a snake his client – the twin sister – had shown him in her apartment. A black-and-yellow ringed Kingsnake. It was one of her pets she kept in a cage.

He then realized his error. The inscription stated the snake was a lethal Branded Krait. Nearly identical to the harmless Kingsnake. After looking behind every rock and branch in the display, Clifford realized the snake was missing.

Is this how it feels? When everything begins to come together?
The dots connecting. Stars forming. The birth of fusion. The eerie
calm that brews inside the eye of a storm?

When I awake to a chasm of missing time I conclude there must
be a logical explanation. As Einstein predicted, we behave the way
we do because forces are always acting upon us, bodies in motion,
under the influence of gravitational fields, so we follow the path of
least resistance.

For example, at age fourteen, Hunter came to be.

I am on a city bus, returning from my mandatory after-school
class in the martial arts. The entire purpose is to "toughen me up,"
in the words of my father who gave me an ultimatum. It was either
this or be sent away to a military academy. *That,* the latter, seemed
a worse fate. So here I am, exhausted after my workout, nodding off,
seated near the back of the bus, on my way home.

The bus is crowded. There is a communal unspoken desire for
silence as we move together, people staring out the window, reading
books, newspapers, mobile devices. We are nameless unobtrusive
passengers with destinations in mind. By chance, we are on the same
trajectory, our proximity meaningless, of no consequence. But our
shrines of private contemplation are fragile. We are vigilant, wary of
strangers, like unsettled stars in space devouring bits and pieces of
each other.

The bus jerks forward, charging ahead like a mechanical beast,
aggressive, unintimidated, over broken lines, through traffic signals.
We brake to a raucous stop, our presence made known. Rumbling,
our engine idling, we swallow up passengers while expelling others.
The horns from smaller vehicles blare outside our shell as we lurch

ahead to cut a path through the commute traffic.

The constant cacophony and rocking motion stirs up my mind, dislodging a remark I made to Mira, the idea popping up like a cork upon a vast ocean. About ontology. Existence. Against improbable odds, two cells unite to make one, to create a life.

My grandmother on the subject: "We're God's miracle, with a special purpose. Don't let anyone tell you different."

My father: "Miracle, my ass. Get real. You fight to survive."

My mother: "Baby, I don't know. But mix me another drink. There's a bottle on the top shelf behind the cereal boxes."

My therapist: "How did their opinions make you feel?"

Self-explanatory. We're miraculous accidents left in the lurch, made to feel incomplete by asking the same question: Why?

I notice an arm reach and pull the cord festooned from front to back of the bus. An elderly woman withdraws her hand at the sound of the bell. Our driver – demigod in his elevated seat – gives a half turn of his head and brings the bus to a stop.

The two who leave are exchanged for one. The man is slender. He examines his fellow passengers as he moves down the aisle. He takes hold of a pole as the bus moves on. His eyes find me, seated by myself in the back. I comprehend his inquisitive stare. I clench my jaw and narrow my eyes. In the animal world, to avert one's gaze is a sign of weakness. It signals an inferior status, so I continue to rebuff him as he advances. He gets the message with a coy defiance, reposing himself several seats away.

My self-defense combat instructor told us this: Animals will usually exhibit restraint to avoid conflict with another member of their own species. The goal in a quarrel is to establish dominance. Not to spill blood. The victor does this for selfish reasons. The longer a fight persists, the more likely both parties will suffer injury, thus warranting other challengers to come forward.

To avoid a confrontation, a dog will cower and tuck in its tail.

A chimpanzee submits to bowing and kissing the feet of a superior. Baboons, both females, and males, will turn up their tail and offer themselves sexually as a sign of submission.

It's a strange pecking order, this kingdom of united cells.

My father: "Go kick his ass! Or you'll be kissing his and every other son-of-a-bitch's for the rest of your god-damned life!"

My mother: "What happened? Baby, you're bleeding. Go put a towel over your nose. Don't use the good ones!"

My grandma: "You were right to turn the other cheek and not fight back. That's how wars get started. I'm proud of you."

My therapist: "How did this make you feel?"

When I don't reply, she asks me whose advice I took.

"My own. I loosened the screws on his bike. He ended up in the hospital with a broken collar bone."

I can still hear my father cackling with approval.

Three teenagers enter at the front of the bus. One of them holds a portable stereo with its volume rupturing the silence. He turns it off. I collect my thoughts and go on alert. They're drunk and stoned. They remain standing. Dangerously unbalanced. They jostle in their close pack, like jackals sniffing, smelling the scent of fear.

"Hey, *mama*. Sexy threads." This voiced by the apparent leader. He leans into an attractive female and cups her breast. She shrieks. A man nearby rises and comes to her aid, but changes his mind when confronted with a switchblade.

"Piss off, *loser*." The cocky teen shoves the man into his seat.

The jackals laugh. Each holds a knife. The alpha male returns his attention on the woman, who cringes as he takes her collar and cuts the threads of her sweater, slicing it apart. The boy tugs at her bra and cuts the cord, detaching the cups. Her breasts exposed, he fondles them, declaring his rights by force and grinning at her face showing fear and humiliation.

The passengers look on, tensely submissive. Our driver, troubled by his demotion of power, glances into his rearview mirror. These kids own the bus. It's theirs for the taking. They stab the backrest of seats and move to the rear exit as the bus slows for the next stop.

Suddenly they are scrambling to escape. Their leader has fallen, face down on the grimy floor. His knife knocked loose. He abandons it to flee and hobble outside to the sidewalk after bursting through the collapsible doors. He looks back shouting obscenities and threats at – it would appear – me, standing.

As the bus pulls away, I comprehend I have missed something. I return to my seat and deflect the stares from fellow passengers. The molested woman is hysterical and hunched forward. A man removes his overcoat and drapes it over her shoulders. She pulls it around her body and sobs. Several watch her, others politely look away.

The counterattack was Hunter's doing, I now realize.

My transitions are like the white noise of a commercial vacuum cleaner transporting me to another place in time.

It is late, early morning, and I am in the Academy of Sciences sucking up the remnants of yesterdays gum wrappers, hair, skin, and dirt. I stare at the Wall of Early Man, at replicas of our ancestors who've evolved into the upstanding beasts of today. Which includes me, performing the task of cleaning. I pass by Eskimos hunting seals and Indians carving canoes. I pull the large vacuum on its tiny wheels and suck up more waste with its long hose.

I enter the Astronomy Hall. The solar system hangs from the ceiling in suspended orbit. Moving like a UFO, I yank the canister through this dark space across the marbled floor. I reach the reptile enclosure and stop at the alligator swamp. I click off the power and look down into the artificial lagoon at these prehistoric survivors. Their species belonged to the Oligocene epoch. That occurred about thirty-seven million years ago.

"Evening fellows. Don't mind me."

They don't, naturally. Their lidded eyes crack open, looking up to take me in, then close me out.

I back away and click on the power with my foot. The vacuum roars back to life. Its industrial-strength roar transports me into a realm of magical wonder.

"We're in Avalon," my mother tells me. "All things are possible in the land of the faeries."

All things are possible to my mother.

Today her name is Glenaa. She is wearing a sparkling summer gown and has dressed me in one similar, yet with tiny wings. She has named me Jenna with the touch of her magic wand. We are looking for signs of faerie rings. She tells me it will lead us to the forts and barrows in which these creatures hide.

"What do we do if we see one?" I ask.

She places a finger to her lips. "Be very quiet." She points to an oak tree. "An elder. The shape a witch takes when it hides."

We walk beneath it very quietly. Once we have passed under its branches and are back in sunlight, she whispers, "Willow trees are known to uproot themselves at night. Remember that. And the trees favored by the faeries are Blackthorn, Hazel, and Oak."

This makes me nervous, but excited to be on such an adventure with my mother. She tells me to watch for leprechauns, and that it's important we see them first, so they will lead us to their gold.

We are to picnic among the faeries. My mother has brought a basket with sandwiches. She also carries a silver flask. She tells me it is a concoction to ward off the dark elves. And to make us safe from the spriggans, tiny and grotesque thieves who kidnap children. She drinks from the silver container, then pushes it into my hands, and instructs me to drink some too.

The taste is horrible but I force myself to swallow several gulps. I don't want to become a slave to the spriggans.

By day's end, I have seen no faeries, though my mother claims to have glimpsed one peeking from behind a large mushroom. I want to believe her. The sky has begun to sprinkle. We run to avoid getting wet. Our car is parked at the end of a road beside closed metal gates. She backs into an oak tree. She fears the crunch of her bumper may have woken the witch and warns me to watch the tree for signs of movement. My mother drives away fast in the rain. I climb over the front seat to look through the back window, to make sure we are not being followed by a witch.

As the sky darkens, the oak tree disappears in the pouring rain. I turn around just as my mother miscalculates and hits a tree.

I wake inside a vehicle in motion. My head hurts. Sirens wail. Paramedics hover around. Their concentration is on my mother, who has a mask over her mouth, tubes attached to her arm, blood-stained bandages across her face.

I wait, seated on an elevated bed, my bare legs hanging off the edge. I am surrounded by green curtains. They get pulled back and shut by doctors who tell me I'll be all right. I ask about my mother. They say she is being cared for. Nothing to worry about. I find that hard to believe. My father slides back the curtain. He sees me there, wearing the sparkly dress with wings.

"What the *fuck!*"

He pulls me off the table. He holds my shoulder to yank out the ribbons clipped to my hair. He grabs a handful of tissues from a box and shoves me from this curtained room.

"Go find the bathroom. Wipe that shit off your face."

I have to stand on my tiptoes to see myself in the mirror, the face my mother has made for me. With tissues, I rub at my blue eyelids, the silver glitter on my cheeks, then my plum-colored lips. My father barges in to find me smearing colors, unable to remove the makeup. He grabs my arm and pulls me from the room.

"Where's mom?"

"They're keeping her overnight. She had surgery."

"Can I see her?"

"No. She's asleep. You're coming home with me."

But we don't go home. Not right away. My father is angry. He punches the steering wheel before driving away. I say nothing, only stare at the lights on buildings in the passing darkness. Our car turns and stops in front of a brick building. It has a neon sign which says, BAR NONE.

"Get out," my father tells me.

I do and stand beside the car until my father comes around and grabs my hand and tugs me through a wooden door. Inside is almost as dark as outside, but music is playing. My father hoists me into the air and plops me onto a tall stool, one that spins. He rotates me back and forth, showing me off to the adults that gather.

"You see what the hell I've been talking about," my father says. "My wife. Her doing. Real *cute*, huh?"

"Hell, Ray, I'd say she's a bit young. Even for *you!*"

There is laughter. I smile, wondering what is so funny.

"Yeah, laugh it up," says my father. "Meet my *son*."

A man on the other side of the long table tells my father, "Ray, you know the kid can't be here. It's against the law."

"Fuck the law. I need a drink. A double whiskey."

"Not in my bar. Take him over there. Here, kid. It's on me. You like Coke?"

I nod and take hold of the glass, which my father takes from my hand. He pulls me off the stool. He leads me to an empty table, tells me to sit, to drink my soda, and be quiet. He then returns to where he was before, among the other men, who look back at me and raise their glasses. I watch from afar as my father upturns his head and drinks down a glass of dark liquid in one gulp, then sets it down with an animal grunt.

"*Another.*" He doesn't look back at me.

I stay there, sipping my Coke, observing, listening to the bursts of laughter which overpower the music coming from a colorful box lit up in the darkness on the other side of the room. While I wait, a woman approaches, touches my cheek, strokes my long hair.

"Hi, Honey. You doin' okay?"

I nod as I suck my soda through a straw. A man trails after the woman and squeezes her bottom.

"Stop it, Roy!"

The man doesn't, teasing her some more. She laughs and slaps his hand away. The man asks me, "Hey, kid, what's with the getup, wearing a dress with wings?"

"My mom, she took me on a picnic. We went into the woods to search for the land of the faeries."

The man nearly falls over laughing. "Land of the *faeries?* Well, congrats, kid. I guess you found it."

I'm confused, because we didn't actually, but I smile.

"You're kinda cute, you know, for a boy." He gives me a wink and tips his bottle toward me. The woman pushes him away.

"Don't mind Roy," she says. "You take care now."

My father's friends are weird. But not as weird as my dad, who bumps into chairs, knocking one out of his way with a swift kick on his way over to get me, hours later. He tells me to get up.

"We're leaving," he says.

Inside the car, I buckle my seat belt. I am afraid we might hit a tree, or something worse. I close my eyes and pray for God to guide us home safely. When the car stops, I open my eyes. My father's head is bent back, asleep against the seat. He grunts, opens his eyes, turns and looks at me.

"The fuck you looking at? Get out. We're home."

He fumbles and drops his keys on the front-door matt. I retrieve them, but he grabs them back and stabs at the keyhole until he gets the key in. Once the door opens, I run upstairs to my room and shut the door.

"Yeah, run. Go to bed!"

The lock on my bedroom door doesn't work. I hear my father lumbering up the stairs, his footsteps heavy. He mutters words I can't understand. I'm scared.

It's too late to hide in the bathroom where the lock works. My father bumps into the walls as he moves down the hallway. I go to my bed and kneel like my grandmother taught me. My hands clasp and I pray for Jesus to keep me safe.

"Dear Father, who art in heaven, hallowed be thy name. Thy kingdom come. Thy will be done, on earth, as it is in heaven ..."

TWENTY-FOUR

Faye blamed Mira. Exhumed memories kept haunting her like the walking dead. Tears had mixed with raindrops as she shivered beneath an awning. She was waiting for the downpour to subside. Her dress clung to her skin and each gust of wind felt like the grasp of icy fingers. The flash of lightning startled her, followed by the sky rupturing in thunder.

Her father burst through her door. "Get up!"

She was on her knees. She kept praying. Her father lunged and grabbed her.

"I said get up!"

Pulled to her feet, she was thrown onto the bed.

"What *are* you?" He cupped her face in his hand, squeezing her cheeks. "Wearing dresses and makeup. What's *wrong* with you?"

"It was mom's idea. She—"

"Shut up!"

Her father looked down at her and closed his eyes. He wobbled before regaining balance. He grabbed the gauzy fabric, confused by the dress with its pink and purple flower petals. The gossamer wings were the first to go, torn off as Faye fought and cried.

Slapped, she was told, "Not another sound. Do you want to be a girl, like your sister? This is what happens to little girls."

Her father unbuckled his pants. Faye closed her eyes. "Jesus," she whispered in a plea, "Save me. Please—"

Her words were smothered by her father's hand.

"Believe this. *Nobody* is coming to save you."

Faye screamed as lightning struck again. She cursed the weather, her stomach too, painfully burning. The martini she drank for lunch hadn't provided the relief she was desiring. Her forehead was damp, also hot. She felt feverish. Had someone at the bar poisoned her? A taxi sped past, ignoring her imprecations.

She watched in a trance as water cascaded off the blue awning. It splattered against the cement. She closed her eyes, wincing at the flashing sight of her mother's face shattering a windshield.

"A penny for your thoughts."

Faye opened her eyes. The voice of her mother was drowned out by the rain. The sound was as distressing as the pain in her stomach. She winced again, reliving the shower of pennies that scattered and rolled across her bedroom floor. She'd earned each penny by playing a game, sharing her thoughts, each worth a coin. And she had saved a whole jarful. Until they were stolen back, every cent.

Searching for happier times, Faye recalled being awakened by her mother before daybreak. They drove over the mountain to the coast. They sang to the radio, sharing Fruit Loops from a cereal box passed between the three of them on the front seat. She ran with her brother and mother screaming across the beach to watch the sunrise at the ocean's edge. Waves crashed and washed over their bare feet as birds scattered and squawked. The sky kept getting lighter. Her mother became confused, then felt foolish. Egon pointed at the sun, which had risen behind them. They laughed and joined hands. Her mother spun them faster and faster until they all collapsed on the sand.

Her mother's warm hands caressed her face. In a soothing voice, she was told, "This is what it's all about, Baby. Remember this day forever. It doesn't get any better than this."

"You wanna share." The stranger's voice startled Faye.

Without hesitation, she stepped out from beneath the awning and took hold of the umbrella. She squeezed close to the man to avoid getting drenched.

"Thank you," she said.

The man's smile was as thin as his hair, combed back, slick with gel. A toothpick was between his teeth. He reeked of onions.

"Had a fabulous meal. Tenderous veal. Absolutely delicious."

"Lucky you," she said.

Faye wanted to hurry his pace which seemed deliberately slow as if each step mattered. And it did. He was stinking drunk. At the next corner, they tugged the umbrella in different directions. Rain dripped onto both their shoulders.

"I live this way," said Faye.

"Fine, fine. I'll walk with you. I'm in no rush."

"You must be psychic."

"Why's that?"

"You're the only one who came prepared for rain."

Rain shook off the umbrella as he laughed.

"How I wish. No. A regular customer. I borrowed it."

Faye focused on the antique umbrella, its spines and its handle made from wood. "You mean you stole it."

"A beauty, isn't she? I love holding beautiful things. A shame when they get destroyed. Sometimes they must."

His words puzzled her.

He added, "I've seen you before."

"I have no idea."

His laughter shook off more raindrops. "Now I remember you. You're that actress."

"I perform in a show."

"No, no. We met at a private party."

"You're mistaken. I would have remembered you."

"Would you? Would you really?"

His pace had slowed. He was no longer staggering, nor were his words slurred. Faye became suspicious and drew away.

"My dear, where are you going?" He pulled her back in. "You'll catch your death."

"I'm already wet."

He touched her hair, clutching it with a forceful tug. "There are better ways to die. Than from pneumonia."

"What are you doing?"

Grinning, he bit down on his toothpick. "You're quite the party animal. And very *naughty*. Fact is, I too can be nasty."

Faye had the presence of mind not to react in fear. She aligned her body with his, rubbed his body with a seductive pull, then push away. "Your place or mine?"

Before he could answer she kicked him in the groin. She struck his windpipe and launched a kick to his chest. Knocked backward, he stumbled into the gutter. The umbrella blew away. Faye saw the knife in his hand and flung off her shoes. She ran barefoot through the pelting rain.

A block away, she stopped and turned. She saw him getting up, gripping himself, unable to run. She walked quickly, glancing back to make sure she wasn't being followed. She reached Egon's house and ran up the stairs. After deadbolting the door, slamming it shut, she leaned against the wall.

She felt monstrous. Looking into the mirror, she swiped at her wet stringy hair, saw the steaks of mascara, saw the stubble beneath the melting rouge, as if transitioning into a werewolf. She saw what her father had seen: an ugly, pathetic, little whore.

Her stomach ached. She gripped the banister and pulled herself up the stairs. At the landing, she saw green mints in a dish. Beside it was a jar filled with lemon drops. What she saw were the pennies she'd collected as a child. She became nauseous and dizzy. Grabbing for a chair to steady herself, she bumped the table.

The jar of lemon drops fell and crashed to the hardwood floor. Pennies, not candy, scattered among the shards of glass.

Faye held the chair and shut her eyes.

She didn't resist as her mind left her body and rose into the air. A feeling of release. A peacefulness that was inexplicable, like the rag doll, the little girl, who she saw lying immobile on the floor.

Her mother was screaming. Her brother crying. Why?

She was free. No more pain.

"*Fuck*," Faye cried out, stepping on shards of glass.

The harsh crash back to earth felt crippling. Faye limped toward the bar. She rummaged through drawers, found a bottle of aspirin, and swallowed three pills, drinking from an open bottle of Merlot. The pain in her stomach became secondary to her throbbing foot. She sat in a chair and plucked with her fingernails to tweezer out the slivers of glass.

Yearning for a hot bath, she hobbled upstairs to her brother's bedroom. Bracing herself against the bathroom sink with one hand, she leaned into the mirror to examine her face. She hated what she saw. It was the face of her brother. She refused to *be* him. To become *integrated*.

Her mother's words returned to haunt: "*It doesn't get any better than this, Baby.*"

Wiping at tears, she noticed the empty terrarium by the window. The top had been left open. She was sure she'd shut it before leaving the house. This was all Mira's fault. Her meddling and psychobabble were causing a loss of identity. She was beginning to feel as absent-minded as Egon. She hated her brother but loved him too. They'd once been close. He was the only person who ever really knew her. He used to tell her *she* was the more imaginative one, and fearless, but it wasn't true. She simply had more courage to react.

Now, with Egon off to perform in New York, she had no one left to confide in. Or blame. Except herself – for thinking that she could outsmart Mira!

Faye winced – glimpsing a doll's head shattering to pieces.

She rubbed her eyes and tried to think rationally. Her pet boa, she realized, would likely be coiled under the bed or warming itself by the radiator.

Faye turned away from the mirror. It still puzzled her why her brother wanted to use her apartment. She'd agreed to this exchange. He wouldn't reveal why, but the temporary switch of residences had something to do with the illusion the Rebel Artists had devised for their grand finalé.

For Egon, Faye had her own surprise.

As for Mira, who was the catalyst, she'd been forewarned.

Faye pulled back the shower curtain to run bath water. She saw her boa constrictor cut to pieces inside the tub. The white porcelain had four words scrawled in red lipstick, as if in blood:

CATCH YOU LATER, BITCH!

The curtain snapped off its hooks as Faye grabbed it and fell to the floor. The contents of her stomach erupted up her throat.

TWENTY-FIVE

I know I am real, visible, a solid presence. But to the audience, composed of murmuring voices as the curtain rises and the cameras search to find me on the empty stage, I might as well be invisible.

On the surface, I am still. Petrified. Inside too. Scared shitless. Afraid of failure. Everything rests on my perfect composure. There is a moment of suspended disbelief as I magically appear. For those watching me from behind, they are baffled by the audience who are unable to see me, then apparently do. The trick is achieved by using an elaborate architecture of mirrors.

Not quite a miracle.

When revealed, I am a statue. One sculpted from white marble. While in actuality, I am a faux-finish treatment of paint and fabric, a replica of Michelangelo's Madonna and Child. A Jesus and Mary. The Virgin's eyes are downcast and pensive, as if aware of her child's tragic fate.

The sculpted vision receives applause.

As this revelation forms in the communal mind of the audience, thirty seconds elapse before the eyes of Jesus slowly open. His head looks up, outward, then peers upward at his mother who remains a statue. Half seated, half standing, Jesus is resting in his mother's lap. He steps away onto the stage.

The lights fade. They return to reveal the child grown into a man, standing upon a mirage of water.

Act One is accomplished by sculpted tapestry (Madonna) and puppetry (the child). The statue of Mary is discarded, replaced by a robed Jesus, who I now portray.

A bolt of lightning signals the end of Act Two.

Darkness lifts to reveal Roman guards flogging a mocked,

scourged, and disfigured Jesus wearing nothing but a loincloth and crown of thorns. Masquerading as the Savior, I carry a wood beam upon my bare shoulders and stumble to my knees. The heavy *thunk* as wood strikes the stage floor in front of a vertical post causes more hushed whispers from the audience.

Everyone knows Act Three. I am expected to be crucified. And we do not disappoint. The television cameras zoom in for closeups as spikes are positioned at the crux of my hands and nailed into my wrists. Metal on metal resounds throughout the auditorium as these nine-inch nails pierce the wood. The audience gasps. The crossbeam I am affixed to is lifted, hooked on the post, and my feet are crossed and hammered into place. The blood spilled is real. Authenticity is what the Rebel Artists of Perception are about.

There is both the illusion of pain and the reality. On this cross, I can see the audience stunned into silence behind the glare of lights. Their unsettled murmurs make me doubt my actions and wisdom in presenting this performance for our final act.

The crowd has yet to boo or hiss, nor has a judge rejected us. No buzzer. No red "X ." My head slumps, signaling the end. Death. A projected light on a backlit sky simulates the sun being eclipsed as an opaque white sheet descends from the ceiling to cover me entirely. Cameras circle the cross draped in fabric to capture my isolation. Garrett holds a spear to portray the execution guard. He stabs me through the heart. Blood spreads upon the sheet and I hear shrieks. The audience is appalled by our attention to detail, unable to accept this suspension of disbelief.

The white cloth is lifted to reveal an empty cross.

Now you see me. Now you don't.

In hindsight, we may have gone too far. Both Jasper and Hunter forewarned me about taking on certain subjects, such as god, sex, and psychosis. Each a social taboo, not topics for entertaining guests at a public gathering.

My initial idea was to include an Act Four, but this got nixed by democratic vote. I had envisioned an ending to echo the beginning. The vision of Madonna and Child closing with Michelangelo's Pieta, which depicts the Virgin Mary holding her dead son. Performance bookends. But too definitive.

Keep the audience guessing, Jenna suggested. So I did not return to the stage with the other Rebel Artists of Perception. The audience and judges wondered if I had been injured. Rumors circulated that I was rushed away in an ambulance. Truth was, I hid within the husks of rolled fabric used to create the Madonna in Act One. I was then deposited into a waiting van. The ambulance was a decoy.

Back in my hotel room – and not the one I'd checked into, but one registered in a fictitious name by my cohorts – I waited alone, watching the news reports of my disappearance. Being a master of disguise, it was easy to check out, passing through the lobby over-flowing with film crews and journalists searching for the story of my whereabouts. At JFK International Airport I escaped undetected by using one of my aliases.

The other Rebel Artists of Perception take the hard questions. Except they love it. I can see it in their faces, lit up by cameras, giving false witness in interviews, while acting as baffled as everyone else. When Mira appears on screen, my heart sinks. I hadn't prepared her for this. She is distraught. A reporter has tracked down a potential story, a connection between us, but she admits to nothing.

The next day I hear from Hunter who informs me he and Jenna will not be returning, but staying in New York. Or maybe departing on a plane to Paris or Morocco. They have deviated from our plan to reassemble in three days at The Comstock Saloon. It is where we will celebrate our victory, which has nothing to do with whether we win or lose this TV competition. The final results won't be broadcast until next week. Technically, we could win, pending my rebirth, if I am found to be alive.

It matters not. We pulled off a hoax. Winning wasn't our goal. Nor was blasphemy, for anyone wondering.

Entertain, Inform & Inspire.

That is our unofficial motto. To perceive what is possible.

Farrah, the bartender who I met at the Comstock, will be there. She is now part of our troupe. Along with Andrea. They had both performed on stage as followers transformed into the disenchanted. From serendipitous encounters, we have become friends, soul mates. This is how we grow.

Meanwhile, I am back in San Francisco, inside Faye's highrise. We've reconciled (agreeing to disagree) prior to my leaving for New York. The truce was initiated by her. I take that as an optimistic sign, even though she declined our offer to join us and participate in our final performance.

Faye was to meet me here afterward. But her place is empty, not counting the many snakes coiled and writhing in cages. Minus her prized boa constrictor, Eve, whom she took with her.

As spectacular as the view is overlooking the San Francisco Bay, I soon become restless cooped up inside. So I opt to travel in a cab. Incognito. No one needs to know. Tomorrow will be the third day, and the world will discover I am alive as I reappear upon the streets of San Francisco. Ta-da. Resurrected, magically, as it were.

I don't think Jesus would mind. Even bad press is good press. Which, I believe, is the current mantra in our media-crazed society. But something strange is happening to me. I feel spiritually haunted after our staged crucifixion. Having played with fire, putting myself so close to the flame, I feel singed. Altered. Maybe it has to do with what Mira explained to me as the integration of forces and fusion of my severed parts.

Maybe I am becoming whole.

From the cab window, I see Italian cafes pass as we travel north on Columbus street. Across Washington Square Park I see the dual white spires extending into the blue sky. They belong to the church of Saint Peter and Paul. I recognize the Jaguar, blue with its tinted windows, parked in front. I tell the driver to pull over.

There is an iron gate barring access to the grandeur beyond the portico's double doors. Undeterred, I go to a nondescript side door, which opens. I enter a rather forlorn entry, the landing to a stairwell that requires visitors to either descend or ascend. I choose to rise.

At the next landing, I turn the knob of a plain wooden door and find myself overwhelmed by the enormity of a glittering sanctuary. It is predominantly white, accented in gold, red and blue, with columns and arches, all of it leading to a towering wedding-cake altar and the image of Jesus presiding from a domed sky.

I search the empty pews, then wander to the rear of the church. I find the detective kneeling in a small shrine. He is lighting a candle and placing it among others flickering in the darkness. The wavering flames cast a spell over me. I am taken backwards to a memory I had forgotten.

In my grandmother's home, a candle was burning day and night. Not any special candle. She had all kinds, shapes, and colors. From room to room she took the flame, transported on a plate or in a cup. Any vessel would do, so long as it was portable and adhered to the candle's pool of melted wax.

"Why do you have so many candles, Grandma?"

In my mouth is the taste of a sugar cookie, the center warm and moist, freshly baked. The tiny flame from her candle is upside-down, reflected in her pupils.

"Because our world is mostly darkness."

"But Grandma. Look outside."

An afternoon sun fills her backyard and small orchard. Bright light is streaming in through her windows. Birds are splashing in a fountain and a squirrel is feeding at a dish filled with seeds and nuts. My vision returns to my grandmother who is clearly in her element, yet burdened by age, moving into another room, taking the candle. This one is on a tea saucer decorated with roses.

I am a small boy, following her like a puppy. To me, she *is* the flame, full of warmth, glowing, fully contained. Also free to waver. I follow my grandmother to her favorite chair. I sit beside her. She smiles as I finish my cookie and she closes her eyes.

"Before God, Egon, there was no hope."

I watch the flame and listen, toying with the hot wax pooling in the dish on the table between us. My finger moves through the flame without burning. It shifts but quickly resettles, pointing up again. It fascinates me, so I keep toying with the flame to see how close my finger can get, and how long it can stay before it burns.

"God divided the dark chaos with light, so hope could flourish. When the darkness overtook the world again, Jesus came to renew in our hearts this light, and to restore our hope."

Half-listening, I wet my finger in my mouth and I dare myself to touch the wick. It sizzles. The flame dies. A plume of smoke rises. My grandmother continues to rock gently in her chair.

"Be a good boy, Egon. Relight the candle."

"I'm sorry, Grandma."

"Don't you worry," she tells me. "He knows the darkness in our hearts and how we all suffer. I know you do. Shall we pray for your father and mother? It's hard to resist the darkness."

"But, Grandma ..."

"What, child?"

"Doesn't the light need the darkness?"

Several candles are flicking as I awake from my trance. I smell the scent of burning wax. Votive offerings glow before an altar.

"I had a premonition you'd show up." The detective is kneeling. "How does it feel to be dead?"

"Rumors of my demise are overrated."

The detective has the demeanor of a priest who finds my humor inappropriate. "An impressive stunt. Did you do it just to be clever? Or were you looking for salvation?"

"I'm looking for my sister. I saw your car outside."

"You didn't come to confess your sins?" The detective stands, holding another candle, this one unlit. His timidity from our first encounter is replaced with a countenance of peace.

"Have you seen Faye?"

"No."

"Do you have any idea where she might be?"

"I do." The detective holds out the candle for me. "Light it. For atonement."

"Atonement for what?"

"Your sins." The detective regards me curiously. He is wearing the vestments of a clergyman. He lights a stick from the flame of a candle and hands it to me. "You don't remember, do you?"

I hold the burning stick in my hand and remember being scared. I'm scared something is not right. I am sixteen. Our new house has been vandalized. The entry floor is littered with broken glass. From pieces of a menagerie. I see a rabbit's head. A hummingbird wing. A fox's tail. All of it from mother's collection of crystal, now destroyed, purchased on a wild shopping spree. My father brags about us being rich, but it doesn't feel like we are. I step through the broken glass. My mother has collapsed on the living room floor. She looks dead. I hear laughter. Followed by applause. I pick up the remote control off the floor and turn off the television.

"Mom?"

She lies perfectly still. Like a fallen statue. Her beautiful face is cracked and fissured, scarred from going through a windshield. Her disfigurement and my inability to put together a clear vision of how she once looked distracts me from her bruised eye and swollen lip. I turn and look for my father. I find him far off in the den, slumped in his favorite lounge chair.

This has to stop. My mind is becoming seized by rage and fear. When I look down upon my mother I notice something in her hand. A small picture frame with a photo I've rarely seen, kept hidden in a drawer, the one of me and my sister as babies, one of our birthdays. We look happy, side by side, held in her arms, all smiles, party hats on our heads. Even my father, who stands behind us, has a big grin. So distant a memory it takes a photo like this to remind me we once existed as a real family.

The house is silent now. No laughter. No applause. I walk into the den and stare at my father.

"Dad?"

He's asleep, passed out cold, with a half-empty glass of liquor tilted in his hand, resting against his side, like a crutch, or loyal pet. He doesn't have to work. He says he's retired. He's stinking drunk. He beats my mother. He shits in his pants. I hate him.

"Dad, wake up."

It would be so easy, I think. I push his leg and get no response. I unclasp the knife he keeps strapped to a boot, extended toward me. A combat knife he carries for protection. I take possession and grip it in my fist. But first, I stop to think. It's called premeditation. And I return to my mother. I carefully, awkwardly, remove her bathrobe. I leave her lying naked on the floor as I put on her robe and return to my father. I raise the knife and fight to summon the courage to stab him through the heart. But I can't do it. He must know this. Or maybe this is what he wants. To be put out of his misery.

His eyes open, squinting. He has a slight smile. Amused to see me conflicted, suffering, struggling to act.

"Not easy, is it? Go ahead. Be a man, for once."

"I am." My hand is trembling. My dad will punish me for this. For now, he laughs and closes his eyes, tired of looking at me.

"No, Son. You're more like her. Your *sister*. Who—"

It's not easy killing someone. The shock of actually doing it, the sound of a blade piercing flesh. I don't know whose screams are the worst, mine or my father's, who lunges but falls back as I leap away, leaving the knife in his chest, fairly certain I have ruptured his heart. Both of us in shock, staring at one another, one last time before his body goes limp, dead. It's nothing like I thought it would be. There is no thinking. It's the absence of thought ruled by rage. The lizard brain taking over, taking me into a prehistoric state of pure instinct, savagely lashing out. To kill or be killed.

My body shudders, shivering. I feel cold-blooded. Unlike my father's geyser of warm blood, sticky on my hands. Also splattered on my mother's robe, which I will remove. I now begin to rethink, considering what the police will find. The broken crystal, the alcohol usage, the evidence of a fight, her battered face, public records of domestic abuse. Her bloodied robe and the knife in her hand. My mother had the right to defend herself. To kill my father.

"Nicely done," I hear a voice say. I'm startled to see Hunter in the mirror, looking back at me with approval.

"That's it, Son," says another voice. "It's good to cry."

I hadn't realized I was. "She didn't deserve that," I tell the priest. "I loved my mother."

My fingers burn. Quickly I light the candle, blow out the stick, and set the candle among the others in the tiered rack.

"God knows what is in your heart, Son."

"How is that possible?"

"We communicate."

I blink, wiping my eyes. The detective has become a clergyman in vestments. The transformation is jarring. It's given me a headache, and I rub my eyes, more confused.

"I thought you were someone else. A detective."

"Kneel with me. Let us pray.

"Sorry, I need to leave."

"Clifford Hill?"

"Do you know him?"

"You've told me."

"Faye, she …"

"Egon, your sister doesn't exist."

"She exists."

"Did. She died."

"You don't understand."

"Let her rest in peace."

The priest's cherubic smile resembles the detective's. "Let her go, Son. You won't find her on Broadway."

The flickering candlelight irritates me and I reply sarcastically, "Isn't that where all performers go to die. Broadway?"

"Don't offend God."

"I wasn't."

"Let Him guide you."

"Where?"

"To the truth. And to this woman you say you love."

"Mira."

"She's the one investigating you?"

"She thinks I'm a serial killer. But, I'm not."

The priest crosses himself before turning to exit this flickering shrine of burning candles and wax.

"Let's hope not. For your sake as well as for hers."

My desire to be with Mira is not a surrender; it's a concession. The mental war has to end between the divisions that constitute me. All of us have become too self-centered. I need this change, to heal, which means accepting a non-divisive inclusion.

But does Mira know what she's doing?

I know now what it means to be altered, divided, locked inside my mind, watching myself from a distance, while parts of me fight a losing battle for independence, in a secession from the union.

But if one of us is a killer? How do I, we, reconcile that?

Faye's highrise apartment, which overlooks the San Francisco Bay, has a panoramic view that allows me to imagine the possibilities of a new life. One where I am whole. And living with Mira, who will need more convincing she loves me and can trust me.

My concerns mount as I wait for Faye. She hasn't appeared as she said she would. The spritely Jenna has left me too, choosing the dark realm where Hunter resides. Which doesn't bode well.

Tomorrow was to be a special occasion at the Comstock Saloon. News coverage of my reemerging self after a staged death would be a victory for the Rebel Artists of Perception, a cause for celebration. I'd planned for it to be the moment to announce my coming out – or, more accurately, my coming together. Admitting to my friends about my disorder. My multiple selves.

Which I suspect will come as no surprise to anyone who knows me. What will, is that I'm on the road to recovery.

At thirty-six stories above sea level, I pace the marble floor and answer the calls from Garrett, Denise, Jasper, Megan, Farrah and others, assuring them that tomorrow's celebration is still on. That I am alive and well. Which is not entirely true.

As Mira explained it, "A full integration is not possible until all the personalities trust one another enough to subsume into one."

There lies the problem. Everyone is afraid of what they might lose in the bargain of becoming whole and healthy.

The sky continues to darken. The lights in office windows are coming on. The vertical cables of the Bay Bridge are illuminated too. It must be happy hour, therefore, I drift over to mix myself a drink, a scotch on the rocks, then return like a sentry at his post, staring out the window for signs of life, and for my sister to return.

I am in awe of the changing colors of the sky, the water, along with the orange, white, and yellow lights generated artificially. In the darkened window, I glimpse a swiggle of motion in the glass. It's a trick, a reflection from a yellow cab on the street, I first think, then look over my shoulder. I see a ringed black and yellow snake slither and disappear beneath the sofa.

My aversion to snakes makes me flinch. Even though I realize it's harmless. Faye's California kingsnake. Nevertheless, I curse her for allowing it to roam freely throughout her apartment. She knew in advance I would be staying here. As I wander, ice clinking in my glass, I inspect her other cages. The other snakes appear to be where they should be: locked up.

They are nonvenomous, but still. They bite.

Despite the visceral unease these creatures give me, I do admire their form and beauty. Sipping my cocktail, I look at her three ribbon snakes – thin, silvery and sleek. The red-sided garter has colorful markings too. As intense in hues as her emerald tree boa, a zigzag of yellow and white over green, entwined like a clenched fist around a branch. Her sunbeam snake, with luminescent rainbow brilliance, dazzles me the most.

Swallowing more scotch, I realize her pets have become a tricky negotiating point. Finding a way to assimilate Faye's love of snakes into my aversion toward them could, potentially, keep us divided.

I resist turning on the television, preferring the city noise rising from ground level into the silence of my thoughts. Rattling ice in my glass, I stare down into the flow of lights, a river of commute traffic. I fight off an urge to call Mira. I want to hear her voice, let her know I'm all right, at least alive. I grab my cell phone off the bar, poke the screen image for her number, but resist making the call.

What do I say? I love you. Take a chance. Come live with me. We can be happy. Even though there's a chance I'm a serial killer, and I could kill you.

If there is an amusing aspect to being a multiple, it's the level of intelligence it takes to negotiate and maintain a convincing front. Also to qualify as a highly-functional human, even a perfectionist, and an overachiever, in certain areas, while dysfunctional in other ways. Garrett has called twice to inform me our agent (that's right, we actually *have* one) has received inquiries from the entertainment industry in both Hollywood and Las Vegas about our availability to meet and discuss the possibility of developing a show.

Assuming I'm alive. Garrett has advised our agent to make sure our prospective buyers stay tuned, giving hints at a surprise ending. But how far do I want to take this?

I wander about, inspecting things. I walk into Faye's bedroom. It's lavish. Decorated to the nines, the same way she dresses. I stare into an ornate wall mirror and brush back my hair, searching for signs of my sister. The resemblance makes me wonder if we came from one egg. Faye claims we are monozygotic, twins with a genetic mutation. She believes she lost a Y chromosome and developed into a girl. That she's magical, a miracle of science.

I push away from the mirror, enter her walk-in closet, surveying her array of clothing hung from racks, her numerous shoes, and hats. Leisurely sipping my cocktail, I walk from the closet and through her bedroom into the hall. I try another door that is locked. Thwarted, I jiggle the handle, now curious. Not one to be deterred, I take from my pocket a knife equipped with a tension wrench and snake rake. I maneuver the internal mechanism and hear the click-release.

I enter and flick on the switch. It's a disturbing sight. The walls of this guest room are plastered with newspaper clippings. There are notations and arrows made by colored markers. Numbers, from one to seven, are spray-painted over each photograph. These are faces I recognize. Victims of the serial killer. What the hell?

I'm sickened by the thought of what Faye has done. Why has she created this shrine of madness? I inspect the clippings to confirm what I fear. Each kill is documented, assembled into seven groups. Lines of text are highlighted in yellow. Articles about the murders. Number seven is the one anomaly. Red question marks surround the news clippings. I can't make sense of all her notations and abandon the effort. I walk over to a file cabinet and desk. I open the middle drawer. What I find hurls me back to another time.

A multitude of pennies. Scissors. Paper. Glue. An assortment of colored pencils. I pick up some of these copper coins and each has a note attached to one side. LUCKY U. SAVE ME. NUGGET. KEEP-SAKE. I toss them into the desk and turn to the file cabinets, sliding open a drawer. It contains hanging files. I pull out a folder and flip through photos. A man is crouching, his hands raised like the paws of a dog begging for a treat, his neck collared, attached to a leash. He is naked. I pull out another file. It contains photos of another naked man, wearing a saddle, a long wig, and a matching tail.

Stored in a lower drawer, I find a ledger. The book is filled with names, addresses, dates and amounts of money scribbled into the columns. Having seen enough to know this isn't good, assuming the worst, I shut the drawers. It's more than I can process all at once. I down the remainder of my drink and exit the room.

Somewhat dazed by these findings, I return to the bar and pour myself more scotch. I drop in ice cubes, then retrieve my phone left on the bar. I awake the black screen with a poke and Mira's number appears, lighting up, tempting me to place the call. But I hesitate and walk over to the sofa to sit, nursing my scotch on the rocks while toying with the phone in my hand. I want to call her. But can I trust her? Whose side is she on?

For that matter, can I be trusted? Each one of the Rebel Artists of Perception vowed to not tell a soul outside our group about our elaborate scheme. So I do nothing.

Until I'm struck by a sharp pain at the back of my ankle, right above my heel. I lurch up from the sofa. I pull up my pant leg and see the bite marks.

"Son-of-a-bitch! You little *shit*. Goddamn you!"

My rage is directed at the snake hiding under the sofa. I take a small pillow and fling it under the furniture. And sure enough, the snake slithers out from under it, moves along the wall, then behind another chair. I reach down and rub my skin where its fangs bit me. No real pain, except I notice swelling. Plus, I feel itchy. Before a numbness begins.

Soon I am feeling light-headed, and I sit back down on the sofa. I stare at my drink and set it down on the table beside me.

Something is wrong. A numbness is overtaking my body, going into my arms, into my chest. Before it fully takes over, I push the number to connect me with Mira. Her phone continues to *ring* and *ring* and *ring* as I gulp for air.

"Hello?"

"Mira."

"*Egon*. You're alive!"

"For the moment ... I am."

"What's wrong? Where are you?"

"I need ... help ... I ..."

"Tell me! What is it?"

"Snake ... bite ..."

I am unable to finish. Cut off by paralysis. I'm done. My hands and mouth won't work. I fall, against my will, to the side, staring out the windows into the sky.

Thank God for GPS. And Mira. Her tenacity. I love her for being smart and relentless. Knowing to call in favors. People who will track me via satellite. My exact location identified by a precise space-based global positioning system.

I am guessing all this. She must know this is an emergency. And so I wait. What choice do I have? None.

Death by neurotoxins is not a pleasant way to die. Paralysis of the limbs means my respiratory system will fail too. I am already having difficulty breathing when I hear pounding at the front door. No need to reply. The lock is destroyed.

Mira enters with the police and a team of paramedics. I admire her initiative and foresight. Maybe she is psychic after all. I am aware of the flurry of activity and all the questions asked of me, but I am not responding well to any of it.

"Find the snake," I hear Mira tell someone.

"Which one? Look. There must be—"

"The one that bit him! We need to ID the toxin."

Numbly, I reminisce about my fake crucifixion upon the cross. A sense of letting go, surrendering to God, to the unknown. I can do nothing for myself but rely on others. I am swaddled like a child, placed on a pallet, and carted off with frantic fanfare.

People crowd the hallways, the lobby, outside on the street, all staring at me in wonder. I wonder too about the sirens and lights flashing as I'm whisked away into a crazy parade. I hate parades. Especially those through a dark valley of towers.

I am going to die. I can sense it. No. I discern this from the absence of my senses. I am a prisoner inside my body, yet my mind races in an effort to find a way to escape and survive.

Finally, my consciousness shuts off. Hallucinations come next. While lying on my back, I feel a weight on my chest. I open my eyes.

Faye is sitting on top of me and smiling. She finds my situation amusing.

"Is this a bad time? We need to talk."

I try to utter a sound but cannot.

"Don't bother," she says, hopping off the bed to let me catch my breath. "This is how it is going to be, if you want my cooperation. To make us whole. Do you want that?"

I nod, at least in my mind, curious about her terms.

"First, I keep my identity. Second, I am an equal partner in this enterprise called *us*. Third, you appreciate me more. Agreed?"

I tell her, "Thank you."

She smiles. "For trying to kill you? You're welcome."

"For the pain you endured. To protect us."

Faye is dismissive, not wanting to revisit the past. "If not me, who? And, if we're going to live, you need to rest."

She seems to fade into me. I close my eyes, then reopen them at the sound of another voice. A hand touches mine.

"Did you miss me?"

Jenna stands beside the bed in all her splendor. She sparkles in the morning sunlight as it enters the room.

"You're a vision," I say.

"You're delusional," she giggles. "I'm the real one."

"Where's Hunter?"

Jenna lets go of my hand and turns to examine the white room, the walls, drapes, bed linens. "Hunter needs more time. You know, this place could really use more color."

"You brighten the room."

"I know. We'll be together soon."

Her delicate hand strokes my cheek, then covers my eyelids as if pronouncing me dead. Her lips kiss me to sleep.

I awake to find myself staring at an angel. My angel. Mira. She is standing in the darkness, looking down at me. Tears fall from her eyes like melting emeralds.

"Are you real?" I ask.

My words startle her. "*Oh*. You're alive."

Alive. A good sign. Mira grasps my hand.

I strain to look down at my body covered with sheets, afraid to ask, but finally do. "Am I whole?"

Her head shakes vertically. "Yes. No amputations. Your leg was saved. Thankfully."

I am relieved to hear this. I give her a faint smile. "Actually, I meant my mental condition."

"Don't worry about that now. First things first."

"Thank you," I tell her.

Her look is a puzzled one, so I explain.

"For understanding. Coming. Saving my life?"

"Oh ... *that*."

Her laugh has a spontaneity. It gives me hope. Mira lifts and kisses my hand. This is new.

"I love you," I tell her.

She squeezes as if tempted to echo my sentiments, but says, "I have feelings for you too."

Not quite what I was going for.

"The integration?"

"What about it?" she asks.

"I think I'm making progress."

"Good." She encourages with another squeeze.

"I'll keep you posted."

Her smile is like an opiate. I close my eyes and sleep.

TWENTY-SEVEN

Flowers. I can smell them. When I open my eyes they surround me. There are baskets of fruit, and cards too. Well-wishers. Which doesn't compute. I don't know that many people.

There is a tap at the door. Garrett, Denise, and Semele enter.

I indicate the flowers. "You shouldn't have."

"We didn't," Garrett laughs. "You deserve a *cactus*."

"If that," Denise adds. She comes over and gives me a kiss on the forehead.

Semele gives me a kiss too. "From your many admirers."

"I wasn't aware I had any."

"Nice stunt you pulled," says Garrett. "I told you not to play with fire. *Or* deadly snakes."

"Tell that to Faye."

"I am," he says.

Garrett makes himself at home in my hospital room. He sits in an armchair next to Denise and Semele. "Your therapist is an eyeful. Very pretty. It all makes sense now."

"I'm glad my disorder makes sense to someone."

"You should have told us," says Denise.

"That she's pretty?" I laugh. "Or that I'm insane?"

"Eccentric, is all," says Semele. "How are you feeling?"

"Catatonic. Relaxed. Better."

Garrett asks, "Great. Because there are a lot of people who want to talk with us. You especially. Are you up for it?"

"Up for what?"

"Interviews," says Garrett. "Reporters are eager for a story. Not exactly what we had planned. But this could be good, and launch us to the next level."

Denise adds, "The police are inquisitive too."

"Police? Why?"

"Oh, nothing," says Garrett. "You had a visitor."

Denise and Garrett glance at each other. Mira enters before they get a chance to say more. She is with two men I don't recognize. Both are large, wearing suits. Doctors, they are not. I say nothing.

But Garrett does, after standing, greeting the visitors with a nod and a look at me. "It's a madhouse around here. People outside the hospital, attempting to sneak in, wanting to get a peek at you."

"Why?" I ask, then address Mira, "Hi."

"This is Joel," says Mira.

"Detective Gulen," Joel adds to inform me of his title.

"Detective Gulen," repeats Mira before turning to the man who appears to be the dominant one. "And detective Faber."

Faber nods, chomping on gum.

"They'd like to ask you a few questions," she tells me.

I electronically adjust the bed to be more upright.

Detective Gulen holds out a photo. "Taken from a surveillance camera. Can you identify this person?"

The blurred images of a man. Inside an elevator.

"No," I say. "Wait. Yes. Faye does."

"Who?" says Gulen.

"His alternate," says Mira. "I'll explain later."

"He assaulted Faye," I tell him.

Gulen frowns, then says, "When was this?"

A few days ago. Near my home in the Marina, by Fort Mason. He had a knife. Same guy."

"Yeah, well," says Gulen, "there was a botched attempt to kill a security guard last night. Same method used by our serial killer. Blunt trauma to the jaw. Neck twisted, but no break. And no "X" cut into the skin, that we could find."

"Yet." The only utterance voiced from Faber.

Gulen continues, "Did this man visit you last night?"

"Not that I'm aware of."

"Meaning?" says Gulen.

"I was *asleep*. "What are you implying?"

"Gathering facts is all," Gulen says.

Mira picks up a card by a bouquet of flowers and brings it over to me. "Do you know who sent you this?"

The note reads: YOU ARE BETTER OFF DEAD.

"A fan?" I grin, but the message is alarming. "I suppose it *could* be interpreted as a joke?"

"Yeah," Garrett chimes in. "Funny."

"I did almost die."

"You got lucky," says Gulen. "How about this one?" He hands me another card: YOU <u>WILL</u> DIE. COUNT ON IT. BITCH.

"Notice how it's signed." Gulen points to the small "x".

"Jesus," I laugh nervously. "Are they all like this?"

"No," says Denise. "Only a few. But we're worried."

Mira tells Gulen, "His life's in danger. We need to move him."

"He has police protection," says Gulen. "24/7 security."

"Wait." I push the remote control to incline my bed further up. "The police are guarding my room? What else have I missed?"

Faber stops chewing. "Same thing we've been wondering."

Mira tells Gulen, "Joel, you can't *use* him as bait."

"It's my *job*," says Gulen, "to catch this serial killer. Somehow there's a connection here."

"We don't *know* that," says Mira.

"He knows something he's not telling us," says Gulen.

"Hey," I say, elevating the bed to its maximum height. "Stop talking like I'm invisible. I'm *right* here."

Gulen turns on me. "What do you know about this killer?"

I hesitate. "Nothing."

"Explain why there're newspaper clippings about these murders and photos of his victims plastered all across the walls of a room in your apartment."

"Faye's."

"Meaning, you."

"No.

"Right," he mutters, turns on Mira. "Tell him. I sure as hell hope you know what you're doing."

I watch as both detectives leave the room, pausing on the other side of the door to say something to the guard stationed there. The door slowly closes behind them.

"What was that all about?" I ask Mira.

"You're coming to stay with me. Temporarily."

I like the sound of that. "Stay where?"

Garrett pipes in to explain, "We're going to sneak you out of the hospital. Like we did in New York. Disguised. You have this knack for attracting maniacs. Nice work."

"We offered to take you in," says Denise, "But Doctor Skyles, Mira, has extra security in her building. Designed to accommodate this kind of ... situation."

"You mean like a psychiatric ward?"

Garrett laughs. "No. A safe place, for you to heal physically, and mentally, until things calm down."

I look at Mira. "Why are you doing this?"

"Someone leaked information to the press about what the police found inside the apartment. And someone wants you dead, it would appear. You need protection."

"I did this to myself. You're not responsible."

Mira has that look of a clinician, the consummate professional as she speaks, well aware of the audience of my three friends. "You put your trust in me. You *are* my patient. I *am* responsible for your well being. You'll be safe there."

Denise adds, "It's just until the hysteria dies down."

282

"What hysteria?" I ask.

"You," says Garrett. "You're breaking news. On every channel. Should I turn on the television to prove my point?"

"Egon," says Mira. "It's temporary. And for your safety."

"Your house in the Marina was vandalized," Garrett tells me. "Broken into. Completely trashed."

"Lots of graffiti," adds Denise. "More death threats."

Processing this, I look at Mira who confirms with a nod.

"Everything has been arranged," she says.

Semele adds, "I packed your clothing and personal items. The luggage was delivered to Mira's apartment."

"Or, safe house," Garrett jokes.

"It's spacious," adds Denise with an encouraging smile.

Garrett winks. "You know how I revel in the clandestine. Our agent, the press, and any business negotiations can wait."

To clarify, Mira tells me, "This is *not* something I ordinarily do. Although, under the circumstances, I feel it's necessary. I hope you understand how serious this is."

"I'm beginning to."

Mira continues, "Privacy won't be an issue. There are separate quarters. I've scheduled a physician to come by and make sure your leg heals properly. A police officer will be guarding the premises at all hours."

With a slight grin, I ask, "For whose protection?"

Mira resists a smile. "Egon, I have other patients. So I trust you will cooperate and behave yourself while I'm away. While I'm there, we can continue to work on your integration."

"You've thought of everything," I say.

"Detective Gulen is opposed to the entire idea."

"You work with these men?"

"Sometimes. I'm also a licensed criminal psychologist."

I'm relieved she's confessed it. "So when do we do this?"

In the dead of night, I vacate my room dressed as a male nurse with facial hair and glasses. In pain, I minimize my limp. From the underground garage, I am transported in Mira's Mercedes, beneath a blanket on the backseat floor. It feels unnecessary but I admire the degree of subterfuge. I hide again while entering the underground garage to the structure where Mira resides.

From there, it's all above ground, meaning an elevator ride to her spacious suite. I watch the numbers stop on the forty-ninth floor. It becomes clear to me that no one can land at this particular level without authorization from lobby security or by an owner's key.

Detective Gulen is part of my entourage. We all enter the foyer, where a policeman in his blue uniform is seated. He stands to greet us. Gulen makes the introductions, then stays to talk with the officer as I enter the living area. The accommodations are impressive.

I sense ulterior motives at work here. I'm suspicious about this safe house, the whole arrangement. Is this really Mira's apartment? Or is it staged? I say nothing, except, "Nice place you have."

"Did you want to see your room?"

"I'd rather see yours."

"Egon, be serious."

"I know. I can feel the gravity of my situation."

"Don't make me regret this."

"Proceed. I'll play nice."

And I do. Play nice, that is. Cooperate. Behave accordingly as the perfect guest.

I've been here almost a week.

The voices in my head have subsided, but I can still hear them assembling, conversing as if at a cocktail party, expressing opinions. Hunter has yet to reappear. Meaning he knows something that I do not, which worries me. He is a missing piece to my puzzle. There could be more loose ends and Mira, God love her, is determined to find them. I've been instructed not to use my cell phone. It's been confiscated for my own good. Nor am I to use the land line in case it's been bugged. So, lacking the concentration to focus my attention on a book, and having scouted the Bay Area like a hawk imprisoned inside its nest, I've been forced to watch endless television.

I am sick to death of incessant replays of my crucifixion on the evening news and the talk-show channels, with all the commentators voicing speculations on my whereabouts and opinions on my recent disappearing act from the hospital. It has inflamed the fascination of many. Fueled further by leaked information about the serial killer striking again, but failing in his attempt to commit murder. Pundits interviewed on talk shows have speculated about my involvement, spewing innuendos that *I* may be *him*.

I fear this will not end well.

Also, several prominent men have been named in a sex scandal. The details not yet released. And, if that wasn't enough, the populus is on a scavenger hunt to find rare and valuable pennies distributed around the city.

Detectives Gulen and Faber came to visit today. More questions to ask me. Gulen sat, facing me, while Faber stood, looking down.

As a preamble, Gulen reads me my Miranda rights.

"We watched your performances on that game show."

"It's not really a game show," I say.

"It's a competition," says Gulen.

Faber says, "A *game* show."

"Whatever," I concede.

"The Rebel Artists of Perception. Why that name?"

"Sounds edgy." I grin and decide to direct my attention on Joel, who displays more civility. "It was the only one we could agree on, as a group."

"We?"

"There's several of us."

"It takes a lot of imagination to do those performances."

"Is that a question?"

"To execute them perfectly. Isn't that right?"

"Absolutely."

"Pretty damned elaborate, those illusions."

"They are. Your point?"

Gulen's smile is not exactly pleasant. "Have you ever imagined killing someone?"

"Sure."

"Is that so?" says Faber.

His question draws my eyes upwards.

"If you've watched our performances, you know I get killed. I've imagined being a detective too. Investigating and apprehending criminals. I admire the work you do."

Gulen doesn't smile. "Is that why you plastered an entire room with news clippings of murdered people?"

"Victims of the serial killer," adds Faber.

"That was Faye's doing."

"Your sister?" Faber sniffs a laugh.

"A twin," says Gulen. "Who died. How many *years* ago?"

"You don't understand."

"I think we do," states Gulen. "Let's talk about your blackouts. Oh, I forgot, you can't. You don't remember things."

"Not everything, but Mira's been—"

"You *sister* assaults men," says Gulen. "She gets herself arrested for it. Then praises the work of this killer. Denies knowing anything about him. Except, it's a lie. She's fascinated by this killer. Collects and decorates the walls with news articles. She makes notes, posting photos of his kills. And now you're telling us – as your *dead* sister? – you've imagined yourself as a murderer?"

"As I *imagine* you have too. Wondering about the psychological motives? What makes him tick. What kind of person would do that? Why not be direct. Ask me the question. It's what this visit is about, isn't it?"

Gulen tilts his head with a sour grin. "You think you're smarter than us, don't you?"

"No. Because I hardly know you."

"For the record," states Gulen. "*Are* you the serial killer?"

I smile, shake my head. "You could have led with that question. If that's all you came to ask me. It would have saved us a lot of time. No, detectives. I am *not*."

Gulen stands. With a sarcastic sniff, he says, "Well that's a load of worry off my mind."

"Glad to help." I follow his lead and stand too.

His sarcasm shifts to a threat. "Mira. Don't you *fuck* with her! If I find you've harmed her in *any* way—"

Faber pulls Gulen away from me, then adds, "You understand what we're saying?"

"Loud and clear, detectives. I'd never harm Mira. I care—"

"She's a *sister* to me," adds Gulen. "Mira's ... headstrong."

I smile and agree, "She definitely has a mind of her own."

"How's the leg?" Gulen's emotional gears shift rapidly.

"Better. Pretty much healed."

"Good. Don't leave town unexpectedly."

"I wasn't planning to. I wasn't aware I could leave."

"Right. So that's clear." Gulen takes a signal from Faber. "We'll be having a talk with Mike outside. Then we'll be off."

"Thanks for the visit. Stop by anytime."

Both Gulen and Faber give me a strange look, not appreciating my stab at humor. With not even a nod, they leave.

Since the informal interrogation, the television has been turned off. For hours, I stare into its black nothingness as I wait, listening for the sounds of Mira's return.

I hear her talking to my guardian at the gate. As she enters, she turns the deadbolt. No doubt the police have a means for gaining quick access. I also imagine there are hidden cameras to keep watch over me. Mira sees me seated in the white leather sofa with my body facing the television's blank screen. No music. Nothing.

I smile and joke, "Welcome home, Dear."

She's not amused, then realizes it's somewhat funny. "Have you become stir crazy? Sorry. Bad choice of words. Are you enjoying the peace and quiet?"

"All the above. How was your day? And your other nut cases? Everyone good? Safe and sound?"

"I could use a drink."

"Me too."

As you can see, or infer from what I have so far described, our relationship has become, you could say, abnormal. You could also say I am a voluntary inmate housed in her highrise psychiatric ward. I get up off the sofa and move to the bar to mix our cocktails. A dry martini for her. Scotch on the rocks for me.

"What did the doctor say?" she asks.

"I'm healed. Good as new. We should celebrate."

Mira comes over and takes the martini from my hand. It's like we're married, yet there is no kiss. A familiarity. An indication of affection flowing somewhere deep within we've yet to explore. I am her captive, and I think she enjoys that I am. I wonder if it's unsafe for me to be seen on the streets. Or was this all a setup? Were the death threats in my hospital room planted, fake, like all the flowers? I'm sure Detective Gulen and his investigative team have scoured my residences by now, looking for clues to incriminate me (maybe resort to *planting* evidence?) in order to have grounds for my arrest.

I expect this scenario to happen any day. My arrest. I expect a lot of things to happen, that don't.

I toast Mira and wonder if this is a ploy to get me to confess to being someone I know not. I know this – she is curious about me. Fascinated to a fault. Her attraction toward me is both mental *and* physical. For I have captivated her too. She likes to psychoanalyze. And I am what she had been waiting for all her life. She returns my toast. We taste our toxic drinks, eyeing one another. I can feel the sexual tension. Maybe it's only my imagination.

"Tomorrow is all for you." She kicks off her shoes and settles down upon the sofa.

"All for me?" I ask. "How do you mean?"

"We're going to search deeper for that root cause."

"*Ah*, to find the lost cord of my disorder." I smile to make light of this hydrotherapeutic excavation into my mind.

"If you're willing to trust me." She takes a sip of gin.

"I trust you." I follow with a smile. "Should I?"

As far back as I can remember I have always been influenced by dreams and the ability to imagine the *what if*. Able to see myself on a small island, so small the ocean waves can be seen all around me. Or see myself floating skyward in a hot-air balloon through the clouds, and disappearing, before reemerging in the blue sky, getting higher and higher as the people, the trees, the houses become smaller and smaller below.

I count backward from one hundred, ninety-nine ...

I hear Mira's voice like a pilot from inside a cockpit, announcing very gently over the intercom that we have arrived.

Missing is a lapse of time. Scorched earth no more.

I am a child again, sucking my thumb, huddled outside a hole in the ground. Mira is holding me. I am trembling, but comforted by her touch, the firm hold, keeping me warm and safe.

I pull back, wiping tears and snot from my face. Mira hands me tissues and I blow my nose.

"What happened?"

Mira has tears in her eyes and is noticeably moved.

"Egon?"

"I'm here. Why are you crying? And smiling?"

"We made a breakthrough."

"How so?"

"How do you feel?"

"Better."

I do, looking around, becoming cognizant of the elevation we are at, somewhere in the sky, inside a building, the picture windows showing the approaching night. I *do* feel better, lighter. Like a bird, released from its cage, I feel I could fly.

I stand. A weight has lifted. My mind feels clear. I walk to the windows and look down at city lights reflecting on the bay. Darkness has taken over. But I have no fear. The sky is spectacular. A beautiful mess of black ink.

I muse aloud, "Time is so strange. It was daylight a minute ago. Now it's happy hour."

"Did you want a drink?"

"No."

I turn back and stare at Mira. Still seated, she is watching me closely.

She asks, "What are you thinking?"

When I don't answer, my thoughts are obvious. I want her.

When I awaken next, Mira is beside me. We are both naked in her bed. And I have a lucid memory of how this happened. Which is a surprise. A revelation. This ability to recall. We managed to defuse the suspicions we have, or had, of one another. And to accept the consequences. Accepting each other. As is.

It's a breakthrough for us both.

Yet I can't recall the last therapeutic session – the place she took me. I do sense the release of pain. Something was excised. Performed like surgery. Or magic. Except this is no trick. It's real.

My fingers brush across her cheek. She wakes.

I scold her playfully, "Very unprofessional."

She shuts her eyes, reopens them with a smile. "I don't care."

"Me neither. But what about your license?"

She turns on her side to face me. I stare at her lovely breasts, how her nipples contract. She doesn't try to hide from me. "You are no longer my patient."

"Since when?"

"The moment you put your penis inside me. And we made love. Right then. At that moment."

I laugh. "You're methods are unorthodox."

"For some. Only you. How do you feel this morning?"

"Much, *much* better."

"I set you free."

"You're a miracle worker."

"You're welcome."

"What about Detective Gulen? What will he think?"

Mira closes her eyes and falls back into her pillow. "He's a good man. But another story. He thinks you're the serial killer."

I prop myself on my elbow. "I figured as much. And you?"

"You're not a killer."

As I start to protest – horrid images resurging of murdering my father – Mira covers my mouth with her hand.

"Egon, you're not. I trust you."

"That's a relief." If we are being filmed, I don't care. My free hand caresses her breast. She lets me roam. I travel to her stomach. My fingers search between her legs. Her eyes close. She is wet with desire and I've become hard again. I want to be inside her. I tug her gently into me. We connect like a plug into a switch, becoming one, electric.

Upon climax, I remain inside of her, and she holds firmly to this commitment to stay attached and pulls me tighter. We look into each other's eyes. I say, "Will you run away with me now?"

"To where?"

"Does it matter?"

"Yes, it does. It won't be easy."

"Living with me?"

"With me."

"I don't care."

"Egon, having sex is one thing. Living together is another. You might find out you don't like me."

"I love you."

"You don't know me."

"Tell me what I need to know. You know all about me."

"Not everything."

"True." Having gone soft, I ease out of Mira. She rakes fingers through my hair, kisses me, and we snuggle under the bedsheets.

"Let's take it slow then."

She studies me. "You call what we did slow?"

I smile. "I've been working on you for months, years."

"So have I," she counters. "But I never expected to fall in love. This is against my better judgment."

"Because you like order. Not disorder?"

"Because I *never* get involved sexually with a patient."

"Ordinarily."

"Ordinarily. You're my first."

"And last, I hope. Let's go to the beach."

"Why?"

"To breathe in fresh air. I've been cooped up here too long."

"Egon, it's only been a week."

"We can walk through Golden Gate Park, picnic, then end up at the Sea Cliff. Say yes."

"I have a better idea."

"Ah, it *begins,*" I tease. "A need to outdo me. You were right. I'm not sure I like you anymore. This competitiveness."

"You'll like my idea. I promise."

She has me intrigued. "Do you need permission from Gulen?"

"He doesn't control me."

"Good to know. When do we leave?"

"Tomorrow I'll clear my schedule. There are a couple of people I need to see first, then we're good to go."

"Okay."

A beach house. Stinson Beach. About an hour's drive north of San Francisco. The back porch abuts a scattering of rocks, plumes of sea grass, and white sand. The ocean is a stone's throw away. I am enchanted immediately by the sound of its perpetual roar.

I set down my luggage. "This is yours?"

"My little hideaway."

"You've been a busy girl. Nice. You must be rich."

"Not as rich as you."

"Says the doctor who cured Oedipus Rex."

As Mira flicks on a light she gives me a puzzled look. "Come again? I'm afraid I overlooked that complex."

"Regarding my dumb luck. Inheriting a fortune. Like Oedipus, I killed my father and fucked my mother. I never dreamed she'd get sentenced to a mental institution, then kill herself. So, inadvertently, you see, I fucked her."

"Your mother suffered from tremendous guilt," say Mira as she pulls back a curtain.

"I never blamed her for the death of my sister."

"Consciously."

"Maybe."

"She blamed herself. For the accidental death of her child."

"I did love her. As screwed up as she was. It does still haunt me. Had I known, I would never have done that to her."

"Have sex with your mother?" Mira gives me a smile.

"That too." I laugh, amused by Mira's wicked sense of humor which I'm discovering. "Seriously, it never occurred to me that I'd be inheriting a fortune from my brilliant yet sadistic father."

"Who suffered from post-traumatic stress."

I watch as Mira takes charge of the interior space, opening more drapes, unlatching windows. "You're right. I guess I should cut my dad some slack. He was a war hero. Not always a shit."

Mira stops to stare at me. "Egon, he traumatized and molested you. Good god, you *are* a mess." She looks me over with a playful, teasing smile. "I may need to do more work on you."

Her place is immaculate. I am learning this about Mira. She is a neat freak. Everything is organized, thought out. Arranged. Ordered. Cataloged. Filed away. I wait for her to tell me what I can do, but she seems to have a precise procedure for opening the place, readying it for the living to inhabit this inanimate enclosure.

"Mix us drinks?" she suggests.

"I can do that." I look around for the bar. She points.

As Mira moves about, I do too, finding what I need, deciding to make martinis for us both. Shaken. Dry. Three olives. I present her with the fruits of my modest labor. She accepts it with a click of her glass to mine. We drink, then pause to look around and take in the fact we are actually here, vacationing together.

I toast her playfully. "To our honeymoon."

"Hmm," she says, raising an eyebrow as she takes a sip of gin. She sets her glass down on one of the many coasters. "Can I ask you a question?"

"I've never been able to stop you. Ask away."

"Do you feel the fusion is working?"

"Ah, the fusion. I believe it is."

"The integration is holding?"

"Everyone says hello. We're all doing fine. Holding steady."

"I'm serious."

"So am I. What's bothering you, Mira?"

"Something Faye said to me."

"About?"

"What she saw during college. In the cemetery."

"The cemetery? Means nothing. I'll ask Faye. Let's see if she's in a talkative mood."

Mira shakes her head. There is something she wants to tell me but is afraid to ask. Faye has something on Mira, a secret they share. To be honest, the integration is not entirely working. Faye is being a bitch, giving me the silent treatment.

"No response," I joke. "I'll try calling her later."

"Forget it." Mira picks up her bags. "Shall we unpack?"

I follow her into the bedroom with my luggage. I stall at the doorway, surprised by the canopy bed with four large black columns supporting an ornate metal canopy top. The comforter is silver with black bed sheets and fluffy multicolored pillows arranged against a padded headboard. "Wow, that's quite a bed."

"Do you like it?"

"Mira. You need to get naked, like, immediately."

I drop my bag and start removing my clothes. Mira is too slow, meticulous, removing her leather coat, folding it over a chair, before unbuttoning her blouse. I intercede, stopping short of ripping it off her body. The bra goes next, flung with her blouse toward a chair. I drop to my knees, pull down her pants, along with her panties, and bury my face between her legs. She shrieks, laughing.

I grasp her bare bottom, lift and drop her onto the bed, where she lands with a playful bounce. I yank off her boots and pants, then situate myself between her legs. On my knees, holding her by the ankles with both hands, I extend her feet into the air. Awaiting my next move, she looks up as I look down, admiring her pink terrain like a pilot preparing to land. Her groomed pubic hairs are snipped into the shape of a directional pointer, providing instructions. And so I descend onto her runway, touching down smoothly, gliding into her warm body. I am home.

I love how we make love, our ceremony of sex.

No words are spoken. Only rhythm. Sensation. Pleasure.

We come to a standstill. I place my hands beneath her and raise her bottom up, our bodies still attached. I slide my legs under her to lay upon my back. Her body is now on top of mine, straddling me. She likes this maneuver and looks into my eyes.

"You've had practice," she tells me with a smile.

"All in preparation for you."

"Liar."

"Go ahead. Ask me anything."

"Ask you what?"

"It's a game. We ask each other one intimate question."

"Only one? Anything?"

I nod as our bodies rock and roll together.

Mira is like a beautiful flower rising from my body.

She asks me, "You're hiding someone. Who?"

"Very perceptive. Hunter. He refused to partake in our fusion. He'll eventually come to his senses and join the party."

Mira shows a flicker of concern, then says, "Your turn."

I point. "Why do you hide that beautiful teardrop scar below your left eye? I like it. It reminds me of a girl I once knew."

Her reaction surprises me. A shudder ripples through her body and spreads in waves into me. She regains her composure and smiles as if nothing has happened. But she doesn't answer me.

She sways back and forth to soothe us both.

"Tomorrow," she finally says.

"What about tomorrow?"

"I'll tell you everything about me. I promise."

PART 3

MIRA:
Inevitable Fusion

"I saw the angel

in the marble

and carved until

I set him free."

— Michelangelo

MIRA

Don't decide to hate me until you have heard my entire story. Then you can hate me if you want.

My name is not Mira. Or Miranda. Not even Mirabelle. It's Clarabelle. What in the hell possessed my parents to name me *that?* Didn't they know it would scar me for life?

I cried for weeks when I discovered it's meaning.

"It means 'bright and famous'," my mother explained to me all smiles. My father nodded and insisted the origin was Latin. *No. Wrong.* I discovered its meaning at a birthday party. At my party. When I turned five. When a boy named Sid from the neighborhood, who was three years older and who I would never have invited since I despised the sadistic shit, screamed:

"Clarabelle is a cow!"

That was his present to me. This cartoon picture of an ugly big-nostriled, bug-eyed cow staring at me when I unwrapped the box. The cartoon face scissored from a comic book he had slipped inside without his mother knowing, I assumed since she slapped his face. But it was too late. The damage had been done. My so-called close friends were rolling on the floor in fits of laughter. The grownups trying to placate this *kids-will-be-kids* name calling with no success. I ran to my room and hid beneath my bed sobbing into a pillow. I refused to crawl out until everyone was *gone–gone–gone!*

Days later I discover the name Clarabelle was not only a cartoon cow but also the name of a clown. A fucking joke! I wanted to die. Or kill my parents. Someone. Anyone.

My parents decided to perform surgery and amputate my given name to Clara. As if *that* was going to help. I was already scarred, henceforth known by my peers as "Clarabelle Cow."

— ☙ —

This candid confessional to Egon has left him speechless. His expression reveals surprise but not shock. There is love in his smile. It is early morning. We are lying naked in bed. The sheets lightly draped over our lower halves. A beautiful sunrise is behind us now, shining over the top of my beachfront house to brighten the ocean. Frothy waves cascade rhythmically along the sandy shore, which we observe through the wall of sliding glass doors.

A moment ago Egon's head was between my legs, spread wide to welcome him. His lips kissing mine, nibbling at my tender flesh, his tongue probing me, my body and mind melting, going soft. Eyes closing, lost in pleasure, as I fantasize. "Egon" is a warrior's name. A man captured, turned slave. Slashed by whips, enduring ridicule, beaten and worked like a savage animal, he has struggled to survive. His magnificence is noticed by the queen. He is rewarded with a hot bath – his muscles lotioned with oils and doused with perfumes, his mane of hair combed and plaited – then brought to my bed.

Egon removes his tongue from inside me, having paid homage to my fertile port, a sanctuary he honors. With a parting kiss, he then travels slowly in a snail's trail of wetness from my groin to my navel. His tongue lingers to circle this small pool, this tiny oasis, before making the trek across my stomach and rising uphill to my breasts. He suckles my nipples like a newborn, gums becoming teeth, softly biting, having grown into a man. His head lifts, his eyes meeting mine, to acknowledge we are equals. My vagina opens to engulf and devour his penis as it penetrates me.

He is a courageous warrior, who has risen to make love to the queen, once untouchable, this woman superior, therapist and savior, who has become his lover. He rides upon me as if upon a wave, many waves, until we collapse, intertwined.

Our lovemaking feels like a dream, but it is real.

My ambitions and hard work have paid off, and I am happy.

Egon has surprised me by bringing breakfast to bed.

He pours more champagne into my glass, toasts me in silence with a nonchalant grin, leans into me with a kiss, telling me my past doesn't matter. Words are unimportant. Names are not what should define us. He confirms this with his eyes, so blue I want to cry. He nods for me to continue, only if I want. So I tell him more.

— ⋟ —

When I was twelve years old I was viciously raped. What am I saying? All rapes are vicious. And brutal. My father went ballistic, mentally unraveling from a desire to inflict violence on my attackers. My mother withdrew into a hate-the-world depression for God to have allowed this deflowering of my innocence. I had lied to protect them. I imagined my dad being sent to prison for murder. My mother left alone, unable to care for herself, much less me. The revelation to lie came to me while I lay exposed in a cold emergency room being probed and examined in places I'd been told to never let strangers touch. The male doctor even resembled one of my rapists, an older version, and was doing exactly that, touching my private parts while nurses swabbed my naked body open for public viewing. All that was sensitive to me had gone frigid and numb.

Initially, I'd been excited by the prospect of my body changing, the pink budding breasts, the flow of blood and the surge of desire stirring between my legs. I was pleased boys were taking an interest in wanting to be my friend. Then I was raped.

I kept a journal. My silly fantasies of worlds where Little Ponies flew over rainbows and lived in clouds evolved into flights of fancy about first kisses from a boy, and so many scribbled dreams of love. Then my entries went noticeably darker. Which says this about me. I am meticulous, unrelenting, and patiently tenacious. And vengeful. I was hatching a plan. I knew the three boys who'd raped me. Even though I lied to my parents and the police. Nobody would find and capture the nonexistent abductors I'd described, who'd abducted me in their off-white van, drove me into the woods, and had their way with me. I decided: Why should I let the police, prosecutors, defense lawyers or some judge – who had no skin in this game – be the ones who decided how these bastards were to be punished?

My rapists kept their distance from me, for a while, though they lived in the same neighborhood. A whole year passed before they turned brazen. Feeling they had gotten away with it, they teased me with lewd looks, even spread lies about the incident. They said I had asked for it, and that I was engaged in sex with numerous boys. So, when I entered high school, I had a reputation that preceded me. And my rapists, who were all seniors, I'd see daily in the hallways, the cafeteria, or on the football field playing hero.

I kept to myself. Instead of opening up into a beautiful flower that I imagined I'd be, I grew up damaged, stunted, and malformed. I nervously ate too much, had put on weight, wore baggy clothing, prescription glasses and (to add insult to injury) I needed braces. Oh, did I mention the acne? With so many distracting features going on with my face, the scar below my left eye – a knife-wound reminder from my rapists – was barely noticeable. Lucky me. Yes, it was safe to say, I was not pretty.

I needed to catch up fast, I realized. They were three grades ahead of me, about to graduate and go to who-knows-where. So I doubled-downed on my academics. I attended summer school. Took AP courses. Received extra credits. Jumped grades. My SAT score landing me in the top percentile. The sum total of my efforts allowed me to graduate at the end of what would normally have been my junior year. My guidance counselor objected to my higher-education choice. My options were unlimited, he advised me. But I already had my sights set, having applied, anticipating my early release, and was accepted into the college where two of my rapists were attending. On scholarships. One for football, the other one for baseball. They were jocks. And not very smart. For if they'd been my equal, they would have had some *clue* that I would be coming after them.

During those nose-to-the-grindstone days, my body underwent a gradual transformation. I was determined to get fit, to fit in, and become social. I lost weight running track. And one by one I began to lose the rest of my handicaps – acne, braces, glasses. I bleached my dirty-blond hair. If my plan was to succeed, I had to become an extrovert, not an introvert. Emerge from my shell and be a butterfly, not a snail. And appear authentic. So I joined a few clubs, displayed school spirit. I didn't make the cheerleading squad, yet the popular girls nudged into my life, desiring to be my friend. Like I said, I am meticulous, unrelenting, and patiently tenacious. And vengeful.

Another required step in my elaborate scheme was to undergo a name change. My dad and mom refused. At seventeen, I didn't need my parent's consent, legally. Except they threatened to cut me off financially. I called their bluff. I told them I didn't care, that I'd forgo college and run away if they didn't permit it. In the negotiation, we agreed on Miranda instead of Clara. And my last name was changed from Skiver into Skyles. Unfortunately, my school records would have both names on file, including the college I'd be attending.

As my reward for academic achievements and new social graces, my parents presented me with a white Rabbit, a used Volkswagen equipped with a black convertible top. I convinced my parents I needed to be independent and drove from Northern California to Oregon by myself. On my arrival, the sky was dark and raining hard, the campus barely visible in the downpour. My determination to be fearless got temporarily derailed. I felt lost navigating through the hordes of students searching to locate their assigned dormitory and unload their consolidated belongings. I began to cry.

As I ran back and forth from my Rabbit clutching suitcase and boxes, I realized I never had to wonder again how much water could fall from the sky all at once. I was running through sheets of liquid. My tears got washed away as I dashed from my car to the dormitory.

I was laughing with the other students who were drenched too. My roommate was already in our room. She was drying her hair with a towel. She was sitting on the top bunk, her feet dangling off the bed she had chosen to be hers.

I dropped my luggage and examined the prison-sized cubicle I would be sleeping in. I then looked up to lock eyes with my cellmate who was smiling. There was something about her I liked right off. Her black hair had a streak of red. She had a sharp chin, cool grey eyes, and a pierced nostril. Not a classic beauty, but pretty.

"So what's up, Roomy-Tuesday?"

It was a Tuesday when we met.

"I'm Mira." I reached out and shook her bare foot.

She laughed, clenching her toes to grip the touch of my fingers. Her toenails were painted black. My fingernails were blood red.

"We might get along," she assessed.

"You're Gwen?"

"Ah, you've read the *dossier*," she said, tossing the damp towel to the floor and proceeding to shape the plume of her hair with flicks of her black fingernails. "What happened to Clara?"

"She died. I'm afraid you get me instead."

"I can live with Mira. If that's who you are. Need help?"

"No." I lifted and set down a box of items on the uncluttered desk, assuming this would be mine. "I'm good."

"By the looks of it." Gwen hopped off the bed. "But I'm a bad judge of character. So I suppose you could be."

I glanced up with a quick smile as I unzipped my suitcase.

"You travel light." She leaned against her desk. "I like that."

"You're from New York?"

"Uh-hum. You?"

"California. Bay Area. You came a long way. Why?"

"No college would have me." Gwen pushed off the desk to look at herself in a hand mirror. "My father was an alumni, so he pulled strings, got me into the summer program. You do the time, pass the courses they require you to take, get above a certain GPA, and they have to take you. Them's the rules. So here I am."

I paused to absorb this information. "That means you know this campus pretty well already. I mean how it works?"

"I know my way around." Gwen squinted, curious. "Tell me what's on your mind, Mira. Or should I be calling you MIA, as in Missing In Action?"

I shoved my suitcase in the closet, having unloaded my clothing into drawers. I slapped my palms. "All done. No particular reason. No hidden agenda."

"I'm not buying it. Not you." Gwen was still assessing me as I removed my blue jeans, leather jacket, boots soaked from the rain. She eyed my tight-fitting grey cashmere sweater that accentuated my breasts. "You're pretty. What's your game? I like the scar."

"Excuse me?" By her comment, I realized the rain had washed away the makeup I wore to disguise my knife wound.

"What are you here for? Higher education? Sorority princess? Catch a husband? Party your brains out? All the above?"

I smiled. Gwen wasn't an easy read. She was dangerous, or so she thought. She was someone I might not be able to control.

"I need to use the bathroom," I told her.

She pointed. I nodded and exited our claustrophobic room to turn left down the hallway.

— ❦ —

Egon is intrigued by my story. His arm is crooked, head angled against one hand while his other hand holds a glass of champagne. He takes a sip and playfully arches his eyebrows to indicate he wants to hear more. He has yet to abandon me. I've implied he might. But he's only seen the tip of my iceberg. I bite my lip in a smile, hesitate, then keep going.

— ❦ —

I had acclimated fairly well, given the fact that existence on this campus was like living in a terrarium. Lush from so much rain. And when it wasn't pouring, it was usually misty. Then suddenly the sun would break through the grey matter. It'd be glorious, stopping me in my tracks. As if God had parted the clouds to have a look down, shining light to remind me this earthly garden was amazing. The sun always shined. Somewhere, just not here. And as the sky darkened, I would walk on, meandering along paths through rolling mounds of green manicured grass, admiring the brick buildings.

Rush Week came and I anticipated the worst. I geared up my mind to be enthusiastic and come off as outgoing, yet blasé enough to not appear wanting, or needy, and thus present myself as someone these female tribes would desire to have among them as a *Greek* who would pledge. Being accepted into this bond of sisterhood was part of my plan, so I inquired, asking other students which sororities were the favored houses. Gwen wanted no part of submitting herself to these institutionalized cattle-calls, describing the ritual as "a mad-cow inquisition conducted inside a slaughterhouse disguised as a fun-loving social gathering."

"I won't be made into a Barbie doll," she said, defiant, as she twirled a streak of her blood red hair. "To be groomed and mated with a Ken doll? It's ridiculous. They have no genitalia."

"Aren't you the least bit curious?"

"To enter into those estrogen-fumed fantasylands. Absolutely not. No way."

I taunted. "No one is asking you to join, Gwen. So what's the big deal?"

"I could get them to want me," she challenged. "If I wanted to be wanted—by *them*—which I do not."

We had been seated back to back at our respective desks, talking like this and getting no work done. I finally turned around in my chair and poked her backside.

"For the adventure. You have to come."

"Stop molesting me." Gwen turned to defend herself. "On one condition. Stop nibbling your eraser heads."

Surprised that I had been, embarrassed by my habit, I removed the pencil from my mouth. "That's it?"

"No. I did research on these *geeks*, I mean Greeks."

"They were defeated by the Romans."

"Gamma Phi."

"What about it?"

"They're the worst house. That means the best."

"How do you figure?"

"They have a reputation for independence and taking drugs. Recreationally. They like to party. They fraternize with the frats but reject their culture of *bro-ness*."

"What's that?"

"Where sisters are subservient to the brothers."

"I didn't know that," I told her innocently.

"I've been here longer than you."

"Okay. Gamma Phi is on our list."

Gwen shook her head, scowling at the idea, before slapping my pencil to the floor. "Aren't you majoring in psychology? You should know what signals you're sending when you chew and suck those eraser heads. *Jee-zuz*, Mira."

— ≋ —

Egon is amused by this detail I've included. He knows my bad habits. But only some. He tips his head, wanting to hear more.

— ≋ —

Gwen and I pledged Gamma Phi. I had requests to join several sororities. Gwen had only one. I pretended I was doing this for her. That I was debating on the others. I wasn't. I knew right away what I wanted. This was the house that Eve built. Adam never stood a chance. The apple was damned-well coming off that tree. There was no turning back. My only hesitation and regret came when I had to succumb to my initiation into this twisted sisterhood of greekdom. Gwen and I and the other pledges were blindfolded and taken off campus and hog-tied with duct tape, plied with liquor and drugs and dowsed in a foul-smelling mud, then tattooed with magic markers – our face, arms and legs defiled with hieroglyphic symbols, the kind seen on bathroom walls – which were painful and hard to scrub off. Of course, this incident never happened. Hazing was forbidden, a nonsanctioned university turn-a-blind-eye tradition of denial.

I avoided going home, venturing south only to present myself for Christmas. With my parents willingness to provide financial aid, I was able to co-rent an apartment with Gwen, who also remained in Oregon through the summer months, by getting assistance from her father. We both managed to land jobs working at a pizza parlor to finance our extracurricular needs. My designated targets – two of the three boys who had raped me – whom I had tracked here, both vacated the campus. But I knew they'd return. Because this was their big senior year. Roger Dossen, who was nicknamed Roger-Dodger, was the star running back on the football team. While the other one, Brad Fuller, played baseball as an outfielder, and got less acclaim since this third-semester sport had sparsely attended games and did little to fill the university's coffer.

They were both frat boys entrenched in the ATX "jock" house, which I discovered the first week of my neophyte year. I also learned what Gwen meant about their culture of bro-ness. There existed an underground (although well known to many students) lexicon for this misogyny. By using the word "target" was to mean (or rather *demean*) a girl. "Pie" was a vagina. A "gullet" meant a girl's mouth. Rating a "grip" was in reference to a target's pie. Not to mention, yet I will, the pie code. Aka *menu*. Strawberry Pie: a white target. Blackberry Pie: a black target. Cherry Pie: a barely-legal target. Pumpkin Pie: Latino target. Lemon Meringue Pie: Asian target.

Once I knew about this sexist terminology, I hated being known as a Gamma *Phi*. Pronounced by all as Gamma *Pie*, with emphasis on the latter word when used by Frats. But then I decided to embrace the name. Gamma meant a unit of magnetic intensity. And Phi, aside from meaning the twenty-first letter of the Greek alphabet, meant *Pie*. So I wore the label with pride. I *was* a Gamma Pie.

When my sophomore year commenced, both Gwen and I moved into the large tutor-style Gamma Phi house. It had a pervasive sweet candy smell from an assortment of perfumes which, at times, fought with a primeval whiff of mold. Outside its walls, the university had a splendid mixture of natural scents. I fell in love with the smell of decaying fall leaves, fresh cut grass, pine trees, needles and cones, and the wild aromas from native flora. I had to admit it was a lovely campus, this lush terrarium, a forest with winding concrete paths through a rolling landscape of groomed lawns and architectural structures composed mainly of bricks.

It was easy to get distracted, to forget my resolve and the reason I had come to this place. For an education. That too, but topping my list was my mission of revenge.

I frequented the Fishbowl, the centerpiece of the campus. Made famous by the movie Animal House. It was an expansive restaurant with curving glass walls where students hung out, sat and ate, met and talked, observed the goings-on of others and, *being* a college, came to cram for exams. This is where I first saw the boy I would fall in love with, and who would break my heart.

— ≋ —

Egon turns to look at me. We are moving from the bed to the veranda overlooking the ocean. It's a balmy morning, unusual for the coast. Wearing nothing but shorts and t-shirts, we settle into two lounge chairs, angled to face each other but also towards the beach. I love Egon. I don't want to lose him. Not now. Considering all I've done to get us to this place.

— ≋ —

It was hard not to have noticed this boy. I was seated beside the window, inside the Fishbowl, of all things studying. I happened to look up. I'd never seen anyone so handsome. He was standing on the first tier of the patio, on the curving rampart overlooking the court-yard and flood of student bodies moving along the many paths. He was alone. His stance was relaxed, yet dramatic, as though he was echoing the mood of the sky, a complex structure of cumulous clouds with diffuse sunlight shining through to brighten random trees or a stretch of landscape. It was a flickering atmosphere of darkness and light which changed gradually as if I was viewing a motion picture. I saw the masculinity, despite the shoulder-length black hair blowing backward from a light breeze, exposing his features. He looked like a vagabond warrior. Wearing weathered black jeans, leather boots, a white linen shirt half-buttoned, he stood, arms hanging at his sides. One hand held a book, his fingers tapping the cover. I imagined to the rhythm of music inside his head. A solemn song. He could have been a prince overlooking his kingdom.

I had looked away momentarily, distracted by someone's food tray crashing to the floor and causing laughter. When I turned back, he was gone. Weeks passed before I thought I saw him again. It was at a fraternity party, following a football game. Gwen and I had strategically (my doing) hooked up with two brothers of the ATX house, from which two of my attackers belonged. They invited us to an after-game party. The courtyard had live music from a local rock band and beer kegs, which we were hovered around, filling our cups. While scanning the crowd of drunk and stoned dancers, I thought I saw the boy I'd observed at the Fishbowl or some facsimile of him. His sister, maybe. Possibly his twin. It had to be. Because their faces were so similar, except for the lipstick, eye shadow, golden earrings. There was not a trace of masculinity in this slender, well-toned body, only feminine features, and curves, wearing a sapphire dress.

What I was seeing was so disturbing, with my constant double-takes, it caught Gwen's attention.

"What?"

"Nothing," I told her.

"Something. Tell me," she demanded.

I tipped my head. "See that girl?"

"Specifics. There's lots of them, Roomy-Tuesday."

"In the blue dress. Dancing."

"I see her," said Gwen. "So?"

"Notice anything strange?"

"That she's prettier than me? Can dance better. No."

"Forget it."

Gwen pulled me back. "Secrets, uh-uh. You must divulge."

With the loud music, I had to lean close, a hand cupped, trying to whisper but shouting. "I saw her two weeks ago. As a *boy*."

I had Gwen's total interest now. Then uncertainty.

"Bullshit."

"I'm serious."

"Seriously hallucinatory. It's from blowing in the weed. That's the answer, my friend," she joked, referencing her idol Dylan.

Our dates had begun to pull us with drunken vigor to the dance floor. Toward this girl, or boy. My confusion over what I had seen, or had not, was making me light-headed. I imagined being tugged into a circle of hell. My date, whose face sported unshaven bristles, was grinning, resembling a satyr.

"I'm not that stoned," I shouted to Gwen, attempting to talk over the noise. Our dates yanked us apart as we danced. I disliked being twirled so much. When the song ended my head was spinning. I told my date I needed a place to sit or lie down.

He took that as a signal I wanted to get laid. Gwen continued dancing, eyeing me as I departed. All the chairs and couches were occupied with bodies, so he suggested we chill out in his frat room upstairs, which had a sofa. I desperately needed to rest my head and thought nothing overly suspicious about his offer, considering the swarm of people moving up and down the stairs and in and out of all the rooms. I hadn't noticed he locked the door after we entered. I immediately collapsed on the nearest piece of furniture, the sofa, the one thing he hadn't lied about. I closed my eyes, still dizzy.

The bounce of his body sitting next to mine signaled a minor ripple of alarm as to what would come next. I felt his hand stroke my hair, softly at first, as though he cared about my feelings. His hand then drifted to my neck, rubbing my shoulder, brushing my cheek next. I felt his other hand tentatively touch one of my breasts. I felt woozy but wasn't averse to the idea of his hands massaging me. It felt good. It was calming me and had stirred erotic notions. It's not like I wasn't expecting a kiss. My eyes stayed closed. I didn't resist. I recalled his face, which wasn't all that bad, making me think of an energetic golden retriever, panting, eager to please.

While one hand kept caressing my neck and jaw, his other hand departed from my breasts. All these sensations got scrambled in the midst of drunken passion. I was anticipating his hand to travel up my sweater. But when it locked on my crotch I bolted. Except that he pushed me back down into the sofa and, with his other hand, he gripped my throat.

"*Hey*," he demanded as if firmly controlling a skittish mare on the farm where he told me he had been raised. "Relax–*relax*."

He tried to kiss me again but I turned my head away and made another effort to free myself. A mistake, he conveyed to me by using a stranglehold with his thumb and fingers pressed into my trachea. "Hold still. Come *on*. It's all good. I have protection. Okay?"

He had single-handedly unbuttoned my pants, had leveraged his hand down my panties, and was busy worming his fingers against my clitoris. Fighting tears and an urge to scream, I didn't know what to do or what kind of psychopath he might be. I could hear the noise of people outside the door, moving down the hall, along with the band bellowing from the courtyard. I doubted anyone would hear me or acknowledge my cries for help.

As if reading my mind, his hand covered my mouth and began shoving me down upon the sofa, onto my back. His other hand and fingers wedged inside me. I felt like a fish he'd hooked, fighting to return to the sea, the full weight and muscle of him lodged against my efforts to resist him.

He told me this, in a very calm but threatening tone, as though he had done this before: "If you scream I will hurt you. *Really* bad. You don't want me to do that. Now, slide off your pants."

I did what I was told and hated myself. It wasn't easy. With both his hands remaining where they were, one over my mouth and his other squeezing the cusp of my genitalia. Somehow I managed to kick off both shoes, then push off my pants, twisting out of them. Prior to the worst and most humiliating act of all. I did nothing, staying silent when he removed his hand from my mouth and placed a finger to his lips. Never taking his eyes off me, he removed his other hand from inside me, unbuckled his pants and pulled them down with his boxers. I considered screaming, kicking him in the balls, scratching, biting, running for my life. This flurry of options stormed through my mind. But I did none of these things. My fierce resolve had been broken. Again. I lay on my back in fear and abject defeat.

True to his word he removed from his shirt pocket a thin pouch which he ripped open with his teeth. It contained a prophylactic. He rolled it over his erect penis. Then, to demonstrate how stiff and primed it was, he cocked and released it to spring back and forth, meant to amuse me, prior to shoving it inside me. Repeatedly. And I lay there, taking it, staring at the posters pinned to his wall – Green Day, The Clash, Sex Pistols, Rancid, Red Hot Chili Peppers, Dead Kennedys, System of a Down – as I plotted my revenge.

When he got off me, he stood, looked pleased with himself. "There. Felt fucking awesome, yeah?"

— 〜 —

"What are you going to do?"

Shaking with rage and shame, I looked at Gwen.

"*Tell* the police," said Gwen. "You have to report this."

"Tell them what? It's his word against mine."

"You can't let him get away with it, Mira!"

My head was throbbing, imploding, close to being snuffed out. I felt disconnected from my trembling body, the victim of a home invasion. My sacred temple had been trashed again. It left me feeling as if it was no longer entirely mine. I refused to cry. "He won't."

"What are you going to do?" pressed Gwen.

We were back inside the walls of Gamma Phi, on my bed, yet nowhere felt safe or structurally sound. "For one, I will never get wasted again at some *stupid* party. And lose my advantage. The next time I *date* that pick, Rick, that's his name, I will be as focused as a laser beam."

"The *next* time? Are you mad?"

"Extremely. Seriously mad. And he won't see it coming."

"See what?" Gwen stood, agitated like I'd never seen her before, then sat down beside me. "Jeezzus, Mira. Who *are* you? I mean, besides being *Clara*."

"Clara's dead. I told you."

"Right, except she attends classes and receives grades."

"That's not me."

"Really? Then tell me who you are."

So I told her. About being raped at age twelve. About my two attackers, two of my three rapists who were attending the college, who I had purposely followed to this location to get revenge.

"Three of *four* rapists now," Gwen corrected me. "So far your vigilante plan has *really* worked out great, Mira. Sorry. I want to

318

help. Tell me."

"Rick, that shit, is no different than the rest. A self-absorbed jock who thinks he's entitled to rape women. Thinks he's invincible. Because, why? He's a fucking hot shot on the basketball court."

"I know his type. So?"

"His *frat* brother who lives in the same house, known as Roger-Dodger, was my first rapist."

"Holy shit, the football star? He's going to be drafted into the NFL. He stands to make millions."

"He won't. He'll be going to prison."

Gwen was intrigued, but made uneasy, squirming on the side of the bed, rubbing her legs. "Why? How?"

"I could seriously use your help."

"Sure. Okay."

"This isn't your fight."

"The *fuck* it isn't." Gwen tentatively raised her hand, touched the scar beneath my left eye. I allowed her, but it made me flinch. The slight disfigurement was only noticeable if I didn't conceal it with foundation and makeup.

"Yes," I confessed. "They cut me after they fucked me."

"Jeez. I never understood why you covered it up."

I explained to her, "When they knew me in high school I didn't look like this. I had acne, braces, wore glasses. And I was fat. They did that to me, Gwen, and made me what I am. This scar is the only reminder to them of who I was."

"I get it." Gwen looked past me at the wall. "When I was a kid I had this babysitter. She was in high school with my brothers."

"You have two, right?"

"Yeah. One was the same age as her. And I thought she was the raddest thing. Really bad-ass beautiful. Funny-sweet and smart. I said I wanted to be like her. They laughed, saying, '*No*, I didn't.'"

"Your brothers?"

"Yeah, and it pissed me off. She was voted sophomore princess. She was cool. I thought her boyfriend was too. He was in a club my brothers wanted to be asked to join. He was a senior, and they knew about him, and told me, 'Seriously, you *don't.*' But they refused to explain why."

I watched as Gwen twirled her nose ring, then stopped, looking directly at me. "Her boyfriend was a total shit. Treated her like he owned her. When she wanted out, breaking up with him, he beat her. Knocking her up before knocking out her teeth. Last I heard she lives on child support, raising this kid, with a restraining order against the bastard dad, a not-so-popular barfly, fat and bald. So, yeah, I refuse to let a scumbag ruin my life. *Or* yours. I won't. Okay?"

"Okay." I told her what I'd learned about their fraternity. Aside from being known for recruiting athletes, ATX was known to deal drugs, specifically cocaine. Which was no secret to any student who wanted to obtain the drug. The main distributor was someone inside their house. "We need to find out *where* the drugs are being kept."

Both Gwen and I were recreational users of this white powder, as were others in the Gamma Phi sorority. It was a key bond between our two houses. The use of drugs and a reputation to party. I was watching Gwen's reaction. I told her, "It's the reason I joined this sorority."

"Not because of me?" Gwen smiled, then turned serious. "So, is there a plan? I mean, what happens when we discover this stash of cocaine, and identify who's the kingpin?"

"It's Rick-the-Prick Brandt."

"No. Are you sure? I've never seen him sell."

"He wouldn't. He has others doing it for him. It's the reason I'd initiated our double-date."

"Wait, *they* asked us."

"They thought so too. That putty in their head, the grey matter, shut off when I dangled sex before their eyes. Higher reasoning goes straight to the brain between their legs, much easier to manipulate."

"You got *raped*, Mira," restated Gwen.

"I got stupid," I countered. "I made a mistake. By drinking too much and getting stoned, I lost my advantage. Never again."

"I'll help you," said Gwen. "But that doesn't mean I'm going to go all-out *sober*. Join a twelve-step. Or give up sex."

"I wouldn't ask you to." And I meant it, every word I told her. "Sex is both our weapon of pleasure and choice. We're out-gunned otherwise. How else do we compete with their muscle and might? We use our *minds*, and our—"

"Gamma Pies."

We laughed. "Gwen, you know I don't hate men."

"Yeah, but these guys deserve to get fucked. Go ahead, tell me about your plan. Elaborate."

"It could get ugly."

"Ugly how?"

"We have to become their friends. We do what needs to be done for them to trust us."

I could tell Gwen was contemplating the negatives, reassessing her commitment to help. "Mira, people go crazy apeshit when you mess with their drugs. Cocaine especially. When money's involved. Stealing. Shit. People *die*. How far do you plan to take this?"

"Whatever it takes to incriminate Roger-Dodger and his pals, Brad, and Rick. Even suck their cocks. I want them humiliated and sent off to prison. That's how far I'm willing to take this. Are you?"

Gwen braved a smile. "Blow them away? Sure."

So lost in my desire for vengeance and the righteous certainty of my cause, I was sacrificing more than I realized.

"No one is going to die," I added, to reassure Gwen. "They just need to suffer. To pay for what they did to me and others."

"Jeez," said Gwen. "You're scary serious about this."

"I am. My degree in psychology will launch me into the field of criminology. And once I gain access to the prison system, I will make their lives – caged like the feral animals they are – a living hell."

"How long have you been planning this?"

"Since the day I was raped."

— ⇒ —

Egon is mixing himself a drink. The celebratory sparkling wine has been replaced by hard liquor. I imagine the Titanic, the Zeppelin, the Twin Towers. I can't avert my thoughts from envisioning icebergs becoming visible, hydrogen igniting, planes bursting into highrises. A disaster, that's what I'm trying to avoid.

But I swore I would tell the truth, despite the consequences. The truth could destroy the delicate bond I've created. I want our lives to be good together. Especially after "psychoanalyzing the shit out of him," as he jokingly describes the nature of my work.

I owe him that much. Knowing the truth about me. We all need to hear the truth about each other before we die.

— ⇒ —

One day while seated by the window inside the Fishbowl, I saw something extraordinary. In retrospect, it could have been a miracle. If I believed in such things. Or the supernatural. But I don't.

I happened to look up from my book and saw one of my targets, Rick-the-Prick, initiate a fight. It was with the strange boy who had a twin sister. He was walking along the upper plaza when Rick, for no apparent reason, yanked his long hair.

The boy, whom I'd decided to name *Sasha* (of Russian origin, which meant defender), spun around to face Rick. I couldn't hear through the glass what words were exchanged, but it ignited a brawl. Rick grabbed Sasha who removed the hand with an evasive twist. Rick swung at Sasha who deflected the punch with an upward flick of his arm to the wrist. He moved away, raising his hands, a signal for Rick to back off and leave him alone. A crowd had formed. With Rick's prowess called into question, my rapist was not about to let this go unfinished. He lunged for Sasha. This time, Rick was flipped. He landed on his back, still conscious, but stunned.

I was in awe and intrigued. Sasha was not much bigger than me, yet he took down this giant, my fucking rapist! Unbeknownst to him, Sasha had become my hero. I desperately wanted to know how he had accomplished this feat. But, by the time I'd gathered up my books and went outside, this boy was walking away. I lost sight of him between the Lokey Science Complex and Cascade Hall.

— ❦ —

Egon laughs and says, "*Sasha?*" He shakes his head and upturns his glass filled with vodka and soda, taking a gulp.

I understand his amusement of my name selection. "I had to call him something." I pour myself a glass of wine and continue.

— ❦ —

The David and Goliath episode circulated the college. At the campus gym, I inquired about classes taught on self-defense. That's where I met an instructor who was older and shorter than me but built like a tank.

"From what you're describing, it sounds to me like a combat form of Krav Maga."

"What's that?" I asked.

"A tactical martial arts developed in Israel. Noncompetitive, essentially a technique for self-defense. And maybe a mix of Aikido, Japanese-based, used to redirect the force of the attacker rather than opposing it head-on."

"Noncombative?"

"Essentially. You only harm when you need to."

"Okay," I said. "And if I needed to? How does it work?"

"Very effectively, Miss."

"Does it take long to learn?"

"Years."

"I don't have *years*. How soon can I start?"

He laughed. "You're eager. I like that. Seven. Tonight. And be prepared to sweat and tolerate my abuse."

"As long as I get to hit you back," I said, smiling.

"You're welcome to try."

He winked at me. Not flirtatiously. But as my future mentor, who would teach me to become what I needed to be.

— ☰ —

I talked Gwen into joining me. She scowled, hating the idea, then began to love it once she became fit. We pounded leather pads held by men, our punches aimed at the jaw or neck. We practiced for hours kicking the shit out of bags held to protect the delicate spot between the legs. Working with bags allowed us to strike with full force and not hurt our joints. Body momentum, not body power, was used to deliver bursts of impact. The hips turned, not the torso. For maximum effectiveness, we were taught to combine hand and foot blows. Also, this: never stop until a threat is neutralized, disarmed, knocked out, or *dead*.

We were taught a hybrid combat version of Krav Maga, with several Aikido spinning throws and disabling pins mixed in for fun. I decided we needed to test our skills. We went to bars downtown, not the nice kind, and faked getting drunk, using our bodies as bait for any loser to hit on and try some ugly aggression. But nothing ever happened. We'd walk back to the Gamma Phi house pissed off that no one wanted to attack us.

There had been reported incidences of a stalker on campus who would molest girls late at night. Gwen and I decided we would try working solo. One of us watching from afar while the other strolled beneath the misty street lamps. We figured no man was desperate enough to pounce on us during a rainstorm, so we waited for ideal conditions, for the fog or mist. And, still, nobody tried to rape us. Kicking leather bags had become boring. Then, *finally*, someone stepped up to the plate. A man sprung out from behind bushes and startled Gwen. He spread his coat, exposing his naked body. A way-too-easy target. But Gwen enjoyed delivering a swift kick to his ball bearings and extended rod. He collapsed to his knees. Next, Gwen body-chopped his neck and he dropped further. She forced him to lay flat on the pavement, face down.

"Fuck *that*," she told him, and pressed her foot onto his butt, showing off, for my benefit. We ran back to the Gamma Phi house screaming with laughter. So elated by our first successful mission, our adrenaline so pumped, we woke up several sorority sisters while running into the house with shouts of victory.

— ≈ —

The day was unusually warm, one of those blustery afternoons in late autumn, leaves swirling in the air, signaling winter was near and snow to be falling soon. I was taking advantage of the weather, wearing black, skin-tight gym pants that stopped below the knees, spongy sandals, and a pink halter top exposing my naked stomach. It was time to step up the game. I was prepared to be the extrovert, the alpha girl, and walked with an insouciant strut of confidence into the lecture hall.

For months, I'd avoided the ATX house and the frat brothers. Some of them were also taking Abnormal Psychology. Which seemed fitting, being what they were. Misfits possessed by deviant spirits or just fuck-ups harboring maladjusted minds. It felt like I was walking through a snake pit. I maneuvered through and took an unoccupied seat amidst Rick-the-Prick and Roger-Dodger. Their heads turned to look up at me, then down at me as I sat.

"Hey," I said with flat emotion.

"Look at you," said Rick. "And I thought you hated me."

"What is there to hate?" I said back.

"So you like us," said Roger.

I returned a slight smile. "What's there to like?"

"Ah, then it must be *love*." Rick grinned.

The others around him thought this funny.

I smiled and played along.

"Is that what you're calling it, Rick? What we did? Wow, no wonder you've signed up for this course. You *are* delusional."

This got a couple of laughs. A sign of respect.

"Don't be a stranger." Roger had on his sunglasses. "Hey, we're having a party tonight. You should come."

"You're *always* having parties," I said.

"Yeah, true, but not like ... with a *theme*, you know?"

This from Brad, I realized, coming from behind me. "No, I don't know. You mean a costume party?"

Rick-the-Prick pulled out a flyer from his binder to show me the artwork, which read: THE DEATH OF SUMMER. Party scene images, a grotesque illustration of Dracula, The Bride of Frankenstein, other creatures, half-naked, wearing swim suits in the dark, in the rain.

"Cute," I said. "Oregon doesn't do summer."

"Everyone has to come in beachwear. That's the theme."

"Can I wear a coat? It might get cold."

"Optional," said Rick. "But it's gonna be *hot* inside."

"It's the whole idea," said Brad. "You know?"

No, but I knew the ATX house was known for lots of things, including weird parties. Exclusive scenes. Mountains of coke. Pole dancing women. Girls offering their gullets and grips in exchange for snorts of cocaine. So I had to think about how I should handle this *invite*. Screw it, I thought. Swim with the sharks.

"I suppose you'll want to fuck me."

My bluntness, like some invisible jolt, got Rick's head to jerk backward. He recovered with a grin. "No disrespect, Mira. But like, I *did* you already."

"You *did* me? Really?"

"No offense," he added.

"None taken. You can't keep raising your flag. Or it's sure to end up at half-mast someday. I totally get it. Save your mojo."

"Fuck you," he told me.

"I was joking, asshole."

"Yeah, well, so the hell was I."

As the lights began to dim, I asked, "Does that mean I'm still invited to your beach party?"

"Whatever. Bring your friend, what's her name."

"Gwen?"

"That's the one, yeah."

"So you can *do* her too? She'll be flattered, I'm sure."

Rick turned his head, amused by my raw humor as if to tell me without the effort of words that I was okay. But I wasn't.

— ≋ —

"Dissociative identity disorder," I said, telling Gwen about the lecture I'd attended. "It's this fascinating psychological abnormality. Previously known as multiple personality disorder."

"You *sat* with those animals?" Gwen couldn't believe it.

"They didn't bite or attack me."

"Because they're *out* of their habitat."

"They invited us to a party."

"*In* their habitat. Swimsuits! Seriously? We're going?"

Gwen had put on muscle. I could see it in her shoulders, arms, legs and buttocks as she moved about our room, taking off one item of clothing in exchange for another. We were never shy about being naked in each other's presence, as with real sisters, I assumed since I was an only child. Gwen grew up around brothers. When I first met her she presented this image of one who was tough, but she wasn't really. Although now she *could* actually punch out someone's lights. I too had acquired this ability, in theory. Neither of us had put it to a real test.

During our first year at college, we'd heard stories about girls raped under the guise of drunken consent. But no one ever filed a complaint. It was a pattern of misbehavior that persisted, pandemic within *one* fraternity. The ATX house. Rick's words kept resonating inside my head:

It's all good. I have protection.

I finally grasped the meaning and true intent. Aside from the obvious, preventing pregnancy, it also meant there would be no incriminating evidence to be used against the rapist. No effective way to prosecute. Always *his* word versus *her* word.

So Gwen and I strategized how we could poke a hole in their bubble-tight prophylactic system. We would collect specimens from each frat brother to refrigerate, categorize, and distribute as forensic evidence, donated to a victim when needed, to incriminate the rapist. Granted, it was a simple plan. But one that could work.

"I think we're ready," I told Gwen.

She glanced at me with a face of twisted smiles and concerns, pulling up the bottom half of a bikini. "Girls Gone Wild? I've seen the videos. It has no *fucking* plot. And no good ending."

"But no one dies," I said. "You look great. Nice body."

"Those guys don't deserve to see my tits."

"So *wear* the top."

She laughed and flipped me off.

I was having doubts myself about this invitation. Being dressed, or undressed, as we were. Second thoughts about going.

Gwen articulated our concern. "Don't you think we're offering ourselves up too easily, showing our willingness to partake in their perverted sacrificial ceremony?"

I joked, "Thank *God* we aren't virgins." My nervous attempt at humor was to defuse the tension.

"Oh, I doubt they *care*," said Gwen.

"They'll be wearing swim suits too."

Gwen sniffed. "That means, '*what*, I can relax?'"

"I know where Rick's room is. And I've had time to study their house. As long as you keep distracting Rick—"

"The Prick."

"I'll sneak in, collect things, and hopefully locate where he hides his stash of drugs."

"In the middle of a party?" Gwen fastened her top.

"Everyone'll be drunk and stoned, which is how we'll be acting. No one is going to suspect us."

"*I* suspect you."

"I'll come off as another dumb party doll. And besides, Rick will be zoned-out and zeroed-in on you."

"Cause he aims to *fuck* me. Gee, did I mention 'thanks a lot' for setting me up on this date?"

"Gwen, the place will be packed. Stay where you'll be seen and you'll be fine."

I picked up my beach purse, a sizable canvas bag with zippered compartments.

Gwen picked up hers, saying, "We're kleptos. Okay, so remind me what we're collecting?"

"Any items that our targets touch."

"Fingerprints. Got it."

"A cup. A glass. Even a roach."

"*Seminal* fluid. No, wait, you have *that* covered."

Her words gave me a shiver, reviving the memory of being raped by Rick and feeling as disposable as the used rubber he had tossed in a trash bucket.

Gwen wrinkled her nose. "I can't believe you thought to collect his sperm as a souvenir."

"My instincts kicked in. What can I say?"

"Instinct?"

"Ingrained from taking criminology classes."

"Super gross, but smart thinking. I'm impressed, I think."

I chewed my lower lip, half in a smile, half worry. "Gwen, you don't have to go along with me on this."

"The *fuck* I don't. Rick and his fuck buddies? I want to screw them like they screwed you."

I was tempted to hug her but resisted. I was hardening my mind for the task: us being vigilantes, partners in crime. What the hell, I thought, and blew her a kiss.

Gwen comically ducked to avoid it, then mocked a sultry stance, as if posing for a fashion magazine. "I am *so* looking forward to this party! *Excited*. You?"

— ☰ —

It was getting dark and we were moving with a trail of others, mostly girls, toward the ATX house. On the porch were two frats seated in taller-than-average red chairs, the kind lifeguards use at a public pool. Both guys were dressed in bright red swim shorts, black flipflops and nothing else but gooseflesh, since the balmy night was turning brisk. They were not there to save anyone, only to check for cell phones. I was glad I had the foresight to purchase cheap beach towels to drape around our bodies for warmth, and stay in costume. I was also glad I'd noticed a warning stating in bold type along the bottom of the flyer Rick had flashed in my face: 'Absolutely NO Cell Phones!' In bold red text. So Gwen and I were prepared and didn't whine like many of the girls who were being forced to forfeit their mobile devices.

"But—*why!?*"

Three girls before us were complaining and holding up the line. They were refusing to write their names on an envelope and drop their phones into a barrel.

The leg of one lifeguard blocked the doorway with his sandaled foot flat against the door jamb "No photos. No videos. No texting. No worries, eh? What happens at ATX, stays in—

"This isn't Vegas, *Richard*."

"Sarah, *lose* your phone or leave. Or come back later with a better attitude. Minus your cell. That's our rule, sister."

The three Zetas, whom I recognized, scribbled their names and scornfully dropped their sealed phones into the barrel.

"You," said one of the guards to me. "What's in the bag?"

"Cosmetics," We both spread open our bags.

"Mighty large bags for tubes of lipstick and pencils."

"It's a *beach* bag," Gwen said flirtatiously. "And a *theme* party. Is it not, Dick ... Head? That's your name right?"

"It's *Hed*ingham."

"Dick *Hed*-ingham," she corrected. "My bad. Sorry."

He grinned nastily. "Okay. You two. Enter."

We found a closet to hide our colorful beach wraps. I neatly folded our towels and stuffed them on an upper shelf.

The music was deafening. The hallway led to the main chamber, where a DJ was spinning a throbbing dance mix with filthy hip-hop declarations of sex and rage. A few girls had shed their bikini tops and were dancing, entertaining the crowd. On a couch were several frats and soros leaning over a glass table to snort lines of cocaine.

Everyone was scantily dressed. Someone had an idea to include decorations. Surf posters lined the walls, which gave the place an artificial beach ambiance of fun-fun-fun in the sun. Maneuvering our way through the party, we saw kegs of beer but passed them to reach a station where there was hard liquor.

An open bar. All the better to get us drunk. We both got vodka sodas with a twist of lime to better manage our alcohol intake. The plan was to sip and spill off the liquor as we moved about, refilling our cups with water so we could guzzle our cocktails in the spirit of wantonly getting hammered. I kept myself vigilant for our targets. Roger was easy to spot, taller than most. He was surrounded by a throng of his fans. Wearing sunglasses in the dark, hair slicked back, he projected a confidence, aware of his good looks and popularity. As if to say he'd be hard to tackle, more likely to score.

He saw me and gave a wave. I was surprised that he would even notice me. I waved back and reminded myself to be an extrovert. A Gamma *Pie*. His smile seemed nice and it bothered me. I hated him for it. Brad was holding court on a sofa, using a razor blade to chop and slice the medicinal powder into white lines upon a table. It didn't take long for Rick-the-Prick to find us.

"*Gwen*," he said, with an emphasis on her name, then, "Mira. You both made it. Awesome." He stepped in front of us to block our path. We looked up to avoid staring at his curly black chest hairs. He was just short of seven feet tall. "You got yourself drinks. Excellent. Some smoke? Blow? You name it, it's here."

"We're good," I said. "For now."

Gwen chimed in, "We *are* determined to get wasted."

"That's the school spirit." He laughed hoarsely.

I might have failed to mention we were the Oregon *Ducks*. Our closest rivals were the Oregon State *Beavers*. It inspired misogynic rebel yells and chants from students directed back and forth during stadium games. The Ducks were playing the Beavers the following weekend. It was considered the *big* game.

"Go Ducks. Fuck the Beavers," Gwen said as a joke, which she immediately regretted.

Rick narrowed his eyes in a salacious smile. I imagined a snake sensing a mouse. His tongue even poked from his lips for a second and gave a laugh. "They will be *fucked*, for sure, next Saturday. Hey, come watch me at practice on the court tomorrow."

This was directed at Gwen, not me. He meant the basketball court. The transition from football into the basketball season overlapped. Rick was envious of Roger's greater fame at the college. Roger had the NFL swarming over him. It seemed all but certain he would be a first-draft pick. By contrast, Rick was struggling to get noticed, overshadowed by others players, and lucky if his name even made a *beep* in NBA's roving radar.

"Let me give you a tour of our house," he offered.

"You *did* already, remember?" I gave him a sour smile.

"I meant Gwen. You had Stan that night, yeah?"

As if either of us could forget. "Well, you two kids have fun," I quipped. "I'll be wandering off to find myself a partner."

"Yeah, you do that," said Rick. "We'll be fine."

Gwen gave me a parting look, a pulse of determination in her eyes: Game on. I was confident she could handle herself, as long as she stuck to our plan and kept Rick from going upstairs. Where I would be rummaging through his room. To avoid any suspicion, I went in the opposite direction of the stairs and ran into Roger, alone, which was unusual. He was strolling down the hall toward me.

"Mira," he said and stopped.

"Roger. Where's your entourage?"

He smiled. I hated him for being nice since it stirred something warm inside me. He was all muscle, from all that constant running, to avoid being tackled, and from weight lifting to take the hits. My eyes went from his bulging shoulders and swelling pecs to his six-pack of abs. I glanced down and got embarrassed. I was slow to pull my eyes away from his crotch.

"You wear those to the beach?"

He gave a self-deprecating grin, a head shake. "What beach? I never have the time. This is all I could dig up. Honestly."

Form-fitting workout shorts. Not a once of body fat to hang from the elastic waistband. The only soft bulge I could detect was his masculinity, down below. I shivered involuntarily.

"You cold?"

"What? No. Hot, actually. In here. Inside the *house*."

That slow grin of his again. "We turned the heat way up."

"Feels nice. Otherwise, we'd freeze to death." I laughed. "I was off to get another drink."

I told him this impulsively before checking to see if my cup was even close to empty. I was not handling this sudden face-to-face with my attacker well. ("*Jeezuz*, Mira," I could mentally hear Gwen hiss at me, "Pull yourself the fuck together.") I did, chastising myself, and gave a smile. "Can a girl buy a guy a drink around here?"

"It *is* free," he grinned. "But sure, why not?"

I resisted being too eager to take his proffered cup and pinched the rim with my fingertips. "A beer?"

"Yeah," he said. "Although I'm not supposed to."

"Not supposed to what?"

"Imbibe. The big game and all. Two can't hurt. I was on my way to the head, so … thanks."

Imbibe. A five-dollar word. His whole demeanor was starting to throw me off. I pointed toward the bar. "I'll meet you—"

"Right back here," he said, finishing my sentence. With a smile he turned and launched up the stairs, taking two steps at a time.

— ☡ —

I deposited his plastic beer cup into my beach bag as I moved through the dancers and the stoners to the bar. I grabbed a new cup from a stack on the table. After working the beer spigot, I went back the way I came. I saw Gwen dancing with Rick. She widened her eyes at me in a *what-the-fuck* look, seeing I was downstairs when I told her I'd be upstairs searching for the drugs. I tilted my head at the beer cup as if that would explain everything. She got pulled away by Rick who spun and twirled her. Roger was already waiting for me in the same place.

I handed him the beer. "Where's the head, again?"

"Upstairs, third door to your left." He took a sip. "Or use my room, end of the hall. Name's on the door. It has a private toilet. The privileges of seniority. I'll wait here for you."

"No," I told him. "I'll find you."

"Promise?" He toasted me as I ascended the stairs.

It *was* a promise, one I had made long ago. To *find* him, *all* of them, to make them pay for what they did to me. The fact he was being friendly and wasn't acting conceited, given his magnetism, or whatever his appeal was, had clouded my mind. I took in a breath and went straight for Rick's room, hoping no one would be inside. In case there was, I planned to excuse myself, explain my error in thinking it was the bathroom.

No one seemed to be paying much attention to the activities of others in this long hallway. People were entering and exiting rooms, one couple kissing as I passed by, another having a spat at the far end of the opposite stairs. I opened Rick's door and closed it behind me. Finding no one there. I locked the door and began my search. In a trash bin I fished around with a pencil for recently used condoms, Finding two candidates, I slipped them into a ziplock bag tagged with the letter "B" for Brandt.

I searched through his drawers but found no bundles of cocaine. I stared at the walls and ceiling. It had to be hidden somewhere easily transportable, able to be moved in a hurry.

The door handle jiggled. I froze. Then whoever it was gave up and left. Not Rick. Gwen was with Rick. But what if this someone told Rick his room was locked? *Fuck Fuck Fuck.* I scrambled to find the drugs.

I was about to give up and try later. *Later—like when? Shit, Mira!* (I chastised myself) *think like a thief, a drug dealer, a criminal!* If I was Rick, where the hell would I hide cocaine? I searched his small refrigerator. Inside a carton of ice cream, I found a frozen block of something concealed in plastic.

In my beach bag was a small knife. I used it to cut a hole in the bag. I scraped the contents, tasted it, but wasn't sure it was cocaine. I scanned the room and saw a large orange plastic circular Gatorade tub beside a pile of clothing. I snapped off the top. It was filled, not with liquid, but with hundreds of colorful packets of candy mints. That was my first impression. But they were prophylactics. I scooped several out, buried the solid brick of what I hoped to be cocaine at the bottom, then covered it over with the candy-colored condoms.

I quickly scattered Rick's jersey shorts and tank tops around and on top of the container as they'd been before. Unlocking the door, I pretended to be drunk and disoriented. I bumped (intentionally) into a girl in the hallway who looked equally wasted. "Sorry, I can't find the bathroom." She pointed and I weaved past several doors before turning, to make sure she was gone, then hurried down the stairs to the main level.

With newfound sobriety, I went in search of Gwen to update her on my progress. I found her in a room with Rick, who held a paddle, playing beer pong with his frat brothers. I discreetly pulled Gwen aside and whispered, "One down; two to go." Then left.

As I navigated through the dance floor I was stopped by Roger. He left the girl he was dancing with to sidle into my path.

"Are you avoiding me?"

"Oh, hi," I said. "No. I got lost looking for the bathroom."

"You? No way. Doesn't compute."

His comment set me on edge, into panic mode. "Why?

His lips pushed into a smile. "Because you fascinate me."

Again, I thought, "Why?"

"You just do. You remind me of someone. You're smart and ... well, pretty."

I grimaced. "Thanks. That's a compliment. Right?"

Roger laughed. It was the first time I'd seen him do it up close. "Would you consider going on a date with me sometime?"

"So you can *fuck* me?"

He scowled, jerked his head away. "Mira. Why so crude?"

"I don't *know*, Roger. This culture surrounding me—maybe. Why don't you go ask your best buddy *Rick*."

"Listen, I know all about that."

"Along with everyone else. Nice talk. Time to go."

He pulled at my arm but I shook him off.

"Mira? Forget it." He turned to leave. "Just so you know, I'd never do anything like that to you."

This stopped me cold. I wanted to shout in his face that he was a fucking liar. That he'd already raped me! My heart was pounding fast. I bit my tongue to stop myself from saying something I would regret. He actually looked sincere, as if he believed his own lies. I wanted to laugh. Or cry. Or die.

I left without responding.

Once out of his sight, I swiped at a renegade tear. Something was happening to me that I didn't like, and hadn't anticipated. I was desperate for fresh air. I pushed open a sliding door that went into the courtyard. The cold night assaulted me. It was no longer balmy. Because of the warm interior, I'd forgotten I was half naked. I felt stupid standing there, wearing a bikini in winter weather.

"Fuck!"

My shout startled shadowy activity beside a leafless tree. Within the faint light of one functioning exterior lamp, I saw a man with an erection standing over a girl on her knees.

Repulsed by this carnal fuck-fest, I went back inside. I glanced around and confirmed the inebriation factor was still in high gear. No one was paying attention to me. The communal desire for more drink and drugs and fun was my perfect camouflage. Once again I fake-staggered my way upstairs and blended in with the crowd, in search of the next room. I was aiming for the end of the hall where Roger-Dodger told me I would find his name on a door. Just then, Brad Fuller walked into the hall.

"Hey," I said, as he passed. Brad returned a stoned and drunken nod of recognition, then disappeared down the stairs.

Assuming the door he had exited was his room, I went back and walked in as if invited. Seeing no one home, I closed the door behind me. The lock was broken. Undeterred, I went straight for the trash cans. This was a room that harbored two beds. I searched to identify the desk-and-bed unit that would be Brad's. My purse had a packet of tissues. I removed one to wrap around a glass of water on his nightstand. After first dumping the remaining liquid in a withering fern, I deposited the glass into my bag.

Digging through his trash, I discovered a dried-up condom (of questionable forensic value). Yet I speared it with a pen, transferred it to a baggie marked "F" for Fuller, and felt marginally successful. I walked toward the door.

It opened and Brad walked in.

"What the hell are you doing here?"

"Nothing," I said, like an idiot. "I was looking for you."

He wasn't buying it. His eyes lowered to my beach bag.

"What'd you steal?"

"From this dump? Nothing I'd ever want."

I laughed and tried to pass him but he grabbed for the bag. He missed but caught my arm instead. When I was twelve, Brad had towered over me. But he had remained that height, and now wasn't much taller than me. What he *did* have over me was muscle. He had the strength to throw a baseball all the way from left field to home plate. He gripped my arm tighter and gave me a lewd grin.

"You said you were looking for me. Why?"

I did the only thing I could think to do at that moment. I went on my knees and pulled down his bathing suit. And it worked. His cognitive thinking shut off, relegating power to his penis, growing, stiffening, aided by my mouth working it hard.

"Wow ... okay," was all he could think to say at first.

I wasn't sure why Brad was so angry, but I knew he suffered from a short guy complex amidst his taller frat brothers. Or maybe it was because no baseball scouts were coming to watch his games with any thought of drafting him (the minor leagues his only bet). Or maybe it was failing grades. But something was eating his mind.

Something fierce and scary. Because he grabbed my hair with both hands and pulled me hard into his body. Which hurt like hell. I was unable to scream because his penis was engorged and rammed into my throat.

"Bitch! *Hard* enough for you? Suck me, you bitch! I'm gonna fuck you, bitch!"

With every "*bitch*" he used I wanted to pull away and bite down on his penis. Except he had a firm grip on my hair and controlled my head with each yank. I clawed at his arms to make him stop. But he was determined to fuck me in the mouth, as he kept saying. In point of fact, it was my head he wanted to fuck. And he did.

When his sperm exploded in my throat I gagged and fought the instinct to swallow or throw up. He let go of my hair and I scratched his neck. He pushed me away. I scrambled to get distance, snatched my beach bag, and fought to keep my wits while holding a mouthful of his sea-stench jism dripping from my lips. He pointed and laughed as I staggered to my feet and wobbled out the door.

Shaken and furious, I looked both ways to make sure the hall was clear, before spitting his sperm into a ziplock bag. I then made my way for the bathroom. I washed out my mouth under running water from a sink faucet. No one in this bathroom, male or female, seemed to think my desperate appeal for water was anything to question. When I raised my head a third time, after flushing my throat, I noticed the girl beside me. She was rubbing traces of white power off her nostrils. She checked her lipstick, adjusted her bikini top, then looked down at me.

"You okay?"

I splashed water on my cheeks. "Fine."

"What a party, huh?" She swiveled on her toes and left.

On my left a guy was peeing circles into a urinal.

I grabbed my beach bag of specimens and walked back into the hallway feeling dazed. I craved liquor to numb me. Brad had fucked my head and I wasn't thinking clearly. I went downstairs to check on Gwen. Through the loud music and swarm of dancers, I spotted her. She looked relieved to see me. I gave her a two-finger message. Two down. One left to go!

She signaled with a scrunch of her eyes for me to hurry. Behind her, I saw Brad walk in. He spread two fingers in a pseudo peace sign. And to mock me, he opened his mouth to form an "O" while sliding his hand into a girl's bikini top. She shrieked with laughter. I flipped Brad off, turned and nearly bumped into Roger. He was with a new girl who was taller than me. Her expressionless stare made me think of a model posing for a magazine cover.

"What's wrong?" This from Roger.

"Nothing," I said.

The mannequin looked down to agree I was nothing.

"I'm fine." I wondered if I'd missed washing off traces of my recent blow job.

"Not enjoying our party?" His expression emitted concern. The girl beside him stiffly turned and stared at the wall.

"No, it's great. You guys know how to throw a party."

A mild squint from him as if reading some signal I wasn't clear I was sending. He gave me that soft smile. As we parted, he told me, "Take care, Mira. I meant what I said. If only to talk. Okay? I'm not a bad guy. See you around?"

I nodded. My plan was to ruin his life. My head felt sullied and addled. I had a strong urge to get drunk, which I fought off. Roger turned and went upstairs while the tall girl remained at ground level and veered off. Too much coke? No one seemed lucid or focussed on anything but to have fun. I was envious.

I waited a few more minutes before I ventured one last time upstairs. I felt invisible as I walked down the hall as if magnetically drawn to the end. To Roger's door. Where I saw his name stamped on the wood. I stopped.

I hesitated to go inside. Half of me hoped he wasn't there, the other half wished he was. And alone. Waiting for me. To what – talk? It was stupid, I knew, but I was having second thoughts about him. Did he know who I really was? Had my senses gone haywire? Was this a kind of Stockholm Syndrome where the victim gets drawn into a desire to be loved by their abuser? Or did I have it all wrong? Had he changed and become a halfway decent guy?

At twelve, I thought he was cute, that he had feelings for me too. I now had scrambled fantasies of us falling madly in love, that he would apologize and I would forgive him, and we'd tell our children years later about the improbable story of how we met as children, during a rape, our lives reconnecting, the hate that once was defused. Subconsciously I knew this fairy tale infecting my mind was absurd. But I opened the door and believed I might find something good.

Roger's bare ass was moving back and forth between a victory sign comprised of two long thin legs spread wide into the air.

"*Out!!!*"

The model was a slut, and she had a voice, one that screamed plaintively before it turned to an angry muffled berating. I shut the door fast before Roger had time to turn and see me.

From her: "*You didn't think to lock the door!*

I retreated to the bathroom where I hid, waiting in a stall, head upon the beach bag held in my lap, as I sobbed.

I hated myself for getting derailed by sentimentality.

Roger *was* what I thought he was. A hypocrite. Someone who could charm and marry a pretty pedigreed girl, be adored by fans, make a fortune running downfield clutching a pigskin, and *screw* with impunity anyone he felt like screwing.

It reconfirmed my desire to destroy him.

I wiped my eyes and composed myself. I swung open the toilet door. I pretended to stagger and appear to be dizzy.

"*Okay.* Way too many." I laughed and went to the sink where

I splashed water on my face.

"Lightweight," a girl muttered.

I raised my head and flashed her a defiant smile. "Good to go. I'm off to party, heavyweight."

The girl looked down to reevaluate her midriff. I hung a left and went to Roger's room. I didn't' care if he was still there. If he was, I planned to react with innocent belligerence and remind him *he* was the one who had invited *me* to use his bathroom.

The room was empty. I went over to where he'd been fucking on a desk. His used condom was an easy find. I speared it from the trash and deposited it into a small baggie labeled "D" for Dossen. Mission accomplished. Now I was eager to escape undetected.

I bolted from his room but stopped quickly.

Standing before me in the hallway was the girl I'd seen wearing a blue dress at a previous party. The twin sister of *Sasha*. She wore a white bikini with a fringed bottom and top. Though small chested, her body was well toned. Black liner and eye shadow highlighted her blue eyes. Pearl-white fingernails raked back her long black hair.

"You were in Roger's room," she stated.

"I was. I needed to use the bathroom. He said I could."

"He would. He's generous that way. I'm his cousin."

"I'm Mira."

"I know who you are. Nice to finally meet you."

Then, with a benevolent look, not quite a smile, she passed me to enter Roger's room and shut the door. It was only afterward, when I was halfway down the hall, that it occurred to me she hadn't told me her name.

Once I reached ground level, I went searching for Gwen. The crowd of dancers in the main room had thinned out. The party was not quite on life support but was dying down. Only die-hards were grinding to an electronic beat. The rechargers were snorting coke at tables, a few standing, supported by walls or door frames as they talked and gazed vacantly.

Few people were mingling at the bar. Several guys had passed out in chairs. I maneuvered past a couple passionately kissing. I started to panic. I ran upstairs to Rick's room and barged in to find it empty. I was overcome by a horrid sick feeling. I looked at my bare wrist where I used to wear a watch. I had no cell phone. I had no sense of time. Only that it was late.

The downstairs was littered with remnants from the burst of energy now diminishing. There were plastic cups, beer bottles, half-eaten pieces of food, puddles of liquid, even abandoned articles of clothing – thongs and shoes. The hall closet was now mostly empty. Both our beach towels were there. Meaning that Gwen had not left. She was here. I wrapped one towel around my shoulders.

I recognized a familiar face, a Gamma Phi sister.

"Have you seen Gwen?"

She gave me a bleary-eyed headshake to indicate, "no." The lifeguard chairs at the front door were abandoned and the barrel moved inside. Stragglers were talking in the entry while others searched for cell phones. I wandered down the hall and slid open the glass door to the courtyard. The silence felt strange. Through panels of glass, I saw the DJ packing his equipment into a case. The courtyard had a concrete fountain at its center, half-filled with an assortment of sports equipment and trash.

Gwen wouldn't have left without me, and not without the beach towel. I was not looking forward to barging into all the frat rooms. About to go inside, I was stopped by a noise. A heaving whimper. It came from the bushes. I heard it again. A rustling of leaves, along with a moaning sound. Cautiously, I went over to investigate.

I saw the leg first, visible through a cluster of plants. I pushed into the small clearing and found Gwen naked on her back, sprawled in the dirt and leaves. I dropped to the ground beside her.

"*Gwen.*" There was no point in me asking, *What happened?*

because it was obvious. I *knew* she had been raped.

I touched her face. Her lips moved but only a heart-wrenching gasp came out in her effort to talk. Her right eye was swollen. Her nose was bloodied. Her nostril sliced open and her nose ring missing. I examined her body and saw no cuts or blood below her neck. But her legs were spread, arms limp at her sides. I saw the yellow top and bottom of her bikini tossed into the bushes.

"Mira."

I looked down at her.

"Where *were* you?"

Her words stung. I removed my towel and covered her body to keep her warm. Each of her words came in painful gasps.

"I'm *sorry*. Gwen, you need an ambulance."

Her fingers touched my arm. They had a feathery coldness and a weak grip, transferring a chill to my skin.

"I tried ... to fight ... get him ... off ... me."

"Rick?"

Her head rocked. She shut her eye. "He overpowered ... me."

"Don't talk." I began to rise "I need to call a—"

"*Mira*. Listen."

I fought off the urge to run for help.

"What we ... planned. You have to. He ... can't ..."

I nodded fiercely. "He won't get away with it, I promise. But you need medical help."

She held onto me and squeezed my hand.

"Make him ... *pay*. Okay?"

Her plea fired my mind with an angered determination. I knew exactly what I had to do. I reached for my beach bag. "It's all here, Gwen. I have everything."

"Have what?"

"The evidence we need. You were *gang* raped."

She shook her head. "Only Rick ... he—"

"Gwen. No, you have to tell the police you were raped by Rick, Roger, *and* Brad. I'll testify as a witness. We'll win this."

"What are you ... doing? *Mira?*"

Gwen couldn't see but felt me rubbing something between her legs. "DNA. Semen. Forensic evidence. Our stories have to match. Gwen? Do you understand what I'm saying?"

She gave a nod. I showed her one of the used condoms, before flinging it into the bushes, along with the others. I unzipped the bags with the cup and water glass, dropping them nearby.

"Gwen, repeat to me what you're going to tell the police."

"I was ... gang raped. By Rick ... Brad ... Roger."

"Exactly." I stood. Gwen looked so fragile. Her fingers were crooked, clasping the towel like the talons of a bird Her swollen face looking up at me with one eye. She was shivering.

I dropped back to my knees, almost forgetting more evidence I could plant. I lifted Gwen's hand and scraped her black fingernails beneath my blood red nails to transfer Brad's skin and blood DNA. The exchange was intimate and binding, more than I realized.

"I'm coming right back."

I ran with tears streaming like blood from my eyes, seeing red. It was the dead of night. I raced out the gate and crossed the street to bang on the Theta Chi Omega house. When the lights came on and the house mother answered the door, I screamed, "Call 911! We need an ambulance! Call the police!"

— ≋ —

I stood in the street and heard the sirens first, then saw the red flashing lights. I waved my arms and directed them to me. The police and ambulance arrived almost at once. The nearby houses began to light up, including the ATX house. I led the police to Gwen. With my rudimentary knowledge in criminology, I very calmly yet forcefully told the officer in charge to tape off the area. This was a crime scene. The man blinked at me incredulously, at this girl in a bikini ordering him about.

"Now hold on! We'll—"

"No! You listen. My friend was assaulted and raped! During a party at *this* frat house. There could be evidence of the crime. Seal off the area before it gets destroyed or *removed* by somebody. God-damn-it, I'm serious!"

The officer could see I was, his hand on his gun. As more police cars arrived on the scene, along with a crowd gathering, he signaled to have everyone moved back, away from the area. I was right there, on his heels, following his every move. I could tell he wanted to swat me away like an annoying mosquito.

As two paramedics were examining Gwen, I asked the police officer, "What about the crime tape?"

"Back off and let me do my job, for Christ sake," he said. "First, identify yourself. Who are—"

"My name is Mira. Friend of the victim. I witnessed the assault and saw her attackers before they fled. I called 911."

"You're a student at the university?"

"Yes, I am. And I'm majoring in criminal psychology."

The officer, a dark and brooding sort, sucked in his cheeks as he thought. Both of us were watching Gwen being placed on a gurney. "Listen, Miss, I appreciate—"

"Have you called for an investigative unit?"

This officer in charge had picked up his radio. "What?"

"A *forensic* team. To collect the forensic evidence. DNA. This is the only chance you'll have to collect it. It's what I've been taught." I paused to show deference. "Before it's *contaminated*."

He was stopped by the use of my word "contaminated." It sent a prickle of concern to his brain: perhaps imagining the ramifications of a botched job, and questions he'd be forced to answer at a trial.

I followed with, "It's standard protocol. For a crime like this. Assault and rape. What should I call you? Officer … ?"

He blinked at my forwardness. "Rifkin. Officer Rifkin. And for your information, Miss—

"Mira Skyles."

"I was just about to *call* it in." Prior to doing that, he shouted, "Stivers! Tape off this entire area! Do it now!"

I stepped away to let Officer Riften do his job, pleased with my efforts to control the situation, then I shifted back to Gwen moving past me on the gurney. My laser-focus energy scattered momentarily. She was pale and showed no sign of life.

"How bad is she?"

"We've sedated her. To keep her stable."

"Where are you taking her?" I was following in their wake to the ambulance doors.

"Sacred Heart Medical. Did you want to come along?"

I let go of her hand. "I can't. I'm needed here. Gwen. I'll be there soon. I promise!"

The doors closed on me. The paramedics pulled away. I stood watching it leave in the middle of the street. The flashing lights faded into the dark cold morning mist.

I shivered and hugged my shoulders, then went back to locate Officer Rifkin. Standing among the crowd of ATX frats were Roger and Brad. Rick was there too. He watched with intense interest as I reentered the taped-off area.

— ≋ —

The investigative unit arrived while I was talking with Officer Rifkin. He asked me about the party, Gwen's assault, her assailants. My involvement. What exactly I'd seen. What I saw at that moment was an officer grabbing my beach bag. I started to panic.

Officer Rifkin noticed my reaction and looked over his shoulder at the officer. "Burt, for God's sake, don't touch anything. Leave it for forensics to collect."

It was Gwen's bag, I realized. Mine was beside me. "We each

brought beach bags."

Officer Rifkin looked at me, then at the bag I picked up.

"It was a theme party. Like I'd mentioned. It's the reason I'm in a swimsuit and *freezing*." I spread open the handles of the bag to show there was nothing much to see. "For our makeup. That was Gwen's bag." I rubbed my shoulder. "I'm really, *really* cold. Can we do this after I've changed into warm clothes? I live in the Gamma Phi house right up the street."

For a second, I thought Rifkin was going to offer me his coat, perhaps confused by what to do with this girl standing beside him in the cold night and wearing only underwear. Shivering again, my eyes widened with a pleading kitten's irresistible desire to be loved.

"All right, go," he said. "Put something warm on. Then come right back. I have more questions to ask you."

"Absolutely, officer, thank you," I shivered and wasn't faking it. I was damned cold. The adrenaline that had been keeping me numb from the shock was not working anymore. I made my way through the police and crowd of watchers assembling on the street. I moved fast, wanting to run, but held back. I was someone escaping with a satchel of incriminating evidence. Evidence I needed to destroy.

The sirens had stirred up activity on the campus. As I entered the sanctity of my sorority house, I was accosted by questions from my curious sisters. They'd been standing on the porch and looking toward the commotion coming from the ATX fraternity.

"Gwen was raped," I said. "And I *saw* who did it." I ran up the stairs. I locked myself in a bathroom stall. I opened my beach bag and flushed the plastic bags down the toilet.

As I exited, several girls asked at once, "Is she okay?"

"*No*. Gwen was beaten really bad. The police want me to come right back. I need to change."

I broke from the group hug to go down the hall to my bedroom. As I put on clothing I was crying, the shock hitting me again. I stuck my head through the holes of a t-shirt and sweater, then grabbed my leather coat. On my way out the door, I pulled tissues from a box on my nightstand. I blew my nose and thanked my sorority sisters, who were offering support.

— ≋ —

"Let her through," said Rifkin, waving me in.

The ICU detectives had set up floodlights, illuminating the area where I'd found Gwen. I saw them searching the leaves and bushes. A condom was being bagged. My eyes scanned the periphery to see half the crowd of frats still in attendance, watching the proceedings, Roger, Brad and Rick among them. A threatening glare from Rick. Which was meant to—*what?* Intimidate me? I glared back to let him know that I knew *he* was the one who'd raped Gwen.

"I need to go over a few things," said Rifkin, notebook in hand, leading me away from the bright lights. "You said you thought you caught a glimpse of who did this to your friend?"

"No," I told him. "I *know,* for a fact, who raped her."

Rifkin was prepared to write down names.

"I'd prefer if ... I'm afraid to say who, right here."

Rifkin glanced over at the frats behind us.

"I need to see Gwen. She needs me. *Please.* I have a car. I can meet you at the hospital. I'll tell you everything there."

"I'm not sure that's a good idea," he stated, slapping shut his notebook and sliding it inside his coat pocket.

"What do you mean?" Panic rippled through me.

"If it's safe or not. Under the circumstances."

"Not safe, how?"

He lifted his chin, to indicate the crowd in the courtyard. "For you to be driving there alone. If you get my meaning."

I did. Rick's eyes were riveted on me like a wildcat.

— ≋ —

Egon's eyes are watching me too. Not like a wildcat, but with a cat's attentive curiosity. He rattles the ice in his glass.

"That's, wow, a hell of a story. I had no idea, Mira. I mean, what you went through. Horrible."

He has no idea the extent of it. Yet.

He gives me a sad encouraging smile. "I'm sorry. I want to hear it all. But I may need to make myself another drink first."

I may need one too.

— ☞ —

Officer Rifkin opened the squad door to let me ride up front with him. I was relieved not to be caged behind him in the back seat like a suspect. We said little on the short drive behind the campus to Sacred Heart Medical Center. I was wondering about his generosity. Was it police strategy? To allow me to stew in my own silent juices, to simmer until I reached a boiling point and everything bubbled out of me at once.

"Gwen was my closest friend," I said.

"Is," he corrected me.

I looked over at him, tears welling up again. I wiped my eyes with the tissues I'd brought. "*Is.*"

"Stay positive, Mira. We're almost there."

He called me by my name. That was a good sign, I thought. God—what was I thinking? I had broken the law. I was riding in a police car. A criminal myself. Yet my motives were justifiable, I told myself, determined to punish these monsters. Each guilty of rape. What I was doing was right. Even if *technically* wrong.

I sensed I was falling into the trap of over-thinking my actions. Officer Rifkin was right. Stay positive.

"You're awfully quiet."

"Sorry. I'm in shock. I guess."

"Completely understandable. Here we are."

He pulled right into the front of the emergency building like he owned the place. I opened the door and ran through the electronic sliding glass doors, which opened as if they'd been waiting for me. A receptionist looked up from her computer.

I almost yelled, "The girl assaulted at the university. She was brought here by ambulance. Where is she?"

"Her name?" The woman looked past me.

Officer Rifkin came up from behind me. Gwen's name would mean nothing. Unidentifiable, arriving naked, except for a towel.

"She had no clothing," Rifkin explained.

"The Jane Doe. Are you a relative?"

"I'm her sister. You have to let me see her. Now!"

"Sorority sister," Rifkin corrected, with a nod. "It's all right. We would like to see her."

"She just came out of surgery," said the woman.

I stifled a scream. "Surgery? How bad is she?"

"The doctor will explain. She's been taken into ICU."

Officer Rifkin knew the way and led me. He held out his hand and I grabbed hold of it, grateful to be held, not sure if I could have made it down the hallway without his help.

I could barely recognize Gwen with all the tubes and wires and monitors attached to her arms and mouth. Her face was bruised and swollen. One eye was completely shut, her eyelid a purple egg. Her sliced nostril was stitched. A choked wail escaped from my lungs, a surreal sound, accompanied by the life support monitors hiccupping their robotic chorus.

"Gwen, it's me. I'm here. *Gwen.*"

"She's sedated," came a voice. The doctor. A woman. That's all I remember. Except she was kind, not hopeful.

I was terrified to ask. "Is she going to be okay?"

"One lung was punctured. Five ribs were broken. And she had internal bleeding. We had to remove a kidney and her spleen."

"*Jesus.*" Someone touched my shoulder. Rifkin, knowing I was unstable, was there to steady me. "What does that mean?"

"We have to wait and see," said the doctor. "There's nothing else we can do for her right now. She might make it."

Might!?

I wanted to scream. I wanted to tell Rifkin that this was all my fault. That I led her into this house of horrors. But I fought off the urge. I collapsed into a chair.

Rifkin helped me to my feet and brought me to a waiting room, guiding me to a sofa, where I sat. My mind was throbbing with guilt and rage, I wanted to tell him everything, but I couldn't. I owed it to Gwen to finish what we'd started.

— ≈ —

"Mira," said Rifkin very softly. "This is the worst possible time to ask you this, I realize, but ... it's important. For Gwen's sake."

I looked up at him. He sat beside me on the sofa.

"I spoke to the paramedics. Before they sedated her, she told them she'd been raped. Actually, gang raped. She said three names. Rick. Brad. Roger. Do you know who she's talking about?"

"Yes. That's who I saw running away from her."

"You're absolutely certain?"

"I am. I *know* they did it. They raped her! Look what they did to her! *God!*"

"Calm down," soothed Rifkin and patted my arm. "I know. All right, then. Do you have parents I can get in touch with?"

"What? No. Not now. Please don't tell them."

Rifkin shook me gently. "Mira? They need to know. They'll want to help you through this."

I shook my head.

"What about Gwen?" pressed Rifkin. "The university has her information. But do you know her family? Who to call? A phone number would help, so we call her parents."

In the scramble to get dressed, I'd forgotten things. "I have her dad's number on my cell phone. In my room. Both our phones were left there. I can't leave here. I won't."

"I understand, Mira. I'll have someone bring your phone. Call your parents. Before the university, legally obligated to do so, does it first. Do you understand?"

I nodded. "Thank you. For everything. And please don't say it's only your job." I tried to make a smile.

He touched my shoulder. "I'll be back. I have a squad car out front. Just in case."

"In case of what?"

"You never know. In case ... you should want a ride over to the sorority house."

"For my protection, you mean?"

"Like I said, you never know. I'll be back soon."

Of course, he would be. He liked me. He also felt sorry for me. He had touched me already, several times. Appropriately. And I had information he needed. It was like we'd become partners.

Once Rifkin had left me, I sat waiting for another hour or more, until the door opened and in walked the doctor, her eyes as black as a night sky void of stars. She told me Gwen had died.

— ≈ —

I lost it, the moment I was told Gwen was dead. I knew I was responsible for leading her down this path. And there would be no eternal reward for me now *for wasting the dawn.* Why this line from a Doors' song emerged to haunt my head, I'll never know, only that I trashed the waiting room in a blind rage, breaking lamps, flinging books and overturning tables. Maybe it was because I was terrified by what I knew would be coming next.

When the news broke, it *was* dawn. A security guard had called the police, who were conveniently parked out front, stationed there, in case there was trouble. They most likely had not expected it was to come from me. Officer Rifkin was only a few minutes behind the two women officers who came into the room and calmed me down.

They cornered me so I couldn't cause more damage. I remained on the floor, unwilling to budge, with my head wedged between my knees, weeping into tissues the officers kept feeding me.

"Mira," I heard Rifkin say, crouching beside me. "It's normal to grieve. I know that. I understand. But you can't do this."

I looked into his eyes. "I just *did*."

"You know what I mean. Self-control."

I normally *was* in control. I was self-admittedly a control *freak*. But I had lost it. And I didn't care. At that moment, I felt cleansed. Then I looked around at what I'd done. I felt ashamed.

"I'm sorry. I feel horrible."

Rifkin stood and held out his hand for me to take. I took it and he pulled me to my feet. "Normally a person never experiences what you're going through. Fortunately. So who's to say. Maybe I would have reacted the same if I were in your shoes."

I looked at his big shoes, then my boots. I sat on the sofa he'd lifted and flipped back onto its four legs.

I said, "I need to tell you something. It may help. Or not."

He pulled out his notebook, resting it on his leg as he sat on a chair next to me. "Tell me, Mira."

"There were drugs."

"Where?"

"The ATX house. Where Gwen was murdered." I wiped away more tears. "Lots of cocaine. Rick Brandt, one of the guys that raped her, he's a dealer. I'm pretty sure."

Rifkin wrote nothing down in his little book, only staring back at me. "Are you involved in it?"

"What? *No*. It's common knowledge among students."

"Mira, we're aware of the drug trafficking. We've had several anonymous tips. About this fraternity."

"Why haven't you arrested anyone?"

Rifkin tapped his pen. "We've had undercover agents purchase

354

cocaine. We know a hierarchy exists. We need to know the source. Do you know who it is?"

I shook my head. "But I know something that might lead you to the source. There's a brick of cocaine hidden inside an orange sports container, buried underneath a sea of rubbers."

"A sea of rubbers, you said?"

"Condoms."

Rifkin raised his brows, shook his head, then wrote in his book. "And you know this how?"

"I placed it there."

He stopped writing and looked at me.

"We were doing our own investigation."

"Who? You and … your friend?"

"Gwen. She was keeping Rick distracted while I searched his room during the party. I found the cocaine in his freezer, inside an ice cream container. I changed locations."

Rifkin pulled out a packet of gum, offering it to me. I declined. "Is there more you're not telling me?"

"Like what?"

"You tell me. It was dangerous what you did. Foolish. It might be the reason why your friend got … assaulted."

"*Murdered.*"

"Yes."

"He's a *rapist*. He raped me. He's raped others."

Rifkin frowned. "There've been no reports filed—"

"No one ever talks," I said. "If you were a girl you'd know why that is. *His* against *her* word. If any girl speaks up and files charges she'd be an outcast on the campus. That's why."

Rifkin was working his mouth, chewing, stopping to turn the gum around with his tongue and teeth. "What about the others?"

"What do you mean?"

"The ones you saw leaving after your friend was assaulted."

"They also have a reputation for raping. Brad Fuller and Roger Dossen."

"The running back?"

"Same one."

"*Shit.*" Rifken began to chew harder.

"What?"

"The publicity. It's gonna be a *fucking* media circus. Sorry."

"It's okay. I swear all the time."

Rifkin snapped his notebook shut. "I have to warn you, Mira. It's different now, being a homicide. Unless detectives find concrete evidence, it's still going to be *your* word against *theirs.*"

"Someone else might've witnessed the rape."

"Maybe. But from what you've told me, their MO is to leave no trace behind. Meaning, it's unlikely there'll be any evidence to nail them on a rape and murder charge."

I bolted off the sofa like a frightening spring-loaded jack-in-the-box. "Jesus Christ! I saw them do it!"

Rifkin stood. "Hold on, Mira."

"No! They killed Gwen! You can't—*not* arrest them!"

"Listen," said Rifkin. "We'll start with a search warrant for that cocaine you hid. You shouldn't have. But, hell, what's done is done. One arrest. Might lead us somewhere. And there will be a coroner's examination. Forensics might find evidence."

"You need to run a blood test on me right away."

Rifkin was walking me out of the waiting room. He glanced at the mess I'd made. He squinted at me. "What for?"

"To prove I have no drugs or alcohol in my body. The findings on a toxicology report will prove I was sober when I *saw* what I saw. When I testify in court."

Rifkin mouth stopped, began chewing again more vigorously. "Criminology major, you said."

"Psychology too. My goal is a career in law enforcement."

I could tell I was winning Rifkin over. He'd fight hard for me. Possibly even bend a few rules if push came to shove?

After my blood was siphoned into a vile, Rifkin escorted me through the hospital. He paused at the sliding glass doors to let me go through first. The perfect gentleman, opening the police door for me too. Before he shut it, he gave me a look of encouragement.

"Rest assured, getting those forensic results is my top priority. Let's be hopeful, okay? Those detectives know what they're doing. They might find something useful."

"Let's hope," I said, working my grateful eyes on him.

I watched Rifkin walk around the front of the squad car. He heaved his body into the driver's seat and reached for his radio.

"I'm sorry about your friend, Mira. I truly am. Stay positive. There's a chance we might get lucky and nail these guys."

— ⋟ —

I notified my parents of the death of my roommate. They flew to Oregon the following day. The murder, a gang rape, the nefarious parties, and the disillusionment of what my parents recalled college life as being – once predicting to me that, "These will be the best years of your life, Clara"– was the reason they kept insisting that I transfer to another university. Which was never going to happen. I needed to stay where I was and get revenge.

Rick Brandt evaded arrest when he saw police cars parked in front of the ATX house. Having anticipated they had come searching for drugs, and for him, he fled in his Porsche on Highway 5, heading south. A BOLO alert for his apprehension caught the attention of an off-duty California Highway Patrol officer in Weed, who spotted his vehicle at a gas station. After calling in for backup, the CHP took a proactive stance to delay Brandt's departure and confronted him. Strung out on cocaine, Brandt sensed a threat. Feeling paranoid, he shot the plain-clothed cop. He made it three blocks before a squad car crashed into his Porsche and forced his surrender.

The warrant for his arrest had been possession of cocaine, found inside a Gatorade bucket. This warranted a more thorough search. Hidden beneath the floorboards in his room were kilos of cocaine, LSD-laced Altoid Mints, psilocybin mushrooms, and marijuana. All total, an estimated street value of half a million dollars.

The capital offense for killing a police officer overshadowed the charges against Brandt for trafficking drugs, even the alleged rape and murder of a college student.

The three students I'd accused of rape and murder were forced to submit DNA swabs and fingerprints. Rick Brandt's was sent from California where he was being held for murder. Within a few days, the computer results provided DNA matches and arrest warrants for the remaining suspects. Brad Fuller and Roger Dossen were taken from the ATX house in handcuffs.

Rifkin had been right. Since Roger was a football star, Rifkin's prediction of a media circus proved accurate. The disruption caused Roger to miss the big game against Oregon State. The Ducks lost to the Beavers. Our undefeated status ended. We lost all the remaining games, which resulted in a dismal finish in the college rankings. My name was mentioned and broadcasted on the sports channels, along with the evening news. I was not the rape victim, so it became open season on me. I was to blame. Roger Dossen, an exemplary athlete, popular on and off the field, had enormous support from those who refused to believe his guilt, despite the circumstantial evidence.

Several college girls reported accusations of rape following these arrests. Nine were filed against Rick, one accused Brad, and no one vilified Roger. Instead, many students publicly attested to his good character. Rallies took place on campus with students holding signs in support of Roger-Dodger. They clashed with the other protesters who held signs denouncing rape: NO MEANS NO. RAPE NEEDS JUSTICE. YOU RAPE, WE CHOP. BECAUSE I HAVE A VAGINA DOESN'T MEAN I AM A WHORE!

Gwen's death began my Collegiate Years of Hell.

I could no longer sit in the Fishbowl and gaze out the windows, or go anywhere with anonymity. Almost everyone had an opinion they wanted to share. Some simply glared at me. Others wrote letters or commented on the social media platforms. I was exhausted after months of being barraged by the media. I provided statements to the prosecuting attorneys, who grilled me on my timeline and memory of events. Then, finally, after a year of continuances and delays, the trial commenced. I was called to testify under oath, and I pledged to tell *"The truth, the whole truth and nothing but the truth, so help me God,"* and committed perjury.

Killing a police officer trumped the charge of rape and murder of a college student, so California wasn't about to release Brandt to stand trial in Oregon. That is until the defense attorneys for Dossen and Fuller combined forces to pin the crime exclusively on Brandt. The defense team brought forth several witnesses who testified that Roger and Brad could not have been involved, thereby poking holes in my timeline. In addition, there was sworn testimony by students claiming only Brandt had been with the victim prior to her death. But given the decadent nature of the party, involving the use of drugs and alcohol, these statements were deemed unreliable.

The defense team also sought to exclude the forensic evidence, stating, through expert witnesses, there had been contamination. DNA from an unidentified woman was discovered mixed among the defendants' DNA. Fortunately, the defense never thought to test me nor suspect this DNA was mine. The prosecution was quick to rebut and remind the jury that the rape and murder occurred during a wild drug-fueled sex party. And that the DNA matches to the defendants provided substantial evidence of their involvement. The motion to exclude the DNA evidence as inadmissible was overruled.

The expense and heightened security required for transporting a cop-killer made the request for extraditing Brandt a contested item.

But since neither the defense nor prosecution had asked for delays in his trial, Brandt received an unprecedented and speedy conviction. California relented, permitting Oregon to extradite their convicted felon to stand trial. The Dossen-Fuller attorneys had argued their clients would be prejudiced without Brandt's inclusion since he was a key suspect in their theory that Brandt, alone, had committed the crime. Several legal pundits surmised the extradition was political, sanctioned because of Dossen's celebrity status. He'd been an ESPN early pick for the Heisman Trophy, also a top candidate for the NFL draft. The rape and murder prosecution had vaulted Dossen into the national news, creating a firestorm of controversy and social media outcries which provided the necessary leverage to justify the expense of a state-to-state transfer.

As officer Rifkin had predicted: the trial was a media circus.

One could assume this was the worst time of my life. Not the college experience my parents had hoped for. And up to this point, maybe it was the worst. Little did I know, it would get even worse. The defense attorneys tried their best to damage my credibility and shame me into admitting I was a liar. They even resorted to publicly disclosing that I had been raped when I was twelve.

Out of desperation, Dossen confessed to his attorneys he'd been, years ago, an unintentional participant to what escalated into a rape. A horrible incident he deeply regretted and wished he could undo, yet could not. Since the rape victim had been me, he believed it was why I had lied and had wanted to send him to prison. To punish him. Of course, he was right. But this Hail Mary pass by Roger didn't work. It failed to wedge a crack in my emotional framework.

I denied it. Roger never raped me. I had never pressed charges. Three men, who never got caught, had abducted and gang-raped me. It was on the record, yet sealed under juvenile protection laws. His confession only made him look worse and lose what credibility he still had. Roger had admitted to being a rapist. Even his legal team began to doubt him.

What did haunt me was the presence of Roger's cousin, whom I'd met the night of the party. She could easily have discredited my timeline and alibi. I saw her watching from the public seating area each day, and I became nervous, expecting the defense to call her as a witness. Her piercing blue irises, framed by eyeliner and shadow, made them seem iridescent as if they were silver daggers.

My testimony was not a smoking gun. A forensic psychologist explained to the jury an eye witness is not as conclusive as one might think. Human perception is faulty. Memories are elusive. The mind will imprint what it wants to believe, and reinforce a misperception, unintentionally contaminating the truth. The defense hammered me on this item. But the lab test I'd taken on the night of the party had proved my sobriety, which cleared doubts in the jurors' minds. And my steadfast demeanor under pressure, even with tears trailing down my cheeks at key moments as I spoke about Gwen, along with my status as an honor student, made me a convincing witness.

There was also the damning DNA evidence – the condoms, semen, fingerprints on plastic and glass, and skin tissue scraped from Gwen's fingernails. One by one these exhibits piled up. And as they did, I watched the defendants all spruced up in suits, opposite to how they normally dressed, become more uneasy. Brad was progressively fidgeting, eyes glazed, while imagining (I suspected) the horrors he would experience inside prison. Roger was more stoic, taking each hit like a running back and, I imagined, hoping for a victory, defying the odds, while his hope of freedom diminished.

Against the advice of counsel, Brandt waived his right not to testify, his arrogance winning out. He sneered as he placed his hand on the Bible. From the stand, he stared down at me. The look he gave communicated that, given the chance, he'd kill me. He denied the charges, claiming no involvement in the rape and murder. He admitted only to spending time with Gwen at the party and dancing with her before she left on her own around midnight. Someone else killed her. He had been inside the house with Roger and Brad when the murder occurred, as witnesses had testified.

The Dossen-Fuller defense team rebutted by reminding the jury that no one had vouched for *Brand's* whereabouts. Also, Brandt was a convicted felon. A fact his counsel had fought to exclude, arguing it prejudicial, yet lost their motion. And Brandt's drug trafficking, his attempt to escape justice, his cold-blooded murder of a police officer, all helped torpedo his credibility and highlight his depravity.

When asked to explain all the forensic evidence pointing at him, Brandt lost his composure. He shouted, "It's total bull*shit!*"

It only helped convince the jury of his guilt. The prosecution closed by restating my testimony and corroborating accounts from students who'd been at the party, along with the forensic results and opinions from expert witnesses. Police officers also gave testimony, including Rifkin who, at one point during the proceedings, gave me a puzzled look. I imagined that he was thinking how unlikely it was, uncanny even, that all the dots had connected so perfectly.

The jury reached a unanimous verdict and found the defendants not guilty on the charge of first-degree murder, but guilty on all the lesser counts of assault, rape, and manslaughter. It was not a gleeful moment for me. I was not high-fiving anyone. I did manage to smile in appreciation of the judicial system. Justice being served, at least, for Gwen's sake. I vaguely recalled a few hugs and a handshake from my attorney. I embraced my mother and father, also Gwen's parents. After that, I wanted to avoid the questions from reporters and simply find a hole in the ground to crawl into and hide.

— ≈ —

Egon tells me he remembers the trial. He should. Even with a dissociative identity disorder. It was pandemic, all over the news, and difficult to miss. But he claims he hadn't made the connection, until recently, that I was the girl at the forefront of this sensational murder trial. I suspect this is not entirely true. However, I let these suspicions go, for the sake of love.

— ☙ —

I omitted a significant incident that occurred during the trial. Perhaps intentionally. Some memories are better left forgotten. My grades were suffering. The pending trial overwhelmed me. There were the constant trips to Portland, meetings with the attorneys, rehearsals for my testimony. I couldn't concentrate on my courses. I tried to anticipate blind spots I might have overlooked that would be used to discredit me.

I had lost my ally. Gwen had been my confidant, had known my secrets, and had remained a loyal friend despite them. She was my true sister. And now she was gone.

When I wasn't in a class or cloistered at the Gamma Phi house, I spent hours at the library. It was a cozy hideaway, an antiquated building emblematic of the original brick architecture. I'd wear my Oregon Ducks sweatshirt, the hood over my head as camouflage, to help regain my lost anonymity. I would stay inside until closing time, nine pm, then emerge to walk incognito to my sorority. The shortest way home was through Pioneer Cemetery, a beautiful grove full of headstones. I had thought that it was odd, having a graveyard in the middle on a college campus.

The sky was dark and sprinkling snow. Walking along the path, I gazed around at the tombstones and branches highlighted in white. Snowflakes touched and tingled my skin, and I enjoyed the moment. My face and hands were chilled while the rest of me was warm inside my clothing.

I began recalling memories, of being a child, once traveling up a winding road in the early morning, half asleep, seeing the heads of my parents in silhouette in the front seat of our car as we drove to the top of Mt. Tamalpais. They wanted to surprise me with my first snowfall. I remembered catching icy flakes on my tongue.

I was lost in this wonderful reverie when something fell in front of me with a thud. A black cat. Unmoving. Dead.

"Hello, Clarabelle."

I was shocked to hear my birth name spoken. But more startled to see the menacing presence of Sid, who I hadn't seen since he left high school. He was standing next to a redwood tree.

"Why aren't you inside playing house with your sisters?"

"I have a class."

"Not at this hour."

I backed away. "I'm studying for a test."

"So many lies, Clarabelle."

"Don't call me that."

"Mira. What's with the new name? And lying in court."

"I didn't *lie*."

Sid let that remark float in the air like a snowflake as his hand reached out to collect a few on his black glove.

"Leave me alone." I attempted to go around him. He grabbed my wrist but I twisted my arm, which removed his hand. He seemed amused by my little escape trick. Undaunted, he kept coming at me. I backed away and flipped off my hood to see more clearly.

"I've checked on you. Shit, you even made the dean's list."

"You *do* that in college, *Sid*. You educate yourself."

"I've learned some things too."

"I can't imagine what."

"A smart-ass like you can't put two and two together? I'm the *supplier* you dumb twit. I deal drugs. Is it starting to compute? I live in the real world, *Mira*."

His aggressive maneuvering and taunting drove me into a grove of trees beside of group of tombstones. "What do you want?"

Sid chewed his upper lip. His lower canines caught light from a street lamp. It gave him a werewolf grin. "What do I *want*? For you to tell the truth. Have you forgotten how that works, Clarabelle?"

"Stop calling me that."

"I don't give a flying fuck about your name. What I care about – you little *cunt* – is what you've cost me. Rick, he's not getting out of jail. The cocaine ain't coming back, sweetheart. How do you plan on repaying me?"

"Fuck you. I owe you *nothing*. You raped me!"

"That's old news. And that's not what I heard you tell the judge and jury after *swearing* under oath."

"Stay away."

He was amused by my show of hands, palms held in front of my face as I took a defensive stance.

"Surrendering?" He joked, "I don't take prisoners."

"*Leave!* Or I'll scream," I warned him.

"Here's the thing. You're going to change your testimony."

I noticed the glint of metal in his hand.

"Why would I do that?"

"No particular reason." He turned the knife vertically to display its sharp point. "The truth? I know it gets twisted. Truth is, I sorta like your parents. Decent folks. I saw they came into town for this. To support you. I'd hate to see them, you know ... suffer."

"You bastard. Don't you—"

"Then *do* what I tell you!"

Snow fell off a branch. It splat on my cheek. I swiped it away. His smile puzzled me. He pointed the knife blade at me.

"Nice work. If I do say so myself."

I squinted, silently transmitting a seething – "*What?*"

"My mark. The kind you carve into a tree."

The wet snow had washed off my makeup and exposed my scar, his handiwork. He was enjoying this, seeing my fear.

"It makes you *mine*. Like we're lovers."

I jabbed with a kick at Sid's crotch. It caught him off guard, but he was able to avoid it by jumping away. Now angered, he squeezed the knife handle and repositioned the blade at me.

"You want to play like that? Let's do this."

Sid slashed the air with back and forth strokes to frighten me, before lunging with his knife. As trained, I knocked his arm away in a lateral motion and smashed his jaw with the ball of my other hand. I followed with a jab to his throat, then a body chop to his neck. He dropped to the ground with a stunned look on his face. I kicked him hard in the face.

I went down on my knees, tightly cradled his head with both my hands and snapped his neck in one swift motion. It happened fast. I glanced around and heard a surreal silence. Nobody walking nearby, that I could see. Nobody witnessing this nightmarish act. White stars were falling like cold floating angels all around me.

I'm not sure what possessed me to remove one of his gloves and slip my fingers into the rabbit-fur lining. To not leave any prints, that had been ingrained in me. But why I picked up his knife and carved a succinct love note into his forehead. That came from somewhere deeper and meaner. A more basic instinct.

— ❧ —

Egon stops me. "You *murdered* someone?"

"In self-defense. I had to. I *had* to. What?"

Egon shakes his head, then rubs his eyes. "Now I know what Faye *had* on you. She knew about it. Didn't she? I'm right."

"She threatened to tell."

Egon wanders away to the sliding glass doors to stare into the crashing waves and approaching darkness. "I doubt that's all. What else? What else does she have on you?"

"Nothing. I swear."

I follow him to the glass doors. He doesn't flinch as I place my head against his. "You know I love you. We've made it this far. It'll be okay. But you need to hear to the rest."

— ❧ —

A dead man discovered unburied in the college cemetery caused renewed excitement throughout the campus. I knew it was a matter of time before I would become a suspect, a person of interest, given that both the defendants knew him, were childhood friends, and someone I'd grown up with too. And who'd be identified as someone in attendance during the trial. Like I said, it was a matter of time.

Officer Rifkin stepped from his police car to approach me. I was walking with my parents toward the courthouse building.

"Mira, good morning." He gave a friendly nod to my mom and dad, then asked them. "Could you give us a moment, please?"

My dad and mom went ahead as I prepared myself for what I presumed would come next. "Hi, what's up?"

Rifkin gave me his half-and-half look, an affectionate frown. "You heard about the murder in the campus cemetery?"

"How could I not? It's horrible."

Again, a half smile, half scowl, as if Rifkin wanted to reach out and either hug or shake me. "He was a known *drug* dealer."

"Oh," I said.

"And he knew you."

"He knew me? How? Who was he?"

"Mira, his name is Sid Meyers."

"Oh. *Oh*," I said, faking belated recognition. He was from my neighborhood. I knew him in school. Not well. But, why ..."

Those piercing, sensitive eyes. They were sending mixed signals, tugging at my emotions to confess, before easing off. His intensity subsided. "I was hoping you could tell me."

"I can't. I haven't seen him in years. Since he graduated from high school. And to be blunt, I *hated* him."

"He was friends with Dossen and Fuller."

"Are you asking me? They were, I think. I'm not sure how close a friendship. They were a few grades ahead of me."

"Had you seen him while he was here?"

"No."

"Hum, apparently he came and sat in the courtroom. He was ID'd by a number of people."

"I swear, I didn't see him. I mean, I barely look at the jury."

"I understand. I believe you, Mira."

"Thank you. For telling me."

"I guess that's it. But if you think of anything useful, about this guy that might be pertinent to … all this. You'll tell me?"

"I'll tell you," I echoed back. "Of course."

With a smile, a concerned frown, he stared directly into my eyes, my soul, before walking with me to the courthouse.

— ☰ —

I'd been emotionally shaken by the trial, yet my resolve was not. They were all guilty of crimes. Only one, for murder. The other two, Roger and Brad, unlucky by association, swept down the river with Rick who deserved what he got.

I was not in court for any sentencings. My excuse, final exams. The following day I had a test in human physiology, a course called Evidence, Inference, and Biostatistics. And for psychology, two term papers were due the next week. One was on *Male Sexual Aggression*, the other, *Dissociative Identity Disorder, and the Creative Arts.*

I would have enjoyed watching Rick's reaction when a judge in California pronounced his death sentence for killing a cop. Gwen's parents had been there and were distraught he'd never be prosecuted for the murder of their daughter, yet were relieved he was sentenced to death row. I had mixed feelings. I wanted him to live and suffer for as long as possible. And I planned to make that happen. I would have enjoyed giving Rick a *fuck-you* sendoff, looking at him straight in the eyes – as a bug I had crushed – with a stare that said, "you are under *my* thumb now."

Brad, who I hated minutely less, would now discover that life in prison was the ultimate bitch. Roger, whom I had less hatred for, and whose fame and fortune I'd transformed into notoriety, was the one I'd have had trouble facing. So I'd made a point of staying away.

I had grown fond of my college terrarium, this campus of lush greenery and weather conducive to studying. I'd kept a few friends in the Gamma Phi sorority, but girls would whisper shit about me behind my back. I had managed to attain a dual status of being both a hero and a traitor. Not an easy accomplishment. Boys would ask me out on dates, but often to glean juicy details about the night of Gwen's murder, which I was unwilling to give, or *put* out. It came as no surprise I'd been stigmatized by media over-exposure, deemed by many on campus as a "man-hating-bitchy-feminist" who ruined the promising football career of Roger-Dodger.

I considered transferring to another school, but doing so would signify an admission of defeat, a minor victory for the other side, and so I stayed. I was turning back into what I'd fought to overcome – an introvert. My social plate was empty, except an occasional date and sorority-sponsored functions I was required to attend.

One day, with my head down, reading a textbook, and feeling under the weather, I was seated at a booth inside the Fishbowl. I was hearing the downpour of rain which seemed to echo my melancholy when someone slid into the seat across the table from me.

"You look lonely. Need a friend?"

Roger's cousin startled me. "Hi," was all I could think to say by this unexpected encounter.

"I've been watching you," she added. "And I know you've been watching – sometimes following – me."

"You're Roger's cousin, you said."

"At the party. I did. Roger sends his regards."

I tensed, closing my book. "I doubt that."

Up close this girl was even more striking. Her shaded eyes and silvery-blue irises distracted my focus. She said, "That's not to mean I've visited him in prison, only that I know how he felt about you.

He was infatuated with you. As am I."

"What do you want?" I was prepared to get up and leave.

"We should be friends."

"Why?"

"Female intuition. My name is Faye."

I stared at her hand extended toward me across the table. Long graceful fingers with pearl-colored nails. I wondered if others in the Fishbowl were watching us.

I shook her fingertips briefly. "Mira. But you know that. And you have a brother, a twin? Who goes to school here too?"

"Hmm." She sipped from a can of Coke that she'd brought to the table. "I don't want to talk about him. And you don't want to talk about Roger. Call it a truce?"

"Okay," I said neutrally, not sure where this was going. She'd made me curious, I had to admit. Under different circumstances, had we met freshman year, I would have easily accepted her invitation to be friends, instead of what this was: A *detente* between nations with a history of espionage and mistrust.

"You're a psych major?"

"I am," I said. "You?"

"Liberal arts. I like to paint and sculpt."

"Are you any good?"

She smiled. "I'm here to learn. But yes. Are you?"

I was warming to her, against my better judgment. She had an insouciance. It seemed genuine and was infectious. "Do you mean *good* at psychoanalyzing people?"

"Are you?"

"I'm learning to be," I smiled and straightened papers spread upon the table. She was observing my tidiness.

"Your friend," she said. "I'm sorry what happened to her."

I stopped fussing with my stuff. "Her name is *Gwen.*"

"I know. I felt a need to tell you. So I did." She crushed the Coke can with a squeeze of her hand, tapping the metal with a fingernail. "If you want me to go, I will."

"No," I said. "You're right. I could use a friend."

"It won't make me popular. Especially at the ATX house. You can bet on that. But I don't care. It was brave what you did."

My openness, like a flower, closed a fraction.

"For *women*," she added. "It sent a strong message."

"You don't hate me? Roger was—*is*—I mean, your cousin."

Faye upturned and emptied the soda. "Roger will get over it. He's incredibly resilient. Prison might do him some good."

I didn't know what to make of her. Could she be serious? I had ruined her cousin's life. Plus, she likely knew I had lied to get him locked away. I sensed she wanted something from me, but I had no idea what. Yet I couldn't resist being pulled into her world. She had that kind of charm and power. Making it inevitable that our lives would be connected.

She said, "This is destiny."

I cleared my thoughts. "What was?" I watched but didn't move as she reached over and took hold of my hand.

"That we become best friends."

— ≋ —

"*Sasha* is Faye? Then. Wait. Because ... *Shit*."

Egon is having difficulty processing this.

"In college, you became close *friends?*"

Normally (but what is normal?) the dominant personality in a dissociative identity disorder is aware, to some extent, of the goings on of the alternate personalities. So I am taken by surprise. All this time I believed Egon was playing me. That he knew the truth about Faye and our friendship. That he had remained silent about it for our sake, to hold us together. To preserve our love.

"I wouldn't say we were ever close. Friends, maybe. Egon, I honestly thought you knew about this."

"*No*, Mira. Faye told me practically nothing about your *prior* relationship. She kept me in the dark. I knew she met you briefly in college. But that's it. What else do I *not* know? I mean, you're the f— ing shrink! I trusted you! *Jesus.*"

"Egon."

"Don't talk to me. I don't want to hear any more."

He turns away, towards the ocean. The windows are black. But we can hear the waves tumbling and roaring.

"Egon, please. Don't let this change things. I love you."

He looks at me, wondering, then turns away, retrieves his glass, tosses more ice cubes and pours more liquor. After a fast swallow, he says. "Yes, Mira. I still love you. Regardless."

"Then you have to hear the rest."

"Why? I don't *care.* Mira, just leave it be."

"I owe you the truth."

"We don't have to do this."

"We do. It's important you know who I am."

Egon rattles his cocktail, drops back into a chair, and waves me on, reluctantly signaling for me to continue. So I do.

— ⇌ —

As I'd suspected, Faye was as devious as me. Maybe more so. And, though our friendship was sporadic – spontaneously meeting for a drink, or coffee, sharing the weeks triumphs and travails – it wasn't long before I realized what I was dealing with. The realization made me almost giddy. I couldn't believe my luck. It was what I had been studying. Instead of vicariously experiencing the phenomenon through recorded accounts, I was directly witnessing a textbook case of dissociative identity disorder. And, admittedly, I was drawn like a moth to the flame.

I met Egon (you) by accident. I don't think Faye had meant to introduce us. Though I could be wrong about that. She suggested a local bar where a bartender she knew was lax about serving liquor to college students, not of legal age. Faye came dressed as I was, in jeans, boots, leather jacket. Her loose black hair fell in slight waves over her shoulders. She wore only a hint of makeup. She was a vision of feminine beauty. Yet I had begun to suspect the truth about her.

You would think it'd be obvious to discern a person's gender. But Faye was different, very convincing. I was mesmerized by her total belief that she was whom she believed she was. When Faye was present, she *was* female. So complete was the transformation that I would have wagered money that nobody in that bar had suspected otherwise. We were conversing as we usually did about our classes, professors, politics, and Faye's passion, the meaning of art.

I wasn't even sure where Faye lived. Certain topics were either off limits or simply ignored if I asked. She'd call on her cell phone, suggest we meet somewhere, sometimes for a concert or sports game, then afterward say goodbye with a wave to disappear mysteriously into the crowd of other students. Then reappear a week or so later, after she'd called me to make a date or suggest a rendezvous.

Our friendship was based on a truce not to *ask*, merely accept. Besides, I was busy. I had overloaded my schedule with courses for the purpose of graduating early, so I didn't question our on-again, off-again friendship. Which is not to say I wasn't curious about her. I enjoyed the theatrical aspect, which was part of her mystique. She acted like a carefree femme fatale. *That* was her persona.

She had me laughing. She was in the process of telling me about a painting she'd composed called *Kisses To Succeed* when her entire demeanor changed. She'd seen something behind me, someone who had entered the bar. I watched with fascination as her face changed from feminine to masculine. The eyes squinting, muscles tensing at the jaw, teeth clenching. A thoughtful line forming on the forehead. The body readjusting its posture in the chair.

A sharp nod, then, "Hey. What's up?" The voice much deeper, directed at whoever was approaching us.

"Bro, you're *freak'n* unbelievable. A new love?"

I recognized both frats when their faces came around to survey who I was, staring down at me. "Holy shit. Not *you!*"

"Man, that's low rent. If Roger was here he'd beat the living shit out of you, *Egon*. Oh, wait, he's *not* here. Maybe *I* should."

"Defuse, Jay. We don't know if he's *fucking* her. Are you?"

Alarmed, my senses on edge, I looked at Egon whose extremely calm composure relaxed me a bit. He looked at me from across the table with a playful smile. "I don't know. Are we?"

At a loss, I blurted. "I'll be sure to let you know *if* we ever do."

My remark resulted in unexpected laughter.

I smiled too, but hesitantly, fearing what might come next.

The merriment died quickly. I was still a pariah.

"Man, you'd fuck anything," spat Jay, then both frats walked toward the bar.

The other one muttered to Egon, "Later, bro."

The vacuum they left behind was chilling. Yet strangely it did not seem to bother Egon.

"Why am I here?" He said with a smile.

"You invited me," I said. "I mean ... Faye did."

"Ah. Faye. Okay."

Confused, I added, "How does this work?"

"It doesn't. What exactly did she say about me?"

"We don't talk about you. Or Roger."

"Off limits. Makes sense."

Not to me it didn't. I was mesmerized. Was this an act? Could this be the same person I had watched from inside the Fishbowl, the one who I saw standing on the wall as if overlooking his kingdom. I recognized the aloof yet penetrating gaze, only now those eyes were looking directly into mine. The intensity was making me melt.

"So," he said with a squint. "Have we officially met?"

"I've only seen you around campus."

"So, no. I avoided the trial. I try to avoid the news too."

"Like the plague?"

Amused, he gave me an easygoing smile. "The world has a fever. It's getting worse. It might be contagious. A precaution I take."

"To be misinformed? Then why go to school?"

"To study the classics. Aristotle. Descartes. Confucius. Locke. Aquinas. Nietzsche. Kierkegaard. Spinoza. Jung. Watts."

"Strictly old-school? A traditionalist?"

"A few great books and movies are still getting made."

"It's not the death of intelligence, then?"

My words made him grin. He took hold of the beer in front of him and toasted me, clinking his glass into mine. "To us, against the world? The two surviving optimists?"

"On the good days I am," I said, then drank my beer.

He waved a hand. "It's all stylistic today. Less about substance. I'm interested in theater. What it can do. That interests me."

"The drama department? Are you an actor?"

"I'm learning how *not* to act. To be in the moment. Then it's not acting. About as close to reality as it can get."

"I'm confused," I said, dead serious. "Meaning, what?"

"Our natural state. As humans?"

I started to wonder if my diagnosis of his mental state had been premature. Was this all an act? Or was he living with a dissociative identity disorder, harboring multiple personalities? "Do you mind if I ask you a question?"

He sipped his beer. "Shoot."

"In the ATX house? You live there?"

"That surprises you?"

"I mean, how do your fraternity brothers react when they come across Faye? How does that work?"

"How does *what* work? Faye's an exhibitionist. A bit of a joke. She entertains. The whole house is weird. They like her. At least, they tolerate her."

I had no follow-up, and I wasn't sure how to broach the subject again. I was curious to know if there were other personalities. Other characters in his performance. On the assumption he was acting.

"We mostly get along," he added. "It helps to play sports and be *macho*. I play lacrosse. And I'm pretty good. I also know how to defend myself."

"I've seen."

Egon frowned. "First semester? You were there?"

"I was watching from inside the Fishbowl."

"Hunter did that."

"Who?"

"Listen, I didn't start that fight."

"I know," I said.

"Like I said, we *mostly* get along. Rick Brandt and others, they had a problem with Faye. But she fixed that."

"How?"

"You'd have to ask her." He grinned. "Having long hair, being a bit of a freak. Some guys get jealous. Especially when I'm the one who often scores the prettiest girls."

"Am I supposed to be impressed?"

"No. No. You're reading me all wrong."

"How should I be reading you?"

"It happens. I don't connive. Or try. Girls are attracted to me. And me to them. It's no big deal. Listen. It's Mira, right?"

I nodded as if this was our first date.

"I'd never force myself on anyone. I mean, *rape* them."

"Good to know."

I glimpsed a scowl, the first tinge of hostility I'd seen from him. But just as quickly it transformed into a self-deprecating grin. "Mira, I swear. I wouldn't. And, for the record, neither would my cousin Roger. Not now. Not here. Not anymore."

Egon (you) then got up from his seat, looked at me with a sad smile, a parting gesture, and walked out of the bar.

— ≋ —

I stop to ask, "You *seriously* don't remember that?"

Egon rattles ice in his glass. "Vaguely. It's coming back. Okay, so we met once. There were lots of girls. And that incident, the one that happened to your friend—"

"Gwen. She was *murdered*."

"Horrible, I know. Sorry. But the trial, it was a blur. Years had passed. Mira, when I saw you again, you looked familiar, that's all. What can I say? It's how my mind works, or doesn't. Okay?"

I sit on the corner of the bed. Not okay. This is not going how I thought it would. I rise from the bed, shake my head, and go over to the bar. Egon grabs my wrist lightly, getting me to stop, pulling me down to kiss me on the lips.

"Be happy," he tells me. "If I had remembered that day then this would all be, like, what? A charade. Right? It's not."

I can't believe I'm drinking more wine. I want to be in control. I set the glass down, still filled to the rim, and leave it on the counter. I wander over to look out the windows, stare into the blackness, hear the waves crashing, see an occasional glimpse of white foam cresting. I turn back to face Egon.

"Are you ready to hear the rest?"

"Do I have a choice?" He smiles.

I eye my drink from afar and continue my story.

— ≋ —

I graduated a semester early with a degree in psychology. The phone calls from Faye became less frequent after my encounter with Egon. I wasn't sure why. But I'd been too busy with schoolwork to care. During my last two semesters, I lived off campus. I had moved in with an architecture student whom I met while we both took a physics course. It could have been love. He filled in the gaps when I wasn't immersed in my course curriculum and helped ease my stress with his sense of humor and optimism. I didn't know if we had a future together though he entertained me with notions of our living in a skyscraper, one he would design, establishing his indelible mark upon the world. We had planned to reconnect during the summer. He sent me a postcard from Arizona, where he'd found employment working for a small firm that designed shopping malls.

My ex-boyfriend wrote to inform me he was engaged to marry. I was at Florida State University doing my graduate work in criminal psychology. I replied with a postcard. It had a cartoon of two female alligators standing and conversing. "Nice purse," said the one. The other replied, "Thanks, it's my ex-husband."

My note: *Congratulations. You'll be better off with her than me. Bon voyage. Best wishes. Love always, Mira.*

That was my kind of humor, which I knew he'd appreciate.

I transferred to Palo Alto University, where I completed my PhD in clinical forensic psychology. The subject of my dissertation was *Traumatic Sexual Abuse, Identity Redevelopment, and Dissociative Consequences.* My internship consisted of working three-month clinical rotations in a California psychiatric ward. I evaluated the disturbed and delusional. I was astounded by the number people who, driven by hallucinations, did harm to others and those they had vowed to love. A toxic mix of voluntary inebriation and childhood abuse was often how these demons manifested. It made me question my own mind. Were humans really capable of free will?

Later, as a licensed psychologist, I gained employment working for the district attorney's office. My job was to assess the mental state of individuals seeking an insanity plea, analyze the competency of a defendant to stand trial, scrutinize the credibility of a witness, and interpret polygraph data. I also worked hard to make political connections within the courts and law enforcement community, and to be admired by my peers, thereby establishing a reputation for my thoroughness and competency.

After five years I launched my own practice. I had endorsements and testimonials from key personnel I'd strategically cherry-picked. This included Office Rifkin who'd risen in rank and whom I'd stayed in contact since college. My clients were public defenders, state and private-practice attorneys. I was hired to interview violent criminals, analyze crime scenes, and testify as an expert witness. I was good at being grilled by the opposing side. I had early training at college.

As part of a community outreach program, I volunteered my time and services, pro bono, to work as a correctional psychologist inside the prison system. I specialized in anger management classes. I worked at two prisons. One was San Quentin, closest to my San Francisco office. The other, Oregon State Penitentiary, which was near my alma mater, where once a semester I was a guest speaker for the psychology department. I'd made a concerted effort to keep in touch with my professors.

By virtue of training and reputation, a forensic psychologist is a certified expert who helps assist a court of law to determine whether or not an inmate has paid his debt to society and should be released back into society. In other words, to be able live beyond the confines of a cage.

I had become one these officially-appointed experts. And I was determined to reap the benefits. My master plan was in place, set in motion on the day of my rape many years ago. I was now ready to take my next step in avenging my rapists.

— ≋ —

It was no coincidence that all of my rapists, minus Sid Meyers, were caged at San Quentin Prison and Oregon State Penitentiary since Brad Fuller and Roger Dossen had been convicted in Oregon, and Rick Brandt had committed his crime in California.

I could not (and refused to) forget or forgive what Brandt had done to Gwen, nor what Fuller and Dossen did to me at age twelve.

I had nearly died. Despite my training as a licensed psychotherapist, I had let my hatred fester and go untreated, nurtured like a bastard child. I knew all this subconsciously. But I couldn't stop myself.

I was clinically trained to recognize the warning signs, but I was blinded by hubris. My elaborate plan required me to call in favors. Penal institutions, by nature, are prone to corruption. I had arranged for two special visits to Oregon State Penitentiary.

— ≋ —

The hour flight, plus the hour drive in a rental car to the prison, gave me ample time to second-guess my actions. Instead, I selected a bestselling crime novel from a store at SFO to occupy my mind while in the air. Once on the ground and moving in my rental car, I located a radio station to take my mind elsewhere. To this day, I can't recall the book I stared into nor any of the songs I heard which were like white noise pulsating in my brain.

I had always made a point of befriending the correction officers (COs), prison staff and guards, once I'd started working in the penal system as a volunteer corrections psychologist. I was known as Dr. Sims, to protect my true identity. It was for my safety, in case some wacko wanted to track me down after his release from incarceration. The State Board of Corrections Department understood my reason for wanting anonymity and permitted this subterfuge.

First on my list, that day, was to visit Brad Fuller, who'd been imprisoned there for seven years. During that time, I learned about Brad's evolution, or rather the reverse, how he had devolved inside this prison culture. From day one of arriving, things had not gone well. His size and youth were contributing factors. Fuller had been singled out as a Fish (new inmate), classified a Cupcake (one easily manipulated and harboring feminine tendencies), forced into being a Strawberry (giving blow jobs and other sexual favors in exchange for drugs), before succumbing to his current role as a Cockglazer (one who was once forced into giving sex but now gave it willingly).

A six-foot-six gang member of the Black Guerrilla Family had spotted Fuller, witnessed his early abuse, intervened, and made an offer. To be his protector. In exchange, Fuller became the property of another. A slave. A white nigger who performed menial tasks for his owner, and traded for sex and drugs. This became his new life for three years until he became an informant for the investigative special unit (ISU). For his cooperation in exposing the drug trafficking, he was transferred to the "Sensitive Needs Yard," a protective custody section exclusive to misfits of a different stripe. Child molesters, rapists, transgenders, gang-banger drop-outs, and snitches.

When I entered the visitation room, Brad was seated on a stool. Standing on opposite sides of him were two female guards. His arms were handcuffed behind his back. He was humming in a rapid sing-song rant with his eyes closed. His hair was shoulder length and was braided into corn curls. His file stated he was a heroin user. He didn't bother to acknowledge my presence. He had less muscle and was thinner, from when he was in college. His blue pants were rolled at the ankles, exposing shaved legs. His bare feet were tapping the concrete in his thongs, showing off shiny pink toenails.

When he finally looked at me, and the recognition of who I was came into his cognitive focus, his mouth opened – in surprise – then shut to hide his gums. Both his upper and lower teeth had been knocked out by his former protector. I'd heard of this ugly practice. This was to ensure that the Ho or Pussy All the Time (a sexually assaulted male who couldn't retaliate) would be unable to bite back while giving oral sex.

It was rude of me to smile, but I did, showing my teeth.

He sputtered inarticulate expletives at me before shouting, "You lying bitsh! Get her out! Thish is all her doing!"

The guards were unmoved, pushing Brad down onto his stool. His missing teeth gave him a noticeable lisp. With his wrists shackled and guards holding his shoulders, he did the only aggressive thing he could think to do. He spat at me. Most of the phlegm drizzled off his chin onto his shirt.

I stood, unflinching, armed with my folder. I shook my head to express displeasure and pretended to write copious notes.

"I shoulda killed you – you *bitsh!*"

Expressing further disappointment, I tapped on the pad of paper with my pencil.

"I was told you'd changed, and become *sensitive*," I said.

Brad blinked, then frowned at me, confused.

"What you just demonstrated to me was pure male aggression," I stated. "Therefore, I will be recommending that you be transferred from the Special Needs Yard and placed back into the general prison population."

Brad flinched, reverting to a dog who'd been kicked and beaten. "*No-no-no.* Y-you can't do that."

"I can," I glanced at the guards. "Tell him."

"She can, Brandy," said one of the guards.

"I'm the corrections psychologist assigned to evaluate you."

"*You?* Evaluate me? Come *on*, that's ... inshane."

"What was that, Brad? Or should I call you Brandy?"

"I'll be killed. I *will*. They ...You c-can't shend me back."

"You should have thought about that before you expressed your desire to *kill* me."

"I-I didn't mean it," he sputtered weakly. "Please. Why are you doing thiss? Haven't you scwrewed with my life enough?"

"Screwed with *your* life? Did you forget what you did to me? You once tried to kill me. Are you calling me a liar?"

Brad's emotions were in turmoil, not sure what to say.

"Are you?" I demanded.

"N-*no-no*," he whined. "What is it you *want* from me?"

"For you to demonstrate how sensitive you've become. I want to know you've changed. Or I'll recommend you be transferred."

Brad's eyes were tearing up. "Why are you doing thish? What is it you want?"

"Who is Brandy? Let me see her."

"What?"

"Would she get on her knees and beg for forgiveness?"

"You want ... me to ..." Brad glanced up at the guards before he slid off the stool and went down on his knees.

I had requested a banana. The guard handed it to me. I peeled back the skin and held out the phallic looking fruit as an incentive, and tapped my foot as if training a dog. "Come here."

Brad scuttled on his knees, hands locked behind his back.

"Show me your sensitive side. Put your lips around my banana, Brandy. Show me how gentle you've become."

Brad was nervously quivering, but hesitantly opened his mouth and did as he was told, giving fellatio to the banana. He glanced up twice for my approval.

"Good girl." I petted his braided locks. "I am going to allow you to stay where you are. But I have one last question."

He looked up at me.

"Who's the bitch now?"

— ≋ —

My second stop on this Day of Reckoning was to visit Roger Dossen. What I had planned for years was coming to fruition. My misconduct, if found out, was minor in the scheme of things. Bribing correction officers could get me in trouble. I could lose my license. Even be charged with a criminal offense, and arrested.

I knew the risks. But my plan was foolproof, I believed.

Inside the prison gates, I was always accompanied by a male officer, which was protocol. He was waiting for me as I exited the visitation room. As he escorted me down the hallway the clamor accosted my senses. There were the lewd catcalls and ever-present threats of molestation. Also, there was the occasional inmate who would be punished for violating Rule 38, public masturbation in front of a female visitor or a guard. I would catch glimpses of these over-sexed and sex-deprived men exposing themselves and stroking their penis from inside their cell. All of which confirmed to me these dysfunctional animals belonged in a zoo.

I entered another interrogation room where Roger was standing between two female guards. Both were armed with taser guns. Roger had his arms crossed in front of him. They were not shackled. But his ankles were. He had become a model prisoner, according to his file. A diligent worker in every capacity or employment assigned to him. During his years of incarceration, he had read law books. He assisted other inmates by writing letters of appeal. He could likely pass the bar if tested. He participated in a program called Insight Prison Project, designed to transform inmates into compassionate humans who were accountable for their actions. He had become a facilitator himself and taught classes on meditation to help expand an inmate's self-awareness. He also led prayer groups in the chapel.

Feeling somewhat queasy about this meeting, I walked to the opposite side of the room before turning to face Roger. He showed no emotion upon seeing me. He was stoic. As if in a football stance, in a line-up, on the field, waiting for kickoff. The two guards were big but lacked his height and muscularity. He looked dignified. For a moment, I forgot the speech I'd rehearsed.

My mind dislodged from present time and transitioned into an imagined past – inside the holding cell beneath an ancient stadium, where gladiators waited to fight for their life before a roaring crowd who desired this bloodsport. It was a fantasy not so far removed from what might have been for Dossen. A college football star with a promising career of wealth and fame. Now a faded dream. And I had caused his fall.

By contrast, I lived in a San Francisco highrise apartment with security guards at ground level. I had a successful career. My rapists had lost. And I had won.

I inhaled, my confidence returning. "Take off your clothes," I told Dossen.

It was the first chink in his armor. He blinked, surprised by my request. He glanced at both guards, who gave curt nods. He shook his head and began unbuttoning his blue shirt. When removed, he handed it to one of the guards. He lifted weights. It was obvious, from his muscular frame. It was hard to keep my gaze professional and unemotional. He pulled down his pants and underwear. Both prison guards were drawn to his penis, exposed for them to stare and examine as he straightened himself and looked back at me.

I walked toward him. "You made me do this once."

"You know that wasn't me who—"

I surprised him – and the guards – by cupping his testicles in my hand. "No? How does it feel? To be surrounded by the opposite sex? Naked. Vulnerable." My other hand touched his penis, stimulating an erection. "What's the matter, Roger? Are you embarrassed?"

I literally had him by the balls. It was as if I had him strapped to a lie detector. So I asked, "Why did you rape me? We were friends, I thought. And that you ... liked me."

Roger answered, "I did. We even took vows—"

I squeezed and he winced.

"Clara—*Mira*, I mean. It's true. I swear."

"Then—why!?"

"None of it was my idea."

"I don't *care*. You were a coward."

"You're right. I was."

"You ran away. You left me there to *die*."

"No, I was going to—"

"*Yes!*" I shut my eyes, shuddering as I recalled the fear overtake me again, the humiliation of being raped, the pain, the abject terror, then abandonment. The loss of self. And the will to live.

"Mira?"

I recalled where I was. I stared into Roger's eyes. His voice was calm. A comforting voice that made me yearn for a semblance of normalcy and love. A belief there was hope left in the world.

"You can let go now," he said.

I'd forgotten my hand was holding his genitals. I let go and backed away, embarrassed by my behavior. I was ambushed by a memory of Roger as a boy, who had brushed my hand, then laced his fingers through mine. A sensation of first love. My heart had felt lighter, fluttering with joy. Before it got crushed.

"I understand, Mira. It's all right. I forgive you."

I awoke from my stupor and snapped, "*You* forgive me?"

"I wanted to stop what happened to you but—"

"You didn't."

"I was scared too. I'm not the same person as that boy."

"Nor am I the same." I took another step back. I noticed both women looking at me strangely as if they'd shifted their loyalties.

"Mira," said Roger. "People can and do change."

"Oh, I've *heard*. I've read your file. All your *good* deeds. You found *God* or something. A born-again *good* guy. A fucking saint! Good for you, Roger. Good luck with that."

"Mira."

I stared back at him, naked before me.

"It's okay to let go."

His words held a different meaning, I realized. I had achieved victory yet the conquest felt like a city in ashes.

"Can I get dressed?" he asked.

I nodded and turned away, retreating to the table that held his file. I was confused by my unraveling emotions. When I turned back, Roger was dressed in his blue prison attire. He then did something that made me go weak. He gave me a tender smile. It felt genuine.

"You need help, Mira. I hope you find peace."

— ☱ —

The plane lifted off the ground and my heartbeat became rapid. I felt light-headed and fought back the urge to reach for the oxygen mask overhead. I didn't feel capable of engaging in idle conversation with my fellow passenger seated beside me. A student, attending the University of Oregon, and majoring in psychology, of all things. His enthusiasm for the subject garnered all but a frozen smile from me. I encouraged his efforts and lied, telling him I was in pharmaceutical sales. I opened my unfinished paperback but only stared at the pages (they might as well have been blank). Nursing wine in a plastic cup, I closed my eyes and listened to the repetitive swoosh of blood surge through my head like a coastal storm as it pounded wave after wave against a shore of jagged riprap.

— ☱ —

The next morning I drove to San Quentin prison. I was to meet with Rick-the-Prick. I had arranged a surprise reunion. The copy of Brandt's file chronicled his aggressive behavior while incarcerated. After being strip-searched and issued a prison wardrobe, he was locked up with a cellmate whom he almost beat to death. While he was being admonished for his despicable behavior, Brandt had spit in the warden's face. This landed him in solitary confinement.

Later the same year, Brandt made a knife composed of melted plastic, which he honed, then approached a Latino gang leader and sliced the inmate's head and neck, scarring and almost killing him. This earned Rick respect and entry into a white supremacist gang. He subsequently advanced to become a leader in this racially-and-ethnically-charged jungle called a rehabilitation facility.

In his fifth year, Brandt had stabbed to death an inmate and was transferred from Death Row's East Block to a high-security section of the prison called Ad-Seg, short for Administration Segregation.

I had been warned what to expect. So I orchestrated a private setting where I would feel safe. Anchored to the cement floor was a solid metal table. The tabletop was equipped with iron locks and chains clamped to each of his wrists. This is how he was when I walked in the room. I had not seen him for more than six years. His eyes seemed wilder and more savage than I'd remembered

Rick jerked at his restraints as I entered as if smelling me first, with an animal's heightened sense. On the days I visited a prison, I always wore a brunette wig and glasses to disguise my appearance. After entering this high-security room, I removed both items. Once he saw it was me, he tensed, like a snake coiling, prepared to strike. I forced a smile and held my breath as I stood over him.

The two guards present had been profiled, by me, in advance. A man and a woman. I knew them both and had chosen them partially because of their ethnicity, which Rick espoused to despise as dictated by the code of his gang affiliation.

Female guards were typically restricted beyond certain areas, but I'd pulled more strings, paying hefty bribes to make this happen. Both guards were of sizable girth and strength. They stood on both sides of Brandt and appeared to appreciate their inclusion.

The physical transformation of the boy I had known in college came as a shock. Rick's head was shaved. And the areas of his skin that were visible, including his face, were tattooed with snakes and numbers and symbols. Since his effort to frighten me had failed, he settled back into the straight-back chair with a cocksure grin.

"Well look at *you*." He spat a laugh, "all dressed up, fancy-like. Going to a funeral? *Bitch*."

"And look at *you*," I gloated, taking my seat to face him. "It's how I imagined you'd turn out. Dressed in orange. It *suits* you."

He lunged at me but was yanked back by his restraints. His act of aggression only exposed his present state of impotence.

I smiled to show him I knew this. "I've read your file."

"Good for you. You can read."

"You killed a cop. You're not getting out of here."

"I'll deal with that. As I will *deal* with you."

"Is that a threat?"

"Hell, no. A *promise*. Hey, I don't need to be on the outside. I've made friends. Who are, yeah, on the *outside*."

His remark sparked a twinge of concern.

He grinned wickedly. "I *got* you. You *felt* that, eh?"

"I feel *nothing* for you."

"Liar. Keep it up." Rick sat forward, elbows on the table. He rattled his chains. "You think you can intimidate me, bitch? I didn't know it was *you* who'd come for a visit. So you can go to hell. I'm done here."

Rick looked up to signal the guards. No one moved.

"I said I'm fucking done!"

"No, you're not," I told him. "You need to understand the full extent of what I can do. You're like a bug I've caught. Who is known to hide weapons. And you just *threatened* me."

He sat back. "I'm chained. What? Not enough?"

"No. Because now I'm required to make sure you're *unarmed* before I release you back into the sewer. Guards. Search him."

Rick swung his head left and right, unable to defend himself as his chair got knocked out from under him. "Hey!"

The guards took hold of him, but he fought back. Even chained to the table, he was a threat. A savage animal until the male guard shouted the magic word.

"Taser! You want to *feel* what I can do to you, *boy?*"

Rick stopped thrashing.

"Better. Now get up! You know the drill. Bend your ass over. Head down on the table. Now!"

The female guard pulled Brandt's pants down around his ankles. She lifted his foot, then the other, and removed his pants. She kicked at both legs to spread them apart. She then lifted his shirt. The other guard held Brandt's head against the table while the woman snapped on rubber gloves.

With a powerless glare, Rick looked up at me.

At my smile. Which I knew he felt. Deeply.

The guard who'd be conducting the cavity search clicked on her flashlight. She gave me a *paid-in-full-thank-you* smile. My generosity in monetary terms was an extra bonus, expressed in a grin she was unable to conceal, "If you wanna leave, Dr. Sims, you can."

I glanced at his file as if interested in the psychological outcome, then slapped the folder down in front Rick's face.

"I plan to stay and watch this.

— ≈ —

The composite clang of metal, cages slamming, the shouts and whistles, seemed to pierce me and reverberate to my core. I couldn't leave San Quentin Prison fast enough. It wasn't elation I was feeling but depression. The mind-fuck retaliations, which initially satisfied a base desire for revenge, especially for Rick Brandt and Brad Fuller, now sickened me.

Everything started to backfire after facing Roger Dossen.

I dug into my purse for my car keys. The locks disengaged with a beep. I opened the door, tossed my briefcase inside, entered quickly, then closed the door. I started the engine. I gripped the steering wheel to steady my nerves. I was shaking and took several deep breaths, trying to calm myself as I drove past the prison gates. The looming yellow structure disappeared in my rearview mirror.

A surge of panic forced me to veer off the pavement onto a dirt embankment. Braking hard, I stopped short of plunging into the bay. I was sobbing uncontrollably. I didn't know what had come over me. Something inexplicable was happening. I detested those who'd raped me, and I'd fought hard to get even. But in the process, I now hated myself. Our roles had reversed. Roger had become a decent human, and I had become a monster.

— ≈ —

Egon does not dispute this. He is processing my story. Shaking his head, he gives me a sad smile. He thought he knew me and now he does not. I wonder if I know myself. His glass is empty, and he glances at it but doesn't move from the couch to pour himself more liquor. He nods for me to continue.

I'm the one in need of a stiff drink, but I choose water.

— ☰ —

Wiping my eyes, I pulled down the visor. I stared in the mirror. A thought occurred to me. Cell phones were restricted during visits. I retrieved mine from the locked glove box. I noticed messages. My receptionist had left three voicemails to call the office. It was urgent. She didn't give any details.

"It's me," I said. My yearlong employee was someone whom I guardedly considered a friend. "You called."

"It involves the police."

I tried not to sound alarmed. "What do they want?"

"Do you know a Faye Norwood? She was arrested and is being held downtown. She asked for you. She had our number and called our office. She said you would know who she was. Do you?"

"Yes. But … years ago. What did she do?"

"She was arrested for assault and battery. But now she's being held on suspicion of murder."

"Murder?"

"It's strange."

"Strange? In what way?"

"She's … well, actually a *man*. And carrying no identification. She refuses to talk to anyone but you. You didn't answer your phone. I didn't know what to do or—"

"Call the police. Tell them I'm on my way. I should be there in thirty minutes, depending on traffic."

"Where are you?"

"I'll tell you later," I told her but knew full well I would not be telling her much of anything about my day.

The drive back through Marin down 101 was uneventful, a mild commute at midday. After passing through the tunnel atop Sausalito, I descended into fog cascading over the headlands. It swirled into the red towers of the Golden Gate Bridge. The bay was sparkling below, and the San Francisco peninsula was like a miniature city far in the distance. A spectacular view worthy of erasing the chaos sloshing around in my head. But only for a few seconds.

I began to wonder and worry about Faye, aka Egon. How long had she (or he) been in San Francisco? How did "they" know where to find me? What had *Faye* done to get arrested? And why was *I* the one who was called instead of an attorney?

I thought of the recent murders. The evidence was leading the police to believe it was the work of a serial killer. Each victim had bruises to the neck and jaw. And the cause of death: a snapped neck. The final link, which tied all victims to one murderer, was the "X" carved into the skin. A very small and precise marking, which was never in the same location.

The memory of killing Sid rippled through me.

The news of these unsolved murders had spread nationally, and the deranged killer was being called, "The X Murderer."

I felt sweat dampening my armpits. I turned on the fan to blast cool air into my jacket and lifted the lapels to dry my blouse. I was so engaged in worries, I drove too fast across the bridge and through the toll gates. The downtown congestion of cars and the traffic lights made me anxious to move faster, yet I was unable to. By the time I had reached the County Jail and parked in the lot, I was shaking again. I didn't want to be seen like this. I knew most of the police officers and they'd notice how jittery I was acting. So I swallowed a Valium, remained in my car, and waited for the drug to take effect.

An officer I knew, from working with the Forensics Department, escorted me to see Faye. She was waiting in a room reserved for attorney-client private talks. She was alone beside a table and seated in one of the four metal chairs. The walls were off-white and blank. She stood out, dressed in a chartreuse jacket, black shirt with accent colors, black stretch jeans, and alligator boots. Her legs were crossed at the knees. Both hands rested on her leg, with fingers splayed. She was examining her nails, displaying boredom.

Faye looked up as I entered. Again I was struck by her beauty. Her silvery-blue eyes, as if from another planet, were set off by dark lashes and eyebrows, as I'd remembered. Her hair was the same length as it was in college, coffee-black, flowing over her shoulders. So convincing was her smile, the intimacy it implied, the little pout, I had to remind myself she was a man. Not genetically a woman.

My colleague in blue gave me a nod. He shut the door to leave the two of us to converse in private.

"I knew you would come," said Faye.

I placed my leather briefcase on the desk and sat. "Why?"

"You owe me. It's good to see you. Nice colors."

Her eyes were indicating my red purse, matching belt, necklace, and bracelet, all set against a dark charcoal blouse and business suit. "Thank you. How do I owe you?"

"The night of the party. When your friend was murdered. Oh, and keeping quiet about that incident in the cemetery."

I flinched and wondered if she'd noticed. "I have no idea what you're talking about."

Her eyes never left mine. "Can we not play innocent?"

I said nothing, sensing that her moves were ahead of mine.

She clarified, "I was following you, way back when."

I was being out-maneuvered. I didn't like where this seemed to be headed. Was she threatening me?

She raised an eyebrow. "So, you'll help me?"

"Yes, of course. But what have you done?"

Her smile was slow to form. "You tell me, Mira."

In a defensive lateral move, I reached for my briefcase, snapped it open, and brought out my notebook. I kept my eyes down and busied myself, selecting a mechanical pencil. I clicked it twice to load the lead, in preparation to write down pertinent information. When I looked up Faye was observing my fastidiousness.

"You're very organized," she told me as if to complement, yet I wasn't sure the remark was meant as one.

"I try to be." I positioned my pad and pencil on my lap.

"It's what I had predicted. Remember?"

Prepared to write, I wrote nothing. "Excuse me?"

"Us being friends. It was inevitable."

"It would seem so." I smiled, then wrote her name at the top of my ledger. "Now, let's start with why you were arrested."

Faye indicated a minor tear to the shoulder of her jacket. "I was involved in a frivolous altercation."

"Where did this occur?"

"In a bar. The Mix."

"That's on Market and Castro?"

"Then you know?"

"Know what?"

"About the place."

"I know it by name, but I'm not familiar with it."

"You should. It's quite fun there."

"Tell me about the incident."

Faye looked at her fingernails. "Some prick insulted me and I struck him over the head with a pool cue. What else is there to say? A total bastard. He deserved it. I'm sure you know the type."

I was used to dealing with a variety of misfits, even psychopaths, but Faye made me more uneasy. "How do you mean?"

"Being a woman."

"Right. I see. Did this man hit you back?"

"He tried. He didn't lay a hand on me. He was unconscious

394

after I knocked him to the floor. Where he pissed himself."

"Your jacket," I said. "How did—"

"Oh, *that*. Jeffery. A friend. He tried to stop the fight and I'm afraid I hit him too, by accident. I'll make it up to him. It was over fast. But someone called 911. Now I'm here."

I tapped the notepad with my pencil. "I understand the fight, or altercation, and why you got arrested. But do you know why you are being held?"

"I suppose it has to do with something stupid I said, off the cuff, while inebriated. It was taken the wrong way."

"What was it you said?"

"I don't recall." Her lips spread into a smile. "Isn't that the line everyone uses? In my case, it happens to be true. Apparently, I said I *admired* whoever was killing those men. The recent murders. You've been following these killings?"

I nodded, indicating for her to continue.

"Hideous men, each victim. All known rapists and pedophiles. They *all* deserved to die. Or have their balls chopped off, which is what I would have done, had I been given the chance."

"You said that to the police?"

"I waived my rights. Stupid me. It's now recorded. The police have indicated that I have become a person of *interest*. Normally, I would enjoy that title. I try to be interesting. But not in relation to being a *murderer*."

I held my thoughts.

"Now," she concluded, "they think I'm somehow involved."

I hesitated, calculating my next move. "Are you?"

She echoed back, "Are you?"

Same words, but said neutrally, left ambiguous as if to let me know she could be as calculating. I wondered if she did know about the murders. Also, how much did she know about me?

It felt like I was being led to a slaughter.

"Mira?"

I blinked, focusing back on Faye.

"Are you? Going to help me or not? I know you have influence with the police. You'll know how to handle this. Am I right?"

— 〰 —

Coincidently, I had been called in to work with the crime unit assigned to investigate these serial killings. I knew what they had in the way of leads. Nothing. And Faye had told them nothing that could incriminate her, or hold her against her will. The contributing factors that caused suspicion were that she carried no identification. Also, their discovery that she was actually a man, her inflammatory statements, and her one free phone call that had been placed to me, of all people. They assumed I could fill in some blanks.

I informed my colleagues I had known Faye briefly in college. My diagnosis back then was correct. This individual suffered from a mental illness called dissociative identity disorder. The root factor of this psychological syndrome was childhood trauma, often involving physical abuse of a sexual nature. I had treated patients who had this disorder, I told them.

I suggested a strategy. A plea-bargain which would require both Egon and Faye Norwood (albeit the same person) to attend weekly sessions with a court-appointed psychologist for anger management. By agreeing to these terms, the assault and battery charge would be dropped since no one had been seriously injured.

When I explained the details, Faye said, "Fabulous. I wanted to hire you anyway."

"Why?"

"To evaluate my twin brother."

"Egon?"

"You met him during college."

"I did. Once. But why?"

"I fear he may be the serial killer."

So began our therapy. Based on lies and mistrust. Egon, when he appeared, was to be told that Faye had volunteered them both to seek family counseling. And by using hypnosis, I hoped to discover the root cause of their disease and, with any luck, integrate their two personalities. To use a popular adage, I soon discovered there were several elephants in the room. It was not uncommon in cases such as this, for there to be many alternates, or *alters*, a term coined for these dissociative states of mind. And, gradually, more alters surfaced to introduce themselves.

This is how I explained the syndrome at lectures:

The human organism is a complex system needing equilibrium. To maintain this critical state it uses integration and differentiation to adapt and defend its core. If threatened, this established sense of self can break down and fracture into diverse patterns of behavior where portions of the brain are not aware of the other parts. This is called dissociative identities. Each identity has its own awareness but experiences episodes of amnesia, comparable to the left hand not knowing what the right hand is doing. This alternating memory loss is a psychological illness called dissociative identity disorder.

The aforementioned description is taken directly from lectures on the subject, and what I say as an expert witness in court. Egon's mental split created alternate forms of reality. The root cause came from childhood trauma. The specific nature and extent of this abuse I had yet to discover. Coping with a traumatic event, such as child abuse, the mind creates an *alter* or an imaginary personality. The purpose: to displace the pain onto another who, the child imagines, is better equipped to withstand it. This mental detachment forms an expedient means for a child to endure the shock of abuse. In essence, it is a built-in mechanism for survival.

Because of this human need for equilibrium, an individual with multiple personality *disorder* seeks a form of *order*. A maladjusted form of stability, which is developed over time. And continual stress creates additional fractures and personalities. In order to function, these alter-egos find a method for resolving their internal conflicts. They establish boundaries. And each of these alternates is created to fill a specific purpose, and each has its own point of view. Once this equilibrium is established, any attempt to undo the integration will receive resistance.

Which is exactly what I encountered. My efforts to treat this psychosis was considered a threat. Some of the alters threatened to destroy me, manifested in aggression, seduction, even sabotage.

For protection, I sought advice from my advisor, who suggested I hire security, as a precaution. Which I had considered. I decided to, instead, purchase a handgun.

— ≋ —

"Destroy you? Did I ever, even *once*, threaten you, Mira?"

I calmly tell Egon, "No. You were never violent."

Egon is standing, leaning against an island counter between the kitchen and dining room. In one hand he holds a bowl of cashews. His other hand catapults single shots into his mouth. As my story escalates, reaching this court-ordered timeline when we met again, the rapid-fire of nuts into his mouth stops. He sets the bowl down hard. The clang of wood onto marble startles me.

I wait, expecting words to follow, but they don't get released. I deduce from his conflicted expression this newly-formed integration of personalities is battling it out, each wanting to tell their version.

I remain poised on a loveseat, projecting a balance of relaxed composure and mindful concern. I sip my glass of ice water and wait for Egon to say something. He is a gifted artist, but words fail him. Despite his disability, he has managed to channel his intelligence into becoming an imaginative and brilliant performer.

Egon has combined the skills of an illusionist, mime, magician, and ventriloquist to invent phenomenal art, statues that come alive and transform into otherworldly beauty. His poetic heart has made mine want to be in sync with his.

But I am wondering if this fusion has worked. Newly formed, his integration is fragile, capable of disintegrating or exploding like a nuclear warhead that appears to be dormant.

Silently he watches me, then gives a playful smile.

"Faye and Hunter send their regards."

This is meant, I hope, to let me know his emotions are under control. A sign for me to continue.

— ≋ —

"Who are you?"

There was a noticeable adjustment, a realization that he is not where he had last remembered being. A puzzled look of acceptance, of not knowing how this situation came to be, or who I was, or why he was facing me in an office environment. Adroitly, he charmed me with a mischievous smile. He followed it with this opening remark, a non sequitur:

"My God, you are so beautiful. I am going to make love to you in my dreams tonight. I hope you don't mind."

I could feel blood flooding my face as if an admission of guilty desire. With one stroke of a few words, he'd scattered my tightly organized world into pieces that I'd not be able to reassemble easily. This college boy I had admired from afar, who had looked so regal on campus, was now in my office. His blue eyes were as stunning as Faye's, obviously, since housed in the same body. And yet different. Seductively warm and piercing. A male persona.

His smile was disarming. "How do I know you?"

"We met in college. Do you remember?"

"Vaguely. I feel like we've known each other before. In another lifetime? What's that called?"

"Déja vu."

"That's it."

"It also means, "an anomaly of the memory.""

Egon laughed and looked around. "Makes sense. Since I'm not sure how I got here. No memory. Sorry. Why *am* I here?"

I smoothed my skirt at the knee, an unconscious habit Egon's eyes homed in on. "Because of Faye."

"What has she done to bring us together this time?"

His wry smile was infectious, a drug infiltrating my brain. I was biting the eraser of my pencil, and he noticed. It made me conscious of another of my behavioral ticks. I glanced down at my notes.

"Faye was arrested for assaulting a man in a bar."

His levity faded. "No surprise. That's serious, I realize."

"It is. The judge issued a court order for Faye to undergo anger-management therapy. Which included seeing you too. Because of your relationship."

"Our relationship?"

"Family counseling is normal."

He laughed. "Does that mean she told you?"

"Told me what?"

"That we're estranged. What else did she say?"

"Well—"

"Wait."

"What?"

"You're *her*. That girl ... Mira something?"

"Skyles."

"You probably told me already."

"I did."

"You were a psych major, right? Wow, this is crazy."

"How do you mean?"

"Us. Now. Here. You know?"

I was unsure of his meaning. "That we'd attended college at the same time? And now I'm your therapist?"

"Don't you mean Faye's?"

"Yes. I suppose the coincidence is unusual."

"And embarrassing. That we're having these problems."

"You and Faye?"

"Mira, I really don't know you, yet. So, yes. Faye and me." Said as a playful taunt, he grinned. "Although, if it *was* you and me, I can't imagine us ever fighting. Can you?"

I felt another involuntary tingle of blood gush to my capillaries, prickling my skin. Trying to mentally fight it off, I looked down and made more notes as a diversion.

"You'd never hide anything from me, would you, Mira?"

"Excuse me?" I looked into his eyes.

"About you and me. Or about Faye and me?"

"There is a confidentiality aspect to these sessions. And for us to get to the root cause of the problems you're having, with Faye, you need to trust me. And be completely honest."

"Fair enough. Faye's made my life a living hell."

"In what way has she?"

He pointed at my book. "You don't have to do that."

"Do what?"

"Write down everything I tell you."

"I don't. But I'm required to take notes. It's not something I share with Faye."

Egon looked at me with suspicion, then shifted to indifference. "Faye used to mention you. Even recently, come to think of it. Which is why your name suddenly registered."

"She mentioned me, how?"

"What you did in college. It was brave, she thought."

"Regarding the trial?"

"Yeah."

Egon seemed to anticipate the question I avoided asking.

"Unlike Faye, I've tried to erase that episode. Roger was always nice to me. But, you did what you felt you had to do. Right?"

I nodded instead of parroting the word. I had to remind myself this *was* Faye. At least, she was part of his mental architecture. And, as his alternate personality, she could be aware of our conversations. The theoretical understanding of precisely how the mind assimilates and functions when suffering from a psychoneurotic condition was just that: *theoretical.* Documented cases were rare and varied with regard to a success rate. So I proceeded cautiously.

After all, Faye had seen me come out of Roger's room the night of Gwen's murder. She could have poked holes in my testimony by introducing doubt about the timeline. Yet she remained quiet during the trial. Why? And now I learned she'd been following me. And, she intimated she'd seen me murder Sid Meyers. It was all supposition, but enough to make me fret.

The eraser had found its way to my mouth again. Egon got me to smile, making me conscious of my habit. I lowered the pencil and made a note. Faye *talked* about me. She had admired what I'd done. Which meant, what? My vigilante form of justice?

Had I spawned a copy-cat killer? Or worse, was Faye planning to set me up and link my past to these recent murders? Could this be payback for what I'd done to her cousin? As a safeguard, I reassessed my therapeutic approach. I needed to erase parts of Faye's memory. It was possible, in theory.

— ≈ —

I was reminded of the myth of Narcissus, who fell in love with his own image. Attempting to kiss his reflection in a pond, he had drowned. Because he was unable to differentiate between what was fantasy and what was reality.

This was Egon. But what was I? The deadly pool?

As time passed I realized, against my better judgment, that I was falling in love with Egon. It was unprofessional. Also unethical. To become romantically involved was taboo. As was he, mysterious and alluring. Faye had beauty and charm too, but of a different kind. She was the *id*, as theorized by Freud in the division of the mind. She was that portion of the psyche driven by instinctual needs and desires. Whereas the *ego* was ruled by perception, as strongly influenced as the id was to instincts.

I was ashamed to admit that Egon had cast a spell on me. I tried to resist him, but I could not.

Faye, on the other hand, had a habit of interrupting.

"Where are we with Egon?" she asked.

I was constantly readjusting to this "changing of the guards" – the shifts from male to female persona. "Faye?"

"Mira. Are you making progress?"

"How do you mean?"

Faye tapped her nails on the armchair. "You *know* I've hired a private investigator."

"Clifford Hill," I said. "Yes, he introduced himself."

"Against my wishes." Faye rocked her crossed leg and flung a strand of hair from her face. "He betrayed me. He has a guilt-ridden conscience. I had hoped for better results."

Did she mean me? I wasn't sure. "From who?"

"*Clifford*. Mira, pay attention. I hired Clifford to investigate Egon. To see what he does when I'm not around. Not a difficult task. Then I discover he's been moonlighting. Hired by another person to investigate these murders."

"Hired by whom?"

"I don't have names," said Faye. "I got him drunk one night and he blabbed. He has a friend in law enforcement, who's been leaking information to him."

"Why?"

"How should I know. But get this, he was asked to investigate the crime unit investigating the case."

"The serial killings?"

"Mira, what else are we talking about? Yes."

I had no idea if Faye was being truthful. Or if this was a mind game to get a reaction out of me. I gave only a facade of professional curiosity. I *was* curious, alarmingly so. I was working on my follow-up question when she surprised me with her own.

"Shouldn't we tell the police?"

"Tell them what?"

"That they have a snitch in their department."

I tapped my pencil, considering this new information, whether it was true or not. "It's possible they already know."

"Then they do, is what you're saying?"

"No," I said.

"Then what *are* you saying?"

"Faye."

"Mira." Her crossed leg stopped rocking. "Don't you think it's important?"

"It could be. I'll be sure to inform the proper authorities about what you suspect."

"Don't act coy. You're a criminal psychologist."

"How did you know that?"

"I had Clifford investigate you."

"For what reason?"

"Because I'm mentally ill, yes? Suspicious of everyone? Whereas you, trained at discerning the sickos from the sane, should know that, and not have to ask."

"Faye, I've never called you ill or sick."

"You've never called me sane either." She raised an eyebrow.

"You realize it was a plea bargain reached by attorneys and a judge that resulted in you being assigned to me."

"I know the reason why we're here," said Faye.

Her remark was edged with aggression. "Let's talk about how your week has been."

"Let's not."

"What would you like to discuss?"

"Anger management."

"Okay. Have you lost your temper this last week?"

"I'd never be that careless," said Faye. "I keep my anger close at all times. It is *that* precious to me."

She got me to smile, and for a moment it felt like we were back in college, drinking coffee or beer, talking and laughing.

She added, "Ah, you mean have I struck someone over the head with a pool cue lately? No. Though I've wanted to. So there, you see, I have my anger managed nicely."

My college-student demeanor reverted back to that of a licensed therapist. "Good. Anger is about devaluing others. When a person lashes out, it's often triggered by a perceived threat to one's self. A knee-jerk reaction to feeling devalued."

"By stupid people who deserve to be *devalued*. I agree."

"It's a vicious cycle, don't you see?"

"Yes, I see it clearly," said Faye. "Here comes the sun, and then the moon. It's cyclical. And with each new day more stupid people. It's like an infestation. Someone needs to stop them. Isn't that the reason we're both in the same profession?"

I paused to deconstruct what Faye had said. "When you said 'we,' what business were you referring to?"

"Anger management, law enforcement, delivering justice, and punishing guilty pricks. Take your pick."

"Aggression only perpetuates more violence."

Faye had that bemused look I recalled from college, a playful pout to imply she had me cornered into checkmate. "And how have you learned to manage *your* anger, Mira?"

"Faye, these sessions are not about me."

"Maybe they should be." Faye cut me off with a smile. "You've been a naughty girl. Haven't you?"

"Excuse me?" I straightened my posture.

"I know what you've been up to."

"What are you implying?"

"Can I stand?" She did anyway, without waiting for permission. She wandered around my office to survey my certificates and awards of merit along the wall, pausing to examine photos of me with police chiefs and heads of state. "When I discovered you were practicing in San Francisco, I came. I was drawn. Curious."

"About?"

"You. Why so close to San Quentin Prison? The three inmates you've *managed* to incarcerate. All of them penned in strategically placed locations. As if brilliantly *managed*."

"I had no control over—"

"No, of course not. But you've managed to control your own anger quite impressively. Look at the results. I'm impressed."

I felt boxed in. Uncertain of my next move. I needed to control the situation, not lose it. Yet I desperately wanted to know what she knew, and how.

I asked, "Have you been following me?"

"That would be interesting. If I could be your shadow or a fly on the wall. But the amount of security in most of the buildings you frequent would never allow me. There are so many rules that go along with your daily schedule, Mira."

"Faye, is there a point to what you're telling me?"

"Yes. My detective has been following you."

"Why?"

"Why not? If you've nothing to hide."

A trickle of sweat rolled down my back. "I'm surprised, is all."

"Being investigated? No one likes it."

"Faye, why do you think your brother is the serial killer?"

She kept circling around me, and I craned my neck. I motioned with my hand for her to return to her chair. She shook her head and collected her purse.

"I'm not sure."

"Not sure he is, or not—"

"Sure of nothing, Mira. How sure are you?"

Faye swept up her purse, motioning her hand toward the clock on the wall and moved toward the door. "I need to go. You should have told me our time had expired."

— ⇝ —

Our time had expired.

Faye's parting words kept resounding within me.

Time management. Like anger management, both coined terms. And philosophies I adhered to in principle, incorporating these skills into my daily life to maximize my work schedule. But my world was becoming unhinged by three concurrent events: the return of Egon (aka Faye) into my life; the escalating murders of the serial killer and; the self-awareness of my own mental disorder.

Seven years had passed since Roger Dossen and Brad Fuller had been convicted of rape and manslaughter. They were both scheduled to have their first parole hearings. Each would be reviewed by a parole board. Rick Brandt would not be. His chances for parole were negated after killing a cop, then murdering an inmate.

I had requested to make statements at both hearings. Attorneys appointed by the Board of Parole Hearings (BPH), who represented Roger and Brad, had also filed requests that I attend. In addition, the district attorney, who might oppose their paroles had summoned me to appear. This was highly unusual.

Some of the factors reviewed by the Department of Corrections and Rehabilitations panel would be counseling and psychological evaluations; disciplinary notices and/or laudatory merits; vocational accomplishments, and; participation in self-help programs.

On the morning of Roger's parole hearing, I entered the Oregon State Penitentiary and stopped to use the public restroom. I splashed cold water on my face to calm myself. A correctional officer then ushered me into the fluorescent-lit room.

I was fifteen minutes early. From behind, I watched Roger and his attorney consulting with each other at a long table. It faced another table and seats, slightly-elevated, reserved for those who'd determine Roger's fate. He noticed me and looked away. What had I expected? For him to smile? To welcome my presence? I was the person who had perjured herself to lock him away. I searched my pockets and found mints. The cinnamon tasted artificial and formed a sour brew with my breakfast of black coffee.

The state prosecutor arrived next, giving me a nod as he took a seat at the opposite end of the table where Roger sat. Neither lawyer took much notice of the other. Then a woman I didn't recognize at first entered the room and sat in a seat toward the back of the room. Since she was not wearing her guard uniform I was slow to make the connection. Only when her eyes avoided mine, refusing to make eye contact with me, did I realize who this person was. She was one of the prison guards I had bribed.

Shit. Hadn't I paid her enough? I feared the courtroom would fill with the other prison guards I'd worked hard to befriend, who would now turn against me. I was tempted to get up and leave. But how would that look? Where would I go? There was no escaping. I had no idea what to expect, only clues.

Crime victims or their families were entitled to present a fifteen-minute statement. Neither Gwen's parents, nor siblings, planned to attend. I'd been in contact with her family and told them I would see that justice was served. Any person (and I was not *any* person) was permitted to submit information to the review board concerning an inmate requesting a parole.

I was relieved when no one else entered the room. The place felt empty and sad. Gwen's spirit had been long gone, disposed into the Dustbin of Forgotten Souls. The commissioner, who presided over this Initial Parole Consideration Hearing, together with his deputy, entered and took their seats.

As the hearing was called to order, I heard the door shut behind me. I turned and saw another person I recognized take a seat next to the women guard. I'd hired him too. Two uniformed police officers entered next and took seats beside the door. Their presence caused a sensation that felt like a roller-coaster drop.

It felt as if my heart was pressed up against my throat.

Was I to be arrested?

What the *hell* was going on?

I wanted to check for messages on my cell phone, an item not allowed inside these walls, so I stared at my hands and pretended to inspect my nails.

I mentally fought the perspiration surfacing on my forehead. The commissioner was speaking but I barely heard his words. The state prosecutor stood to make a comment, followed by a rebuttal from the defense attorney. The volley of words, from one side to the other, went by so fast I was startled when I heard my name called.

I was being asked if I wanted to make a statement. I did.

Addressing the parole board, I came forward and sought control over my nerves. This is what I read to the BPH:

"Since his imprisonment, Mr. Dossen has maintained a blemish-free conduct record and has strived to enhance his ability to function within the law upon release. He has successfully taken college-level courses and has held skilled jobs such as law librarian and custody captain's clerk. He has availed himself of an array of self-help and therapy programs, including Alternatives to Violence and Breaking Barriers, along with advanced classes. He has published more than 300 articles in Prison Legal News and has participated in the Men's Advisory Council.

Psychological reports and evaluations, including my own, have repeatedly found that he does not suffer from any mental problems. He has received numerous favorable reports from correctional and mental health professionals and has maintained solid relationships with his family throughout his incarceration. His prison record is spotless, and while in prison, as mentioned, he has worked hard to acquire new skills and additional education in order to make realistic parole plans. His work has been exemplarily and praised.

Based on all these factors, including my own firm conviction of his rehabilitation and my belief that he will return to society as an asset to the community, and by no means be a detriment or threat, I implore that Mr. Dossen be released from prison to parole.

I thank the board for listening and for your consideration."

I sat down, in a puddle of sweat (that's what it felt like). I was relieved my speech was over, but now terrified of what would follow. I felt queasy, even nauseous. I expected Roger's attorney to launch a counter-attack on my credibility, my improper conduct as a criminal psychologist, and my *criminal* abuse of power. I watched Roger and his lawyer as they consulted in hushed voices. I heard not a word of it, but I did notice Roger vigorously shaking his head.

My heart fluttered erratically when one of the prison guards was called forward to speak. She spoke on Roger's behalf. Praising his prison conduct and civility. Stating Roger was a model inmate. The other guard came forward too, echoing similar sentiments. Roger, when questioned by the board, was thoughtful and articulate.

I was stunned when no recriminations against me followed. No one spoke of my misconduct. I would not be chastised, arrested, or led away in handcuffs. At least not today. The panel left to convene in private for several minutes. Upon returning, the commissioner announced his decision: Roger would be granted parole.

I didn't move. My emotions were still in a tailspin, yet striking nothing. I had averted disaster.

It was because of Roger, I intuited, who decided not to punish me. Granted, his decision was based on logic. If he had attacked my credibility, it would have weakened his case for receiving parole. Also, my prepared statement was genuine and heartfelt, which I had

410

hoped he knew and appreciated. A good deed that had inadvertently worked to my advantage too.

I wanted to approach Roger to say or do something. But what? Give him a hug? Say congratulations? Ridiculous. Me, the one who was instrumental in taking his freedom away, who was now willing to help him. I felt shame, and couldn't face the prison guards either. I waited with my head down, pretending to make notes. I fought back tears and dabbed my eyes with a tissue, careful not to disturb my makeup, then stood and walked out of the room. My CO escort was waiting. Through the din of caged men and the series of security doors, he led me out of the impenetrable structure.

I felt lucky to be leaving.

— ≋ —

I made an appeal for Brad's release too, although he didn't have Roger's stellar record. He was a recovering heroin addict, had been a drug runner and a prostitute for a prison gang – and was currently housed in the Sensitive Needs Yard for being a snitch. My statement to the BPH asked the board to take into consideration the abuse he'd received while imprisoned, his forced slavery and coercion by gang members to participate in illicit acts. I cited his courage in reporting the drug trafficking to the Investigative Special Unit which, by doing so, endangered his life.

Also, Brad had enrolled in a self-help program to stay drug-free. It was my belief, I stated, that he no longer posed a threat to society. His rehabilitation would improve better if in a healthy environment. There were beneficial reentry programs to mentor and counsel him. Behind prison walls, he was in danger of being killed, as retaliation, for cooperating with the ISU.

Brad was almost unrecognizable to me from the boy and college student I knew who had brutalized me twice. He was struggling now with his sexuality. His blond hair, no longer braided into corn curls, was brushed straight and shoulder length. His posture was straight, poised to listen. He nodded attentively at each question and willingly answered. The high register of his voice and toothless lisp sent chills of guilt throughout me. He made a quavering plea to be released and set free. When he was denied parole he wept loudly.

I felt something break inside of me. As if my glass heart had shattered (is what I'd imagined) from his high-pitched piercing cries. I was responsible for this tragedy. What I had set in motion years ago had exceeded being a vengeful act of justifiable retribution, and now out of my control. Our eyes made brief contact before he was taken, in shackles, out of the room.

I was left shaken. I felt a slow rigor mortis seizing control of my muscles as I stood. Trying to convince myself that I was still human, I walked stiffly through the prison and across the parking lot to my rental car.

The plush interior felt like a coffin as I closed the door.

That night I slept like a corpse but woke with a start, in shock. I was still alive. I fell back into an unsettled sleep. I had nightmares of being shackled, forced to strip naked, squat, and spread my legs as a mirror at the end of a stick was placed beneath my vagina for a guard to peer inside. I heard subterranean laughter.

I awoke to the sound of glass breaking inside my head. A noise that reverberated, unwilling to leave my senses. My silk nightgown was soaked in sweat. I was shivering. Even a hot shower took several minutes to warm me.

That was my life. *I had made my bed, so now I had to lie in it.* Wasn't that the expression? At my office, I awaited the arrival of my first patient who was scheduled to meet me in thirty minutes. I sat sipping from the styrofoam cup of coffee cradled in my hands. I kept hearing faint sounds of glass breaking. What had I become? A fraud? One who gained success and prestige from listening to the problems of others. Professing to cure their ills when I, myself, was mentally crippled by my own form of madness.

In my defense, I was methodical and respected by my peers. My record of achievements was exemplary. I'd received certificates and awards. I served on the board of two charities and donated my time and money to several nonprofit organizations. I worked long hours, lived atop a skyscraper. My wardrobe was impressive, calculated to make the right impression for whatever environment I was called to work in. And my jet-powered bathtub helped soften the edges after a long, hard day.

My love life, by comparison, was not so rich. My brief relations with men ended on various off-key or minor notes. A surgeon I had dated ended our affair by telling me I psychoanalyzed his every move and made him second-guess his skills when operating. His excuse for breaking off our engagement, he claimed (saying he still adored me), was for the sake of his career. Then there was an investment banker. He consolidated his love for me by ignoring his children, an ex-wife, family, and friends. He bought me expensive gifts. And he expected my exclusivity. He was smart, witty, and loving to a fault. One night, I awoke to find myself locked inside a vault, a soundproof basement room where he'd imprisoned me, and slowly smothered me with sex, until death. A nightmare, thankfully. Yet, subconsciously, I realized the dream rang true. I was the one who ended the relationship.

There were other lovers, a short list, not worth mentioning.

My staff, colleagues too, had nicknamed me The Ice Princess. *Hot face, cold body.* The inside joke was that men felt threatened by my mind and feared their sexual asset would freeze, maybe snap off, over time. When I accidentally overheard this moniker used about me at a conference, I pretended to be amused. But I was wounded. Hurt, that people thought this about me. I was aware that I came off cold, at times, but I was a loving person, warm-hearted, beneath the surface. I appeared aloof by necessity, given the intimate nature of my business, the emotional involvement and the disclosure of secrets from patients during therapeutic sessions.

To disregard these client-patient boundaries allowed a greater chance for transference to occur – the process by which attitudes and desires associated with another, such as a parent, a sibling, or spouse, were unconsciously redirected onto the analyst. These were hazards of my profession, and I was aware of them. It was imperative that I be clinically precise in my actions and judgments at all times.

My clients had issues that ranged from phobias and depression to psychosomatic complaints and fears. I had to face psychopaths who would kill me without a second thought. These face-to-face encounters were intense, often frightening. The socially-violent ones needed to be institutionalized. My psychotherapeutic skills provided a valuable service to the community.

The problem was, I had my own screw loose. I was vulnerable. It was my Achilles' heel. And I wondered, was my nemesis, the one who could deliver the arrow shot, about to walk through my door. My next patient was Egon, Faye, or an alternate, since I never knew who I'd be facing.

I sensed a masculine presence when the door opened. But the cocky swagger, the hesitation before choosing a seat, the bemused grin, signaled a new persona.

Once my patient was seated, I asked. "Egon?"

"I'm Hunter. Egon is indisposed. Rehearsing for a show."

"Have we met?"

"Not formally. Egon's my mate. He keeps me informed. And asked me to come in his stead."

Hunter looked at my office space as if he was debating whether to rent or buy it. "Nice place. You've done well, Mira. Or should I be calling you Doctor Skyles?"

"Mira's fine." I smiled and tried to dredge up his name when I'd heard it before. "I believe Egon's mentioned you."

"With a smile on his lips? Spoke well of me?"

"Yes. Regarding a college incident, a fight on campus?"

"I'll need reminding, love. I've had a few squabbles."

"At the University of Oregon. In front of the Student Union? Outside The Fishbowl? Rick Brandt had—"

"Yanked my hair. The bastard had it coming."

I had no guidebook to refer to, nothing to prepare me for this, so I went with the flow. "How long have you known Egon?"

"We met in high school. He was shy. Unlike my dad, who could be funny, but a sadist bastard. He forced me to learn the martial arts. To toughen me up."

"To be a man."

Hunter laughed. "His words verbatim. He'd push me into fights which I hated."

"In high school?"

"Yeah. 'Kick his ass!' he'd yell at me. Fighting with guys I had no grudge against. But there I was. Caught up in a brawl."

"That sounds horrible."

"Horrible? God-damned *surreal*. Fancy this. When I realized I'd outgrown my old man, I beat the living shit out of *him*. Now that was surreal. And the last time he ever told me what to do."

"How did that make you feel?"

"Satisfied. Sad. Alone. Fucked. But, independent."

No case-study or medical journal had prepared me for this, so I relied on instinct. "How would you describe your relationship?"

"With Egon? I'm not sure what you're asking me, Mira."

"You were close friends? Mates, as you put it."

"What's *that* imply?" He leaned toward me, grabbing a chunk of his hair. "That I'm a *fag*? I'm not a queer, sister!"

Confronted with a fight or flight response, I did neither. I held my ground, remaining calm. "I wasn't implying you were."

"Good." He leaned back in his chair. "I don't carry prejudices on that sexual orientation shit. Neutral free, okay?"

"Okay." I smiled neutrally. "Can we talk about Faye?"

Hunter grunted, "No. I'm here on Egon's behalf."

"All right. Tell me about Egon."

Hunter padded his coat pocket, looked up at me. "No smoking, I'm guessing?"

"Optional."

Hunter rubbed his mouth. "He's gifted. A true artist."

"Egon?"

"Have you seen him in the park? Performing his art?"

"I'm afraid I haven't."

Hunter winked. "*Afraid?* Mira. You're a doctor."

"Therapist," I clarified.

"You can't be spending your life indoors. Get out, breath the air. You're not even curious?"

"What can you tell me about his art?"

"Experience it yourself."

"I might."

"Come Sunday."

"Where? When does—"

"Union Square, nine am sharp."

I wrote this information down. "What do I look for?"

"A sign. Can't miss it. Okay. Time to go."

Before I could think of anything to say, knowing instinctively it would be futile to try and reel him back in, Hunter rose, gave me a departing nod and was gone.

— ≡ —

Sunday morning I walked into Union Square, ascending the row of steps past a large colorful heart sculpture elevated on a pole. I had always loved to watch people. And there were plenty to watch, from tourists talking in foreign languages to the downtrodden jangling cups for spare change. I stopped to buy a coffee, then drifted through this urban park paved in a glistening pattern of marble.

I had arrived early so I would have ample time to find what I

GOD, SEX & PSYCHOSIS

was looking for. A sign, Hunter had said. But how obvious was it? There was a clown twisting balloons into colorful animals. I stopped to observe a man moving robotically to electronic sounds. I tossed a dollar into his upturned top hat on the ground.

The park's centerpiece was a several-story-high column with a bronze statue of a woman balanced at its top, on a ball. Her raised arms held a garland in one hand; a trident, in her other. I knew what the monument represented – the death of an American president, combined with a victory at sea. I moved closer to refresh my memory and read the plaque.

I noticed a sign nearby:
SHOW STARTS @ 9 AM SHARP.

The words were written on a miniature easel, placed before what appeared to be a large vertical block of cement. I walked over to examine the structure. I tapped the surface with my knuckles. It felt solid, but softer than concrete, plaster maybe, and produced a hollow sound. I backed away and found a nearby metal bench to sit and wait for the hour to arrive.

At nine o'clock sharp two women approached the nondescript block. Each wore a white artist's smock. One was carrying a metal urn; the other, a stepladder and a satchel. With mechanical precision, like automatons on a clock, one set down the ladder and removed a bronze bell from the sack. The other removed a hammer and hit the metal, producing a mellifluous gong.

One woman held the ladder while the other, holding the urn, climbed to the top. She carefully poured the contents into a hole in the block, which erupted a gush of steam into the air. She descended the stairs, then she held the ladder while the other women ascended. With the hammer and chisel, she chipped at the block until a crack formed. She worked at this fissure. It cracked open. The walls fell in sections to the ground.

Left standing was a bronze sculpture of a naked man, wearing only a hat and boots. He stood on a pedestal. His long hair flowed in curls over his shoulders. One arm was cocked, fist at his side, while his other clenched a long sword that touched the ground. A large severed head was at his feet.

It took me a moment to register I was looking at a replica of Donatello's David. An amazing feat of art. The noise in the square had quieted, which was so unusual, amidst the clanging cable cars. The two women in smocks were miming alarm and consternation, and pointing to the sculpture. A portion of the plaster had remained attached to the body. It extended from the ground and concealed his genitals, which were exposed on the original statue.

One of the women pushed the other up the ladder. The hammer and chisel were positioned to remove this defect in the unveiling when suddenly a whistle sounded. Pushing through the crowd came a policewoman. Wearing a blue miniskirt, halter top, and knee-high boots, she held a badge while tooting her whistle. She was signaling to stop the removal of this last vestige of decency.

The crowd laughed, realizing the humor. Each of these three women was disputing artistic freedom, yet no words were spoken. This was when the sculpture of David came alive. His eyes opened first, observing the debacle. He lifted the sword above the women, as if to smite one, maybe all, before reconsidering. Instead, he lifted his foot off the head of Goliath. He speared it like a cocktail olive and raised it into the air. The three woman seemed unaware that the statue was moving or the crowd laughing.

I was in awe, enthralled by the performance. This David, whom I recognized to be Egon, removed the head of Goliath from his sword and placed it on his fist. Which he raised, displaying the head before the crowd, claiming victory. The eyes of Goliath opened, expressing shock – alarmed to be without a body – staring at David, who stared back with equal disbelief.

This theatrical pantomime and illusionary puppetry continued for several minutes. The performance ended when the policewomen detached the sword from David's hand and stabbed Goliath's head. As it toppled to the ground, she impaled David too. An audible gasp arose as the sword penetrated his chest and emerged from his back, the tip sticking out. Egon, portraying David, remained on his feet. But his head fell forward. Both his arms hung limply at his sides. And slowly he became rigid, a statue again, transformed.

The applause was delayed. Nobody knew if the show was over. When the three women aligned to take a bow, the ovation was loud. I was on my feet too and clapping while moving closer to witness the artistry. The attention to detail was impressive, the resemblance to Donatello's dark bronze statue. He looked so authentic, as if poured from metal, then honed and burnished. Now reconfigured.

His cockiness vanquished, impaled by his own sword.

So enchanted, I stayed to watch Egon hold this pose for more than five minutes. I was drawn to his body, physically toned yet graceful. And like the original statue, his nakedness was on display. I felt embarrassed, but unable to keep from staring, scrutinizing his body, seemingly cast in bronze, yet knowing this was a real person, a patient I was treating.

— ≋ —

"You came," said Egon, approaching me. "I'm glad."

I was rather star-struck at the face and body encased in a patina of bronze. "I can hardly believe what I saw."

"That's the point."

I looked at the sword sticking out from both sides of his torso. His genitals were concealed with a bronze-colored fig leaf, the last remnant of plaster now removed. I averted my eyes to stare into his light blue irises. "The sword, how is that done?"

"It's an illusion."

"I realize that ... that you're not *dead*, but ..."

He smiled and pulled out both ends of the sword. One of the

performers came over to hand him a robe, which he put on, synching the cord at the waist.

"Hi," she said to me in passing.

"You were great," I told her.

"Thanks," she said with an ounce of flirtation, before moving back to help the others gather up the props.

I told Egon, "I'm surprised I've never heard of this. How long have you been performing?"

"Here? Months. But this is all new."

"What is?"

"David and Goliath. You saw the debut performance. How do you think it went?"

"It was wonderful. I mean, you must know that."

"I can't see myself. If I could, I would. Maybe." He smiled. "Well ... I should go, help clean up the mess we've made."

As he turned, I said, "Thank Hunter. He told me I should come. I'm happy I did."

Still wearing the hat, Egon tilted his head, leaned forward and kissed me on the lips. "Until we meet again."

I felt as if I'd been transformed into a statue. I couldn't move, and wasn't sure if I should try. I hadn't anticipated his kiss. Any kind of intimacy was unprofessional in a doctor-patient relationship. But now I realized, I had wanted him to kiss me. His lips were scented and texture from his bronze makeup. I backed away and bumped into someone. "Sorry."

I walked across the sparkling marble. I felt weak in the knees. *Weak in the knees – from love.* Was I? I wasn't sure what I felt or how I should be feeling. I began to second-guess Egon's intentions. Had it been an affectionate peck, to show gratitude for my coming? The way he might kiss a relative, or an associate?

No, I decided. It had meant more than that.

I was walking up the hill to retrieve my car parked in a garage when, on an impulse, I veered to my left and pushed through glass doors to the Grand Hyatt Hotel. Continuing up a flight of stairs, I arrived at the restaurant bar. I sat on a stool in front of the bartender to receive faster service and ordered a Bloody Mary.

To my superego, that region of my brain that patrols my social behavior, bans my unacceptable desires, and doles out permissions, I said – *Screw it*. This was the weekend. I had a right to enjoy myself. Out loud, I muttered, "Pull yourself together."

"What's that?" asked the bartender.

"Nothing. Thank you."

I stirred my breakfast cocktail with the celery stem and rewound the morning events in my mind. Aside from one couple at a corner table eating breakfast, I was alone with my thoughts. The bartender was preoccupied checking his inventory of liquor. I enjoyed the quiet atmosphere. It allowed me to daydream, wondering how to best deal with my next encounter with Egon, Faye, or whoever happened to show up in my office.

How did one part of the mind compartmentalize and function automatically from another? I couldn't comprehend how the switch process worked, how divergent personalities continued to disappear and reappear.

The medical community still considered it an unsolved mystery. A prevailing belief was that each personality was developed to fulfill a specific need. I knew this from research, but directly experiencing someone whose mind altered drastically was difficult to fathom. And despite a patient's professed desire to unite these personalities – to become whole and function normally – no identity wanted to forfeit his or her independence, for fear of being eliminated.

I had to remind myself to keep on good terms with all the ego states involved. The documented cases did not indicate there was a reliable success rate for merging these personalities into one. And, even on the assumption that this fusion could hold, what would the end result be? I speculated it being comparable to a married couple who, despite the inevitable conflicts which had the potential to unravel its bond, stayed together.

What was the magical ingredient? Sacrifice. Submission. Trust. Commitment. A belief that the union is greater than the individual? No person was the same all the time. Everyone had moods and, to varying degrees, attractive and repulsive sides.

Nursing my drink, I decided everyone was a composite of selves, multiple personalities. Only not fractured and disassociated.

"Let me buy you a drink."

This was from a man who sat next to me. A large man, not fat but muscular. I noticed a tattoo with flames on his neck poking up from his shirt collar.

"I have a drink," I told him.

"Why not two?" He showed me a glitter of gold from his teeth as he smiled.

"I allow myself only one. But thanks."

He signaled the bartender with a snap of his fingers. "I'll have what she's having."

I had no right to prevent him from having this close proximity to me, even though there were plenty of empty seats.

"That was one hell of a show," he said.

"Excuse me?"

"In the park. I was there too."

"Oh," I said, "Yes, it was."

"I was watching you."

"Weren't you supposed to be watching the performance?"

"I'm good at multitasking." He took hold of the Bloody Mary set before him and guzzled down half the drink. "I was thirsty."

"I can see. You followed me here?"

"Happenstance. Serendipity. Don't you believe in it?"

"Not really." I turned away and sipped my drink. His intensity, the vibe he was projecting, made me uneasy.

"I thought I'd take this opportunity to meet you."

"Very flattering," I said, "But I'm already spoken for. Married, you see?" I held up my hand to show him the wedding ring I wore to ward off advances like this.

"Liar."

"*Excuse* me," I said, expressing annoyance.

"I am too. It takes one to know one."

I pushed away in preparation to leave.

"Stay." His large hand grabbed hold of mine.

"What are you doing? *Don't.*" I tried to pull my hand away but his grip was firm. The tattooed head of a snake poked out from under the cuff of his shirt sleeve. "Do you want me to scream?"

He released my hand. "You won't."

"I might. What is it you want?"

"To give you a message. Rick sends his regards."

This sent a chill through me. "Who?"

He huffed a laugh. "Like I said, about us. Being the same. You know *damned* well who I'm talking about."

I decided not to deny it.

He upturned his drink and swallowed down the rest, then set it hard on the bartop. "God *damn*, feels good being free. Doing what you feel. Having a Bloody Mary on a Sunday morning. To hell with going to church."

"Who are you?"

"Who *am* I? There's a brain teaser. Let's say I'm one of many friends on the outside. Friends of Rick. Yeah, the *Prick*."

When he pushed away from the bar and stood to go, I should have felt relief. But I didn't. He unbuttoned his cuff and pulled up his shirt sleeve past his elbow to show me snakes coiled around his arm, before covering them back up.

"Snakes. Harmless, except when they get *pissed* off."

"Are you threatening me?"

"Do I look stupid? I'm here to introduce myself."

"You're not going to murder me?"

He laughed. "If Rick wanted you dead, it would have been done long ago. Like six months. No, we've better plans for you."

I felt the injection of venom, felt numb, sickened, made worse by his parting remark.

"Your time is coming. *Clarabelle.*"

— ≋ —

Egon interrupts me, saying, "Wait."

So I wait. We have moved from inside to outside, standing on the deck overlooking the ocean. It is night and all we see now are a couple of campfires, a half moon, and the luminescent row of waves arching and cascading, crashing onto sand. Water spreads toward us, a shimmering liquid that varnishes the dark stretch of beach, then recedes, swallowed back into the sea.

"This man. His arms were tattooed with snakes?"

"I saw only the one arm," I say.

"The serial killer."

"What about him?"

Egon turns toward the ocean. "His last victim had tattoos of snakes on his arms. Also a dragon across his chest."

"It was the same man. I saw his body in the morgue."

He turns toward me. "Pretty strange."

"I know."

"Did you tell Gulen and the others?"

"About our encounter? Yes," I say and lie to his face. And hate myself for doing it.

Egon reaches for his drink on the railing and takes a swallow of the diluted scotch. "Are you getting any closer?"

"Closer to finding the killer?"

His head tilts. Of course, that was his question.

"I believe we are."

"Aren't you scared?"

"Of Rick Brandt, yes. I'd be lying if I said I wasn't."

"He's never killed a woman."

"He murdered Gwen!"

"I was talking about the serial killer."

"Can we not talk about this?"

Egon finishes his drink. "What, then? The mystery of who you are?" He raises an eyebrow.

I take the initiative to get closer and wrap my arms around him, rubbing his back. "Don't be sarcastic. He did scare me. What would David do? The victorious, or the vanquished? You choose."

This gets Egon to smile. "You like that guy, huh?"

"After he kissed me, I fell in love. With you too." Our bodies come closer and touch. "Make love to me."

"You're very forward."

I take hold of his neck, lift my legs to wrap them around him, and rest my head on his body. I close my eyes and rock gently to the motion of us moving as one. I hear the crash of waves fade behind us as we enter the bedroom. He lays me down upon the bed. I feel his fingers undo my robe and spread it apart. I open my eyes and watch as Egon casts off his robe, standing like David, mythical and magnificent, about to impale me with his sword. I open like a flower to accept him.

Love is the truest and sweetest sacrifice. A mutual surrendering, a desire to become one. Two bodies. Two minds. Reforming to create a new beginning and a climactic end.

We collapse in each others arms, searching with our mouths for a last kiss before snuggling.

In this somnolent aftermath of lovemaking, I feel warm and happy. My hand moves over Egon's chest, my fingers dance lightly, nymph-like on his immobile flesh. He murmurs his contentment and rolls toward me. I muse, *Why can't we stay like this forever?*

"Why?"

"Why what?" he asks.

"Why can't we stay like this forever?"

"Who says we can't?"

I have no good answer. I wish we could. But we can't.

"Do you want to tell me the rest of your story?"

Not really, I want to say. Not now.

But I do tell him. Because I can't help myself.

— ⲍ —

I did make an effort to help myself, trying to imagine how this might work. Could it work? Who would I be living with from one day to the next? From hour to hour? I knew little about Egon, only from our sessions. There were multiple aspects to his mind, defined personas inside this one person. It was possible I had not seen them all. In my heart, I wanted to believe I'd dismantled any danger, and that none of his personalities was capable of murder.

Egon was not the serial killer. He was an artistic, gentle soul. "Very *Zen*," was what I wrote in my notes about him. He lived in the moment, very attuned to the elements of change like a shifting wind, adaptable to surprises. He had to be, in order to survive. As we all do. I fantasized about us having a relationship. Foolishly, I imagined it being not that dissimilar from other married couples. The mind, like a house, had many rooms. A domain that sheltered many personalities, from one space to the next, fashioned by colors and decor, each with its own character and ambiance.

No one was ever the same person *all* the time.

People changed. As had Roger Dossen, Brad Fuller, and Rick Brandt. I'd kept track of them all. Roger had been granted parole. But to ensure public safety that an oversight hadn't occurred, it was subject to further review. The governor had the power to overturn the verdict. But Roger got released. And I was relieved.

From a distance I followed his post-prison activities, receiving reports by people who worked in the Department of Corrections and Rehabilitation. His vocational training landed him an entry-level position working for a construction company, removing demolition debris. Not the promising career expected of this rising football star. He joined a nondenominational church. Twice a month, he worked at an outreach shelter which provided food to the disenfranchised. From a model inmate, he transitioned to a model citizen. His parole officer told me that Roger had begun coaching at-risk kids, teaching them how to play sports and become leaders in their community.

I wanted to take partial credit for the good man he had become, but I had no right. It was my guilt I was trying to alleviate.

I learned that Brad was striving to become an inmate in good standing. He was making efforts to change. Roger sent him letters of encouragement. He advised Brad to attend the self-help programs that had helped him achieve an early release. Brad became discreet with his sexual interactions. And he was trying hard, as if cramming for college exams, preparing for his re-evaluation and appeal.

Rick, however, was incorrigible, locked in solitary confinement. He refused to comply with the rules. He defied authority by defiling his cell window with excrement – to force his extraction. The prison would deploy an army of guards wearing helmets with faceplates, padded gear, and groin guards. A pointman held a plexiglass shield and discharged a stun gun. Sometimes pepper-spray projectiles were tossed in his cell. This is what it took to contain the savage force of Rick, who spent his waking hours building his muscles.

During an extraction, Rick would scream, "Has that *bitch* been caught yet? I want that cunt in a box! Tell me—God-damn-it!"

Nobody, except me, knew who he was talking about.

His threats stung like inoperable shrapnel lodged in my brain. They festered and flared up – again, as I stared down at the corpse of the latest victim. The investigative unit consisted of two seasoned detectives, Faber and Gulen, a rookie assigned by the DA to the case, our forensics specialist, and me. And, unofficially, the coroner.

The man was naked on the table. His cause of death, a snapped neck. Overhead lights highlighted his tattoos. Snakes were coiled around his arms. A fire-breathing dragon took up the terrain of his torso. Its flames reached his neck. From his forest of pubic hairs rose a green snake. Its forked tongue encircled his navel.

By contrast, his penis hung limp, resembling a deflated snake. This man, who frightened me still, was dead in the morgue. He gave me the chills.

"Christ." said Phil, who was heading the investigation. "I can't say I'm *heartbroken* this one's departed."

"Ex-con," said Joel, the lead detective. "Got released from San Quentin seven months ago."

"Your killer really knows how to pick 'em, eh guys," joked the coroner who had become all too familiar with our case.

"You sure it's our guy?" From Bitner, new to the team, whose first name I kept forgetting. "There's no x-marks-the spot."

"Skyles. Thoughts?"

"Well," I said. "No motive for murder that's obvious."

"Envy, I'd say," joked Harvey, our forensic specialist. "Take a look at the size of his ... well, *snake*."

The men burst into laughter. Proximity to dead people triggered strange emotions. Postmortem humor.

I smiled. It was funny. "Do you mind?"

The coroner moved aside as I selected from his tray of tools the large extraction forceps. I reached and plucked the victim's penis. The laughter died as I pinched it by the tip, lifting and examining the appendage clinically. I let it drop, clicked on my small flashlight and followed the snake tattoo rising from his groin to his navel. "There," I said. "Cuts. Traced into the tattoo."

My male partners in this investigative team huddled closer to see what I was referring to.

"I'll be damned," said Faber.

The forensic specialist said, "I had time only for a preliminary. I was about to do a thorough—"

"Harv, relax," scolded our boss.

"Tracing its tongue?" said Joel.

"I missed that," said the coroner. "Fresh cuts."

"Not exactly an 'X,'" said Bitner.

"No, it's a 'Y,'" I said.

"Exactly," added Bitner.

"No," I explained. "The *letter* 'Y.'"

"Well that makes no sense," said Joel.

"Unless he's sending us a message," said Harvey.

"Nice work, Skyles," said Faber.

"You think it's our perp?" said Joel.

"Maybe a copycat killer," I speculated.

"Fuck," said Faber uncharacteristically foul.

My discovery of the "Y" mark caused the forensic specialist to shift into competitive gear. "I noticed something different too. This is the first time our *vic* got his eyes pepper sprayed."

"More like a woman to do that, right?" said Joel.

"From a purse, you mean," said Bitner.

"Not necessarily," I said. "A serial killer would come prepared. Rules out gender. Based on your can-from-a-purse theory."

"Yeah, plus this guy's big," said Joel.

"No way a woman could take *that* down," said Bitner.

"That may be true," I conceded. "But using pepper spray gave him, or her, an advantage. Could be either sex. My opinion."

"Good point," said Phil. "Which leaves us nowhere."

"You're forgetting the blood sample," said Harvey.

"Along with the windfall found in his pockets," said Joel.

"Tell Skyles," said Phil. "You'll find this interesting."

Harvey gave a pleased smile. "The killer got nicked this time. I found specks of DNA on his shirt. Could be from our perp. Lab's running the tests now."

"Good work, Harv." Phil turned to Joel. "Tell Skyles."

"What?" I braced myself for the unexpected.

Faber walked away from the corpse. He moved his bulk around as if carrying the weight of the world with him. The investigative team re-huddled nearby.

Joel broke the silence. "A newspaper article was in his wallet. About a murder committed years back, with the same MO as our serial killer. A broken neck. And guess what? An "X" carved into the middle of his forehead. Take a guess where it happened?"

I shook my head, feeling trapped, groping for a lie to use.

"Your alma matter. Ring any bells?"

The inside of my head was clanging. I acted as if a lost memory (completely forgotten) had suddenly reconnected. "Oh, my God! It happened while I was there. On the campus. A boy was killed in the cemetery. Was that the murder?"

The forensic specialist stopped chewing his gum. "How the hell could you let *that* one get by you, Skyles?"

"Are you kidding me? My best friend had just been murdered! I was traveling back and forth to Portland. It happened during the trial. Officer Rifkin ... he, I remember, pulled me aside and told me. I avoided watching the news. And I didn't bother *reading* the news. I was too focussed on the trial and my classes. What?"

Everyone was looking at me. Joel took the initiative to touch my shoulder with a shake. "Get a grip, Mira. No one's accusing you of falling down on the job. Geez, you were a college kid. Your best friend *died*, we get it. But this is good. It's a solid *lead*."

"Yes," I said with conviction. "Someone attending the college, or living in the area, was involved. Who moved to San Francisco. Who could be the serial killer. This *is* good."

"Now you're with us," said Phil, finishing with a smirk, before lumbering for the door with his crew following.

"I know someone who can help," I said. "He's a police officer."

"Rifkin?" Joel held the door open for me. We're way ahead of you. He remembered you. Said to say hi. Stop by this afternoon. Photos are being sent. See if you can ID any suspects."

Joel slowed his pace to walk beside me.

"My last appointment ends at three. I'll be by afterward."

"Perfect. By the way, I pulled your case."

"My case?"

"College murder. Those three who got sent away? One of them was paroled a few months back. Roger Dossen."

"He couldn't have done it," I said too quickly.

"I'm not saying he did, Mira. But he might know something."

"You're right. I went to his parole hearing."

Joel slowed to look at me, then regained his speed.

"I spoke on his behalf. Roger has turned his life around."

Joel gave me a strange look. "That's rare."

"Not really," I said. "Prisoners, some, do get rehabilitated."

"That's not what I meant."

It was my turn to stop and wonder.

"He *murdered* your best friend."

I resumed walking so I wouldn't have to look him in the face, then said, "I'm trying to learn how to forgive."

"Hmm. Don't think I could. Anyway, you never know, it might lead us somewhere. He lives in the East Bay."

"Oakland," I told him.

Joel stopped again. "Maybe you should come along, talk to him with me?"

"I don't think that would be a good idea."

"Maybe not. I understand. I'll see you later then."

As we left the building, we angled off in separate directions for our cars, and he shouted at me. "A new Mercedes?"

"You know it's the same one."

"As *last* year." He smiled his big burly grin. "Psychiatry? Who knew talking to crazy people paid so well. I'm the *head* detective. I talk to crazy people all day, and I'm the one gets to drive a Buick! *Used.* Mira, let me take you on that dinner date you keep avoiding. I'll let you read *my* mind."

"I can already read *your* mind. You have a wife."

"Leave her out of this," he joked.

We both laughed. He played at being my ardent admirer, one who would run away with me if I would only say the word. Maybe he was in love with me and would. But he was like my big brother, someone who'd always have my back. At least, I hoped.

— ❦ —

"Where's Egon?"

"Why do you care?" said Faye. "You get me instead."

I was disappointed by this but tried not to show it. I clicked my pencil, loading the tip with lead. "How has your week been?"

"I heard you went to see Egon perform. Is it true?"

"I went to observe what he does? Yes."

"It'll never work out," she told me, twirling a strand of her hair around a finger, then letting the curl uncoil.

"How do you mean?"

She was staring directly at my breasts. "I'm jealous of your *girls*. Grown cats to my kittens. Egon is fond of them."

I waited patiently for her to continue.

"You're not the first," she added. "He's done this before."

"Faye, you need to be specific."

"Falling in love. *Now* with you. His therapist. *Our* therapist. Shame on you. I hired you!"

"You were assigned to me by a court order," I corrected.

Faye crossed her leg and wiggled her foot. "Do I need to spell it out for you?"

"Please do." I didn't like her tone or the look in her eyes.

"Mira, I admired you in college. So I followed you. Fascinated to know what motivated you."

Faye let her words sink in.

"I saw you kill that guy in the cemetery."

My pulse increased, my heart was thumping. I avoided moving to appear calm, in control. "It was done in self-defense."

"I could see that. He was a horrible person."

"He was. Who did you tell?"

"Nobody." She smiled. "That I can recall. I may have blabbed something, to someone, back in college. Why?"

"My life is being threatened."

"Join the club. I'm not judging you, Mira. Or for how you lied in court. We do what we have to do. I broke a billiard stick over a man's head to get arrested. So you'd come running. I'd anticipated the court ruling. Didn't Egon warn you? *This* is how I play."

"What is it you want?"

Faye wiggled her foot, seeing she'd broken through to me now, and had my undivided attention. The playing field had shifted to her advantage. Her smile scared me.

"I want you to remove Egon."

I was desperately trying to hold onto my emotions. I folded my hands to keep them from shaking. "Remove him, how?"

Faye sighed, disappointed in me. "While we were in college you never insulted my intelligence, so please don't start now and act like you are smarter than me. I know what you've been doing."

I bit my lip to stop myself from asking, sensing it wiser to let her talk. In uncharted waters, I feared capsizing and drowning.

"I understand the concept of fusion," she finally said and leaned forward to touch my bare knee. "And your intent with us. The only difference will be me, the dominant personality in this arrangement.

Becoming the *host* personality. Not Egon."

She had power over me. I felt it. Feared it. I was dealing with a highly intelligent and charmingly devious amalgamation of the mind. I knew not how, exactly, but she controlled my fate. She had learned lessons from me in the art of manipulation. She now had me trapped in an uncompromising situation, and could make my life miserable. Even ruin me if she didn't get what she wanted.

I wondered how much danger I was in. As strong-willed as I was, or wanted to believe I was, I realized, I'd do almost anything to avoid getting arrested and sent away to prison.

Faye was offering me something white. A white flag, was what I foolishly visualized, at first, my mind going soft, my vision blurring from the onslaught of a blinding migraine, before realizing it was a handkerchief bordered in lace.

"Mira, you're perspiring. Take this."

I wiped my forehead and thanked her.

She explained to me very sweetly, as if we were engaged in play, partners in crime. "If you help me, I am willing to help you. Now, you must tell me how you plan to elevate me into this single person and relegate my brother into, well, nothing."

— ⇝ —

"For Christ's sake, Mira!" yelled Phil, "This—this *psychopath* you're treating? You *knew* him in college? And when he was a kid too? Why the hell didn't you tell us?"

"He's not a psychopath," I explained. "And I didn't know him at all, really. Hardly at all. I didn't think it was important."

"Everything is important!" said Phil. "*You* tell her."

Joel told me, "Mira, he committed a violent offense. And then praised the work of this serial killer. That's not nothing."

"Or *she* did," grunted Phil. "Whatever the fuck he is."

"He's suffering from a rare condition known as dissociative identity disorder."

"It's not *known* to me," said Phil with disgust. "I want to *know* if he's capable of murder."

"Which *is* what I'm determining. I don't believe he is."

Joel tilted his head, gearing up to turn the screws as gently as he could on me. "So we're clear. Both of you went to the same college. At the *same* time when this first murder took place?"

"Yes. But—"

"Anything else *not* worth mentioning?" said Phil.

I looked from Phil to Joel, preferring his kinder eyes.

"We grew up in the same neighborhood."

"Jesus," said Phil, pushing back his chair and standing.

"Was he mentally ill back then?" added Joel.

"I don't know. He moved away when I was twelve."

"And just *happened* to resurface while you were in college."

"He was a year older. I didn't consider it unusual that he would come there. Roger Dossen was his cousin. And he knew Brad Fuller, one of the other assailants who got sent to prison."

"For *murder*," said Phil, punctuating his annoyance.

"They came from the same neighborhood, but were older, and I hardly knew any of them."

Phil was prone to pace. And my boss was burning up the floor of his office while Joel stayed seated with me. He gave me a firm but encouraging nod. "With this ... condition you mentioned. Are there blackouts involved?"

"Not exactly. It varies," I said.

"Varies how?" said Joel.

"Dissociation has been described as a form of amnesia."

"*Shit*," hissed Phil. "Blackouts!"

Joel was trying to be careful in his phrasing. "Has ... *he* shown any violent behavior while in your presence?"

"No," I said.

"Threatened you in any way?"

I hesitated. "Not really."

"Not *really*," mocked Phil with a huff. "I want him brought in here for questioning! Now!"

"Sir?"

"What?"

"The stress of an interrogation is liable to—"

"What, Skyles?"

I feared more what Faye could do to me than my boss at that moment. So I calmly explained, "The interrogation could fracture him even further, and make his condition worse."

"Speak *English*," snarled Phil.

"Using methods of hypnotherapy, I've managed to reach most, if not all, of his personalities. And they've begun to stabilize."

"Again, Skyles—English."

"It's called fusion. The patient's mind becomes whole again and forms a healthy equilibrium. That's the goal in these cases."

Phil sat on the edge of his desk, tired of pacing. "Frankly, I don't give a rat's ass if *he* or *she* breaks to pieces. I want this serial killer caught, locked up, and off my streets."

"Sir, I respectfully ask that you allow me to continue treatment, so I can find out through psychotherapy if he *is* the killer. Trauma from an arrest and interrogation won't get us desired results."

"*Trauma* from an arrest." Phil, sarcastically echoing my words, looked down at Joel for his opinion.

"What harm is there?" he said. "We can't hold him on anything substantial at this time. We'll set up 24/7 surveillance and see where it leads us. I trust Skyles' expertise."

"Do it then," said Phil. "Now *get* out. Skyles?"

I was already on my feet headed for the door and turned.

"I want results."

"Yes, Sir."

I was glad to have escaped Detective Faber's office. Joel tugged me by my arm to indicate I was to follow him. We went to his office, the door closing behind him. "Have a seat."

"What now?"

"I went to visit the parolee. Roger Dossen."

"Oh."

"Aren't you going to ask?"

Trying to lighten things, I smiled. "I figured you'd tell me."

Joel's face scrunched, a smile of sorts, then sat behind his desk. He found a stress ball to toss into a small hoop on the opposite wall. Missing the shot, he returned his focus on me. "Dossen told me you knew the victim. One *more* kid from the neighborhood?"

"He was. I hated the prick."

"Jesus Christ! So you *knew* them all?"

"Not well. I don't see why—"

"Mira, what else are you *not* telling us?"

"Nothing. That's it."

"Those three boys didn't rape you when you were twelve?"

"No. Did he tell you that? He's lying."

"I know," said Joel. "You denied it during the trial."

"It never went to *trial*. Oh. You mean in Oregon. Yes."

"Dossen was pretty insistent."

"I'm sure he was. What else did he tell you?"

Joel leaned back in his chair. "That you tampered with evidence, obstructed justice, perjured yourself in court. That, you mean?"

I felt myself blanch but said nothing. "He's lying."

"He never said any of it. Didn't have to."

"What do you mean?"

"It's all on record, Mira. I read the entire transcript. I prefer reading crime novels while lying in bed with my wife at night, but I found it rather compelling. A real page-turner. You know why?"

I gave a terse head shake to indicate "no."

"Because of *you*, Mira. I care. What happened to your friend, and what you went through. Really awful."

"I've tried to put it behind me."

"I admired your bravery."

"Thank you."

"Now get out of here. Let's solve this damned case."

"I'm trying to. Believe me."

— ⇛ —

All animals, man included, have a region in the brain, a network of cells, called the "rage circuit." If electrically stimulated, violent aggression is triggered. And it will convert a passive individual into something unrecognizable. Mahatma Gandhi, Mother Teresa, Jesus Christ, in theory, could have transformed into vicious killers had their rage neurocircuitry been tampered with. Or damaged. It was one of many theories we were kicking around.

"Serial killers don't think they are doing anything wrong," said Dr. Hilts, sharing his insights and his expertise on serial murder cases to our investigative team. He was a supervisory special agent with the National Center for the Analysis of Violent Crime (NCAVC), a component of the FBI's Critical Incident Response Group (CIRGI). We were seated around a table, and I could tell my colleagues were reticent to accept this notion being presented. Dr. Hilts continued, "And they are incapable of recognizing self-deception."

"What the hell does that mean?" said Joel.

"Evil-doers think they are acting morally," I added.

"Bullshit," said Faber.

"Take Hitler—" said Hilts.

"I'd rather not," said Harvey.

"He was an idealist," Hilts went on. "Hitler believed he had a moral vision. That the heroic sacrifices of others would bring about a thousand-year utopia. His actions were justified, according to his mental view. Same rationale as a Jihadist."

"Where are we going with this?" stated Faber.

"Serial killers see themselves as victims, not as perpetrators," said Hilts. He had a smile that twisted downwards on his left side and squinting eyes darkened in their sockets. I wondered if years of studying these sinister people had forced these mannerisms upon his physiognomy. "They often feel cheated out of a childhood. And this sense of victimization is carried into adulthood. Dismiss the myths you've heard that serial killers are dysfunctional loners; white males; motivated by sex; prone to change locations; unable to stop killing; evil geniuses who want to get caught. These are fallacies. Most serial killers hide in plain sight within a community. They span all racial groups. Their motivations vary, which can be revenge and attention seeking. They generally kill in defined geographic areas. Their killing spree can stop suddenly. And though they might have a debilitating mental condition, they are not above average intelligence, normally. And lastly, it's not that they want to be caught, they think they *can't* be caught. And *that* is the key."

"How do you mean, key?" asked Joel.

Hilts clasped his hands, and I imagined him invoking us all to pray with him by the look of his shuttered eyes and the downward tilt of his head. But no, he looked up. "They leave crumbs."

"Crumbs?" said Bitner.

"Scraps of evidence. A psychological *need* to have an identity, create a unique signature and leave this trail for us. This is what I find so fascinating. These people, what drives them? It's the reason I enjoy this line of work."

"And *catching* them?" said Joel, with a bit of sarcasm.

Hilts brushed the criticism aside. "That too, of course. Here's a checklist an associate has developed to measure distinct personality traits and social pathology of these killers. They fall into four types: interpersonal, affective, lifestyle, and antisocial."

Faber began scrolling through email on his phone.

"The *interpersonal* traits include glibness, superficial charm, a grandiose sense of self-worth, pathological lying, and manipulation of others. The *affective* traits include a lack of remorse and/or guilt, a lack of empathy, and failure to accept responsibility. The *lifestyle* traits include stimulation-seeking, impulsivity, irresponsibility, and unrealistic life goals. The *antisocial* traits will show poor behavioral control, early childhood behavioral problems, juvenile delinquency, and criminal versatility."

Faber looked up from his phone. "Please tell us something we don't already know. Like how to nail this prick?"

"The crumbs." Hilt's eyes darkened, narrowing. "From what you've shown me, you've found a few. Hairs and fibers."

"Which haven't led to any matches," said Harvey.

"As yet," cautioned Hilts. "The newspaper clipping found on the latest victim provides a link to his first kill. Out of state. Almost a decade ago. He moved here. Why? There has to be a connection. Plus, we now have blood DNA. Ah, and the penny found."

"Valued at roughly five grand," said Bitner, who'd followed the lead and had a numismatic authority appraise the coin.

"Impressive sum," said Hilts. "And more of these rare pennies have been scattered throughout the city? More golden crumbs. The dots are beginning to connect, gentlemen."

Harvey intervened, "What about the "Y" he carved in the last victim? No "X" was found. Explain that?"

"*He,*" said Hilts with a twisted half-smile, "could be a she."

"A copycat killer?" said Faber.

"Possibly," said Hilts. "But not likely. The 'X' changed to a 'Y' construes, to me, he's intentionally left a clue. For us to solve."

"Same thing Skyles said," said Faber, "Thoughts?"

"I agree. Same killer. He's sending us a message.

Joel tapped his laptop. It awakened, projecting a screen image on the wall. It displayed the enlarged photos and newspaper articles found in Faye's apartment. "I say we focus on this message. Each of these murders, including the one in Oregon, is on display." Gulen clicked through the exhibits to the last one. The news clippings and photographs of the seventh victim were circled with question marks. He turned on his laser pointer, scribbling the image with a red beam. "He claims to know nothing about this killer. *That* is not nothing. Norwood sure as hell has a keen interest in this case."

"That was Faye's doing," I stated.

Joel snapped back, "His *twin* sister? Who died as a child? Who doesn't exist. Alter ego or some shit. Let's get real here."

"She *is* real to him," I countered.

"Fuck that," said Joel. "I say he's our guy."

"There's no DNA match," said Harvey.

"Fuck that too," added Joel and clicked to another slide.

Harvey added, "The blood came from someone else."

The next projected image showed the open desk drawer. Joel scribbled over the pennies with the laser. "And these, same as the one found in our snake-man's pocket. And forensics ID'd a partial print. Guess what? Matches a whorl from your boyfriend's fingers."

"He's not my boyfriend. He's my patient."

"I *see* the way you look at him."

"Enough," warned Faber.

"What are you saying, Joel?" I said. "That I lied – covered up for him? That I'm compromising the case!"

"You've lost your perspective on this one, Mira."

"Screw you, Joel. Go to the next slides."

Gulen clicked forward. "Why? To show what a sick bastard this guy is? Sure." He clicked to the photos showing Faye in a leather corset, holding a whip, a naked man handcuffed to a bed. "Hell, we could arrest him on extortion charges alone. He kept records of the transactions. Not to mention these photos as evidence."

Faber interjected, "Which are *not* to be made public."

Harvey laughed. "Only the ones of Bitner."

"Fuck you," said Bitner. "You do the undercover investigation next time! See how you like it."

"Looks to me *you* did," added Harvey.

"Those prints had better be destroyed!" shouted Bitner.

"Relax, Peter," said Faber. "Everyone, refocus. We have a killer to catch."

"I'm not sure it's even blackmail," said Bitner.

"How's that?" said Faber.

"I mean, technically, he never collected a cent. He made copies of the letters. And from what we have so far, no money was ever exchanged or extorted. He mails the photos with letters of gratitude, and recommends the recipient be merciful and to, quote, 'find in his heart' the desire to make a monthly donation, including a suggested amount, to be sent to a non-profit organization. They differ."

"Yeah, but demanding specific amounts," said Joel.

"*Suggesting,*" corrected Bitner. "The wording is cleverly precise, non-threatening, and not incriminating, according to legal. I ran this through several departments."

"And we've investigated each man's bank accounts," I added. "Monthly checks were written to Safehome, the Shelter for Abused Women and Children, and the Coalition Against Domestic Violence, RAINN, which is for rape victims—"

"Fuck," grunted Faber. "You mean charities. All of them?"

I said to Gulen, whom I still loved like a brother. "What kind of sick fuck would orchestrate something as altruistic as that, Joel?"

— ❦ —

Egon pushes away from me and slides out of bed.

"I have to pee," he mutters.

I am left alone with my thoughts, my confessions. In the dark, I pull the sheets up to my neck and lay there listening to the rhythm of the ocean waves. It's a sound that is ever present, like a heartbeat, increasing in volume, then fading, but always noticeable. Making me aware I'm still alive. Mixed into this background noise is the sound of Egon flushing the toilet, turning the faucet on and off, and rattling around. Busy doing something.

When he reemerges from the bathroom, he moves shadow-like, in silhouette, over to a counter, leans against it and looks at me.

"Come back to bed," I say.

"Is your house bugged?"

This snaps me from my lethargy. "What?"

"I *said*, is it bugged? Wired to tape our conversations?"

I sit up against the pillows and backboard. His tone of paranoia makes me paranoid. "No. Why would I—"

"Oh, I don't know, Mira. From what you've told me. Working *hard* to find this serial killer. Still on the job. And *why*, exactly, did we come here? Is this part of your investigation?"

"It's a vacation. I love you."

"Umm. Right. Me too."

It's dark but I don't want to turn on the lights. I hear clanging and realize Egon is making another drink. Ice in a glass, the gurgle of liquor comes next.

"You want one?"

"Sure," I say. "Since it's our honeymoon. *Ha-ha*."

I see his hand extend toward me and I take the glass of scotch. Not my favorite, but it'll do. He taps his glass against mine.

"To us," he says.

"To us," I say, then take a sip. "Egon, I know it's not you."

"Ah, the serial killer, you mean?"

"I never suspected you."

"But maybe Faye? Or Hunter? Or some other *sick* part of me? That's what you've been *thinking*, Mira. Am I right?"

I become alarmed. "Who am I talking to?"

"Me. I'm here, still in one piece. You do nice work."

It wasn't exactly a compliment. "Egon?"

"What?"

"You have to trust me."

"Why?"

"I love you. I'd never let any harm come to you."

"Is that meant to reassure me?"

"Yes," I say. "Don't you trust me?"

A full pounding heartbeat of waves passes as I wait.

"I'm trying," he responds.

I select my words carefully. "It's possible the serial killer won't kill again."

"Why would he not?"

Egon shakes his ice cubes. I imagine a rattlesnake. I tell him, "An "X" wasn't left in the last victim. Instead, the letter "Y" was cut into the tattoo of a snake's forked tongue."

"Interesting. Like asking a question. Why?"

"Those were my thoughts too. To communicate he's questioning his actions. He wants to end this killing spree."

"How'd you arrive at that?" I can barely make out Egon's face. He rattles his ice again, then sips his drink. "Could be he plans to go through the entire alphabet, A to Z."

"I don't think so."

"Why not?"

"It's over."

"*Gone*. Poof. Like magic?"

"Come back to bed," I ask him gently.

"You know something you're not telling me."

"Yes. If you'll let me finish."

"Finish what?"

"My story."

The cubes have melted, the rattle is softer, almost gone.

"Okay. I'm listening."

— ≋ —

It was already dark when I left my office. For over a week my receptionist received calls from a man who scheduled appointments and never showed, using the name of Rick Brandt. Of course, he was not going to appear. He was in prison, on death row. I had assumed it was the tattooed man trying to intimidate me. Whoever it was, it was working.

I had returned to my office after attending a fundraising event downtown for the anti-sexual violence organization, RAINN. I was the guest speaker that evening. The next morning I was scheduled for a court appearance. I was an expert witness for a domestic abuse and rape case, and I'd forgotten my notes. It was close to midnight by the time I locked up and rode the elevator to the underground garage. From my purse, I removed a canister of mace. I always took it out as a precaution during late hours. I first peered through the reinforced windows of the metal door before pushing it open.

I was pushed backward into the stairwell and slammed against the elevator. A hand gripped my throat. The man who'd confronted me in the bar had been waiting for me.

"I made an appointment!"

"How did—?"

"Not the question you should be asking." He held me in place, arm extended, fingers locked around my throat. My purse and notebook fell to the granite floor, but I kept hold of the mace in my fist, clutched at my side.

"What do you want?"

His calm demeanor had a forceful intensity. "I haven't decided. You're pretty. In a tight-ass rich-bitch sorta way."

"You're a real charmer."

My neck was squeezed tighter. By not responding as I should, I had unleashed a seething rage.

"I can see why Rick fucked you. You wanted to be raped. You had it coming. You asked for it. Didn't you?"

He was choking me now.

"Didn't you? Say it!"

I could barely breathe. "Yes."

He grinned. Gold teeth sparkled. As he relaxed his choke hold a fraction, my eyes looked for the eye of the surveillance camera. I saw its nodule covered with duct tape.

"Did you think I'm stupid?"

I saw myself reduced and turned upside down inside his black dilatated pupils. Fear had overtaken me and was causing paralysis. I willed myself to stay strong and focused, but it wasn't working.

He shook me by the throat and I felt fragile, a bird toyed with by a savage alleycat. "You're a good listener. That's what you do. Well, listen to this. Sid. You remember Sid. What you *did* to him?"

"He tried to kill me."

"Can you blame him? I don't. *Relax*, if I wanted you dead, you'd be dead."

With his free hand, he stroked my head with his fingers – before yanking out a few hairs.

"DNA, it's easy to get. And to plant at a crime scene. Yours too. Are you following me? All the evidence piling up. Each victim traced back to you. From a statement you made in court. A judgment made after an interview in a holding cell. You knew each one. You despised them all. Each victim. Didn't you? Say it!"

"Yes."

"Can you *feel* it now? Time closing in. After an anonymous call, they'll want to check *your* DNA. Yeah. Right after your next kill. Too much DNA evidence to ignore. All the connections leading them to you. Can you *feel* Rick now? You bitch!"

He held my torn hairs in front of my eyes. My hand was sweaty, and I feared the canister of mace would slip from my fingers.

"In prison, you have plenty of time to plan your revenge, hatch a strategy. Like a string of murders. All pointing to you, Clarabelle.

Payback for Sid, Brad. My buddies."

"They raped me!"

"Did I *say* you could talk?" His hand choked me again. "Good. Plead your case in court, then tell all the other inmates how innocent you are. How you were framed. No one will believe you."

"You killed them? All of them?"

"No, Clarabelle." He kept his hand on my throat. His other hand grabbed mine and lifted it to his lips as if to kiss my fingers. He smiled, showing his gold teeth, before biting into the knuckle of my index finger. My scream never left my throat, squeezed tighter. He let go of my hand to spit my blood and skin into a plastic baggie. "You're the one, Clarabelle, who gets to be the serial killer."

The pain woke me from my fear-induced paralysis. I lifted my arm and sprayed mace into his eyes. The toxic solvent was effective and unlocked his grip. I bolted away. He blindly struck the elevator door with his fist. I kicked him in the groin. Delivering several sharp strikes with the heel of my palm to his jaw, I followed with several body chops to his neck. He was hard to bring down, but he collapsed to his knees. I kicked him hard in the face. Then, with all the strength I could manage, I clutched his head and snapped his neck.

I stood, in shock. The fluorescent lights above were humming, hissing a kind of silence. I recalled angels floating like snowflakes all around me. The polished granite floor under me sparkled with stars. I looked up at the blinded security camera. I went to the doors and peered into the garage and confirmed that the surveillance eye inside had been duct-taped too, allowing me a safe passage out.

I hesitated, heart pounding, trying to regather my frayed nerves to function properly. My attacker was lifeless, sprawled on his back. I stared at his tattooed arms. His sweatshirt, bunched at the elbows, had separated from his black jeans and exposed a tattoo surrounding his navel. My curiosity overcame me and I went down on my knees. I removed a handkerchief from my purse and unbuckled his pants.

The red eyes of a green snake, poised to strike, greeted me. It jolted me with fear and anger. The memory of Sid, his taunts and threats, came rushing back. On my keychain, I kept a miniature knife.

This had to stop, I told myself. I cut a "Y" into the snake's forked tongue, then wiped the blade on his jeans.

I gathered up the baggie with my skin, placed it with the knife in my purse, along with the can of mace, the handkerchief, and what I could find of my pulled hairs. Holding my notebook and purse, I stood. As I looked into the fluorescent lights flickering intermittently, I saw angels floating like snowflakes all around me.

— ≋ —

The adjustment was difficult, having killed again. I wondered, what had I become. I was staring down at the man I had murdered, who now lay in the city morgue. I had lied to people I cared about, who I trusted, and who trusted me. Who was I?

Time passed. I wondered about free will. Did unconsciousness rule our conscious thoughts? I delved deeper into the mind of Egon. To gain his trust I needed to convince him, which included the hostile personalities, that I was there to integrate all aspects of his fractured self, and not eliminate or harm anyone.

Faye wanted none of it. When the dust settled, she wanted to be the dominant one. I reassured her this would be the case. My role had become that of a diplomat attempting to convince nations at war, with a long history of distrust and violence, to cease fire, and to agree to a peace treaty that would settle age-old border disputes. By accepting these terms, the benefits would outweigh the negatives.

A delicate balance that could easily backfire on me.

History itself showed that zealots of a maladaptive system of government would desperately fight to keep it in place, willing to do whatever it took to sabotage negotiations and kill a peace process. Well-meaning politicians got assassinated for doing exactly what I was attempting to do.

I knew the risks. But I was committed, too far involved.

Through hypnosis one day I made a breakthrough. A small boy emerged, tentatively. He was at the very core, hiding underground. He'd been living there, he told me, inside a hole in the ground.

"Are you a rabbit?"

I disguised my shock as best I could, professionally nodding and telling this new voice, "I like rabbits. Who am I talking to?"

"Arin."

"How old are you, Arin?"

"Seven. Who are you?"

"A friend. I'm here to help you."

That was how it began, in a seemingly simple dialog to convince a traumatized soul it was all right to come out. The danger was over. I would protect him and guide him from darkness into daylight.

I held my emotions together for the entire session as I brought Egon back to consciousness. He was sobbing and clinging to me.

I was elated, tears streaming from my eyes. He finally let go and pulled away.

"What happened?"

"Egon?"

"I'm here. Why are you crying? And smiling?"

"We made a major breakthrough."

"How so?"

"How do you feel?"

"Better."

After handing him more tissues, he stood to wander across the room. I had an urge to get up and hug him but resisted.

After silently staring out the windows into the darkening sky, Egon turned back to me with a sly and playful smile.

"You know, Mira. You *do* remind me of a pretty rabbit."

— ≋ —

His words got me to laugh. Then to cry.

I overstepped the bounds of my profession that day by letting my feelings for him cloud my reasoning. We made love.

Don't judge me until you hear the rest.

Egon's breakthrough was the catalyst for initiating my own. The following morning I attended to my morning patients. My secretary rescheduled my afternoon appointments and cleared my schedule for the next week. After lunch, I forced myself to take a drive across the San Francisco Bay into Oakland. With no expectations, I arrived unannounced and sat in the back of a recreation room. I felt like a rabbit hiding at the far edge of a field as I watched Roger Dossen. He moved back and forth, engaging a group of young kids who sat attentively, often screaming in laughter at his jokes.

I was tempted to leave a couple times but stayed seated. I knew he saw me, but he kept his focus on these kids. It was obvious they adored him, admiring the person he was, listening to the advice he was giving them. When his pep talk ended, he told them to warm up on the field with the other coaches. As these adolescents left for the outdoors, Roger walked toward me.

He wasn't smiling. He had a squint to his eyes, wondering why I was there. I began to second-guess myself, about why I had come. I stood and didn't know if I should extend a hand in greeting, but chose to keep my hands at my sides.

"You're very good. With the kids. I was impressed."

"I'm surprised you would come," he said.

"I know. I needed to."

"Why?"

"To say I'm sorry."

Roger turned his head and walked away.

"Truly. I *am*."

I assumed he wanted me to leave. But he returned holding a box and held it for me to take. I removed a tissue and wiped my eyes. He gestured toward a nearby table.

"Why don't we sit and talk."

"Thank you," I said, grateful for him allowing me to stay.

I was glad to be seated instead of standing, feeling shaky on my feet. I folded my hands on the table in front of us. I couldn't erase the memory of making him stand naked, then holding his testicles. The embarrassment was all mine now. I felt ashamed. My flattened hands slowly slid off the surface on the table into my lap. Roger looked up into my eyes.

"That was awkward." He gave me a puzzled look.

"I ruined your life. I don't know how to amend that."

"You can't." Roger rubbed at an imperceptible spot on the table as he talked. "To be honest, I hated you. More than I hated myself. I wanted horrible things to happen to you. It was hell, what you put me through. I tried to make the best of it. But, it was hell."

"I'm sorry."

He looked directly at me. "I didn't deserve that. Not the extent to what you did to me. You lied. It wasn't right."

"I know. I realize that. I … I'm sorry, Roger."

I had more I'd planned to say: how Gwen's death had changed everything, committing me to doing things I shouldn't have, and how it all spiraled beyond my control. But words failed me. I wiped at more tears.

"Hey. I can't change the past either, and what happened to you. When we were kids. I can see how that damaged your life."

"I'm doing all right."

His eyes took on a sharper squint.

It got me to confess, "I'm lying. My life is a mess. Sure, I've got my career, and I'm doing okay financially. I donate time and money, doing these good deeds. For causes I *care* about. But it never fixes the pain inside me, this sinking pit of guilt for causing Gwen's death, and for lying in court, ruining your life. It eats at me. On the surface, I look okay, but I'm falling apart inside."

"I like that you're honest with me. It's not easy."

"No," I said.

"It took me time to admit it to myself that I had been a coward. Like you said. I *was* a coward. For letting that happen to you."

"We were kids."

"Doesn't matter. Still makes me a coward."

"People change, Roger. I know about the work here. I admire what you're doing, and what you've done with your life."

This seemed to take him by surprise. Then he nodded. He put his hands back on the table, rubbed at more spots, then spread them both wide. "Most of these kids, Mira, they have no one. You know, someone who can help them stay off the streets, and out of trouble. Gangs eat you alive. Hell, I saw it every day while I was in there."

There. In prison. The unspoken word between us.

"These are good kids underneath it all. I figure this is my way of helping. Giving back. Making some kind of difference."

"You are." My hands resurfaced to rest on the table but were keeping their distance, poised at the edge.

"I try to direct them away from doing stupid things. To be smart with their lives. Not making the mistakes I made," he added.

"Roger, that was *my* fault. You didn't—"

"Hey." He put up a hand. "Don't go there. I know where your rage came from. I've thought long and hard about that. But I've been able to let it go. And forgive you."

I grabbed for the more tissues. "Thank you. But, how do I ever forgive myself?"

"I'm not sure I can help you there." His smile was sympathetic. He gave me a nod. "That's your department. Psychotherapy?"

I returned the smile, then blew my nose.

He said, "I know I'm partially to blame for putting you in that dark place. Because of what happened that day. Just so you know, that was all Sid's idea, not mine."

"I know. I thought I was going to die."

"I've tried to forgive myself too. It's hard. I can't."

"I forgive you."

Roger locked his eyes on me. "That means a lot."

Roger reached over to touch one of my hands, both huddled like frightened rabbits at the edge of a culvert. The contact startled me, then began to calm me. He held my fingers, gently, then let go.

He spoke again, "I heard what you did for Brad. Helping him get released. And the cost involved. I mean, for everything."

With a knowing look, he studied me. I admitted nothing.

"Mira, I *know* it was you. Who else? He has no family left who cares. An ex-con. No money. Dental implants? And that surgery. What's the procedure called again?"

"Gender reassignment."

"You didn't have to do that for him. Or *her*. I keep forgetting. I haven't adjusted to calling him …"

"Brandy."

"Yeah. What the hell. It's a brave new world, I'm told."

"I felt responsible. I wanted to help."

"You did." He touched my hand again. "He doesn't blame you. We talked. It's what he—*she*—wanted."

"If it hadn't been for me, sending him to prison …"

Roger looked away. "Listen, I let *her* know that it was *you* who made that surgery possible. Which *she* wanted, but couldn't afford. And guess what? She cried. Told me to thank you if I ever saw you again. And I'm telling you, it *pains* me to say it, but god-damn it, she looks pretty damned good. Kinda *hot*, even."

It felt good to laugh with Roger. Openly. Without judgment. Both of us learning to accept and be accepting of each other.

I repeated, "I really *am* trying to make amends."

Roger shrugged. "Aren't we all. That is, excluding Rick."

"Who raped and murdered Gwen," I snapped.

Roger let go of my hand. "Well, I guess getting one out of three correct ain't too bad, huh?"

"I'm sorry. Again."

"Let's not go there. Unless you need to?"

I shook my head. "I want Gwen to rest in peace."

"Brandt's dead. In case you hadn't heard."

No surprise to me. I nodded.

"He wasn't well-liked. He finally got that lethal injection."

"Good."

Changing the subject, Roger said, "I hear you've been treating my cousin Egon. I always liked him. I made an effort to look out for him. How's he doing?"

"Good. Yesterday we made a major breakthrough."

"Breakthrough?" Roger squinted. It was as if he saw into me, saw the emotional connection hidden behind my words.

I looked away to avoid his eyes. "I believe I've helped him. And, he's helped me too. He made me understand things about myself I couldn't see before."

Roger tapped the table to get me to look up. "About?"

"My trauma."

Roger nodded, yet remained silent.

I added, "How I became ... the way I am."

"How is that?"

I put on the brakes to stop myself from making a full confession. "That I'm healing. Becoming whole again."

"Glad to hear it. Your partner in crime paid me a visit."

I tensed a fraction, not sure whom he meant.

"Questioned me about Sid. What I knew regarding his death, and our past history. About you too."

"Me?"

"I admitted to raping you. *He* brought it up. It's all there in the transcripts he showed me. From the trial. I didn't lie, Mira."

"I know."

"I never understood why you didn't tell the police it was us."

"To protect my father and mother. Mainly."

Roger nodded, accepting that.

I told him, "I never understood why it happened. I thought we were friends. I wanted you to like me. I thought ..."

His look was one filled with regret. "I know. It's crazy. We're all fighting to be loved by someone, in one form or another."

His hand moved across the table to take mine.

"Mira. So you know the truth. I *was* in love with you."

What he did next transported me to the past. He very tenderly laced his fingers through mine.

— ⚡ —

I wanted my first encounter with love to be beautiful.

And it was.

Until it turned ugly.

It started when Roger's hand accidentally brushed against mine as we were walking up the hill along a path. It was on summer break. We were on our way to pick blackberries. There was a vacant lot at the base of the hill where baseball games took place. Kids would gather and we would scrape together a game. I was one of two girls allowed to play with the boys. Not only could I catch a softball, I had my own mitt, and I'd broken the stereotypical assumption that, being female, I'd throw like a girl. I threw a baseball better than most boys. I could also hit a softball with a bat. Not very far, but effectively. Thanks to my father who, no doubt, would have liked to have had a boy, but got me.

After the game broke up, Roger asked if I wanted to go pick blackberries. Roger was fifteen, a freshman in high school, while I was twelve, in seventh grade. It surprised and elated me that he'd ask. I had a secret crush on him. His name appeared all over the pages of my diary, locked with a key and hidden away so no one would know. We'd known each other for years and seen each other around, but rarely spoke more than a few words to each other.

Roger was cute, for sure. But what also attracted me to him was his size. He was not much taller than me, and I was average height for my age. It made him seem less intimidating. Roger got teased for being "vertically challenged" and had been nicknamed "Runt." Not meant as a mean tease, because Roger was popular. Small in stature, but good-looking. He had a confident bounce in his stride. And, I guessed, the buoyant spring in his step was to make him appear taller and project an attitude of upwardly-mobile optimism.

Needless to say, I was not thrilled that his two friends butted in to join us on this uphill trek. Sid and Brad were considered (and not only by me) the neighborhood bullies. Prematurely tall for their age, they used it to their advantage, stealing bags of candy from kids on Halloween and beating up smaller boys in public bathrooms to take their money. They would tie firecrackers to the tails of dogs and cats and light the fuse to watch them howl in terror from the *rat-a-tat-tat* detonations. Mailboxes got smashed and set on fire. It was part of an initiation to belong to their illegal club.

Sid was the instigator, and Brad his loyal wingman. When they weren't being total dipshits – destructive and cruel – they were funny. Their wisecracks made us all laugh. And they were good at sports, which, I guessed, was why Roger hung out with them.

We carried our baseball mitts. And we were each wearing jeans, running shoes and t-shirts. Roger wore a red and gold shirt depicting a Forty-Niners' Super Bowl victory. Sid wore mostly black and had on an Oakland Raiders' shirt. Guns 'n Roses for Brad. I was wearing a vintage Runaways t-shirt. We were dusty from playing in the dirt. It was late afternoon and warm, but we were shaded by the oak trees that populated the hillside. Brad was holding this bat by the knob and dragging the barrel on the ground.

Sid held a switchblade. He'd fling and stick the blade in a tree.

And as we walked past, he'd yank it out. Brad started lobbing small rocks into the air and smacked them with his bat into the valley. I felt Roger's hand touch mine. His fingers toyed with my fingertips, then were gone.

I turned my head. Our eyes met. I looked away.

A gold-and-black monarch butterfly fluttered in front of us to cross the sun-dappled path, and I watched its wings pulsing like my heart. Was Roger flirting? He had to be. I had wished that Sid and Brad would decide to turn back, butt out, and leave us alone.

When I felt my hand being brushed once again, I knew it was intentional. It was my turn to touch his hand, and as I did, he laced his fingers into mine. And we were holding hands. Our linked arms rocking back and forth between us as we walked along. Our other hands held our mitts. The joy I felt made me buoyant. I imagined walking on a cloud, and I could have stayed there if not for the crack of Brad's bat and the swosh-snap of Sid's knife.

Our secret attraction for each other was finally acknowledged, yet neither of us said a word while Brad and Sid amused themselves with their bat and knife.

"Hey," said Sid, punching Brad in the arm to get his attention. "Look at *that*. Two lovebirds."

"*Shit*," said Brad. "Runt's getting a boner."

Roger let go of my hand.

"Your balls musta dropped," joked Sid. "Mojo rising!"

"Fuck you, Sid," said Roger.

"Runt," taunted Sid, "show her what you got."

"Yeah," said Brad. "Show Clara your junk."

"Piss off," said Roger.

Sid laughed his wicked little snicker. "That ain't how it's *done*. You know nothing about sex. It ain't done with *piss*."

Brad laughed along and knocked another rock high into the sky. It sailed into the trees, cracking into branches. I flinched with each smack of his bat. I wanted to turn back and go home. We'd reached a small clearing. The view was spectacular but my mind was barely registering any of the beauty.

"I'm going back," I said.

"*Blackberries*," said Sid. "Come on, it's why we came. You can't turn back now, Clarabelle."

"Don't call me that. And I can *do* what I want."

"Don't get *pissy*," teased Sid. "It *is* your name."

"And *Sydney*, yours," I shot back.

Sid aimed his knife at me and flung it past my head into a tree. As he bumped past to retrieve it, he said, "It's *Sid*."

I looked at Roger for help but he did nothing.

I said, acting nonchalant. "Have fun. I'm leaving."

Sid said to Brad. "Don't let her."

Brad jumped ahead of me, armed with his bat and slung it over his shoulder like a bouncer at a nightclub. He had a big grin.

Sid laughed. "*Clara*. Come on, I was joking. Don't be a baby. Cause you're clearly *not*. I mean, hellfire, you got *tits* now."

Until that moment I hadn't been especially conscious of them. His remark made them plain as the nose on my face. And everyone but me had their eyes focused on the two bulges. On my Runaway's t-shirt, Joan Jett and the girls looking back in defiance at the boys, but unable to do a damned thing to help me.

"I like the Runaways," said Brad. "Some killer songs."

"*Ch-ch-ch—Cherry* Bomb," sang Sid. He gave us an air-guitar demonstration. "Fuck, yeah! I say we go for *cherries*. Fuck them blackberries, eh?"

I smiled, pretending to think his act was funny but was getting nervous. I looked again to Roger for help and scrunched my brow, signaling him to do something.

"Let her go," said Roger, finally. "Catch you later, Clara."

Brad slammed his bat into a tree. The impact made me jump

backward and shudder.

"No–no–no." Sid squeezed his switchblade, snapping it shut. He dropped it into a back pocket. "You two lovebirds need to finish what you started. It's all good. Stay."

Waiting for Sid's lead, Brad rested the bat on his shoulder. His smile was crooked, like his teeth. His glove was hooked to his belt. He paused to rake fingers through his dusty surfer-blond hair that fell over his eyes.

"We'll make it official," said Sid. "Fuck'n A! Almost forgot I had the power. I sent away for it like my older brother did."

"Sent away for what?" said Roger.

"Right here, see?" Sid pulled out his wallet. He held up a card.

"Your dog license?" I said.

"Funny," said Sid with a sneer. "I'm an ordained *minister* of the Universal Life Church."

"The fuck you are," laughed Brad. "Let me see."

"Bullshit." Roger snatched the card from his hand.

Sid let him look, then took it back. "I knew this would come in handy. Like today. My *dearly* beloved. Who are gathered."

Brad cackled at that. "Minister *Sid*. Has a nice ring to it."

"It does, Brother Brad. Now gather around you two lovebirds who wish to be bound in matrimony."

"It's not funny, Sid," said Roger.

From his back pocket, Sid retrieved his knife and popped open the blade. "Not meant to be. This is serious business. Brad, as the best man, would you escort the bride and groom before me."

I looked at Brad who raised the bat from a resting position on his shoulder, lowered it and poked my back, prodding me toward Sid and Roger. "Move, Clara. Play along."

"I don't like being poked." I moved to get away from his bat. "Stop it, Brad!"

Sid laughed. "*Poked.* Clara said the magic word! You win! You get Roger. You gave him a boner. Love can't be denied. Seals the deal. Now hold hands."

"This is stupid," I said.

Sid slid on his baseball mitt and struck the pocket with his fist. He cocked his head. "Do it. Pretend. I need the practice."

All day I'd seen Sid sneaking off behind a tree and coming back rubbing his nose, eyes glazed. And fired up with more energy. Now I knew why. He took off his glove, dug into his pants pocket, and held in his palm small gold capsules."

"Poppers," he said. "I need a ritual, like the blood and crackers Jesus has going. This'll be *my* thing. Watch and do as I say."

He held the capsule to his nose, snapped and snorted.

"Hallelujah! Praise the Lord!"He blinked, held out his palm and offered us to partake. Brad was quick to grab a capsule.

"No thanks," I said. "I don't want one."

Sid gave me a disapproving grin. "Swear to God, you'll love it. Roger, show her how it's done. Don't be a pussy."

Roger gave me a look and said, "I've done it before. You get a tiny buzz. That's all. You feel good. Lasts a couple minutes."

To demonstrate, he broke one, inhaling. "See, no big deal." He wiped his nose with the back of his hand and gave a shrug.

"Join the party, sister," said Sid. "Act like a *Runaway*. Get wild! We're about to party! Have fun here, yeah?"

"I don't like being *threatened* with a baseball bat."

"Nobody does," said Sid. "Lose the bat, Brad."

Brad let it drop to the ground.

"It's all for fun, you know." Sid grinned and brought his hands together, pressed in mock prayer. They reopened, his palms holding poppers. I took one, glancing at Roger, hesitating before snapping the capsule and inhaling. I felt the immediate rush of vapors – *amyl nitrite* – ballooning inside my head. I became light-headed and felt waves of heat arousing my senses and sparking me to life. I looked at Roger and blushed.

Sid cackled. "It's a gas. An aphrodisiac! I told you."

I don't know what happened to time, but it slowed, then sped into warp speed. I took hold of Roger's hand and stood before Sid, whose crazed grin reminded me of a flying monkey in the Wizard of Oz. He waved his arms theatrically, blessing us, sprinkling leaves, all nonsense, and his antics got us laughing and into hysterics. We were actors in this absurd play, pronounced man and wife, then Sid gave Roger permission to kiss the bride.

At that moment I froze, realizing I was about to kiss a boy. A boy who I had been secretly in love with for more than a year.

My face was hot and tingly, along with the rest of my body. Roger seemed uncertain too, wondering how far to take this joke. But he widened his eyes as if to say "here it goes," leaning into me. I immediately forgot about the blackberries and the hillside and the fact we were being watched as Roger's lips pressed into mine. So ecstatic was the sensation that I didn't want it to end. He must have felt the same because his kiss was not timid, but full-blown passion. The spell was broken when I heard Sid and Brad laughing.

"*Jeezz*, get a room!" Brad squealed, his voice cackling high.

"It's all legal-like now," said Sid. "*Do* her."

The warmth I was feeling quickly turned cold like a hot shower interrupted by a blast of ice water.

"You heard me," repeated Sid. "Fuck her."

"Hey ... no way," said Roger.

"I said *fuck* her," Sid demanded. He shoved Roger's chest.

This awakened me back to a harsh reality. My head throbbing. The switchblade and baseball bat reappeared and were moving in a threatening manner circling around us.

"Take off your clothes," said Sid. "Both of you. Now!"

Brad slammed his bat against the ground and startled me.

"Do it, or I'll cut you," said Sid. "You know I will."

The remark was aimed at Roger. He began removing his t-shirt, kicking off his shoes, then unbuttoning his pants.

"What are you waiting for, Clara? You too."

I pulled off my top and let it fall to the ground. I copied Roger, kicking off my shoes next, then unbuttoned my jeans, unzipping the fly before sliding my pants down and stepping out of them. I was standing in my underwear and bra.

Sid and Brad were both in hysterics.

"There she blows!" shouted Sid.

Brad was pointing. "Look at the size of that thing."

Sid nodded. "Impressive. Who knew the runt was a stud."

I looked to see what he was talking about and saw the erection poking from Roger's jockey shorts. Brad came up from behind and yanked Roger's underwear down to expose his erect penis. I became light-headed. Nothing felt real. I was standing half-naked in front of a naked boy who I had fantasized being in love with, dreamed he would love me too, and foolishly dreamed of one day marrying him, having children. I was trembling and wanted to run home.

"Your turn, Clarabelle. Let's see your tits and pussy."

I screamed as my underwear got yanked down past my knees by Brad, who then went for my bra. I covered my crotch with one hand, struggling with my other to keep my bra attached, but Brad managed to undo the clasp, tossing away my last bit of clothing. I was naked and unable to cover myself. I avoided looking at anyone, especially Roger. I was crying and sniveling.

"Move your hands away," Sid demanded. "Let me see!"

I did as I was told, holding my arms stiff at my sides.

"Glory be!" Sid whistled. "Breasts of an angel."

Sid moved toward me. His hand stroked me. "Smooth as silk. Damn, girl, you're giving *me* a boner." He lifted my chin. "Don't be sad, Clarabelle. It's all legal-like. You two lovebirds can copulate to your heart's content. You have my blessing."

He told Roger, "Take possession of your bride."

Roger didn't move.

Sid flipped open his knife. "Hey, either do it, or I'll cut off your dick. Put your hand on her pussy."

Roger timidly came toward me. I stood there like a statue as he placed his hand on the nest of hair between my legs.

Brad was all jittery, hovering nearby. "Finger her, man."

"If you've got the *balls*," added Sid. "Do it!"

The tip of his finger penetrated me and I gasped, confused by a sensation of fear mixed with pleasure, my vagina getting moist.

"Don't," I pleaded with Roger.

I shut my eyes and prayed for this nightmare to end.

Sid, as the sadistic moderator, told Roger, "Now lay her down and stick it to her, man. Do it!"

When he didn't, Sid shoved Roger aside and grabbed hold of my legs. Brad grabbed me from behind. I screamed and fought as they lifted me. Sid shook me hard. "No *screaming*. Or I'll cut you!"

Whimpering now, I was lowered, weak and cowering, placed on my back in the dirt, my buttock and shoulders pricked by tiny rocks and thistles. Brad kept hold of my arms. Sid stood and looked down at me with his wicked grin. He rubbed the bulge in his pants, then moved away, pushing Roger toward me.

"Don't let me down, Runt."

I shook my head, imploring with my eyes, *Please. Don't.*

Sid tossed Brad his baseball mitt. "Shut her face."

The world went dark and smelled like leather. I closed my eyes and winced at the first stab of pain – void of any pleasure, pushing and tearing into my vagina. His penetration (I would later realize), was gentle, Roger trying not to hurt me more than he already was – the humiliation, his betrayal. That I was being raped in the dirt!

I felt his penis pull out of me. I hoped it was over.

"You're up, best man." This from Sid, like he was calling up the next batter to the plate. "Don't swing and miss."

Brad lowered himself on top of me, but I felt almost nothing, bracing myself for the pain of his forced entry. But he was struggling to push something soft and pliable into me. I heard Sid berating him with laughter. Suddenly Brad was on the ground, knocked aside.

"This ain't *softball*, Brad," said Sid, his voice getting closer, then his body on top of me, his hands squeezing my breasts, pinching my nipples. "It's hardball, jerk off."

Brad was complaining, "I wasn't ready, Sid!"

"You had your chance. Watch as I hit a grand *slam*."

My screams were muffled by the suffocating smell and pressure of leather forced over my face. I feared for my life. Each thrust was vicious, stabbing deep, deeper. It felt as if Sid was trying to strike a target he couldn't reach and wanted to slaughter me in the process. The motion went nonstop, brutal, aggressive, and I knew my vagina was torn and bleeding.

When it ended, there was no relief. I felt only a throbbing pain. And I felt as worthless as the dirt I lay upon.

I remained there, on my back, sobbing. I heard their voices. They were arguing about something. The baseball mitt was still on my face. I twisted my head. It fell off. I glimpsed Sid snorting another popper, loading his head full of chemicals.

"Let me *fucking* think!"

"She'll talk," Brad howled. "We'll be screwed!"

Roger was shirtless but had his pants back on. As small as he was to the others, he was now showing anger, pushing Sid, "That was sick what you did! She's bleeding."

Sid shoved Roger back. "Chicks bleed, dickhead!"

"She needs to be taken to a doctor."

Sid abruptly lunged at him, knocking him to the ground. "Don't be a *pussy*, Roger!" Sid turned on Brad. "You too! Stop whining! I'll handle this."

Sid came over to me. He kneeled, placing a knee between my legs and flicked open his switchblade.

"What are you doing?" Roger raced over.

Sid turned the knife on Roger. "Stay away! I'm only going to make a point, to convince Clara *not* to talk." He looked back at me, quivering, watching as the blade moved in circles above my face. It lowered and came to rest below my eye. "Are you going to be telling anyone about this, Clara? *Are* you?

"No," I said. "I won't. I swear."

"I need to be sure."

"I won't say anything. I promise."

I felt the knife blade press into my skin.

"Please. Don't hurt me."

"Because ... if you do, *shit* happens. Like *this!*"

Sid sliced my cheek. My scream got muffled by his other hand covering my mouth.

"What the *fuck!*" shouted Roger. "You're crazy!"

"You want to be arrested?" said Sid. "Go to jail? Then shut the fuck up!" He looked back at me, bringing his knife close to my face. "And *you*. Scream again and I will kill you."

He got off me and stood.

"You think she'll keep quiet?" Brad said, following Sid.

Sid glared at him. "What do *you* think?"

I saw Sid circling around, looking over the ground, searching for something. He bent down. Next, I saw him holding a large rock. Roger came over and stood between us.

"What are you're doing, Sid?"

"What does it *fucking* look like? Containing the god-damned situation, *Roger*. Get out of my way!"

"No! I won't let you. Brad, help me stop him!"

Brad stuttered, "S-Sid, come on, man."

"Shut up! She lives, we go to jail. No one has to know. We're in the middle of fucking nowhere!"

Sid pushed into Roger who pushed back. He kicked Roger in the groin, then walked past him holding the rock.

Roger screamed, "Stop him, Brad!"

I heard a *swoosh* through the air. Then another.

Sid's head jerked, stuck by something. He dropped the rock. It crushed my head. Or so it felt. The impact shook the ground so hard I thought I had died.

Instead, the rock had struck Sid's toe. And he was screaming. "Fuck me! Son-of-a-bitch! Who the fuck did that?

"Did what?" said Roger.

Sid wiped his forehead and saw blood.

"Someone threw a rock." Sid looked at Brad, backing away.

"It wasn't me!" Brad said.

"*Shit,*" hissed Sid. "Over there!"

I managed to lift my head and saw what they must have seen. Someone was running through the woods.

"He's getting away!" Sid shouted, "Stop him!"

"Who?" said Brad.

"Who-the-fuck-should-I-know, asshole! Come on!" Sid pushed Brad and told Roger. "*You!* Stay here. Don't let her go!"

As Sid and Brad ran off, I willed myself to move, to get up. But I was unable to, drained of any will I once had had.

Roger came over, looking down. His face was full of remorse. Frightened. Panicked. Pathetic. "Clara, I'm sorry."

"I *hate* you. Go away." I began to sob. "Go away!!"

"I'll go get help." He ran off.

Abandoning me. Leaving me there to fend for myself, as I had told him to. I lay there staring into a blank, pale-blue, godless sky, drained of hope, numbly aware that I was naked, bleeding between my legs, afraid to move. And knowing any second Sid would return to crush my head with a rock.

I didn't care anymore. I wanted to die.

— ⇋ —

I was semi-conscious, feeling weightless, drifting up into the sky. Someone was shaking me. I opened my eyes. An angel was looking down at me. I knew he was an angel because his eyes were brighter, more brilliant, than the sky. A silvery-blue. And his face was serene, beautiful, framed within swirls of black hair.

"You have to get up," he urged me. "*Hurry.*"

His voice jolted me back to reality. I recognized him from the neighborhood. A strange kid who rarely came out to play, who kept to himself, watching the rest of us from afar. Everyone knew he was crazy. It was the way he acted, as if possessed, how he talked.

I felt him touch me. "What are you doing?"

He had my panties in his hand and was touching my leg.

"Don't!" I kicked him and was seized by pain.

"They'll be back. I don't want you to die."

This got my attention. I no longer resisted and let him dress me. Once my underwear was on, he lifted my arms and slipped my t-shirt over my head. He helped me to my feet and tried to get my legs into my pants but I could barely stand, nor could I squeeze into my jeans, much less walk. The pain of my torn flesh was torture.

"I can't." I held onto him for support.

He wrapped his arms around my back and lifted me up. As my feet left the ground, I held onto him tightly. My bare feet scraped the dirt as we moved down the path. When I began to slip from his arms, he would set me down, then lift me up again. I would readjust my grip on his shoulders. We were more than a mile from our homes.

"It's going to be all right," he told me.

I felt him laboring hard to hold me, his breathing getting heavy. We were halfway down the hill when he stopped abruptly, turned sharply into the woods, and hid us behind a large oak tree.

If they hadn't been yelling at each other we wouldn't have heard them coming or had time to take cover. The slap of shoes against dirt was heard next, coming fast, running past us on the path.

"You let him get away!" Sid shouted.

Brad yelled back, "The *hell* it's my fault! What about you?"

"I do the dirty work! Cause you're such a pansy-ass!"

"Go *fuck* yourself, Sid."

Brad stopped a few yards past us to catch his breath. Further, down the path, Sid stopped too. "Come on! She's hurt. They can't have gotten far. Let's go!"

Brad pushed off. "Yeah, and then what?"

"Maybe kill Roger too. Run faster, asshole!"

I was shaking again. This boy pulled me closer. "Stay still," he whispered. "We have to wait. It's going to be all right."

He kept whispering this into my ear all the way home. Making me believe him and filling back my emptiness with hope. We moved cautiously the remainder of the way. I feared Sid would lunge out of the bushes and slaughter us. We kept to the side of the path to hide within the shadows. We crept between trees that bordered the field where we played baseball, avoiding open areas, and snuck through the backyards of homes until we had reached a main street. The sky had begun to dim. The streetlights had switched on. There were kids playing kick-the-can in the road. It was close to the dinner hour.

By now the boy was drenched in sweat. I was holding onto him tightly, feeling glad to be held. He'd cradled my bottom in his hands. I was no longer bleeding, but trails of blood had run down my legs. Half of my face was streaked with more blood. Neighbors, unsure what they were witnessing, stopped to look at us. At me, half-naked, carried down the street by this boy. But I didn't care what anyone thought. I felt warm in his arms.

This strange boy had saved my life.

— ≈ —

"That was you," I say.

Egon is standing at the foot of the bed with his hand against the column. I am sitting, propped up by pillows against the headboard. It is late, or early, depending on one's point of view. Around three in the morning. The waves pound the sand with its intermittent roar.

He asks, "When did you know it was me?"

"The night of the party. In college. When Faye told me she was Roger's cousin. It took awhile for it to sink in and make sense."

"I had no idea it was you. I hadn't seen you since we were kids. My dad moved us away. And you'd changed your name."

"What about my scar?"

He shakes his head. "You hid that well. Besides, you'd changed physically." He scoops ice from the watery bucket on the nightstand and drops cubes in his glass. "You'd bleached your hair. Not even Roger knew who you were. Not until the trial."

"During therapy?"

"Not right off. Faye obviously knew. My memory doesn't work like hers." Egon looks toward the ocean as though hearing voices I can't hear. "I couldn't believe it. I'd found you again."

"You followed me here?"

"No. I'm from the Bay Area. Originally."

"Then it was Faye's idea?" I am fishing, letting out more line to see what I might hook. "To move back?"

"It's possible. Listen, I didn't follow the trial. It was ugly. Your friend dying. Roger accused of rape, convicted of murder, sent away to prison. I blocked it all out. I do that sometimes."

"How much *do* you remember?"

"Mira, why does it matter? I'm now communicating with Faye, again, thanks to you. I'm remembering things. And yes, I know my sister is dead. I'm dysfunctional. What can I say?"

I shift my body against the backboard, wanting to understand his mind, this man I love. "But you clearly remember me swimming naked in that pond. While you sat watching in a tree."

He smiles. "I wasn't spying. It happened by accident. Faye had run away. I was looking for her."

"After being raped."

Egon turns to stare at the ocean, at a hint of light on the cresting waves. "I will admit, sometimes I did follow you. You were so pretty. I felt a ... need to protect you."

"You did. You saved my life."

He turns back. "I thought I'd never see you again. Then, five ... six years later, there you are. And I didn't even know it was you."

I shift upwards against the pillows as he pauses to take a sip of liquor. I ask him, "Why did you leave?"

"Because I'd raped you. That's what everyone thought. Me, this crazy kid. Who wandered off alone in the woods. I knew about the rumors. They got to me. I wasn't stupid."

"I know. I'm sorry."

"And that bomb blast during my freshman year in high school? That didn't help."

"I was still in middle school."

"For the record, it wasn't *me* who set that off."

"Of course not."

"It was Sid and his pals, Brad, and Stan."

"Stan Romano," I mutter involuntarily, recalling his face as a boy, then as a man. Images of snakes and death fill my head.

"You had your own problems, Mira. Being Clara. It wasn't my decision to leave the neighborhood. My father made us move."

"You never said goodbye."

My words like delicate iridescence soap bubbles float in the air. They pop as Egon laughs bitterly. "That was never going to happen. My father threatened to institutionalize me."

I shake my head, not knowing what to say. I hold up my empty glass. Egon comes over, grabs ice from the bucket, drops in cubes, then pours scotch. "*Stop.* You'll get us drunk."

"Isn't that the point?" There's a devilish twinkle in his blue eyes as if channeling Hunter. His eyes shift toward contrition and I detect Clifford's voice. "No, you're right. Why are we even doing this? God, it's the middle of the night. We should be asleep."

"I want us to be happy."

"It was your father, you realize."

I hear Egon's voice again. "What about my father?"

"He'd have killed me if I came near you."

"Only because—"

"I *know* what he thought. Your abductors vanish into thin air. Not a trace. Never to be found. A fake story. A *lie*, Mira."

"I know."

"The police went after me. You knew that, right? They scared the *shit* out of me. But they never got the truth." Egon shakes his head and gulps more diluted scotch, before setting down his glass. "They had me take a batch of tests. Psychological evaluations. Wired me to a polygraph. They'd tried everything. Except my DNA didn't match. Which meant they had to let me go. So we moved."

"Again, I'm sorry."

"My dad wanted to send me to a military school. The bargain I made was to become *his* version of a man. So I learned martial arts. I took boxing lessons. I beat up other kids."

"Hunter told me."

"Ah." Egon lifts his glass. "To Hunter."

I toast. It feels strange drinking to one of his alternates. "Thank you," I tell him.

"For what?"

"Saving my life."

"I had to. The Spriggans." I detect Jenna's impish tone.

I can't tell if he's joking. "What about them?"

"They ensnare kids. I couldn't let that happen to you."

I question him with a frowning smile.

He mimics my look. "It was fate. I *had* to save you."

"Why?"

"So you'd fall in love with me."

"I did."

"That's the miracle. The one I was talking about."

My eyes tear up. I reach for him. But his smile gradually shifts, going flat, downward. I detect Faye's presence in this new demeanor. She wants to have a word with me.

"Then you betrayed me, Mira. I should have known I couldn't trust you. You're a schemer, same as me."

I return the thin smile, not sure if this is an act. My hand moves beneath the sheets, behind the pillows where I've hidden a canister of mace. I don't know who I'm talking to anymore. "Is that why you never told the police about me?"

"You told me to lie."

"I was talking about college."

"So was I." It's Egon's voice. "I keep my promises. When we were kids, you told me to lie. To be untruthful. Why stop?"

I sip my drink. "I wasn't thinking clearly."

"I understood you. Better odds if we lied. And you were right. You got revenge on your rapists. It worked like a charm."

"It was wrong."

"Was it?"

My hand resurfaces from beneath the comforter to move across the bedsheets as if to smooth things over between us. "I don't know anymore, Faye – I mean, Egon."

He grins, then says, "Sure you do. You always get your way. Mira. You're tenacious. And vengeful."

The remark gets me to look up from my drink. He has a gun. *My* gun. The one I carry with me concealed in a makeup case inside my purse, which he has searched through and found. I now realize what he was doing earlier while rummaging in the bathroom.

"You brought a gun?" He waves it in the air, then at me.

I push into the pillows. "For protection."

"From me?"

"No. My life's been threatened."

"So has mine."

"I deal with psychopaths. Who've threatened me."

"You mean me?"

"No."

"Who?"

"Rick Brandt."

"Imprisoned. *Dead*."

"Stan Romano."

"Deceased. Assuming what you told me *is* the truth."

"Egon, it is true. And I'm licensed to carry a gun."

He studies it, admiring the make and model. "Nice. Hell of a weapon. I'm learning all sorts of secrets about you, aren't I?"

"Put that down, please."

"Are you sure about our fusion? If it's really working?"

On high alert, my body stiffens. I'm perplexed by his use of the word "fusion." Does he mean the bond of his personalities? Or us staying together?"

He scratches his chin with the gun barrel. "You carry it because of the work you do? Doesn't that includes *me?*"

"Not anymore."

"This whole relationship, Mira, it's been based on lies!"

"Who am I talking to?"

"You know damned well who. You cured me."

I hear a cacophony of voices. "Egon, what's wrong?"

He huffs. He points the gun at my face. "What's right? Tell me. Which one of us is it?

"Is what?"

"Don't play with me!"

"I'm *not*."

"The serial killer! Jesus, Mira! It's the whole f—ing reason why we came here? Isn't it? Or did you make that story up too?"

"Egon, calm down. What are you talking about?"

"The tattooed man? This *pretense* of a vacation? Honeymoon? Shit. Were you planning to *fuck* me one last time – before you had me arrested and sent to prison?"

"Please, stop."

"Admit it. Isn't that the plan? Getting me to confess?"

"No."

"Your house isn't bugged?"

"Egon, think. I just confessed that I perjured myself under oath. So, no, the police are *not* listening or waiting outside."

He glances at the door, then turns back. The gun is still aimed at me. "But you know it's me. I'm the serial killer."

"You're not. That's the truth."

"The truth?" He mocks, "How does that work?"

"I never suspected it was you!"

Egon cocks back the hammer. "Liar. I'm not an idiot!"

"I know that."

"No, I'm a fool. I should've known this was a trap."

Egon points the barrel at my head and I jerk backward, pushing into the pillows with my hand raised, the other twisted behind me.

"Egon, don't! I swear I'm telling the truth!"

The gun shakes in his fist. With his other hand, Egon grabs and flings his glass of scotch – smashing it against the wall. "Or did you *eliminate* Hunter during one of our sessions?"

Tears are in both our eyes. He turns the gun on himself.

"Egon—don't!"

"It's for you. You're not safe around me. I'll kill again."

He places the gun barrel in his mouth, angled upward, thumb in the trigger guard, ready to blow a hole in his brain. I am scrambling mentally for something to say to stop him.

"You would leave me here all alone? I *need* you."

He pauses to consider my words, opens his eyes, stares at me. The tension on the gun slackens.

"I don't want to live without you. Egon, please don't."

I take this opportunity to slowly remove the can of mace I have buried in the pillows. Call it my backup plan, in case the fusion fails.

"Egon?"

He looks at me but says nothing.

"You're right. It's true. At first, I didn't know if you were the serial killer. Or Hunter. Some part of you. Or if it was Faye, setting me up. I didn't know. Now I do. You're not. Please trust me."

Egon is not a violent person. Nor is he is a psychopath. He's a wounded soul, like me.

"Come back to bed," I ask him.

He removes the barrel from his mouth.

"We don't need that." I indicate the gun. He glances at himself in the mirror with a puzzled look before he approaches me.

"You're manipulative."

"I am," I admit.

"I thought I understood you."

"I know."

"Why the "X" mark?"

A good question. I have forgotten myself what possessed me to carve the mark into Sid's forehead. I shake my head. I offer a sad smile. "I guess I felt someone had to take credit."

My confession appears to satisfy his curiosity. Egon sets the gun on the nightstand. He slides into bed next to me.

I tell him, "Thank you."

"Sorry about that."

"It's all right."

"No, it's not."

We kiss. His body is tense. My one hand strokes his face, then his shoulders. This calms him. My other hand grips the mace.

Trust will always be an issue between us, I fear.

We kiss again. I feel him relax, turning into the way I like him, the one I have made. The one I love.

He asks, "What will happen to us now?"

I think of all the incriminating evidence. All the dots that have yet to be and may never be connected. All the possibilities for good and evil. Outside the windows, I see light on the horizon. I smile and tell him, "It's going to be a glorious day."

He laughs softly and grins.

"What?" I ask.

"Maybe that rock *did* land on your head. You could be dead and not even know it. And all this—"

"No. You saved me."

He kisses my forehead. "You told me something once."

"When was this?"

"During our therapy."

"Your therapy." I rake my fingers through his hair. "Okay, yes. I'll concede. Ours."

He likes this, the way my fingers trail down his neck. He shuts his eyes and says, "About my condition. The one I have."

"Had," I correct him, then push the can of mace back into the pillows and let go. "Dissociative identity disorder."

"Right," he says. "My multiple personalities. You'd equated it to the beginning of time. Creation, itself. How humans have this innate dichotomy, a desire to diversify as well as merge."

"I did say that."

His voice is gentle. "Tell me again."

I sense Arin's presence, the small boy who I found in a cave, and has come out to play, now a child in need of sleep. To be told a story. A good one.

"Once upon a time," I begin as a tease.

He looks up, amused by my choice of words. "Go on."

"Darkness prevailed. And God said, 'Let there be light.' And, behold – the universe. Then soon we appeared."

"Us." His head rests upon my breasts.

I stroke his hair. "One God, who became many. The multitude. Stellar dust and starlight. That's all we really are."

In a sleepy voice, he says, "Poetic."

His hand continues to roam and linger between my legs.

"Make love to me?"

His eyes search mine. "That's it. The inevitable fusion."

"What is?"

"The universe. After the Big Bang runs its course and reverses, everything will go back to the way it was."

His body rises in compliance to engage in sex.

His smile is full of love for me. His eyes are so bright, so blue, I want to cry. I feel Egon knows something I will never know.

I spread my legs and my arms around him. "You're right. In the end, there can be only one of us."

Acknowledgments

The idea for God, Sex & Psychosis occurred while I was at the University of Oregon, where I graduated with a degree in psychology. Since then I have read numerous articles and books on dissociative identity disorder and have interviewed medical professionals familiar with this unique mental condition. The list would be very long and of little value because, all things considered, this is a book of fiction. It is a novel, a work of art using words instead of notes or paint to formulate a DNA of indelible visions and emotions to touch the soul. And, in the words of Pablo Picasso: *"Art is a lie that makes us realize truth."*

To my support team, I have much gratitude. Writing is a solitary endeavor. And this novel, in which I endeavored to explore a disturbing psychological condition, was like a journey into a dark labyrinth. It was challenging. And in the end, I received help. Therefore, I want to thank a few people for their suggestions, which significantly improved the final story: foremost, my wife, Helene, and my daughters, Brit and Alexis; also Maureen Crist, editorial consultant; and Kate Johnston, an attorney versed in the social services and legal division of the prison system, who was the first to read the pre-final draft. The comments Kate sent me via email, saying – *"Your book is freakin' amazing – seriously. I could not put it down – even when I should have been fixing Thanksgiving dinner."* – helped reinforce my confidence and propel me over the finish line.